# *Forgotten April*

*A Novel*

by Robyn Bradley

*November 2006*

# Chapter 1: April

When Maggie showed me her birth certificate and claimed my mother was also her mother, I didn't know what to think. I mean, my mom had never once hinted about some illegitimate child from her past. But then I remembered another big secret she kept from me: my father's death when I was five wasn't an accident—it was suicide.

*A sister? I had a sister?*

I looked from the birth certificate to Maggie herself: her staggering height (close to six feet?); her glossy auburn hair (a prettier shade than mine); and her model-like face—familiar since I'd seen it on TV, but also in a way that I couldn't explain. In that instant, I knew. I didn't need evidence like a birth certificate (Maggie had been born here, in the same town as me) or my mother's confession (impossible to get anyway, thank you very much, Alzheimer's disease). I knew in my gut that Maggie and I were connected, that we'd both formed in the same womb, that we shared a partial bloodline.

If she'd only given me one goddamn moment to collect my thoughts, things might have turned out differently. I mean, how long has she been doing this investigative reporting thing on television? Twenty years? Thirty? Long enough to know that when you turn someone's life upside down with a single piece of paper, you should give the person time to process.

But, no. She had to go and make demands. *She* wanted to see *our* mother. She wanted to set up a DNA test. She wanted to film everything for her TV show, starting right then and there.

I'll admit it doesn't take much to get my Irish up, but c'mon. This was more than any old news story. *We* were more than any old news story. Weren't we? Why would she want to exploit us? Why wouldn't she want to deal with everything in private, like a normal, rational human being? That was my first clue that Maggie Prescott was in it for herself, and only herself, and she didn't give a rat's ass about Mom, or me, or the fact we were, well, family. The only functioning family I had left.

My friend Joelle says that instead of kicking Maggie and her cameraman out that day two weeks ago, I should have challenged her, shared what I was feeling, and seen how she responded. Because, Joelle claims, that would have been more revealing of Maggie's true character. This is probably why Joelle is the social worker and I'm the lowly activities director (read: bingo bitch) at Saint Anthony of Padua Healthcare Center. I don't always think things through. I wear my heart on my sleeve. You piss me off, and you're going to know it in fairly short order.

For a while, though, I thought Joelle might have been right. Perhaps I'd been too hasty. I considered calling Maggie and saying, "Let's try this again." But something always stopped me. Why hadn't she reached out to me? It had been nearly two weeks, for God's sake. I don't watch a lot of TV, and I tend to avoid the news since it's too depressing, but even I know that Maggie is good at what she does. Why would she give up on this "story"—*her* story—so easily? Why would she give up on me, her sister? Hadn't she done her research? Didn't she know how hard it would be for me to trust again, love again, take a chance again, and that I'd need a little help, some prodding at the very least?

But then came the second clue, reminding me that my original hunch about Maggie Prescott had been correct.

#

When Maggie waltzed in here this afternoon, alone this time, my heart skipped a beat, like I was in love or something. I was happy to see her, happy that she hadn't turned her back, and happy that maybe we'd get a second chance at this whole sister thing. Then she tossed the envelope at me. She didn't even hand it to me. She tossed it.

"What's this?" I said as I held it in my hands.

"The DNA results. Proof positive."

I looked up, confused. "Whose DNA results?"

She arched her left eyebrow, her eyes wide. "Um, mine and Kate's."

It took me a second to register who Kate was. *Kate. Kate. My mother!* "What? But how did you get—"

"You didn't think I was going to let everything drop, did you?"

"But a DNA test?" I tore open the envelope and pulled out the papers, but the text and numbers blurred together. "I didn't give you permission to do this. To invade my mother's privacy."

"*Our* mother," she said. "Or so it would seem."

I threw everything on my desk. "You don't care about *our* mother. You only care about getting the story."

"I care about the facts. I care about the truth."

"Oh, right. I'm sure ratings don't play into that at all."

"The truth brings ratings, yes. As it should."

"And you'll simply walk over anyone in your way in order to get the truth, is that right? Even if it's family you're walking over?"

She rolled her eyes, but her voice remained even and calm. "I wasn't going to let your so-called concern get in the way of my finding out the truth, no."

"My so-called concern? You think I'm faking concern for my mother?"

"Our mother," she said. "And yes. Considering you've locked her away in this place, I'd say your sudden distress over her wellbeing and privacy came across as disingenuous at best."

I gripped the sides of my chair. "You don't know what you're talking about. You don't know anything about me. Or her."

"Oh, that's right," she'd said and her eyes narrowed. "How could I? She's *your* mother, isn't she?"

#

Joelle, who fancies herself a shrink instead of a social worker, says Maggie was simply attacking a known weak spot. Most people who put a parent in a nursing home have some feelings of guilt. Joelle thinks Maggie was simply exploiting this weakness, she was good at her job, and she was using it as leverage to get what she wanted: complete access to Mom, which, of course, I immediately granted, as if doing so would prove she was wrong, that being in Saint A's was the best move for my mother, and that I didn't have anything to hide.

The problem is, that last part's not true. Even though a big part of me keeps hoping someone will come up with a magical cure for Alzheimer's, allowing Mom's memories freedom from whatever prison they're in, another part of me is afraid of this ever happening. Because some memories are best left dead and buried. Like the way I treated Mom in those last months before I moved her in here. Especially that last night. That last god-awful night.

Maggie's disdain for me is justified. I get that. But the minute she put her career and ratings before my—*our*—mother's needs, she lowered herself to my level.

Thing is, I'm aware of what I am and what I did. I know I screwed up and that I did wrong by my mother. But Maggie? She goes along as if her quest is some sort of noble pursuit. Well, screw her quest. And screw any chance at our ever being sisters.

# Chapter 2: Maggie

"You spending the night?"

Yawning, I stretch and face Serena, my no-nonsense producer. "That your way of asking whether you can go home?"

"Maggie, after fifteen years of working with your brand of crazy, I've earned the right to decide when I get to go home. I was just wondering if I should stop by your condo tomorrow morning and pick you up a change of clothes. Considering you've been living here the last few weeks and all."

I turn back to the screen. "Soon," I say, opting to answer her original question and ignoring the last one.

"Uh huh." Serena flicks off the light, leaving me in a room filled with monitor-glow blue. "I'll see you tomorrow, then."

I don't respond, my mind and eyes already refocused on the barely fifteen-minute footage of the only family I have left in this world. I memorize every detail: the color of their eyes (green, just like mine); Kate's ultra-thin lips (so that's why I need Botox); April's no-nonsense pixie haircut and barely-there freckles splashed across her slim nose; Kate's vacuous expression; and April's flushed cheeks, her anger impossible to mask.

At first, April was nothing more than a nuisance, an obstacle between me and the truth. I'd been in this position hundreds, maybe even thousands of times before, and I'd always emerged unscathed, story in hand, job complete. After all, I'm Margaret R. Prescott. As one former boss liked to point out, "And the *R.* stands for three things: reporter, renegade, and royal pain in the ass." I always chalked up his derision to jealousy. Because, you see, nothing rattles me. Not a bombed-out village in Afghanistan. Not mass graves in Rwanda. Not a gutted daycare center in Oklahoma City. Not shell-shocked students, their T-shirts and jeans bloody, hours after the Columbine massacre. Not when the Twin Towers fell. Nothing.

This is the way it's been for the last thirty years. That is, until I walked into this Hades otherwise known as Saint Anthony of Padua Healthcare Center, where my steely veneer cracked, thanks to sister April, my birth mother, and the buried memory of the woman who raised me until I was ten years old.

#

I'd convinced *New England Journal*, my new television home in Boston, that the story wouldn't be a problem. Was I willing to document, on camera, the first time I met my biological mother and then construct a whole segment around my "journey" as an adopted child, all in time for a special to air later this month? Of course. That's what made me a reporter. A renegade. And another R-word that too many people in the business, men especially, are loathe to admit: *respected*. I go where the story—where truth—takes me, no matter what, or who, is involved.

Sentimental, I am not, and a sister—or half sister, as April likes to point out—delivers little emotional impact on my heart. Why should it? I'm fifty-two years old. I've known I was adopted since I was old enough to read (at age four). I suffered more emotional losses by the age of twenty-five than anyone should have to go through in a lifetime. While I could have wallowed in my grief, mourning my losses, I chose to do the opposite. The vernacular, I believe, is called "making peace with your past," which I did and which is why this new assignment was merely that—an assignment—and one that I hoped would afford me a second chance at a New York gig, despite my age and reluctance to be nipped and tucked.

If only I hadn't faltered the first time I'd met Kate.

#

That fateful afternoon two weeks ago, we'd just left April's office, a shoebox-sized room of chaos filled with DVDs, hundreds of romance books, random tennis balls with holes cut in them (used for the bottoms of walkers, I quickly observed), an employee of the year plaque with April's name etched onto a gold plate, and dozens of pictures of a man with a boy about four years old. April's late husband and son, I presumed. My preliminary research had revealed this fact: they were killed in a car accident over ten years ago.

April was kicking Hank—my intrepid cameraman—and me out of the building because we'd refused to turn off the camera and she didn't want us prowling around. But I know the real reason was because she had to digest what I'd just revealed to her: we were half siblings and shared the same mother, Kate Sullivan. She'd taken the news like anyone else would have— with a combination of confusion, incredulity, and a touch of curiosity—but I didn't care. My segment needed focus; it needed to be about Kate. The look of surprise on April's face when I produced my birth certificate made it clear to me that she knew nothing about my existence. Ergo, she was of no use to me, or this piece.

Her righteous anger over my desire to tape a segment and set up a DNA test didn't surprise me, nor did her decision to escort Hank and me to the front of the building. When we'd arrived at the sliding glass doors, she stood with her arms crossed as she watched us walk onto the semi-circle driveway. Hank winked at me—he liked the chase as much as I did—and lit up a cigarette while I pulled out my Blackberry and pretended to make a call. The whole time, my peripheral vision followed the movement on the other side of the glass.

"She's gone," I said when April was no longer visible. "Let's go." I shoved the Blackberry into my bag, Hank dropped his butt, and we walked back inside. He lifted the camera to his shoulder as I spoke to the receptionist at the front desk.

"We're ready to see Kate Sullivan now," I said. "Second floor, correct?"

The woman beamed, unaware, apparently, of what had transpired between April and me, and charmed, no doubt, to be in the presence of a "celebrity." Or at least the closest she'd ever get to one. She nodded and pointed down the hall towards the elevators, and Hank and I marched on, in pursuit of a story, in pursuit of truth. We passed the dining room and rounded a corner when a stench filled my nostrils. I doubled over, woozy, and Hank practically walked into me.

"Maggie," he whispered. "You okay?"

I placed my hand flat against the raised wallpaper, a maroon and green paisley print, the perfect accent to the shimmering gold banisters, the ornate mirrors, and the chandeliers hanging overhead. We could have been in some posh hotel or the foyer of a mansion. Except, of course, we weren't. The odor—a combination of urine, rotting food, and Lysol—revealed otherwise. And suddenly, just like that, I was ten again, walking hand in hand with my father down a muted green hallway where every obnoxious smell imaginable bombarded us. I'd try breathing through my mouth, counting the interminable steps it took to get to room 142, the place where my mother— the only one I'd ever known, anyway—lay dying.

Whenever we visited her, we passed old women and the occasional token male strapped to their wheelchairs and put on display outside their rooms, lining the hallway like it was Main Street on the Fourth of July. They were always there, waiting. Some would reach out and try to touch me as I passed, their eye sockets sunken, their mouths toothless, their grips surprisingly strong. The whole time I'd be thinking, *I hate it here, I hate the doctors who put her here, and I hate my father for letting them.* That is, until these thoughts were interrupted by her, my mother. Despite my stellar vocabulary and eighth grade reading level, I'd never known until those dark days in that horrific convalescent home that you could define "anguish" as a sound.

"Maggie," Hank said again.

"I'm okay. I'm okay." I stood up, took a deep breath, and I was. The moment passed. It always did. "You still rolling?"

He nodded, and we continued onto the elevator to the second floor where the Alzheimer's patients resided. We walked down the darkened halls. No one noticed us, despite the camera. As we approached the nurse's station, a fat woman behind the desk looked up. I walked to her, smiled, and said, "We just met with April Sullivan-LaMonica. We're here to see Kate Sullivan."

The nurse paused, considering our request, and I could imagine what she was thinking—*How does the employee handbook say to handle film crews from television stations?* But then she noticed she too was being filmed. She touched her limp hair, her dark roots showing, and pointed to the dayroom across from where we stood. In the far corner, a small woman, frail as a bird, sat looking out the window.

I turned and walked backwards while speaking into the camera, knowing we'd have endless editing to do, but also knowing that this raw footage was priceless. "Here I am," I began, "about to meet my biological mother for the first time."

As I crossed the threshold into the dayroom, a TV blasted three ticks louder than it should have.

"Hello, Mother," I called out, and self-consciousness overwhelmed me. I had meant to say *Kate*, not *Mother*. The old woman didn't respond, of course, so I cleared my throat and tried again. "Hello, Kate." She didn't respond to her name either, didn't look up, didn't acknowledge my presence.

I went to her and touched the sleeve of her turquoise sweat suit that was two sizes too big.

She jumped.

I jumped.

And that's when everything changed. When I touched her, electricity charged every cell of my body. I couldn't let go. My eyeballs swam. My palms sweated. My face flushed. The nausea returned. *How could April put her in here, leave her here to die? I need to help her, save her.* I turned to Hank.

"Shut it off," I said.

"What?"

"You heard me. Turn off the camera."

"No."

"What do you mean no?"

"Serena warned me you might say that," he said. "And to keep rolling if you did."

I'd never told a film crew to shut a camera off in my life. Why would Serena think I'd do it now? "I don't care," I hissed. "Shut. It. Off."

"Sorry, Maggie." He shifted from one foot to the other. "Keep going. This is good stuff." With his free arm, he pointed to Kate. "See? She's looking at you."

I charged the lens. "I don't care."

Hank swung around. The camera panned the room, the nurses' station, and the large picture window that looked into the dayroom from the hallway. A man stood, watching the scene unfold. "Jesus, Maggie," Hank said. "Okay. Okay. It's off."

And the tape had gone black.

#

"What the hell," I whisper as I review the footage for the umpteenth time. I'd always been so fixated on Kate and my own reaction to her that I never noticed the person watching on the other side of the window. I play it back and home in on him.

"No," I say aloud even though there's no one in this area of the station, the folks affiliated with *New England Journal* having wrapped up the live broadcast hours ago. "It can't be."

I play it again, this time pausing on him, the image blurring as a result, but it doesn't matter. Even though it's been thirty years, there's no mistaking the dimples in his cheeks, like fingerprints molded in clay.

I lean back in my chair, wondering what sort of twilight zone I've walked into and how many more issues I've "made peace with" plan on rearing their ugly heads.

# Chapter 3: Nigel

I trudge in the darkness towards the church's side entrance, and a floodlight comes on, triggered, no doubt, by my movement. I shiver in the shadows. I've never been a religious man, and churches have always made me uncomfortable. Of course, Homer once said that all men have need of the gods. I wonder if Homer had been in AA, too.

A steep set of steps leads to the basement where, I've been told, a chair awaits me. I ignore them and instead walk in circles, trying to keep warm. It's unusually cold for early November, and I dig my bare hands in my pockets. I pace, stop, pace, and eye the stairs, waiting for what, I'm not entirely sure. But then, as if I'd conjured it myself, the basement door creaks open. A man ascends, an old-timer with craggy skin, a gray handlebar mustache, and Red Sox cap. He nods at me, not at all surprised to see me there, and lights a cigarette. He's quiet for a few minutes. Then he speaks.

"Okay. This is how it usually works." His voice is as wrinkled as his face. I recognize it, too. We've talked on the phone. "You come on down," he continues. "You listen. Talk if you want." He pauses but doesn't look at me. He takes a drag and stares off into space. "Now, I can't make no guarantees about anything, except this. It *won't* work with you standing out here all night."

He doesn't say anything else, simply finishes his business, drops the butt to the ground, and goes back downstairs as if I weren't even there, as if he hadn't spoken at all. I stare at the door, willing myself to move, but my will is gone, my confidence shaken, and I remind myself that no matter what I choose to do right now, too much has happened to ever go back.

#

"What's up with all the hours you've been spending at Saint A's lately?" Zoë, my secretary, had asked this afternoon. "And they're not billable hours, I might add."

"Ruth Frankenfeld has needed a little more hand holding than usual," I said, referring to one of our more notorious clients. "And there may be other prospects."

"Well, I hope these other 'prospects' are paying ones. Being nice and helpful to dying old ladies is all well and good, Nigel, but it doesn't pay the bills."

Normally, I appreciated Zoë's candor, but not today. "Do you get paid?" I asked.

"Before you do." She smiled. "And sometimes before the landlord."

"Then let me worry about the billable hours." I glared, she stuck out her tongue, and I disappeared into my office, knowing that our slightly dysfunctional boss-employee relationship would survive despite my moodiness. Despite everything.

#

What was I thinking? That I was somehow ready to walk into a group of strangers and confess to the bitter truth, when not even six hours earlier I lied to my secretary about why I'm spending so much time in a nursing home? That I was ready to stand up and make a proclamation that I'm not even sure I need to make? That I'd be comfortable "offering it all up" and giving myself over to Him?

Problem is I gave up on Him a long time ago, even before Maggie. It's funny—my life can be divided into two parts. Before Maggie. After Maggie.

The "During Maggie" I've always refused to acknowledge, those memories locked away for good. Or so I thought. So what now? What will I be calling this grand period of my life in ten or fifteen years? The "Maggie Stalker Years?" Those years Nigel Hurst spent lurking behind old ladies in wheelchairs as he spied on the infamous Margaret Rose Prescott, waiting to see if she might recognize him? Is recognition what I'm even looking for? Or am I hoping for more? And, if so, what?

I could tell myself and anyone else who asked—my shrink, my mother, even my sweet boy, Max—that what I had with Maggie was not one, but two lifetimes ago. That we were kids. That it's over, and it has been for a long time. I'm sure I'd be convincing. After all, hasn't that been the bane of my existence, the fact that I can convince a jury of whatever I want through bullshit disguised as beautiful rhetoric?

People think I got out of trial work because it was too much on me, because I wanted to be my own boss, because I had been one of the few who had made some good investments during the dot-com era and got out before it went belly up. But I left precisely for the reason my shrink says I'm never going to get sober: truth. I was tired of the spin, the slant. I was tired of looking in the mirror and seeing my father. So I got out. The thing is, the visage in the mirror never changed. At least, not until two weeks ago when the Nigel of today converged with the Nigel of thirty years ago—and all because of one scent.

I was surprised when I caught a whiff of her perfume as I exited a room at Saint Anthony of Padua Healthcare Center, a place known for its eau de urine rather than chic cologne. Not that I hadn't smelled this particular fragrance on other women over the years, but this time, it was different. It was exactly how I had remembered it being on Maggie—on those delicate places, like the spot below her throat, her wrists, and behind her ears. Despite every effort on my part to avoid it, my brain time-traveled back to 1973.

#

"Is this what you wear?" I had picked up the bottle from the bureau in her Emerson College dorm room. For weeks, I'd been dying to know the name. I had even gone to the store to hunt down Maggie's scent.

"Yeah. Why?"

I pulled off the cap and sniffed the bottle's contents. "It smells different on you."

"That's because," she said, taking it from my hand and dabbing a drop on her wrist, "it reacts with my body chemistry. Two people could be wearing the same perfume, and both would smell slightly different." She held her wrist to my nose. I sniffed. "See?"

"Ah, yes. There it is. Shows how much I know."

Maggie smiled and flipped her gloriously long red hair. "A true connoisseur will know the history."

"There's a history to a bottle of perfume?"

"There is to this one. Coco Chanel created it in 1921. Well, she didn't create it. A man named Ernest Beaux created it for her. He presented her with many versions, and this one—her favorite—was fifth in line, or so the story goes."

"Thus, the number five."

"Exactly. In the olden days, only the very rich bought perfume. This was the first commercial scent available to the masses."

I laughed. I'd been around her long enough to know that the woman was a walking encyclopedia, but still. "How do you know all this?"

Maggie shrugged. "It's called Chanel No.5 for a reason. I wanted to know why." She returned the bottle to her bureau. I noticed her hand linger on the black cap.

"What's wrong?"

She'd turned to me, her eyes wet. "It's funny how we associate scents with people. My mother used to wear this. Whenever I smell it, I think of her. I don't think I'll ever be able to associate it with anyone else."

#

I'm not sure if she jinxed me that day or what, but the same thing happened to me. I've always associated that damn perfume with her, no matter when, no matter where. Luckily, on that day at Saint A's two weeks ago, I ducked before she saw me. Because I didn't want her to see me, right? I didn't want to make small talk about weather or our jobs as if the chasm otherwise known as the last thirty years didn't exist. As if everything hadn't fallen apart one day in Florida back in 1976. There's no sense in living in the past. Or reliving it.

Right?

This is what my logical brain attempts to program into the rest of my gray matter, but my emotional brain knows it's all crap.

#

I'm back in my Jeep now and hover my hands over the heater. "You want a *real* confession, people?" I say aloud to no one. "I've been spending the last couple weeks playing Russian roulette with my heart. Hoping beyond hope that I bump into Maggie Prescott. That her visit to Saint A's wasn't a one-time deal. That she recognizes me, and I see some hint of something in her eyes."

I pause and turn up my favorite country station. "I increase my odds of seeing her by spending even more time at Saint A's." I slap my jeans in rhythm with the music and tap my boots against the floorboard, and the cowboy me emerges. Anything to disguise the real man, the person who's spent the last three decades trying to stamp out any traces of his drunken British father, opting instead to become more like his American mother, right down to masking any traces of his English accent—an accent that always turns up when he's speaking from the heart, with emotion, too fast.

"But at the same time," I continue to my invisible audience, "I'm trying to dodge a bullet of pain and misery that my reconnecting with Maggie is bound to lodge into the most vulnerable and tender part of my soul."

Ahead, the floodlight illuminates a path as people emerge from the basement while smoking, talking, and backslapping. The meeting's over. I've missed it again.

"And that," I say, while turning around and heading home where my wine collection awaits, "is the truth."

# Chapter 4: April

Saint Anthony of Padua Healthcare Center sits on a hill down the street from my childhood home. For the first two decades of my life, I never thought much about Saint A's, never even noted its existence, since high hedges and maple trees barricaded the front of the lot, obscuring most of the mansion-like building from view. Why would I notice it, anyway? Growing up, I played in the park directly across from my house, and in my teenage years, I became a mall rat. Old people didn't interest me. I had no memories of either sets of grandparents, and since my parents were the only children of only children, I had no elderly aunts or uncles or cousins twice removed, charming me with their wisdom and wild stories.

So the day Mom dragged me out for a walk eighteen months after the accident, I had no idea where she was taking me as she led me up the hill toward Saint A's. The only thing I remember is how the sun hurt my eyes. It had been so long since I'd been outside, having opted instead to sleeping ten, twelve, eighteen hours a day in a darkened room for over a year.

"I'm tired. I want to go back," I said.

"The walk will do you good, April. You need to get out."

"Why?"

She stopped and faced me, but I refused to make eye contact. "Because you're still alive."

I folded my arms. "As if I didn't already know that."

"Actually, I don't think you do. You act like you're dead. Or that you want to be. Which I can understand. But that's not your choice."

"Isn't it, though?" I mocked. I felt her eyes on me, burning me more than the damned sun. There's nothing else I could've said that would have hurt my mom more. Suicide was an off-limit word, my father's suicide an off-limit topic. I'd violated the most serious of understood pacts.

She clicked her tongue. "You would have done it by now. Since you haven't, that leads me to believe there's a piece of you, no matter how small, that wants to live." As I opened my mouth to protest, she held up her hand. "Don't. Just don't, okay? I know you're hurting. I know that pain—remember that pain—all too well. You have a choice. Sleep away the rest of your life. Or start to live."

"Living hurts too much."

She started walking again, and I automatically followed. "It wouldn't be life if it didn't," she said.

We were quiet for a while. She stopped, and I almost bumped into her, my head still down. We were standing in a semi-circle driveway in front of a building with a brick façade, two white pillars, and sliding glass doors.

"Where are we?" I peered at the sign above the doors: Saint Anthony of Padua Healthcare Center.

Mom said nothing. The glass doors parted as she approached, and I followed her through. We stood in a hotel-like lobby, complete with a reception desk and fancy waiting area. Mom spoke to the receptionist.

"My name's Kate Sullivan and this is my daughter, April. We called earlier about the activities assistant position. They said to come in and fill out an application."

*We?*

The receptionist smiled, nodded, and handed Mom a clipboard with a job application. She motioned for us to sit in the waiting area. As I plopped onto a rose-colored couch, I said, "You're getting another job?" Mom had worked two jobs for as long as I could remember—waitressing and some tailoring she did from the house.

"No. You are."

I froze as I watched her fill out the application with my information.

"Here." She handed me the clipboard. "You need to fill in the rest and sign it."

"But I can't." I shoved the clipboard away. "I'm not ready."

"It's a low-stress, part-time job, April. You'll be playing bingo and giving old ladies manicures. The HR person is one of my regulars at the diner, and she knows your situation. You're all but guaranteed to get the job."

"But—"

"You need to do something." She covered my trembling hand with hers. "This doesn't have to be forever. But you need to get back on track. Have something to wake up for."

I looked around. Aside from the receptionist, it was just us. It was quiet.

"Give it six months," Mom continued. "You'd be doing my friend a favor. They've been looking for a while."

"Why are they having such a hard time finding someone?"

"Doesn't pay much. Ten bucks an hour, if that. And it's not the most stimulating of jobs."

"Gee, I'm so glad that made you think of me."

She sighed. "That's the whole point. It won't be hard. You can literally roll out of bed, walk up the street, do a few hours, get paid, start to get some credentials and references, and get back in the swing of things."

"I can't."

"Listen, when your father died, I wanted to do the exact same thing you're doing: curl up in a ball and go to sleep."

"But you had me."

"Exactly," she said. "And you have me."

"It's not the same. And you know it."

She squeezed my hand. "But it's something, isn't it? And it's better than nothing. Do it for me, okay?"

I'm not sure what made me agree: guilt, fatigue, or the knowledge that my mother was right, that I couldn't do what I'd been doing forever. I filled out the form. I got the job offer the next day. I started the following week, my mother's words *"This doesn't have to be forever"* ringing in my head. If only she had been right.

#

On my first day at Saint A's, my uninterested boss decided to have me visit the most "challenging" residents in order to "acclimate." There was Norman, an eighty-year-old skeleton who invited me into bed with him; Sheila, a seventy-something woman with boobs that practically dragged on the floor—I know this because I walked in on her as she was trying to navigate her bra; Max, a paraplegic in a powered wheelchair who'd smash into you if you didn't give him what he wanted, which was usually some sort of contraband, like chocolate; and finally Hazel, an eighty-three-year-old woman rehabbing from hip surgery. Or at least that's what she told me, even though she was on the first floor that housed long-term residents, not the sub-acute wing on the second floor that was home to transitional patients.

By the time I reached Hazel's room, I'd been rammed into, yelled at, and sobbed to. I'd seen two naked women, one enema, one shriveled penis (after walking into the men's shower room by accident), and encountered a hallway that smelled like a combination of shit and canned cat food. I was one broken catheter bag away from walking out of the joint, my promise to Mom be damned, when I entered Hazel's room.

She sat in a rocking chair and scowled at me. "Are you the superintendent?" she asked.

"Excuse me?"

"Are you the superintendent?"

"Um, no."

"Are you the nutritionist?"

"No. I'm April. From the Activities Department."

"Activities?" She laughed. "My dear girl, does it look as if I need activities? What I need is food that I can recognize." She shook her head. "What is wrong with this place? It is a good thing I am only a rehab patient, as I cannot imagine what it would be like to live here permanently. I have asked to see the superintendent for the last week to talk about this rubbish they call food." She gestured towards a tray table and an untouched plate on which the only item I could identify was green Jell-O. I bent to get a better look and was about to say something when a woman in a black suit, high heels, and tight bun click-clacked her way into the room.

"Are you the superintendent?" Hazel asked.

"No. I'm Joelle Weiss. Your social worker." She raised an eyebrow and considered me for a half second before turning her attention to a chart. "Ms. Cooke, it appears you have a problem with the food."

"Well, wouldn't you?" Hazel pointed to the tray table, but Joelle ignored her and shuffled through pages.

"As we've explained a myriad of times, this particular diet has been ordered by your doctor."

"Diet? What diet? I have never in my life been on a diet that—"

"Well," Joelle interrupted. "According to this, you are."

"As I have explained myriad times, Ms. Weiss, either everyone here is reading that chart incorrectly, or they have mixed up the orders."

"That's not possible."

Hazel's eyes widened. "Oh? Did you hear that, my dear girl?" she said, turning to me. "They make no mistakes in this place."

Joelle sighed. "Ms. Cooke. As we have explained—"

Hazel held up her hand. "Tell you what. You name three items on this plate, and you will never hear me complain again."

Joelle pursed her lips. "Fine." She leaned over the tray and pointed. "Jell-O and ..." She paused, squinted, and considered the grayish-orange mash that reminded me of Jimmy's favorite baby food: Gerber's sweet potatoes. "And ..." She sighed. "Okay. This food has been pureed. It's probably some sort of vegetable."

"Why has it been pureed?" Hazel asked.

"For easier chewing and swallowing."

"And why, Ms. Weiss, would I need assistance in chewing and swallowing when only two months ago, I was eating corn on the cob the night before my surgery?"

"Your surgery may have—"

"My hip, Ms. Weiss. I had a hip replacement. Not a root canal."

"Well, dentures can—"

"Who said anything about dentures? I do not have dentures."

"Oh." Joelle looked from Hazel to me. I shrugged. "Well," she continued. "I'm sure your doctor has a reason. Doctor's orders, you know."

"But," I piped up. "Shouldn't you check to make sure that someone hasn't made a mistake? I mean, what's it going to take? One phone call?"

Her back arched. "And you are?"

"April Sullivan-LaMonica." I held out my hand. "New activities assistant."

"Right. Notice there's no 'MD' after that title."

"Just like there's no 'MD' after yours." (I guessed.)

She glared at me. "Fine. We'll check."

"Thank you," Hazel said as Joelle stomped out. "That is all I have been asking." She shook her head and turned to me. "I suppose you are the one I should thank."

I looked at the plate of mystery food. "No need for thanks. And if for some reason your doctor did order this crap, I'll sneak you in some fruit smoothies."

"My dear, forget the fruit. I will have a double scoop of chocolate fudge brownie. *With* nuts." She smiled, and for the first time that day, I did, too.

#

It turned out there had been a mix-up with the doctor's orders and that the nurses, aides, and Joelle had all ignored Hazel's protests.

"It's a common complaint, the food," Joelle said sheepishly after she sought me out to apologize for her behavior. "Not just here. At all nursing homes. Listen, you're not going to report me, are you?"

"Report you? You mean there's a place I can go when someone is being a bitch?" I smiled so she could see I was kidding. "Trust me, if that's the case, I can think of plenty of people who'd be at the top of my list before you. But I do have a question."

"Shoot."

"Well, Hazel said that she was only rehabbing from surgery, but she's on the first floor with the long-term residents. Is it possible that's been screwed up, too?"

Joelle shook her head. "Unfortunately, no."

"So is she demented? Or delusional?"

"More like in denial. The truth is, she probably doesn't need to be here. It's her family's decision."

"You mean they went against her wishes? Isn't that illegal or something?"

"It's more complicated than that when you deal with powers of attorney and all the other legal stuff."

"So she knows she's here permanently?" I pressed.

"Deep down, I think she does."

"And she won't fight it?"

"I think she'll simply complain louder about the food."

"Why's that?"

"Because that's something she might actually be able to change. She might bitch about being here, but at the end of the day, she'll abide by what her nephew wants. He's all she has left."

"Wow. That sucks."

Joelle nodded. "Yeah, it does." We stared at each other for a long moment, and even though I sensed how different we both were—that she'd gone to college and graduate school, that she was much worldlier and more refined—I felt an alliance forming. I don't know if it was because of our ages—turns out she was twenty-five, only a year older than I was—or if it had something to do with the fact we'd come out on the other end of a potentially ugly situation relatively intact, but I felt a bond, a connection. "No matter what anyone says," she continued, "and no matter how good they are, all nursing homes suck."

I think that's when I made the silent promise to myself, the one where I swore I'd never put my mother in a place like this or use any sort of deceit or deception when administering her care when she got old. Which now, of course, makes me wonder about the circle of hell I'll be going to in the afterlife.

#

"April," a voice calls out as I walk from the admin offices and across the lobby to help herd the residents into the music room for a performance by a young woman with multi-colored hair named Rainbow. After that first day at Saint A's ten years ago, I worked my way up to activities director within eight months, an impressive feat in any other industry but this one, since turnover—even in the benign area of activities—is high.

I turn and see Nigel Hurst, an attorney who has several clients in the building, including Ruth Frankenfeld who is known for going from zero to bullshit in thirty seconds. I give the man a lot of credit.

"What's up?" I say.

"I'm looking for someone I saw here a few weeks ago. I've noticed she's signed into the guest book since then. And, well, I'm trying to see if she comes at a regular time."

"Who is it?"

"Maggie Prescott."

"What?"

"Now, April, I know what you're thinking. Don't worry. I'm not some sort of celebrity stalker. I actually know Maggie. Well, knew her. Ages ago." He stops and shakes his head, almost embarrassed. "I suppose it's silly, isn't it?"

"Yeah. Probably," I say without even thinking. "She doesn't have a regular time. But she's here every day." Every blessed day asking me if I've considered this drug or that therapy for Mom, as if treating Alzheimer's is as simple as treating a sore throat.

"Right. Thanks."

"Well, good luck." I hurry down the hall towards Hazel's room—first, to see if she's interested in watching Rainbow, and second, to escape any further discussion of Maggie, but Nigel catches up with me anyway.

"One more thing," he says.

"Yeah?"

"Whom has she been seeing?"

I'm surprised he hasn't heard, considering the rest of the building has been abuzz ever since people found out that Maggie and I are related.

"She's visiting her mother."

"Her mother? But she's adopted. And her adoptive mum died when she was a child."

"Right," I say, even though I had no idea. "It's her biological mother."

"Crickey," he says, and with that word, I hear what sounds like a British accent. "Who is it?" he asks.

"Kate Sullivan."

"But wait," he says, stopping. I stop as well, folding my arms impatiently. "Isn't that—"

"Yes," I interrupt. "Kate's my mother, too."

#

When I get to Hazel's room, the door is closed. Again. Been like this all month. Hazel, despite all her complaining, is also one of the more popular residents, mainly because she has all her faculties and can outwit people half her age. Her door is usually wide open, regardless of what her roommates prefer. (She's gone through eight in the last ten years, and not because they all died.)

I knock and push the door open. Hazel looks up, her eyes scared as if she's expecting Death himself. When she sees it's only me, her face relaxes.

"What's with the door, Hazel?" I collapse into a chair and wave hello to Hugh Dooley, who sits across the room by his wife's bedside. He's been here every day since the paramedics delivered his comatose wife, Gloria, seven months ago.

"There is a draft, my dear," Hazel says. "I would not want Mr. Dooley or his lovely wife to get a chill."

Okay, so there's something she's not telling me. Looking at Hazel, you could easily think she's simply a proud old woman who chose the route of teacher and caretaker as opposed to wife and mother. At ninety-three years old, she stands barely five feet tall and still wears dresses, nylon stockings, jewelry, and makeup every day. That's the surface woman, the Hazel you meet when she has her hair done in Saint A's salon or when she has tea with some of the other women in the private dining room. But the Hazel underneath—the woman who's loved, lost, and spent her life alone, and not by choice—is the real woman, the woman I've come to know and love, despite my resistance to becoming too close to anyone, especially someone whose days are numbered.

"So, do you want to come down to the music room and hear Rainbow perform today?" I ask.

She wrinkles her nose.

"Didn't think so. But it gave me an excuse to visit and put my feet up for a while." I prop my feet on the edge of her bed.

"How has your day been so far?"

Nigel's face flashes before my eyes. "Weird. Seems everyone and their brother is interested in seeing Mag—" I pause. "You know. *Her.*"

Hazel's face pales, and her usually commanding voice sounds shrill. "So Maggie Prescott is still spending time here?"

"Yep. But she seems to have given up on bringing in any cameras. Once she's convinced there's nothing she can do for Mom and that there's nothing I can offer her in way of answers, I'm hoping she leaves. For good."

"April," she says, and her voice sounds strong again. "There is something you should know about Maggie. I—"

Before she can finish, someone knocks on the door. Joelle pokes her head in. "There you are. I don't know why I didn't look here first. You better come with me."

"What's up?"

Joelle gives me a *you-need-to-see-this-for-yourself* look. "Just come."

I roll my eyes at Hazel before trotting after Joelle.

"Did you give Maggie permission to bring cameras into the building today?" she asks as we step onto the elevator and she presses the button for the second floor.

I groan. "I was just telling Hazel that she hadn't brought any in since that first day. Looks like I jinxed myself."

"Well, that's not all," she says as the doors slide open. We exit and walk down the hallway towards my mother's room. As we get closer, several voices emanate from inside along with something that sounds like a muffled cry. Pushing the door open, I discover my mom on her back in bed and thin silver needles protruding from her forehead, earlobes, and other various points on her body. A solitary tear makes its way from the corner of her right eye and down her cheek. Maggie is holding her hand, rubbing her thumb along the contours of Mom's index finger. Two women lean over them while a guy holding a video camera captures everything.

I charge into the room. "What the hell is going on?" Everyone looks up.

"April," Maggie says. "I'm glad you're here. I'd like you to meet—"

"I'm not meeting anyone." I turn to the cameraman and hold my palm over the lens. "Turn it off." He jerks away, but I'm already focusing on the two women poised over Mom. "Get out of this room! And get those things out of her!" I reach for the needles, but Maggie's hand holds me back.

"Careful," she whispers. "The practitioners need to take them out."

"Then take them out! She's crying, for chrissakes."

"She was crying, April, but only for a minute. There are sensitive spots, but she's fine now. See?"

I consider my mother's face and notice that the tear has disappeared, leaving a wet mark on her cheek. She even appears relaxed, despite my screaming. "Who gave you permission to do this?"

"You never responded to the information I left in your mailbox," Maggie says. "I mentioned in my note that you should let me know if you had a problem with Kate trying acupuncture. I said that if I didn't hear from you, I would assume you were okay with it."

"I don't remember this note, and you shouldn't assume I'd be okay with something like this. Get them out. The needles, your so-called doctors, and the fucking paparazzi." I storm out of the room past Joelle, who I know will clean up the mess. Maggie comes up behind me.

"April. Wait."

I quicken my pace.

"Will you slow down for a minute?" Maggie grabs my arm, but I shake her off. "Let's talk about this," she says as we reach the elevators.

"There's nothing to talk about." I pound the down button, but nothing happens. Desperate to get away, I head for the stairwell around the corner, plow through the door, and take the steps two at a time. I burst through the door that takes me to the first floor and race down the hall, Maggie on my heels. Finally, I turn and face her as I get to Hazel's room, figuring she won't violate another resident's privacy by following me inside.

"If you'll excuse me," I spit before exploding into the room.

Hazel is on the phone, which is probably the only reason why I don't slam the door shut behind me. I close it enough so Maggie can't see inside.

"Bertha, I will have to call you back," Hazel says into the receiver when she sees how upset I am. Hugh looks up from his book.

"My dear, what is it?" she asks.

"It's her. Maggie."

As I say the name, the door slowly opens. Then, Maggie appears. She's not looking at me. She's studying Hazel.

"Miss Cooke?" she says. "I saw the name 'Hazel B. Cooke' on the door. But it can't be you." She peers at Hazel. "Can it?"

Hazel takes a deep breath and smiles a smile I thought was reserved only for me.

"Margaret Rose Prescott." She clasps her hands together as if she's about to pray. "I wondered if I would ever see you again."

I can't believe this. "You two know each other?"

"Knew," Maggie says.

"A long time ago," Hazel adds. "I was Maggie's teacher in high school."

Maggie shakes her head. "You were a lot more than that," she whispers.

Hazel looks nervously from me to Maggie and back to me. "Well. I—"

"You two will want to catch up," I hear myself say as I turn and walk out.

#

I wander aimlessly around the building and then through the activities room, ignoring the hellos from two residents who are watching *The Sound of Music* for the gazillionth time. Even though I have three shelves filled with old black and white movies, Julie Andrews and the Von Trapp kids always win. I fish through the top drawer of my desk and find my emergency pack of Virginia Slims, matches, and the key that will unlock the door to the patio that's closed off to the residents for the winter.

My thin top does little to protect me from the raw November wind as I plop onto a patio chair. The sun is already setting, and the orange sky casts a bizarre glow on the tree trunks and bare limbs. I shiver, light a cigarette, and cough, a stale taste in my mouth.

"Those things will kill you," a voice says.

"Only if my luck changes." I turn to find Hugh Dooley leaning on the corner of the building where the patio meets the grass. "What are you doing out here?"

"Well, there's this." He holds up a cigar. "But I also thought I should give Hazel some privacy."

"I didn't know you smoked," I say.

"I didn't know you did."

"I don't." I pause, caught. "Shouldn't anyway."

"Me either." He walks toward me, settles into the only other metal chair, and lights up.

"This area is closed off to residents for the winter," I say.

"Well, I guess it's a good thing I'm not one."

"There are places to smoke in front of the building."

"That's where I started out until an old woman with an oxygen tank started giving me dirty looks. I didn't think anyone would be back here."

"The employees smoke on the stoop at the side entrance."

He inhales, exhales, and waves his hand as if he's dismissing me. "Be my guest."

"I meant you."

"Me? But I'm not an employee."

"But I was here first," I say.

"And I was here second. What, are we ten?"

"I wish."

He nods. "Ten was a good age, wasn't it?"

"I'd rather go back to five, actually," I say as my father's face becomes as clear as Venus in the almost-winter sky.

"Why five?"

"Long story. Look, I came out here because I wanted to be alone. I don't mean to be rude, but I don't feel like talking." I take a drag and cough again.

Smoking's a habit that Javier, the first and only guy I've slept with since Vinny died, got me started on when I would hang out with him and the other Brazilian aides. I stopped when he left and returned home to Brazil and to his wife and the litter of kids he forgot to tell me about. I haven't had a butt in nearly two years and I'm clearly out of practice. Not that I ever learned to inhale right.

"She wanted to tell you, you know," Hugh says.

"Who wanted to tell me what?" I sigh.

"Hazel. About Maggie. But she thought it might upset you."

"Yeah, well. Whatever."

"Looks as if she was right."

"I'm not upset. Just surprised."

He nods and says nothing.

"So how close were they?" I ask when I can't stand the silence anymore. "Hazel and Maggie."

He shrugs. "From what I was able to glean from my conversations with Hazel, quite a bit."

"Well, it doesn't change things."

"Nor should it."

"I mean with Maggie. She can't fix my mother, despite what she thinks. And there's no way in hell I'm going to let her broadcast Mom's condition to the world in some pseudo-documentary. She's a meddlesome bitch," I add for good measure, surprised at how angry I sound.

"From what I've overheard you describe to Hazel, I would have to agree."

"Really?"

"Yes, really." He shifts in his chair so that we're facing each other. "But then again, meddling is what families do."

He holds my gaze, and the patio light comes on. The white light reflects off his head, which is an attractive—even sexy—bald, like the guy who plays Locke on *Lost* or Jean-Luc Picard on the *Star Trek* reruns I sometimes catch when I can't sleep.

"You know what I like best about you, Hugh?" I point to the red silk tie poking out from beneath the collar of his long black winter coat. "The fact that you always wear ties for your wife."

"Gloria said she always liked me in ties and crisp white shirts."

"See? That's sweet."

He doesn't respond, but the corners of his mouth turn down slightly, and I get the feeling he doesn't agree, that there's more to the story than that. I don't ask. All I know is Gloria is in a coma due to some sort of fall that caused a stroke. She's sixty-three, young by nursing home standards, and as far as any of us can tell, she's not going to get better or wake up.

"Can I ask you something?" I hear myself say and immediately regret my impulsiveness.

"You may."

"Why won't your daughter sign Gloria's DNR?"

While I'm used to having frank discussions with residents' family members, something feels different about this one. Usually a spouse holds durable power of attorney and controls the healthcare proxy for the other. If someone is divorced or the spouse has died, another person, like a child, is named. But in Hugh and Gloria's case, their daughter Adrienne—someone I've met only once at a care plan meeting when Gloria was first admitted—is the person in charge, not Hugh. What's stranger still is that Adrienne refuses to sign her mother's "Do Not Resuscitate" order despite everyone from the director of nurses to Gloria's own private doctor to Hugh himself believing that she should.

"It all goes back to what I said earlier," he says.

"What's that?"

"Family members who feel the need to meddle."

"Guess we can't escape it."

"Guess not."

"So, how do you deal?"

He tilts his head, considering the question. "By meddling right back."

"But how?"

He gets up, holds his cigar in one hand, digs the other in his coat pocket, and faces the sky, where a few stars dot the night. I'm so used to seeing him in a rocking chair or leaning over Gloria's bed that I never realized how tall he is, well over six feet. He's quiet, and I'm starting to think he's not going to answer my question when the deep sound of his voice cuts the silence.

"By refusing to let her think she's right."

# Chapter 5: Maggie

My first instinct is to walk out and never look back. To leave this hellhole of a time warp and flee to New York or LA or London. It was a bad idea to come back home to Boston and dredge up the past.

"My dear," she says in a tremulous voice. "How are you?"

I face Hazel, her one simple question making it sound so easy, as if a lifetime—her life, my life—hadn't passed in the three decades since I last saw her.

"I'm fine."

She tilts her head, sizing me up. "Are you, Margaret?"

"I don't know what to tell you."

"The truth. Tell me the truth."

I laugh. "The truth, Hazel? You want the truth? You knew I'd been coming here, didn't you?"

She nods and stares at her lap.

"Why didn't you tell April you knew me?" I'm surprised at how hurt I sound.

"It is not as simple as you think."

"No? Let's review. Seems you and April are close. Presumably, she told you about me. Why would you try to hide the fact you and I knew each other?"

She sighs, lifts her head, and finally meets my gaze. Her face is thinner than I remember, and her nose is longer, pointier somehow. In all my reading and research on Alzheimer's, I've also read general information on the elderly. As we grow older, our bodies shrink in height, but the cartilage in our ears and noses continues to grow. Our skin thins and becomes fragile, like eggshells. However, there's something else about Hazel's face—something I don't recall having been there before. It startles me.

"This is a bad idea," I say. "Let's pretend it never happened." I turn and have one foot out the door when she speaks.

"Maggie, wait. Please. Do not go."

"Why not?" I turn around. "Obviously, too much has happened. Too much history for us to overcome."

"Things ended poorly," she says.

"That's an understatement."

"I handled things poorly."

"Agreed," I say.

She sniffs. "It takes two, my dear."

"Once again, let's review the facts. You're the one who cut off all correspondence. After I got out of the hospital, you stopped communication. I'd call, but you were 'never in.' I'd write, but you never responded." I stop, gauging whether I should continue. This is ridiculous. Water under the bridge. So why is my chest so tight? "You must have known," I begin slowly, carefully, "what that would do to me. You rejected me, Hazel. *You* rejected *me*."

"You are right," Hazel whispers. "I am sorry for that, Maggie. More than you will ever know." She stares at me, her lower lip quivering. Making an old lady cry is not my goal, especially if it means inducing tears on my end. I stand straighter, smooth my hands on my pants, and flash my brightest smile.

"Forget about it," I say. "It was a long time ago. I'm sure you had your reasons. Besides, you did me a favor. Once you were gone, there was no one left. I was on my own and made my own way." I stretch my arms out wide. "You must admit I haven't done too bad for myself."

She searches my face, and I can feel her eyes boring through my mask. "But are you happy, Maggie?"

"Are you?" I shoot back, my rookie attempt at avoiding her question.

"I'm ninety-three years old. I live in a nursing home and share a room the size of a linen closet with a woman who is hooked up to machines that keep her alive. What do you think?"

"Well, it's your choice, isn't it? This isn't prison." *Unlike what it is for Kate,* I think.

"It might as well be."

"Whatever happened to—" I shuffle through memories. "Tallulah Falls?" I pause again, more memories bursting from my gray matter. "What happened to Mack's sister? That house?"

Her lips form a tight, straight line. "You are quite good at this. I have watched you over the years, how you steer the conversations exactly where you want them to go."

"What do you mean?"

"You have not answered my question."

"Which one?"

"Are you happy?"

We stare each other down. Finally, I speak. "I'm fifty-two years old. Never been married. No kids. No home to speak of. Adopted parents are dead. Biological mother has Alzheimer's, and biological half sister thinks I'm Satan incarnate. What do you think?"

She shakes her head, chuckles, and plays with the ratty fringe of the yellow blanket covering her lap. I try to hide a smile.

"Hazel," I continue. "What were you thinking? We were bound to meet. You live in the same nursing home as my mother, for God's sake. You know April. Were you hoping I'd eventually give up on all this and go away?

"No, my dear," she says. "I did not hope that. But April did. Still does, I imagine."

I cross my arms, shake my head, and gaze at the ceiling. "Well, it seems to me we have a choice. Pretend this never happened. That we never reconnected." I stop and wait.

"Or?" Hazel finally asks.

Our eyes meet. There was a time when Hazel was the mother I'd lost, the confidante I longed for, the woman whom I turned to for advice and comfort. If anyone had told me thirty years ago that somehow we'd lose touch, that she'd stop being there for me, I'd have said that, barring death, that never would have happened.

"Or maybe," I begin, "we pick up from here. Try again."

She smiles a sad smile. "With whatever time we have left."

*Damn.* The younger me, the version that was, perhaps, a little sentimental would have wanted to run to her, to tell her not to talk like that, to ask her how she's been all these years, to ask her how I should handle Kate and April. These were the types of things she counseled me on when I was on the cusp of adulthood. But I don't. Instead, I glance at my watch.

"Hazel, I hate to do this, but I'm on the air in a couple of hours. I have to go." I walk to her, bend down, and look her in the eye so she can see I'm serious. "But I'll be back."

"And I shall be here, Margaret Rose Prescott." She reaches for my hand. I place mine over hers, which is bony and small. "Maggie, I *will* be here."

#

I'm in such a daze as I stand outside Hazel's closed door that I don't notice him approach. But then I hear …

"Mugsy."

There's only one person in the whole world who calls me that. Who used to call me that.

I face him, convinced that I must be dead, and this is my reckoning, my one final chance to make peace with the most significant people from my past. How else can I explain everything that's transpired in the last few weeks: Kate, April, Hazel, and now …

"Nigel," I say. The man I saw on the tape was him. "What are you doing here?"

"A client," he says, holding up his briefcase. "I was just dropping off some papers."

"Weren't you going into criminal law?" I picture old mobsters and murderers, white-haired and wheelchair bound, sitting in the dayroom down the hall.

"I was. I did. Got out a few years back. I handle estate planning now. Private practice."

I nod and start to walk down the hall. Nigel's stride matches my own, and his arm brushes up against mine.

"Well, aren't you going to ask me why I'm here?" I ask quickly, ignoring my body's reaction, the bat-sized butterflies flapping in my stomach.

"I already know," he says. "April told me."

I glance at him. "So you've known all along, too?"

"What do you mean 'too'?"

More memories: Hazel and Nigel arguing, years ago. Perhaps he doesn't know she's a resident. There's no sense in upending her world even further.

"How long have you known that I've been coming here?" I ask, trying to deflect.

"I saw you in the dayroom on the second floor a few weeks ago. You had a camera operator in tow. I didn't know it at the time, but you were, I believe, talking to her. Your biological mum."

He still can't completely mask his accent. When we first started dating, I asked him why he tried to hide it. "I'm in America now," was all he said.

I nod. "That was my first day here. Almost a month ago."

"Right. I figured I'd bump into you. One of these days."

We reach the main lobby, the same place where April had escorted me out of the building.

"Well. It looks as if you finally have," I say.

"Yes."

We stare at each other dumbly.

"Well, I should get—" I begin, but he interrupts.

"How've you been, Mugsy?"

I laugh at the situation's utter absurdity. First Hazel. Now Nigel. "We haven't seen each other in thirty years, and all you can say is 'how've you been'? As if you'd just seen me a few weeks ago?"

"Well, I did see you a few weeks ago. Technically." He smiles. Typical. Always trying to lighten the atmosphere with a joke.

"Look. I have business here. And, apparently, so do you. It's possible we'll bump into each other again. But let's get one thing straight. We don't have anything to talk about. So let's not pretend. You go your way. And I'll go mine."

His expression grows serious. Age lines appear around his eyes. His face is thin. No, not thin. Gaunt.

"Ah, I see how it is," he says. "You running away. Just like before."

"Don't start with me. I'm not the one who ran away. You never responded—"

"Daaad," a young voice interrupts. "C'mon. I've been waiting in the car forever. And Coach says I can't be late again."

We both turn towards the voice, and a boy, maybe twelve and decked out in football gear, stands in between the sliding glass doors of the main entrance. The doors start to close, then stop, start to close, then stop. I look around for the boy's father, but the only people in the area are the receptionist and us.

"I'll be right there, Max," Nigel says. He turns to me and smiles. "My son."

"I can see that." And I can. The same dimples. The same wild cowlick that won't behave. The same saddle-brown eyes. "So, you're married."

"A couple of times, actually. Max is the product of wife number one."

"Oh? And where's wife number two?"

"Working on husband number three, no doubt. Or maybe it's number four by now." He shrugs. "We divorced several years ago, and I haven't spoken to her since."

"I see. And is there a wife number three on your horizon?"

He clicks his tongue and winks. "Haven't asked her yet."

"Lucky for her. She still has time to come to her senses."

"Ah, yes," he says. "There's the Maggie I remember. Always ready with a witty, albeit cutting, response."

"Wouldn't want to disappoint you."

"Darling, you did that years ago."

"Daaad."

"I'll be there in a second, Max. Go wait in the car."

"It's uncanny," I say as we watch the boy race around the semi-circle driveway towards an idling black Jeep.

"What is?"

"How much he looks like you."

"Yes, I know, poor kid. He'd be better off with my sparkling personality rather than my looks."

"I don't know about that. Your looks never got you into trouble. It was your mouth."

Nigel chuckles and shakes his head. "Why so antagonistic, Mugsy? Can't we let bygones be bygones?"

"As I recall, that's what I wanted. But you couldn't."

"Well." He pauses. "I've changed."

*But I haven't*, I remind myself. I can't change what I did decades ago. And if I ever doubted whether Nigel could forgive me, there's no doubt in my mind now: he can't. Max is proof of that.

He touches my arm. "Maggie? You okay?"

I shake him off. "Fine."

"You were thinking something."

"I'm thinking Max is waiting for you." I avoid his eyes. "And that it's best if you go." I can feel him watching me, but I'm a master of blank expressions.

"Right," he whispers as he turns on the heels of his cowboy boots—wow, he still wears them?—exits through the sliding glass doors, and follows Max's steps to the Jeep. He hops into the driver's seat, tousles the boy's hair, and fastens his own seatbelt. Soon, the vehicle disappears down the long winding drive.

"Right," I whisper back.

#

I'm on autopilot for the rest of the afternoon and evening. It's amazing how I can get through a live television broadcast—the show's annual

Thanksgiving special highlighting local people giving back to the community—without missing a beat. Is he home watching me? Is he alone? Do I care? It's not until the show wraps and everyone heads home that I realize how unhinged I am over today's events. I'm not sure how long I've been staring at my computer when Serena pokes her head in my office.

"What're you doing?"

"Thinking."

"Yeah?" She walks in, reaches for the juggling balls on my desk, and tosses them in the air. We did a recent segment on juggling. It's supposed to be a form of relaxation. "So," she continues as she catches all three with her right hand. "What's his name?"

The question is a joke—one I know very well, since I taught it to her. She laughs, expecting me to join in, but when our eyes meet, she sees that she's caught me. Her smile fades.

Years ago, the question served as my one-line test for weeding out serious college interns from airheads. Whenever I said, "So what's his name?" to any young woman who appeared deep in thought, I'd usually get a giggle followed by ten minutes of gushing over Tom, Dick, or Harry. Serena was the first intern who offered a serious reply. *"I'm thinking you failed to ask an important question in that segment we taped last week."* It was one of the most refreshing moments in my entire career, even though she was wrong about her point. Of course, we still debate that.

"Spill it," she finally says. She leans her rump against my desk and crosses her arms. I try to ignore the way her forehead crinkles and her dark copper eyes remain wide and unblinking as she awaits an explanation I have no intention of giving.

"Spill what?"

"You know what. Tell me about whoever it is you were thinking about."

"Who would I possibly be thinking about, Serena?" I say, while doing my damndest at sounding annoyed. "I spend my life working here. When I'm not here, I'm at the nursing home. Trust me—eighty-year-old men are not my thing."

"Uh huh." She flips her thick black cornrow braids adorned with rainbow beads. "You've been acting strange all afternoon. I figured it had something to do with Kate and all the drama with April. But now it makes sense that there's more to it than that. That there's something else. Or *someone* else, I should say. A man. So, c'mon. Fess up. Who is he?"

I sigh. "If you must know, I ran into an old ..." For some reason, I can't finish the sentence.

"An old what? Boyfriend?" Serena pauses. When I don't say anything, she gasps. "Husband?"

"It was an old boyfriend. I've never been married. You know that."

She shrugs. "Just when you think you know everything about a person is usually when the universe decides to send a cosmic surprise the size of an asteroid."

"You know all my secrets, Serena." Most of them.

"All except one," she says. "What's his name?"

"You're not going to leave me alone until I tell you, are you?"

She shakes her head.

"His name is Nigel."

"Nigel? He British or something?"

"His father's British. His mother's American."

"Does he have an accent?"

"Unfortunately."

She grins and throws one of the balls in the air. "Yeah. I'm with you. Accents are hot."

I say nothing.

"Is he married?"

"Divorced. A couple of times."

"So what's the story?"

I lean back in my chair. "That is the story. I ran into an old boyfriend. The end. What more do you want?"

"What more do *you* want?"

"Who said I wanted anything?"

"Hey—don't get so defensive. I'm not the one staring off into space thinking dirty thoughts about old boyfriends."

"Oh, please."

"Bet you ten bucks that you were on Google looking up info on him."

I smile and move the mouse by my keyboard. The screen saver disappears, and the monitor comes to life.

"No need for a bet," I say. "You're right. I was googling his name. Don't forget—the reason you and I are where we are is because I've always asked questions and been curious. Wanting to know more about Nigel is as natural to me as breathing."

I don't usually play the you-wouldn't-be-anywhere-without-me card around Serena, but I need to put her in her place regarding Nigel. The only way I'll play Twenty Questions is if I get to do the asking.

"So it's curiosity—nothing more?"

"Perhaps a dose of nostalgia, too. Who wouldn't after thirty years?"

"Nostalgia isn't healthy," Serena says as she drops the balls back on my desk and heads for the door.

"Why do you say that?"

"If you're so curious, look up the origin of the word."

I can tell I've pissed her off, but I also know she'll be fine tomorrow. One of the things I like most about Serena is the fact she doesn't hold grudges—an uncommon characteristic in this incestuous dog-eat-dog world of broadcast journalism.

She's right, though. I'm curious what she means about nostalgia, which I've always associated with a longing for the past. I type "define: nostalgia" into Google. Expecting to find a long etymological history and quotes from Shakespeare, I'm surprised to learn that a man named Johannes Hofer coined the word in the seventeenth century to indicate severe homesickness, which, at the time, was considered a serious disease. Soldiers fighting wars often came down with cases of nostalgia. The cure usually involved simply sending them home.

*Home.*

My eyes study the four simple letters making up such a powerful word. I quickly back out of the website, shut down my computer, and gather up my stuff. As I lock the door, I glance at the sheets of paper sitting on top of my printer, articles and information about Nigel Maxwell Hurst. I grab them and chuck them in the trashcan.

Serena's right: nostalgia isn't healthy.

# Chapter 6: Nigel

I complete my fiftieth lap around the loft, or at least, that's how it feels. I stop by Max's bed, gaze at the sleeping lump and marvel at the fact that he's already twelve years old. When I was twelve, life was still good, even though at the time I didn't think that way, impatient little imp that I was, wanting to hurry and grow up. The growing up happened faster than I ever imagined when one year later, my parents separated and I had to choose between them.

As a young man, I swore I'd never make the same mistakes as my mum and dad, yet I surpassed them handily in the egregious-error column a long time ago. The one thing my ex-wife Anne Marie and I agree on is not having Maxwell choose between us. We share our rearing responsibilities equally, and Max divides his week between my home and hers.

*Home.*

I scan my modern loft that I bought five years ago when some developer decided the dilapidated and forgotten GM plant in the bad part of town would make good living spaces for young divorced professionals like me who longed for hip urban accommodations but were relegated to the suburbs because of kids.

The loft is quite impressive with its exposed brick, high ceilings, and buffed honey-colored hardwood floors. The kitchen has more chrome than a Harley Davidson, with its super sleek high-tech gadgets, like the space-age cappuccino machine and Sub-Zero refrigerator that I'm convinced might do my laundry since it seems to do everything else. But when Max isn't here, my supposedly hip bachelor pad seems austere, uninviting, and filled with stuff.

I normally don't believe in flaunting wealth since it reminds me too much of my father, but when Anne Marie left me, I thought money would be my salvation. I was devastated by the divorce. Not because I lost her, but because I was convinced I'd lost Max. Somehow, I'd become my father: successful, rich as Croesus, and divorced with a child who too often seemed to prefer his mommy to me. The only difference was Anne Marie had even more money than I had, and I sure as hell wasn't going to let her extravagant lifestyle lure Max to her side for good. So I bought the most expensive unit with the most expensive accessories to level the playing field, even though I soon realized this contest was only in my head. Max loved me, pauper or prince. Which was exactly how I felt about my father when I was twelve.

#

I glance at the clock. It's late, but if Maggie's work ethic is anything like it was decades ago—and given her success in the field, no doubt it is—she might still be at the station. I dial the number listed on *New England Journal's* website and make my way through the automated answering system until it connects me with Maggie's office line. The phone rings once, twice, three times and then dumps me into her voice mail. I listen to her message, spoken in her deep broadcast voice, which I loathe. When Maggie first got into the business, she was coached on how to speak and how to lower the pitch of her voice so she could sound more authoritative and more like a man. It became one more reason for me to hate television. Towards the end of our relationship, I'd reminded Maggie of this fact constantly.

"For someone who espouses truth as her number one objective, don't you find it strange that you need to disguise your true voice?" I'd lobbed this particular remark at her during her stint at a small Florida station in '76. She began taking vocal lessons soon after her arrival, even though her voice—as far as I was concerned—was fine.

"I need to remain competitive," she said.

"When did it become a competition?"

"If I want a shot at reporting the truth—which is still my main objective, by the way—then I need to be willing to sound like the rest of them in order to get the chance."

"So first you start disguising how you sound. What'll you disguise next?"

But her only response had been a sigh followed by a slamming door.

#

*You're one to talk about truth,* my inner voice admonishes as I listen to my options on how to leave a message and then wait for the beep. I wonder if she's there, whether her phone has caller ID, and if she felt anything when she saw me today. I pause long enough to know that my blank message is being recorded. Then, I hang up.

I stand. I pace. I jog in place. I contemplate going to bed.

The wet bar on the other side of the room beckons. *Don't!* my inner voice instructs, but I ignore it. I'm home. Max is safe. I only need one glass to take the edge off. Some people successfully cut back on their alcohol consumption. That's all I need to do. It's not a problem. Not like it was with my father. How it probably still is with my father, even though I haven't seen him since Max was a baby. Hell, I've been sober before. For five months, even. *That's not sober,* the voice chides. *That's a dry drunk. There's a difference. And you know it. If you want to get sober, you need to admit you have a problem first.*

The bottle is in my hand. I never thought I'd be a consumer of such cheap red wine. I can pick it up by the case at Trader Joe's along with Max's favorite granola bars and the organic milk and yogurt Anne Marie insists he eats. One-stop shopping. No package store involved. No sign of dependency. A little *vino* with supper, that's all. Or in times like this. It's nice to have extra bottles of wine on hand. For guests. To bring to parties. For Zoë when

I've been unusually ornery at work and she's been unusually patient.

I bring the glass to my lips. People don't realize how much the shape of a glass affects the wine's taste. I prefer the oversized dessert-port wine glass, which gives the liquid plenty of breathing room. *What are you talking about?* the voice laughs. *It doesn't stay in your glass long enough.*

Sip.

Gulp.

Sip.

I must go to bed soon. No time to sit and savor. Just enough until I calm down. Feel sleepy.

See? There's still half a bottle left. Okay, one third of a bottle. You know, finishing it up won't hurt. It'll help me sleep, and I need it. I've been dreaming of her, of us, of how it was, and how it could have been. Maybe Zoë is right. Maybe I need to find new clients. But Ruth Frankenfeld! The old gal needs me. I like helping her. I like the people at Saint A's.

"Dad?"

My body stiffens. Is he awake? Sometimes Max talks in his sleep. Maybe I should look in on him. Except the spiral staircase to the loft looks so long. Confusing. Best I stay here on the couch. See? He's quiet. He's fine.

God.

I.

Am.

Tired.

Damn Maggie Prescott. Damn her.

*Damn her? Damn you!* the voice yells.

Yes, I think as I drift off, empty bottle by my side. Damn me all the way to hell.

*Too late*, the voice cackles. *You're already there.*

# Chapter 7: April

I study the pictures of Vinny and Jimmy on my desk. I miss them every day, of course, but holidays are harder, the sadness more pronounced. That's why I always volunteer to work, hoping that being busy will fill the void. It somehow never does.

Sighing, I force myself to pick up the phone and dial the number for the only plumber in the Yellow Pages I haven't tried yet. One ring. Two rings. Voice mail. "Shit," I mutter and slam down the receiver.

"Guess I shouldn't ask if you're having a happy Thanksgiving."

I look up. It's Hugh, leaning against the doorjamb to my office.

"Only if you're a plumber," I mumble.

He tilts his head, curious. "What's going on?"

"Leaking toilet."

"Where?"

"Home."

"No," he says. "I mean where's it leaking?"

"Uh. At the bottom? At least, that's where the water is."

He nods. "Probably a wax ring."

"Great. Simple-sounding diagnoses are usually the ones that end up being the most expensive."

He shrugs. "Not if I fix it for you."

I wait for the punch line, but he simply stares at me. "I couldn't ask you to do that," I say.

"You didn't. I offered."

"But it's Thanksgiving."

"And?"

"Don't you have plans?"

He holds his arms out wide. "This is it."

"Well, I doubt the hardware stores are going to be open. If that's even where you get wax rings."

"I bet your maintenance guy keeps some on hand. He's in today. I saw him a little while ago."

"And you're going to what—walk into his office and causally ask for one?"

He taps his breast pocket, a couple of cigars poking out. "I've gotten friendly with him. Besides, I've seen his office. The man has extras of everything."

"Yeah, including bodies, quite possibly."

He chuckles. "So it's settled. I'll check on the wax ring and then I'll need directions and keys to your house."

"Well, that's easy. I don't keep it locked. And it's right down the street. Literally. Number seventy."

"Good enough," he says while handing me an envelope. "I'm supposed to deliver this to you. It's why I originally came down."

"What is it?"

"Card. From Hazel." He pauses. "She misses you."

#

I stand outside Hazel's room, clutching the card. There's a picture of a sad puppy dog on the front. The inside is blank except for these words: "My dearest April. We need to talk. Love, Hazel."

"Knock, knock," I say as I push open the door.

Hazel looks up, relieved.

"Hey," I say.

"Hello, April."

"Got your card." I hold it up as if she needs evidence. "Sorry for being MIA. It's been busy, you know, with the holiday and everything."

"I am glad you stopped by. I have missed your company." She pauses. "Will you consider stopping by Michael's house after you get off work today? We can save you a plate."

I cringe at the mention of her nephew's name. "It's not *his* house. It's *your* house."

"Regardless," Hazel says. "I still wish you would reconsider."

"I'll be okay."

"Where will you go?"

"I'll stay here. The kitchen makes a spread for all the employees."

"What about your mother?"

"I'll sit with her during the residents' lunch."

"What about Maggie?"

"What *about* Maggie?"

"April," Hazel begins, "We need to talk about that."

"There's nothing to talk about. You two can have a relationship, friendship, whatever you want to call it. I just can't be a part of it."

"Do you forgive me for not telling you about her?"

I go to her side and squat next to her chair. "Hazel, there's nothing to forgive."

"I should have told you right away. I am surprised I never mentioned Maggie in the first place. It is not every day a teacher has a future celebrity as a student."

Shrugging, I place my hand on hers. "You had no reason to tell me. What were the chances she'd show up here and be related to me?" As I say this I recall something I'd once read: that most people live within fifty miles of where they were born. Perhaps we're all more closely connected than we realize. Turns out Hazel taught at the Catholic high school in town, which is where Maggie went.

"My dear, I do hope you take the time to get to know her."

"She needs to take it down a few notches before that's going to happen."

"She means well. I believe she is trying to make sense of it all."

"There's nothing to make sense of. Everything is clear-cut. My mother—*our* mother—is sick. Aside from some miracle, she's not going to get better. I don't have any of the answers Maggie's looking for because Mom never told me about Maggie. I don't think she told anyone. At least, not anyone who is still alive."

"What about the two of you?"

"What about us? Why does everyone keep asking me that? The woman wants to exploit my mother's condition by putting together some stupid documentary. I don't think she's as interested in this newfound family as people seem to think. Once she gets what she wants, she'll be out of here. You watch."

"Try getting to know her," Hazel whispers.

"Hazel. I—"

"Please. For me." Her voice is barely audible. She seems so frail, so old. Despite her makeup. Despite her favorite navy blue dress. "Do it for me."

#

Our conversation plays on an endless loop in my head throughout the morning. It's not like Hazel to use guilt trips on me. Maybe she's right. Maybe I should try a little harder. But as I approach the dayroom to help the aides with Mom, I stop short when I see Maggie calmly and patiently remove Mom's hand from her food. Calm and patient, calm and patient. My mind twists, wringing out the memories from the last night my mother and I spent together when any patience I had left—if I even had any to begin with—disappeared forever.

I shake my head, my eyes searching for something to distract my brain. *It's a Wonderful Life* plays on the TV in the dayroom, a movie I've seen thousands of times since the residents take a break from *The Sound of Music* every December for endless showings of the Frank Capra holiday classic. Seeing it now triggers something inside of me, and I'm not sure whether I want to vomit or scream. I had that happy Hollywood ending, for an eye blink anyway. Then, I didn't. Because my guardian angel had forgotten about me. Or had never existed to begin with.

It's been a decade since I've had a normal Thanksgiving. Vinny and Jimmy were still alive. Mom wasn't sick. Maggie Prescott didn't exist. Well, she existed, but she wasn't a part of my world, like she is now. Every time I turn a corner at Saint A's, I bump into her or people connected to her like some prosthetic limb: Mom, Nigel, Hazel.

Even my house, a place that should be a respite from Maggie, isn't safe. Flipping through the channels in bed, I see commercials for her show. When I close my eyes at night, I survey my memory for answers or clues.

*"What do you want, April?"* When Joelle had asked me this the other day, I didn't have an answer, which surprised me. Today, I still don't know, but I have been wondering what it would've been like had things been reversed—if Maggie had been the one my mother kept and I'd been the one she'd given away.

Watching Maggie fuss over Mom, taking her hand out of the mashed potatoes and wiping it gently with a napkin, I have my answer: I don't know what it would've been like for me, but Mom's life would've been better with Maggie. Maggie's a grownup. Maggie is responsible and makes a lot of money and can afford private care. But most of all, Maggie never would've done what I did.

I turn and walk away, not sure where I should go. Tears fill my eyes, but I breathe deeply a few times and look at the ceiling until the elevator arrives. On the first floor, I head to the employee break room, where a feast is set up. When I walk in, the room is packed and some people look up, smile, and wave, but they're all Brazilian, speaking in their own tongue, and I curse myself for not having learned more Portuguese when I was dating Javier. The thought of him makes me sad—this man who, two years ago, I thought for a half second would save me from all this despair and self-loathing. It seemed too good to be true, and it was.

"April, have something to eat. There's plenty." Paulo, one of the cooks, wears his chef's hat perched on his thick black hair.

I shake my head, knowing I can't stay in here to eat. But I don't want to head back to my quiet office on the other side of the building to eat by myself. That's when I get the idea. No one will miss me for an hour or so. So I start making two plates, piled high with turkey, mashed potatoes, turnips, peas, corn, and stuffing.

Paulo laughs. "You are hungry!"

"It's for a friend. Do you have anything I can cover this with?" Paulo produces a long rectangular box of plastic wrap from underneath one of the tables. "Thanks."

He smiles. "Enjoy."

"We will." I hope.

#

"Knock, knock." I tap on my bathroom door and touch the blue silk tie dangling from the doorknob where his shirt drapes over a hanger. I observe his surprisingly muscular arms and the lean upper body beneath his thin white undershirt.

"April," Hugh breathes. "I didn't hear you come in."

"How's the patient?"

"He'll live. I was just cleaning up." He sits back on his heels, wipes some dirt and dust from the knees of his khaki pants, and scans the yellow-tiled floor before peering at my face. "How's your day been so far?"

With his words, my heart breaks. What a normal scene this would be in an ordinary life: husband fixing the toilet, wife coming home on lunch break, husband asking how her day's been. I miss this lost minutia so much.

"Hugh, I can't thank you enough for doing this. I—"

He holds up his hand, stopping me, and I pray he can't tell how close I am to tears. "No need for thanks. I'm happy to help out." He pauses, tilts his head to the side, and watches me, a question mark hanging from his lips.

"What?" I whisper, knowing that the dam is about to break.

"Do I smell … turkey?"

"Oh!" I laugh, quickly wipe the corner of my eye, and hold up the brown paper bag from Saint A's. "I brought lunch. Courtesy of Saint Anthony of Padua Healthcare Center. That is, if you'd like to join me. The kitchen makes a big spread for all the employees on Thanksgiving Day. I figured you haven't eaten, and I haven't eaten, so ..."

"Is it better than the food they normally serve?"

"You've been spending too much time with Hazel."

"She is rather outspoken."

"It's one of the reasons I love her. C'mon. Let's go downstairs." I touch the bottom of the bag. "While everything's still hot." I wait while he puts on his shirt and washes his hands, and then we descend the stairs together.

"Please excuse the way the place looks," I say as we enter my mother's kitchen. I haven't been able to call it my own, because somehow it doesn't feel right. I grew up in this house, and it bothers me to no end that at the age of thirty-four I'm living in it again.

"Don't worry about it," he says, and his eyes don't reveal any judgment. Maybe he doesn't notice the dishes piled high in the sink or the breadcrumbs on the counter or the fact the floor is in desperate need of waxing. Joelle's forever complaining about her husband and his lack of domestication: "I think the sink could be filled with every single last dish in the house, and he wouldn't notice. But what do I expect? He's a guy after all." As if having a penis is an excuse for not knowing how to fill a dishwasher.

"What can I do to help?" Hugh asks.

"If you'd like to get some silverware from the drawer by the sink and clear a couple of spots at the table. Make one pile of all my little piles." I open the fridge, hoping the Food-Shopping Fairy has stopped by. "Well. I'm afraid I don't have much to offer in the way of beverages. Water. Flat diet Coke. Milk. And I can't guarantee that the milk isn't sour."

"Water's fine," he chuckles while placing two forks, two knives, and two spoons on the table and then forming one neat pile of my magazines and bills. We settle into our chairs, and a wave of fatigue floods my body.

"What should we drink to?" Hugh lifts his water goblet toward me.

"What to drink to," I repeat while raising my glass and realizing I forgot to say any blessing or thanks. I glance at his expectant face.

What to drink to?

Toasts are for weddings and births and the ends of movies like *It's a Wonderful Life*. Toasts are for birthday parties where two sisters have grown up together, loving each other, knowing each other, and not this thing with Maggie.

What to drink to?

After ten years of working in a nursing home, of watching people suffer from cancer or strokes or multiple sclerosis or dementia or plain debilitating old age, I know that every day I'm able to get out of bed on my own is a day

I should be thankful for. But I'm tired of giving thanks for the basics, for the things every human being has a right to, like breathing without machines, peeing and pooping without assistance, eating without someone taking the food and pureeing it in a food processor ahead of time. I'm tired of trying to find all the positive in all the bad.

Fuck it all. I'm just plain tired.

"Yes," Hugh whispers. He clinks my glass. "I couldn't agree more."

I awake from my trance, confused at first, because I'm certain I haven't spoken these thoughts out loud. As I search his face and try to gauge what he's thinking, I recognize the sad, tired look in his eyes because they mirror my own, and my confusion gives way to knowing. Maybe I've found someone who does understand.

# *Chapter 8: Maggie*

I've always volunteered to work holidays, professing that people with kids and family should get the day off. The fact I didn't have a home to go back to was the real reason for my generous offer to work. It never occurred to me that I wouldn't have a choice in Boston and that I'd automatically get Thanksgiving off, thanks to football preempting my show.

Serena's convinced me to join her and her friends for a holiday dinner at Legal Sea Foods in town, but that's not until six o'clock. I have a whole six hours to kill until then, which is why I'm sitting in the Alzheimer's unit at Saint A's feeding turkey and mashed potatoes to my biological mother who has no idea who I am, why I'm here, or what she's eating.

Residents and aides cramp the dayroom. *It's a Wonderful Life* plays on the large screen TV by the wall. It's the scene where George Bailey pays a visit to Mary Hatch and they kiss for the first time. It's an explosive kissing scene for 1946, allegedly shot in one take. Director Frank Capra had to edit it, or so the story goes, to get it past censors. I'm so focused on the scene, its romance and intensity, that I don't notice someone has sidled up next to me until the person speaks.

"Happy Thanksgiving."

I turn and find Nigel standing before me. Max lingers in the archway to the dayroom, bug-eyed as he observes the feeding frenzy among the living dead.

"I'm beginning to wonder if you have your own room here," I say. "Or office."

"Max made a card for one of my clients who has taken a liking to him. We're on our way to my mum's and thought we'd drop it off." He glances at Kate, and I follow his gaze. She has her fingers in the mashed potatoes. Again.

"Kate, no!" I remove her hand, wipe it with a cloth napkin, and hope Nigel senses my exasperation and leaves. Instead, he sits down on a stool vacated by one of the aides.

"Hello, Kate," he says. To my surprise, she smiles at him and pats the side of his face. She leaves a speck of potato on his cheek.

"I don't see her smile much," I say.

Nigel grins. "Who can resist a face like mine?" Before I can answer— before I can even allow my brain to take a mental photograph of his smile— Max walks over. "Maxwell," Nigel says, while wrapping his arm around the boy's waist. Max leans into him. "I'd like you to meet an old friend of mine. This is Maggie Prescott." Nigel turns to me. "Maggie, I'd like you to meet my son, Nigel Maxwell Hurst, the third."

"I didn't realize you had your dad's name," I say.

Max shyly holds out his hand and I take it in mine. "People call me Max."

I smile. "So I hear. It fits you."

"And this, Maxwell, is Maggie's mum. Her name is Kate."

"Hi," Max says. Kate pats the boy's head and laughs.

"I wish I knew what she was thinking when does things like that," I say.

Nigel laughs. "There you go again."

"What do you mean?" I ask.

"I mean your insatiable curiosity and need for answers."

"What do you expect?"

He shakes his head. "Maggie, I gave up having expectations a long time ago."

We stare at each other, but I break the connection.

"So, Max," I begin, "What did your dad's client think of your card?"

"She liked it."

"That was nice of you to make it for her."

Max nods and shifts from one foot to the other. He has on a puffy charcoal jacket with a hood. His face is flushed.

"Well, I don't want to keep you," I say. "You're going to your grandmother's for dinner, right?"

Max nods again. "My nana's."

"She's doing well, I hope?" I smile at Max, but the question is for Nigel.

"Yes. Very," Nigel says. "I'm sure she'd love to see you."

"And what about your—"

"My father?"

"Yes. How is he?"

"He'll outlive us all, I imagine. Virus and disease avoid him, no doubt because they find him as unbearable as I do."

I chuckle, despite myself. How is it that we fall so easily into conversation? We stare at each other again, and the heat rises to my face. Max tugs on Nigel's coat.

"Okay, son." Nigel sighs. "Let's go."

"Nice meeting you," Max says.

"Nice meeting you, too, Nigel Maxwell Hurst, the third."

"I meant what I said," Nigel says. "My mum would love to see you. She was always one of your biggest fans. Perhaps you might like to stop by today? If you don't have plans, that is? For coffee and dessert? She's still in the same house."

I reach for his cheek and remove the speck of potato. His breath is warm on my wrist. I shake my head.

"How 'bout it Mugsy?" he whispers.

"Sorry. I have plans."

He stands abruptly, nodding his head. "Right. Of course you do. It was only a thought. Well. Happy Thanksgiving."

I say nothing, pretending to be absorbed as Kate pounds her left fist into her squash. *She wouldn't be a fan if she knew what I did.* I twist my head and watch as Nigel and Max walk down the hall. *And neither would you.*

# *Chapter 9: Nigel*

"Dad? Can I have another piece of pie?"

"Of course you can," my mother says and smiles. "Can't he?"

"Sounds like the boss has spoken." I tousle Max's hair. He sits on a stool at the kitchen counter, his Nikes dangling above the Mexican tile floor.

"Well, it is Thanksgiving. And he is a growing boy." She slices a piece of pumpkin pie and adds a dollop of homemade whipped cream.

"Keep telling yourself that, Mother." I take an extra long sip of my merlot. "Have you noticed the obesity epidemic in this country? Researchers will probably end up relating it directly to grandmothers like you. You're not doing him any favors." I'm surprised at how perturbed I sound over my skinny-as-a-bean-pole son partaking in an extra serving of dessert. On a holiday, no less.

Mum glances in on the living room where the rest of her guests are drinking coffee and tea and eating from endless dessert platters that she's placed within reach of everyone's paws. She returns to the counter, fiddles with the radio tuned to our favorite country station, and wipes her hands on a dishtowel. She still wears her gold wedding band, even though I know it's been a decade since she's seen my father.

"So," she begins without lifting her eyes, "are you going to tell me what's on your mind? Or shall I guess?"

"I don't know what you're talking about," I say a little too fast.

"I see." She crouches down next to Max, kisses his pink cheek, and digs her shoulder into his. "How's the pie?"

"Yummy."

"Maybe we should give some to Daddy. Sweeten up his mood."

"Dad's sad because his friend couldn't come over today."

"Oh?"

"Yeah," Max continues, "from the nursing home."

"Ah." Mum nods and so do the graying tendrils around her face. "I take it Mrs. Frankenfeld has disowned her children and wants to adopt you. At least, this week, eh?"

"No." Max licks the tines of his fork. "Not Mrs. Frankenfeld. It's Mag—"

"Okay, Max," I interrupt. "That's enough."

Max stops mid-lick, stricken by the harshness in my voice. I notice his eyes fill up; he's such a sensitive child. "But you said Nana wanted to see—"

"Right, Max. Off you go. Finish your pie in the other room with Uncle Harry." I nudge him out of the kitchen and into the living room.

Mum looks from Max to me. "Said I wanted to see whom?"

"You don't want to hear it."

She crosses her arms and leans against the stool Max occupied. "Try me. You told this person I wanted to see him—"

"Her. It's a she."

"Ah, well. That explains it." She grins. "Must be serious."

"Serious?" I shake my head at how far off she is. "Why, yes, Mum. It's serious all right. Seriously insane."

"Why do you say that? It's not as if you've fallen in love with an old woman at the nursing home, right?" When I don't respond, she looks alarmed. "Nigel?"

"No, not an old woman. An old lover." I reach for a tendril that's fallen across her forehead and brush it away. "An old lover with whom I never fell *out* of love."

Mum closes her eyes. "Maggie."

"Bingo."

"But, how? I know she's back in town, but how did you ever cross paths with—"

"Her biological mum, believe it or not, is a resident at Saint A's."

"*Mon Dieu*," she murmurs. "And, I take it, you've seen her? Talked to her?"

I nod and say nothing, because I don't want to provide an all-out confession. I don't want Mum to know that not only have I seen Maggie, but I try to see her. Regularly.

"And you asked her over for dinner today?"

"Dessert. Coffee. I told her that you would have loved to see her. That you were always one of her biggest fans."

"I was. Am still, I guess. It's been so long."

"That it has."

"You still love her."

Mum was never one to mince words—a trait that crazed my father. "Is that a statement?" I ask. "Or a question?"

"I know you've always carried a torch for her. But now that you've seen her and talked to her, is the flame real, Nigel? Or imagined?"

Good, ol' Mum. I hadn't allowed myself to think of it this way, even though I'm sure the notion was in the back of my cerebrum, clamoring for attention, while I dutifully ignored it. I have no doubt that I still love the Maggie I knew thirty years ago. I always have. I always will. But how do I feel about present-day Maggie Prescott?

"I don't know, Mum. I don't know."

"Perhaps you should find out."

"I'm working on it."

"Perhaps," she says while taking my wine glass away from me, "you should work harder."

Mum has made known to me her feelings about my drinking, but always in soft, subtle ways, as she did with my father. It never worked. Part of me wishes she were tougher, even though I know the stubborn me would rebel and run away. She lost my father. I know she couldn't bear to lose me. I break her unwavering gaze and allow my eyes to rest on the wine glass sitting on the counter.

She reaches for my face, cups my chin in her delicate hand, and directs it toward her. "It's about time you unpack the baggage and put it away once and for all, don't you think?"

She stands up straight, smoothes her dress, and leads me—*sans* wine glass—into the living room. She slides into a small spot on the couch between Uncle Harry and Max. The conversation, from what I'm able to glean, is light—weddings, babies, who's applying to what Ivy League school. The television hums in the background, although I don't believe anyone is paying attention to *It's a Wonderful Life*, the most pretentious piece of sentimental rubbish ever put on film. Somehow, I always end up catching most of it every December around Christmas. As George Bailey contemplates suicide while leaning on the snowy bridge in Bedford Falls, Mum's words resonate in my head: "*It's about time you unpack the baggage and put it away once and for all, don't you think?*"

I sit next to my cousin Edward, resigned to the fact that I must feign holiday cheer even though all I want to do is drink and scream at the television, *Jump, George! Jump.*

# December

# *Chapter 10: April*

The December before the accident, Vinny and I decided I'd start an in-home daycare center the following summer. I loved kids, and Jimmy would have been four in February—a reasonable age, I believed, for him to learn to share me with other children. Despite the fact I'd gotten pregnant right away with Jimmy, Vinny and I were having trouble conceiving again. I loved my little boy and took immense pleasure in watching his ever-expanding world, but I missed babies.

I'll admit I became distracted by the idea, devoting much of December and January to "my business," learning about regulations and local ordinances, thinking about how many kids I'd be able to reasonably handle. I still wonder to this day if Jimmy felt ignored.

To make it up to him and to make him feel extra special, we promised Jimmy a new bike for his fourth birthday, one he could pick out. But Mother Nature had other plans: a nor'easter descended upon us on the big day. Vinny's landscaping company plowed during the off-season, so Jimmy and I didn't see him for forty-eight hours straight, and by the time he'd gotten caught up on sleep and some indoor work he'd promised a client, a week had passed since Jimmy's b-day. I, in the meantime, had been busy trying to get my high school transcript to see if the coursework I'd done in early childhood education would be sufficient for the daycare licensing requirements in Massachusetts, "trying" being the operative word. After much stalking and borderline harassment, I finally had an appointment with someone who said my transcript would be waiting for me, and I had a lunch scheduled with a former teacher who said she'd be happy to talk to me about my plans. But it turned out to be on the same day Vinny had arranged to bring Jimmy to pick out his bike.

"Don't worry, hon," Vinny had said. "We men can handle it on our own."

"Yeah," Jimmy piped up, thrilled, no doubt, that his father had referred to him as a man. "The men can handle it."

"Okay," I said. It wasn't like I was going to miss him riding his bike. The roads were still a mess from the storm, despite unusually warm temperatures, temperatures that would end up dropping precipitously that fateful afternoon, although no one knew this at the time. It would likely be a couple of months before our driveway would be safe enough for him to ride, even with training wheels. And I was certain Jimmy would still be glowing when they got back from their shopping adventure.

"Bye, Mommy," Jimmy said, wrapping his arms around me while I sat at the computer working on flyers announcing our daycare. "Love you."

"Love you, too." I kissed his head—I remember that—but I can't recall if I looked at him, if my eyes remained fixed on the monitor, distracted, or if they glanced down at his crown of black curls, his silver-dollar-sized eyes, his soft baby-fat skin. Like many first-time moms, I was always anxious, worried about things like childhood leukemia and pedophiles and freak accidents at amusement parks. I was rarely away from Jimmy for more than a couple of hours and always apprehensive during our separations, even when he was with Vinny.

*Vinny.*

"Come on, kiddo. Let Mommy do her work," he said.

I looked up as he scooped Jimmy into his arms. He stood in the doorway of my cramped "office," which had been the junk room not two months before. He wore the burnt orange mountain jacket I'd bought him from L.L. Bean for Christmas, his hair still damp from the shower.

"Have fun you two," I called out and blew them both a kiss.

I always thought I'd know if something happened to Jimmy or even Vinny, that my maternal and spousal instincts would ping extra loud, alerting me that something was wrong, so terribly, terribly wrong. But I had no clue. None at all.

The days and months that followed the accident were a blur combined with instances of perfect clarity: the image of their bodies cleaned up and cooling, waiting for me to identify them because I had insisted on doing so; the lambasting I gave the florist who claimed he had no way of getting sunflowers, Jimmy's favorite flower, in February in time for the funeral—*You're a fucking florist! Figure it out!*—the confusion I felt when, back at our condo, I kept stepping on Jimmy's toys, the ones I had dutifully packed away in an effort to move on. But what I ignored was the fact that I got up in the middle of the night and tore open the boxes, spreading the Tonka trucks and LEGO bricks on the floor, convincing myself that it was Jimmy who was up to such mischief.

The one constant during the haze and those few lucid moments was Mom. When it became obvious I couldn't live in the condo, couldn't care for it or myself, she handled the rental (and ultimate sale), the packing, and the moving of me and my belongings into her house, the same one where I'd grown up. When I couldn't be in touch with Vinny's family because it was too painful since I saw hints of Vinny in his brother's eyes and Jimmy in his mother's lips, Mom intercepted letters and phone calls and at some point—I don't know when—sat the LaMonicas down and explained that I needed to be incommunicado for a while (which turned into forever). She monitored my eating, my peeing, my pooping, as if I were a child again, which in many ways I was, crying myself to sleep, weeping myself awake from bad dreams, calling out for her. She came. She came every single time. I was lost, metaphorically, and she found me. And therein lies the irony, because neither one of us knew then that eight years later she'd become lost, figuratively, metaphorically, and in all the ways that were important.

#

"So who's Saint Anthony?" I asked Joelle one day while we sat having lunch in her office, about a month after our first meeting in Hazel's room. We had quickly become friends, which thrilled my mother, since I'd all but abandoned the other moms I'd engaged with over the last five years. Joelle was single at the time, although it wouldn't be long before she met the love of her life. I'd be in her wedding, too, holding up one corner of the *huppah*— the canopy held over the bride and groom during a Jewish ceremony. I'd be the person she'd call in the middle of the night when her firstborn, Sam, suffered from a bout of colic. And I'd be the person she'd want to talk to first when she miscarried three times before finally carrying her second child, Jacob, to full term.

But as we ate our sandwiches from the local sub shop, we didn't know any of this. I was only trying to make conversation.

"Patron saint of the elderly," she said. "And finder of lost articles."

"Finder of lost articles?"

"Yeah. He's the name you invoke when you can't find something. Like, 'saint Anthony, please help me find my car keys.'"

"Does it work?"

"I don't know. I'm Jewish."

"Doesn't work if you're Jewish?"

Joelle shrugged. "I don't know. I've never tried it. But the saints are a Catholic thing, I think."

I didn't know much about religion. I'd been baptized in the Catholic church—this I knew, because I'd seen the pictures in my baby album—and I had a few blurry memories of church with my parents. But the memories stopped right around the time my father died. I remember a man dressed in black with a white collar coming to our house after Dad died and Mom crying, begging, and pleading with him about something. The priest, apparently, had refused to perform Dad's funeral since Dad has committed suicide. We ended up having a simple ceremony in the funeral home instead, and my mother cut off all ties with the church after that. As a result, I did, too.

This, of course, became a source of contention when Vinny and I became engaged, his family being devout Catholics and all. We'd promised his mother that I would "take classes and everything," which pacified her long enough for us to get through our wedding with a hip Catholic priest who married us in a backyard ceremony, even though I've since heard of many priests who refuse to preside over weddings outside of a physical church. We had Jimmy baptized. As for the classes I was supposed to take? They never happened.

"The owners," Joelle continued, "name all their nursing homes after saints. Makes it sound less like a business and more altruistic."

"A business?" It was the first time I'd considered the concept.

"Don't let the name or even what we do fool you, April. This is a business, and the owners are in it to make money."

"Wow. That seems so ..." I struggled for the right word.

"Heartless? Ruthless?" Joelle offered. "That's business for you."

"So why do you work here then?"

"Because I figure people like you and me can keep Corporate in check. They may be all about the bottom line, but you and I are providing compassionate care to real people who need it." She paused and when she began speaking again, her voice was barely audible. "You know, that afternoon we met in Hazel's room and I was out of line—"

"Joelle, forget about it."

"But I don't want to forget. I'd only been here a little more than a year, and already I had succumbed to Corporate's way of looking at residents as numbers instead of human beings. You reminded me not to be like that. You reminded me why I became a social worker in the first place. I still can't believe how quickly I lost sight of that." She shook her head. "But I did."

"So this Saint Anthony dude," I said, trying to change the subject since I felt bad Joelle was beating herself up so much. "Can he help me with finding, say, Brad Pitt?"

She laughed, and I did, too, but guilt wrapped itself around my heart for having made the suggestion, even in jest. It bothered me for the rest of the day, and I confessed later to Mom as she sat watching me move my meatloaf around my plate.

"It's been almost two years," she said gently. "It was a harmless comment that you made in an effort to cheer up a friend."

"The logical part of my brain knows that. But I feel like I betrayed them just by saying it." I still couldn't bring myself to say Vinny's or Jimmy's names out loud. Whenever I referred to one or the other, I had to use the plural pronouns "them" or "they," which sounded weird at times: "*Oh, that Cookie Monster bubble bath was their favorite.*"

"Do you think they would see it like that?" Mom respected my pronoun issues, and I loved her for it.

"I don't know."

She placed her hand on top of mine. "And that's okay. Because someday, you will know. And you'll see that it's all right."

#

In the days following their deaths, I'd bargained with God: *Please, just bring them back, even if they're in a hospital bed, hooked up to machines, please just let me see them, touch them, hold them again.* My thought was that as long as they were physically present, there would be hope, and that would be enough for me. Losing them completely—mind, body, and soul—was more than I could bear.

Years later, as Mom descended deeper and deeper into her disease, I would learn that this assumption was false—that a physical presence, but an absent mind, was far worse. When you suffer a complete loss, as devastating as it is, your brain—your logical brain—takes note and begins to process, waiting for your emotional brain to catch up. But when the person you lose remains right in front of you, when the face you've loved your whole life looks at you without a hint of recognition, it not only hurts the emotional brain, but it also defies the logical brain as well.

Over the last three years, I've prayed countless times to Saint Anthony to help Mom find her memories: short-term, long-term, all of them.

"Have you ever considered," Joelle asked me the other day, "that Saint Anthony has answered your prayers?"

"What do you mean?"

"Well, Maggie showed up."

"But that's not what I prayed for."

"Yes, that's true. But Saint Anthony is the finder of lost articles. Your sister was lost all this time, only to be found."

"Half sister," I corrected. "And I wouldn't consider her lost. I didn't know she was missing."

"Your mother knew. And Maggie, too. Maybe you're supposed to give her a chance."

What Joelle fails to understand is that it's hard to offer chances when you're someone whose luck ran out a long time ago.

#

I finally disengage my mind from these memories and lug a box of leftover ornaments and fake tree branches through the activities room, where a mean game of bingo is taking place. I convinced Old Man Garrity, a popular male resident, to call bingo today so I could do double-duty decorating. All the women residents love him except for Blanche who is the most competitive bingo player in the building. After spending five hours erecting four Christmas trees, three menorahs, and countless strings of lights, the last thing I want to do is listen to an old lady bitch about losing fifty cents. But as I walk through the bingo game on the way to my office, where I intend to curl up and die, Blanche follows me in her wheelchair and cackles about Old Man Garrity rigging numbers.

"Okay, Blanche," I say without even looking at her. "I'll call the Massachusetts State Lottery Commission. We'll look into your claim of fraud."

In a perfect world, I'd slam the door in her face, but I don't because deep down I feel sorry for her. Blanche is an overweight seventy-seven-year-old diabetic with a beard, and her only fun in life is bingo and smoking. I know she has four kids—it says so on her chart—but I've never seen any of them visit her.

"Why does she always complain so much?" another resident asks in a stage whisper.

"Because sometimes," Blanche retorts, "complaining is all you got left."

*Amen, sister.* I close my eyes, rub the side of my head, and wish I could get my hands on some Oxycontin.

"Hi, April."

I look up in time to see Hugh place an oversized cardboard box at my feet.

"I've been cleaning out the house," he says. "I thought you could use some extra Christmas decorations around this place."

"Don't you want to keep these?" I say as I push apart the flaps and reach for a shoebox filled with ornaments. On top is a wooden sleigh. "Maybe for your daughter?"

"Adrienne doesn't want them."

I select another ornament, this one a delicate crystal angel. "Why not?"

"I suppose because it reminds her of us—Gloria and me."

He says it so matter-of-factly, I almost think I didn't hear him right. "What about for you, then?" I say. "Don't you decorate at Christmas?"

"Do you?"

"Of course. Look at this place—"

He holds up his hand, cutting me off. "No. Not here. I meant your home."

For a minute, I consider lying. But the truth is I haven't decorated for any holidays since Mom's diagnosis three years ago. "Point taken," I say. "It's too damned painful." I want the words back the minute they exit my mouth. Hugh doesn't need to hear about my crap or my complaints.

"Agreed," he says simply, holding my gaze, and once again, I sense understanding in his eyes. "Well, I should go on up. Hazel is probably wondering where I've been all day."

I watch as he makes his way through the activities room before disappearing into the hall. "But sometimes," I whisper. "Complaining is all you got left."

#

I drag myself through the rest of my day—giving manicures to the women on the second floor, cleaning up urine from a catheter bag I ran over by accident with a wheelchair, and cutting up chicken and trying to feed it to Mom, only to have her throw it in my face.

As I button my winter jacket and shut off my office lights for the night, my eyes fall on a framed photo on my desk. "My boys," I say as the tears form, but I refuse to let them squirt out from underneath my lashes.

I keep their pictures all over the office, and Joelle has mentioned several times that it might be time to leave them at home. She's right. More than once an unsuspecting resident or family member has beamed at Jimmy's pumpkin face and asked, "Is this your son? He's beautiful! How old is he?" and I have to stammer through something about his death, a long time ago, don't know why I keep the pictures, blah, blah, blah. Which is always followed by a long awkward pause.

Most days I can keep the demons at bay—the visions in my mind, the voices in my ears that remind me of everything I lost. I don't stop moving from late November to December 31—dashing to stores for decorations and gifts for the residents; attending colleagues' holiday parties out of obligation; smiling and laughing because that's what you're supposed to do—fake it—like so many other people. It's amazing how lonely you can feel even when you're not even dwelling on it, when you're so tired by the end of the day you crawl on all fours into bed like a cat. I remember last year shopping for Siobhan O'Leary, a sweet resident with a thick Irish brogue. It was December 22—at night. Not a good time to be in the mall. But Siobhan had her heart set on a certain toy for her first great-grandson. I don't even remember what it was. Cash in hand, I accepted my mission with a cheery wave. As I stood in a twenty-person deep line at the cash register, I found myself leaning into the guy in front of me so I could feel a man's body heat next to mine. He was about my age, handsome, sporting a wedding ring, and no doubt buying the video games he had in his red shopping basket for his kids. I remember he glanced back at me and smiled. I expected him to move since I was practically humping him from behind, but he didn't. Maybe he knew I needed him. Maybe he was lonely in his world, too, and for a few minutes, he didn't mind our bodies almost becoming one in the middle of Toys R Us. Or maybe he didn't feel me at all because there's no heat left to feel.

#

The orange and yellow glow from the front window of my house has my mind jumping from memories of heat to the reality of fire. I pull into the driveway, leap out of my car, fumble with the doorknob, and race to the living room while bracing myself for smoke and flames. But I don't find any.

Instead, the house is quiet and dark, except for a Christmas tree decorated in dew-drop creamy white lights and silver and gold ornaments. An angel on the front of the tree holds a piece of paper. It reads:

*Dear April,*

*Maybe we have it all wrong.*

*Maybe a little Christmas cheer is precisely what we need.*

*Hugh*

I cry.

I cry because it's the nicest thing anyone has done for me in a long, long time—perhaps ever—and I don't deserve it. I have Hugh fooled like the rest of world. If he only knew what went on in this house, in the very spot where this Christmas tree stands. I cry for Hazel and the residents at Saint A's, especially the ones who don't have anyone to cry for them, like Blanche. I cry for Maggie because as much as I want to hate her for being who she is, I can't help but feel sorry for her because she's never going to know the reason Mom gave her up. I cry because of the way my brief relationship with Javier damaged me even more, and I cry because I know I need to ignore the way my insides flip-flop whenever I'm near Hugh. I cry for Mom and for Vinny and for Jimmy.

I cry because all I can think about is our last Christmas together as a family. Jimmy was the perfect age for Santa Claus and winter stars you wish upon. We had such a wonderful magical holiday with laughter and smiles and white fluffy snow. But when we finally hauled the Christmas tree to the curb one gray day in early January, Jimmy looked up and down the street— many of our neighbors were on the same timetable, their trees littering the sidewalks—and he fell to the ground in his new navy blue snowsuit and sobbed.

"Sweetheart, what's the matter?" I had pulled his red mittens away from his flushed face, thinking he had hurt himself.

"Mommy, they look so sad."

"Who does?"

"The Christmas trees!"

I sat next to him, the wet pavement soaking the seat of my jeans, and examined the scene from the vantage point of a child. Jimmy was right—the trees did look sad. There was still a lot of life left in them, many with tinsel and broken ornaments attached. But they were kicked to the curb anyway, their purpose in this world over. Hugging him close, I'd sobbed along with him.

And now curled up on the floor beneath Hugh's Christmas tree, I look up through its branches while tears trickle down my cheeks and into my ears until, finally, I cry for me.

# *Chapter 11: Maggie*

Every time I walk into Saint A's, I wonder if I'll find Nigel or April lurking behind corners watching me. Other times I wonder if Kate will finally be waiting for me with her arms outstretched. "Maggie," she'll say, "my dear, dear daughter." With that, she'll envelop me in her arms, never letting go. Then, I wonder about Hazel. I've stopped by her room a couple of times, but the conversations always stall with stiffness. Unspoken words hide in the shadows. We haven't talked about what happened so long ago, why she cut off communication. I have a feeling I don't want to know the reason because there's a good chance it'll make me angry, and it somehow doesn't seem right to inflict my rage on a woman three steps away from death. But I still can't help wondering why.

I also want to know why Hazel's stuck here. Yes, she's old, but she's mentally and physically sound. Since we've reconnected, more memories—more "Hazel stories"—have surfaced: the house in Tallulah Falls and her unrequited love affair with a man named Mack Crawford.

The first time she'd told me about him, I was already in college. I sat cross-legged on her couch, rapt. Soon it became my favorite request. "Tell me about you and Mack," I'd ask. Eventually, I knew her story as well as she did.

"I met him later in life," Hazel would always start, the opening line of her story never changing. "I was already in my mid-forties, had been proposed to twice, and had broken the hearts of the men who wished to marry me. How could anyone expect me to marry a man whom I did not love? And then I met him. The year was 1952. He was a construction worker from Tallulah Falls, Georgia, and had recently moved to Boston so his wife could receive treatment for a plethora of ailments that amounted to nothing more than old-fashioned depression and domestic abuse. Except Mack Crawford was not the one doing the abusing—his wife was the tormentor. Naturally, I did not discover this right away, but rather over time when Mack and I conversed over morning coffee before he would begin his day's work remodeling the kitchen of my family's home. To this day the smell of brewing coffee transports me to summer mornings, haze burning, damp grass between my toes, the air filled with so much moisture you want to wring it out like a towel but instead of your hands dripping wet when you're done, you catch a promise that only the heat and passion of July can produce."

"Wow!" I'd always exclaim, breathless from her description.

"Wow, indeed."

"What did he look like?"

"Oh, Mack was all man. Well over six feet tall and with hair the color of sand. He smelled of the outdoors—dusty country roads, pine trees, autumn leaves. His eyes crinkled when he smiled, which was not often at first. But as the summer wore on, we talked, and he did smile more. He was good with his hands. He was, in fact, a very decent man. He had never thought of leaving his wife until we met. We fell in love that summer, over coffee and my freshly baked banana breads and blueberry muffins."

"What happened?"

"The people closest to me—my mother, my aunt—were concerned because he was married, and even if he divorced ... *well*. My dear, we were Catholic after all."

"So that's it? You fell in love but couldn't do anything about it?"

"No. Far from it. My aunt discovered that Mack had not married in the church, and our parish priest assured Mother and Aunty that only a marriage in the church could be considered sacred."

"That's ridiculous."

"Perhaps. But Mother was able to accept it after that. She had it all planned: Mack would divorce his wife and marry me properly."

I'd always puzzle over this, and Hazel would always remind me of her situation: "I bet you are wondering why a grown, working woman was not in charge of her own life? My dear, times were different then. First, I was a woman. Second, I was still Jasper Cooke's only daughter and one of only two remaining children. Two of my brothers had died—one during the War when he was barely a man, and the other to cancer. I still lived in my father's house. There was the family name to consider."

"But you were a grown up."

"That didn't matter in the early 1950s. Women—at least women like me—were not allowed to command their own souls. Or hearts."

"So what happened?"

"For a long time, we kept my father in the dark, having decided to wait until Mack was indeed divorced. But Father found out anyway. Was he ever furious! So Mack decided to talk to him, man to man, and explain his intentions."

"And?"

"I remember Father descending the stairs, Mack standing at the bottom with his hat in both hands. 'Are you married?' my father asked. The grandfather clock in the hallway struck eight, and they stood there, silent, through eight long, mournful bongs. Finally, Mack spoke. 'In name only.' He tried to say more, but my father would hear nothing of it. He stormed back up the stairs. I had been watching the whole thing from the kitchen. After my father left the room, Mack stood there watching after him, motionless, like a statue. I went to him, touched him gently on the sleeve of his coat, and he looked at me with such pain in his eyes. He stroked the side of my cheek. I remember his fingertips were so rough and calloused. 'Hazel, my darling,' he said. 'I'll come back for you when it's right.' And, with that, he put on his hat and walked out the door. He was dead eighteen months later."

#

As I approach Hazel's room, one more memory returns: Mack had built a house for his little sister in Tallulah Falls, and he'd instructed his sister to share her home with Hazel should something happen to him. At least, that's how I remember the story now. Hazel used to tell me that "someday" she would go to Georgia, perhaps when she retired, but we lost touch before that happened.

"Special delivery," I call out as I knock and open the door to Hazel's room. She looks up from her book. Her roommate Gloria lay motionless, her husband absent.

"What's this?" she asks.

"I told the receptionist I'd drop off your mail." I tap the stack of letters against my palm, not knowing where to begin. I hand Hazel everything except for the one on top. "I couldn't help but notice the return address on this one." I shake the lavender envelope in front of her face, point to the handwriting that reads "Tallulah Falls, GA," and then hand it to her. As I sit on the side of her bed, I tuck one leg underneath the other. "Did you ever go to Tallulah Falls?"

"That's the million-dollar question," a voice says.

Hazel and I look up to find April standing in the doorway. "Okay, maybe that's not entirely accurate," April says as she settles into a chair. "The question I always ask is this: Hazel, *when* are you going to Tallulah Falls?"

"Oh, my. The two of you now!" Hazel exclaims, but I can tell she's happy we're asking. Or maybe she's happy to have us both in the same room.

April sighs and shakes her head. "The answer is no. She hasn't gone. Despite my urging for the last decade."

"I would be a burden," Hazel murmurs.

"How do you figure that? They love you. They keep calling and writing and asking you to come. Besides, you don't belong here."

"She's right," I say.

"Hey, look!" April smirks. "Something we actually agree on."

"Now, now, girls. It was one thing to urge me to go thirty years ago when I was young. Well, younger. But now?" She sighs, and I decide to change the subject, not wanting to remind Hazel of this pain. But my mind blanks. I grope for some common ground for all of us.

"Hazel?" I finally sputter.

"Yes, my dear?"

"Do you remember Nigel Hurst?"

"How could I forget?"

"Wait. You know Nigel, too?" April asks.

"*Knew*," Hazel says. "Why do you ask, Maggie?"

"He's here."

"Here?" Her face pales.

"Not as a resident." I glance at April.

"Don't look at me," she says. "You seem to know more about everyone in this place than I do."

"He's an attorney," I continue. "Apparently, he has clients here."

Hazel nods. "I see. How has that been? Seeing him after all this time?"

I shake my head because I don't know.

"Have the two of you talked?" she presses.

I can tell by her tone, by the slight change in the pitch of her voice as she says "talked," that she's referring to something specific, that time in a Florida hospital when everything had gone bad.

"Not much," I say. "What sense would there be in that?" I know Hazel doesn't believe me, but I ignore her questioning look and turn to April.

"Don't ask me," April says. "Seems your family here keeps getting bigger and bigger."

"Don't be silly," I say. "Nigel's not family."

She shrugs and stands. "Whatever."

I glance at Hazel who nods and gestures for me to follow April, who is already out the door.

"Go," Hazel whispers. "She needs you."

"I don't think so."

"And you need her."

"I don't need anybody," I say automatically, my standby answer to anyone who pries into my private business.

"If I believed you, I would drop it," Hazel says. "But I do not. Go to her, Maggie. Do it for me."

I roll my eyes, but find myself standing up and obeying her guilt-laden directive. I slip out the door and practically walk into April and Nigel.

"*What?*" he says.

"Yeah," April responds as she walks backwards down the hall and juts her chin in my direction. "Ask her."

We watch as she quickly disappears around the corner.

"Ask me what?" I say.

"Is it true that Hazel Cooke is a resident here?"

I point to the placard with Hazel's name on the door. "Yes."

He lets out a low whistle. "Good lord."

"Weird, isn't it?"

"That's an understatement."

"Actually, I just told Hazel about bumping into you."

"What'd she say?"

"Not much."

"Well, that's not surprising. Last time I saw her ..." He pauses and looks at me hard. "Well. You know."

"Yep."

"Not the best of circumstances."

"Nope."

"I may have been a bit harsh. With Hazel." He runs his hand through his hair. "It's been, what? Thirty years. How old is she?"

"Old," I say. "Ninety-three."

"Well, maybe it's meant to be."

"What do you mean?"

"Maybe she's here because I'm supposed to say I'm sorry."

"Sorry for what?"

"For being such a bastard to her." He shrugs. "Maybe God or fate or whatever you want to call it is intervening."

"Since when have you been a fatalist?"

"I used to think you and I were meant to be together. But then you and I ended. So to answer your question, I was a fatalist up until my mid-twenties. I became a realist after that."

"So what brought you back to fate? To this divine intervention?" I mock.

He watches me as if he's considering what to say next. For a second, his lips move and sound emerges, but then—nothing. He drops his head to the floor. "No reason," he mutters. "Guess people have a tendency to turn to God or the universe or fate as they get older, that's all."

"Well, I'm sure she'd appreciate the apology." I point again to the door.

"Would you like to join me?"

"Sorry. I have to go to work. Don't you ever work, Nigel?"

"This is work, Maggie."

I know he intends double meaning, but I pretend not to notice, or care. "Well, get back to work then." I turn, but he grabs my arm.

"Listen," he whispers.

"What now?" I sigh, shaking him off and doing my best to sound pissy because I don't like the tone of his "listen" or the urgency in his eyes or the possibility in his words—whatever those words were—that he almost spoke when I asked him what brought him back to fate.

He swallows. "Forget it."

When I get around the corner, I lean against the wall and shut my eyes, wishing that I could.

# *Chapter 12: Nigel*

I peer at the name on the door: "Hazel B. Cooke."

"This is crazy," I whisper, but even as I say the words, I can hear my sponsor-cum-shrink admonishing me: *"Crazy? It's not crazy, man. It's divine intervention. When are you going to let go and put your faith in the man upstairs?"*

I don't know what step it is in that Big Book, but I do know that asking forgiveness for past sins is a big part of it. For some reason, I felt compelled to tell Maggie all about those sins right before she morphed into a bitch and strutted away.

"Hazel B. Cooke," I murmur as I push open the door without knocking. "Remember me?"

The old woman's head jerks up at the sound of my voice. She's more wrinkled than I remember. Smaller, too. She sizes me up with an icy stare. That, apparently, hasn't changed either.

"Nigel Maxwell Hurst," she says. "How could I forget?"

Indeed. The last time we met was in some dive one block from that hospital in Florida. I'd been banging back shots—of what I can't remember—when Hazel had come to talk to me.

"Go away, Hazel," I'd said when I spotted her walking through the door. "Whatever you have to say, I don't wanna hear it." Music blared from a jukebox. The place smelled of beer and sweat and smoke. She was so out of place, all prim and proper in her skirt and blouse, clutching her purse in front of her.

"I do not have anything to say. But Maggie does."

"Yeah?" I swiveled on the bar stool to face her, but the room kept spinning long after the stool stopped. "Why isn't she here, then? Oh wait! I know!" I slapped my leg as if I'd remembered something. "Because she's with her *boy*friend."

"You have it all wrong, Nigel."

"Do I, Hazel? Do I?"

"Yes, you do."

"Well you know what? You do me a favor. If Maggie's got something to say, she can tell me in person. But not here. You tell her to come back to Boston. To leave this hellhole and get back where she belongs."

"But her job is here."

"Fuck her job." Even then—despite being totally loaded, shit faced, ossified, whatever you want to call it—I felt a surge of heat go up my face. I'd barely ever sworn in front of Maggie let alone a woman old enough to be my grandmother.

Hazel stood a little straighter, chin raised. "What do you mean?"

"I mean it's me or her job."

"You are not serious."

"Do I look like I'm joking? She can come back to Boston and do her little television work there."

"You're drunk," she said.

I feigned a look of surprise. "No shit?"

"And either the alcohol is unleashing the truth from within your soul, or you have no concept of what you are saying."

"Oh, I have a concept all right. There's been nothing but trouble for Maggie and me since she got mixed up in this television business, which, by the way, has never been what she ever wanted to do. She wanted to make films. Documentaries. Not this commercial bullshit." I shook my head. "I can't do it anymore. Not the weird hours. Not her movin' around. Not her runnin' around—"

"She was *not* running around."

I leaned into her face. "Listen. You believe whatever you want. I saw them together."

"You think you saw—"

"No, Hazel. I. Saw. And I don't know if I can ever forgive that. But I know one thing. I certainly can't forgive it as long as she stays down here doing this."

We were quiet for a while, Hazel watching me bang back drinks and calling for more from the bartender.

"I see," she finally said. She twisted her purse straps so hard her knuckles turned white. "Well, then. I guess you are right. There is nothing left to say."

And with that, she was gone.

That had been the last time I saw her. Until now.

#

"So to what do I owe this pleasure?" Hazel asks.

"I bumped into April. She told me you were here."

"And Maggie?"

"Maggie mentioned you were here as well."

She straightens up in her chair, but her back still hunches over. "Well, let's hear it."

"I beg your pardon?"

"This is not a social call, I am sure."

"What makes you say that?"

"Have you forgotten what happened the last time we met?"

I close my eyes and sigh. "No. But I was hoping you had."

"Nigel, have you found that the things we wish to forget, we cannot?"

"Unfortunately."

"Luckily, forgiveness is different. If we wish and pray hard enough, we can forgive."

"Does that mean you forgive my behavior from three decades ago?"

She chuckles. "My dear man, I was hoping enough time had passed that you had forgiven *me*."

"For what? Telling Maggie to forget about the drunken ass you encountered in the barroom that afternoon?"

"No," she says, shaking her head. "For not telling you everything I was supposed to tell you."

"Well, I wasn't the easiest person to reason with."

"True."

"And what was there to tell that hadn't already been told." I say this as a statement, but then her face pales. "What? Are you saying there was something more that I was supposed to know?"

She closes her eyes, which is when I notice her palsy—a slight tremor in her chin and hands. The last thing she needs is stress to exacerbate her condition. I decide to take it down a notch.

"Hazel, whatever it is, forget about it. It was a long time ago." I walk to her side, pull out my wallet, and hold out my business card. "I think it's time we all move on from the past."

She opens her eyes.

"Here," I say. "Take it. If you ever need anything, you let me know."

She accepts the card and rubs her index finger along the embossed black lettering that spells out my name. "You still love her," she murmurs.

"Excuse me?" I choke.

"Maggie. You still love Maggie."

"Hazel, remember what I was saying about moving on from the past? I don't—"

But she holds up her hand to stop me. "While you may think we should move on from our past, I believe you have a right to know what you are moving from."

"Well?" I say. "What is it then? What didn't you tell me?"

"Ask Maggie."

"Ask Maggie what?"

"Ask her," Hazel whispers, "about the letter I never gave you."

\#

I go about the rest of my tasks at Saint A's—the obligatory visit with Ruth and a consultation with another resident and his family in the private dining room—but all the while, Hazel's words keep repeating in my head: "*Ask her about the letter I never gave you.*"

Waiting for the elevator, I'm so engrossed in my thoughts that I don't notice the doors slide open or the person who apparently slips by me until that someone says, "Excuse me, sir? Are you getting on?"

My eyes refocus and before me is the most beautiful woman I've ever seen in this godforsaken place: long blonde hair, model-like body, and eyes so blue they don't look real.

"My apologies." I rush on and lean against the wall. I don't think I've invaded her personal space, yet I'm aware that our shoulders are touching.

"Tough day?" she asks. "I find it's always harder to visit when the weather's bad. Like you can't escape it, you know? Damp and cold outside. Damp and cold inside."

I'm completely speechless as I watch her lips form words. "Right," is all I can manage.

"I'm Trudie." She extends her hand, and I take it in mine and can't help but notice its warmth. "Sorry for being so forward, but I've seen you around here before. Figure it can't hurt to know each other's names."

I squeeze her hand. "No cold or dampness in there." Groaning inwardly, I try convincing myself that I did not utter those words. "Good lord. That was awful, wasn't it?"

"Yes, it was." She smiles. "But I'll forgive you. This place has that effect on people."

"So, come here often?" I quip as we exit the lift.

"I liked your other line better," she giggles. "I'm here visiting my aunt. And you?"

*Oh, you know. I'm stalking an old lover.* "I'm an estate attorney, and I have a couple of clients who reside here." I pause. "This is usually where people insert the bad lawyer jokes."

She laughs. "So an attorney who makes house calls, huh?"

"Yes, ma'am."

We've made our way to the sliding glass doors at the front entrance. A nurse walks in, and a raw plume of air follows her.

"Well," Trudie says. "You never did tell me your name."

"Oh, yes. Please pardon my manners." I extend my hand, and she takes it in hers. "Nigel Hurst. It's a pleasure to meet you."

"No cold or dampness in there," she mocks.

"My dear woman, you'd be surprised."

"Really?" she says, and her voice goes up two octaves. She bites her lower lip before continuing. "Well, surprise me then." She pulls out a card and pen from her purse, scribbles a number on the back, and hands it to me. "Call me some time. Maybe we could get together."

I stare at the card.

"I didn't notice a ring." She gestures to my left hand. "Of course, my friends say that doesn't mean anything these days. So if you're married or spoken for, say so. No hard feelings, you know?"

"Right." The card feels heavy.

She dips her head trying to catch my eyes, which haven't moved from her phone number that for the life of me I can't make out. "So. Does that mean you'd like to get together?"

This time I do look up, and she's as beautiful as I thought she was the first time I saw her, what, five minutes ago. She's probably in her mid-thirties, looking for a husband and father to her unborn children. For all I know, she has one or two kids already waiting at home, hoping Mommy found a candidate for the job, a perfect Christmas present.

I don't get picked up often these days, as gravity has somehow taken over my middle and The Gray Fairy has sprinkled her magic potion on my head. Of course, I don't usually put myself in those situations since I'm doing my damndest at avoiding bars. I don't hang out in other pick-up joints like charity events or the produce aisles of supermarkets, either. The last place I expected to meet someone was Saint A's. It occurs to me maybe that's why I've been spending so much time here, even long before Maggie Prescott showed up.

"I'm … sorry," she stammers. "I didn't mean to put you on the spot. I thought that—"

"I'd love to," I hear myself say.

*Damn*, the inner voice says. *This isn't fair to this girl. This* … I turn the card over because I've already forgotten her name.

"Trudie," I begin. "Maybe we—"

She smiles and looks so happy and relieved that I stop. "It doesn't matter what we do," she chirps. "I'm open to anything. Coffee. Dinner." She pauses. "Rio de Janeiro at sunset."

I laugh. "Rio, huh?"

She shrugs and giggles. "A girl can dream, right?"

"Right," I nod. "Absolutely."

I don't have the heart to tell her that the dreams seldom come true.

# Chapter 13: Maggie

"You should move in." Serena flops onto the couch in our office. "You spend all your time here."

"No I don't."

"Oh yeah, that's right. When you're not here, you're at that nursing home."

"Where else am I supposed to go?"

"I don't know. How 'bout the theater? Or the movies? Remember? Like we used to do in New York? You've been invited to every premiere since we've been here. But how many have you gone to, Maggie? Nada. Zilch. None."

"What are you complaining about? You get the invites like I do."

"And what about the inns in Vermont? That'd be a nice segment this time of year."

I look up from my keyboard. "We're doing a piece on the Vermont inns."

"Yeah. Jackson is. And her producer."

"Jackson is the heir apparent. You know that. I took this gig knowing that."

"Right, but if we wanted that segment, we could have it and could get the hell out of Dodge for a couple of days. You are 'the' Maggie Prescott after all."

"You're starting to sound like April."

"What do you mean?"

"Just because I am who I am doesn't mean I always get my way. Nor does it make me a complete bitch or diva." I pause, but Serena says nothing. "Um, this is where you're supposed to jump in and agree."

"You're far from a diva, I'll give you that. I'd be happy if you acted more like a diva instead of this." She gestures to my desk covered in papers and books on Alzheimer's disease.

"Yeah?" I sigh. "And what do you think 'this' is?"

"Closed off."

"How do you figure?"

"You ever talk to your old boyfriend? That Nigel guy?"

"What's he got to do with anything?"

"Did you?"

"I've bumped into him a few times at the nursing home."

"That's all?"

"Yes."

"And you don't care? You don't want more than 'bumping into him'?"

"Of course not. What makes you think that?"

Serena crawls off my couch and reaches across me for a file folder buried beneath the stacks. She's so close I can smell the hair goop she uses in her braids.

"This is what makes me think that," she says handing me a folder with the words "Nigel Hurst" scrawled across the top. "And don't give me that nostalgia-curiosity crap." She places the folder on my lap and opens it to a picture of Nigel that I found on the Internet. "He's cute," she says. "In an old pompous sort of way. But that goes with you."

"Gee, thanks."

"No, seriously. I can see it. You and him together."

"Serena. How many times do I have to tell you? We haven't been together in forever. A lifetime ago. Besides, even if I did feel anything, he wouldn't be interested."

"How do you know that?"

"I know, that's all."

"Uh huh. So, how do you explain him calling this evening while you were on the air and leaving a message with me?" She digs into her back pocket, pulls out a yellow sticky pad, and throws it on top of his picture.

"Why would he leave a message with you?"

She shrugs. "Who knows? The switchboard and voice mail directory around here are wacky." Getting up, she stretches and yawns. "Oh. And before you say it's too late to call him back, he said he'll be up and to call any time."

While I eyeball Nigel's telephone number, Serena heads for the door. "It's your call." She glances at her watch. "Literally. Well, gotta run."

#

There's nothing in life's rulebook that says I need to return Nigel's phone call—ever. Sure, it might be rude, but he's gotten over worse when it's come to me. It's not as if we can pick up where we left off, and I doubt that's what he even wants. After all, he made that clear years ago.

A ringing sound emanates from under a stack of papers. I root through the pile, find my Blackberry, and glance at the digital display on the front: "Serena Flores."

"What now, Serena?" I say into the phone.

"Have you called him yet?"

"How can I possibly call him when I can't get away from you?"

"Good point. So, does that mean you're going to do it?"

"No. I'm not."

"Party pooper."

"Yeah, that's me."

"It's your life."

"That's right."

"But if you bump into him and he asks why you didn't return his call, you better not lie and claim I never gave you the message."

"God forbid," I say and disconnect. Almost immediately, it rings again. "Serena, listen," I sigh into the phone. "You're not going to convince me to call him, so you might as well stop trying."

Silence.

"Serena?"

A throat clears. "Um, Maggie?"

"Yes?"

"Hi, it's me. Nigel."

*Shit.* "Oh. Hello."

"Your producer gave me this number."

"She did, did she? Well, how convenient."

"For whom?" he asks. "You or me?"

"Neither. For her."

"I see."

"Well." I trace the outline of his face on the picture that's still in my lap. "What do you want?"

"Right. No need to beat around the bush. I was wondering if you'd like to get together. For coffee, perhaps?"

"Now?"

"Well, sure. Now, if you'd like. Or tomorrow. Or the next day."

"Nigel. I—"

"Wait. Before you decline, hear me out. Maggie, a lot of time has passed. I know that. We're different people from who we were three decades ago. I know that, too. But I also believe there's more to the story—our story—than the way it ended. There has to be."

"What makes you so sure of that?"

"Hazel told me."

"Hazel told you what?" My mind races. *What did she tell him?*

"She told me to ask you about a letter."

"A letter?"

"She said, 'Ask Maggie about the letter I never gave you.'"

"But she did give you the letter," I say, confused. "You refused to read it. You tore it up. At least, that's what she told me."

"I was—admittedly—not in the best of shape when Hazel found me in the barroom that day, but I didn't black out. I remember what happened. There was no letter."

"But." My tongue turns to cotton. I struggle to swallow. I had revealed everything in that letter. *Everything.* In my mind, it was a test. If Nigel read it and could forgive me, we'd be okay. "I don't understand," I say more to myself than him as I struggle to remember what had transpired in those dark moments.

#

When Hazel came back to my hospital room that night, she said he'd refused to read it. That he had torn it up. I struggled to sit up in the bed. "I need to find him," I groaned. "The letter was a stupid idea. I need to tell him face to face."

"Shh." Hazel sat on the edge of my bed and directed my shoulders back onto the pillows propping me up. "You need to rest. The hell with him and men who think they know what is best for us."

"What?"

"It is a sign," she continued. "His tearing up the letter. If he truly cared—if he felt the way you do—would he not have read what you wrote? Listened to what you had to say?"

My head spun. The drugs pumped into my system nauseated me. "I guess so." I was tired. I clutched my belly. "But—"

"Rest, my dear. Rest. Tomorrow, you will see things more clearly."

Somehow, I did. But not without a healthy dose of Hazel's vitriol. How come I'm only remembering this now? Why did she lie about the letter? Not that it would have necessarily changed the outcome if he had read it. But I allowed her to convince me that his refusal to even consider my explanation was evidence that he wanted nothing more to do with me. That it was he who had rejected me.

#

"Maggie?" Nigel says. "You still there?"

"Yes."

"Listen. I don't know what happened with that letter years ago, but I'm here now. I'd like to know what was in it."

"I don't think that would be a good idea."

"Why not?"

"It just wouldn't, okay? Why are you harassing me?"

"Harassment, my ass. Why are you always so bloody obstinate?"

"Gee, Nigel. It's hard to believe you're single when you use lines like that."

He sighs. "Can't we even be friends?"

"Do you believe it's possible for old lovers to be friends?" I ask.

"I don't know. I thought maybe, yes. That we could."

"Are you friends with any old lovers?"

"Only Ruth Frankenfeld."

"Who's that?"

"My number one client at Saint A's."

"Seriously, Nigel."

"Are you friends with any old lovers?"

"I asked first."

"This isn't a competition, Maggie." He pauses. "No, I'm not friends with any of them. Are you happy? I guess I lose."

"You said it wasn't a competition."

"Well, what about you? Is Maggie Prescott friends with any of the men she's bedded over the last three decades?"

I consider his question. Being single has never been an issue in my life, nor has finding strong arms to hold me—or for me to hold onto—when I've needed them. Lovers? I've had plenty, but how many of them are still friends? Hell, how many were friends to begin with? Only one, and I'm talking to him now, asking him to go away.

"Right," Nigel whispers, having apparently mistaken my silence for fond old-lover rumination. "It was silly of me to ask."

With that, he hangs up, and I'm left wondering if I'll ever breathe normally again.

# *Chapter 14: Nigel*

When Max was a little boy, he loved those bright-colored alphabet magnets. We had three or four sets of letters on the fridge, dishwasher, and anything else to which they would adhere. I remember the day he learned how to spell his name without assistance; he couldn't wait to tell me. Except he had to since Anne Marie and I began to quarrel when I arrived home, arguing about what, I can't even remember. Exhausted from our row, I collapsed onto the living room couch, a bottle of merlot by my side, while Anne Marie locked herself in our bedroom. I'm ashamed to admit that I'd forgotten all about Max until he plodded his way to the sofa in his fuzzy blue pajamas with rockets and stars and plastic-soled bottoms.

"Daddy, come see." He had toothpaste dribble on his chin and tear stains on his cheeks. Taking my hand in his, he led me to the kitchen where he proudly showed off his spelling talents: MAXWELL HURST.

"Brilliant!" I picked him up, hugging him tight. His blonde curls were still damp from his bath, and he smelled of baby shampoo and Ivory soap. "Okay, sport. Time for bed."

He shook his head. "You next, Daddy."

*No,* I thought. *I'm tired. I need to be alone. I need a drink. You need to sleep.* But then an image of my own father—brushing me off, always too busy or preoccupied or drunk to pay me any attention—zipped through my head.

"Okay, Maxwell. Okay."

Together, we mixed up the magnets, so he could start from scratch. In his little boy voice, he sounded out my name and selected the appropriate letters with his soft, chubby fingers. He got "Nigel" right on the first try, but he paused and looked up at me before continuing the rest.

"You already know how to spell the last name. It's the same as yours," I reminded him.

He nodded, licked his upper lip, and reached for the "H" and then the "U," continuing until he had our last name displayed in electric neon colors. I clapped my hands without even surveying his efforts. "Bravo. Now, bed." Scooping him up onto my shoulders, I pretended to fly to his room. He giggled the whole way.

It wasn't until the next morning when I was having breakfast by the light of the moon—that's how early I claimed I needed to "get to the office"—that I noticed the words on the fridge: NIGEL HURTS.

Underneath it was another line, no doubt formed after Max and I had gone to bed: ANNE MARIE DOES TOO.

#

Trudie's telephone number—555-GRIN—jars this memory loose. I hesitate then dial the number. My frustration with Maggie is going to lead me to do one thing—drink—unless I get my mind off her.

"Hello?"

*Shit! What am I doing? Just hang up.* "Hello," I hear myself say. "May I speak with Trudie, please?"

"Yep, you may. It's me."

"Trudie, it's Nigel Hurst speaking. Many apologies for calling so late—"

"Hi, Nigel. What took you so long?"

"Pardon?"

"What took you so long to call?"

I gape at the phone, wondering if somehow I had gone off on a bender and lost a few days in the process. "We only met this afternoon."

She giggles. "And I've been waiting by the phone ever since."

Realizing that she's joking, I laugh as well, although it's not my best I'm-being-polite laugh.

"So, what's up?" she says.

"I was wondering if you wanted to perhaps get together?" *Wait. I want those words back.*

"I'd love to."

*Damn.* "Right. Excellent."

"What do you want to do?"

"Well, I believe you suggested coffee. Or dinner. Or … Rio." I cringe and pray she doesn't opt—even jokingly—for the third item.

"Coffee sounds great."

"Oh, good." I pause, but the words escape anyway. "I was worried you were going to choose Rio."

"Nah. Coffee to start. And we'll work up to Rio." She laughs again, but this time its warmth and genuineness penetrate the phone line.

"Where would you like to go? Would you like to meet somewhere, or shall I pick you up?" I hadn't even considered where she lived or worked. I turn the business card over in my hand and squint at the print, a jumble of letters and numbers.

"Let's make it easy. We can meet at Saint A's and go somewhere from there."

"Perfect."

We make our plans, wish each other goodnight, and hang up.

*Perfect.*

Perfect not because Trudie and I are meeting; perfect because Maggie might see us together at Saint A's. I'm surprised I don't feel more like a heel for essentially using this young woman, but I quickly rationalize that it's not as if I'm taking her to bed—just for a cappuccino or latte. Huge difference. Enormous. Gargantuan. I won't allow it to get out of hand. I won't hurt this woman with the angelic face, sweet laughter, and telephone number that ends in "GRIN." I won't, I won't, I won't. And if by some chance I do—

I think back now to that morning when I saw Anne Marie's words spelled out on the fridge. I added my own line underneath hers: I AM SORRY.

But it was too late then for forgiveness, and I knew it.

# Chapter 15: Maggie

Confronting an old woman about something that in the grand scheme of things is probably insignificant is the last thing I should be doing, but I can't help it. I need to know why Hazel didn't give that letter to Nigel.

"So," I say, while trying to think of a way to transition from the pleasantries we've been exchanging to the topic at hand.

"So," Hazel repeats. "Why don't you tell me what is on your mind."

"Nigel called me last night."

She nods, her face serious. "I imagined he would."

"He said that you said he should ask me about the letter."

"That is correct."

"He said he knew nothing about the letter. But how could that be, Hazel?" Despite my best efforts, I can't mask the anger in my voice. "You told me you'd given it to him and that he'd ripped it up without so much as glancing at it."

Hazel focuses on her clasped hands on her lap. Finally, she looks up. Her face is pale. "That is correct. That is what I told you. But that is not ..." She pauses and gulps some air. "That is not what happened."

"But I don't understand. I—"

"Maggie, I made an error in judgment. An egregious error, I realize now." She takes a deep breath, and her face pales even more.

"Why?" I ask. "Why did you decide not to give him the letter? A letter that explained everything?"

"The Nigel I encountered that afternoon reminded me too much of my father. Controlling. Overbearing. Drunk." She shivers. "But the truth is I became my father by interfering. By deciding not to hand the letter over to Nigel and lying to you about his response."

My face grows warm and my palms sweat. I can't believe what I'm hearing.

"It is true that we become our parents," she whispers, her voice hoarse. "Destined to make the same mistakes. I never believed this until I realized I had essentially done to you and Nigel what my father had done to Mack and me."

My brain spins on its axis. What if Nigel had read the letter? What if he had known the truth? Would he have come back for me? Forgiven me? No. It would have killed him. He wouldn't have come back then, and he certainly wouldn't be showing this interest in me now. Hazel's done me a favor.

"Maggie," she gasps. "I am sorry."

I jump out of the chair and sit on her bed, taking her hand in my own. It feels clammy. "Hazel, wait. There's no need for—"

She interrupts and attempts to squeeze my hand. "Yes, Maggie. There is. There is a need for forgiveness. And the truth. You must tell Nigel the truth."

I sigh and shake my head. "I don't think that would be a good idea. What's the point? I can't do anything about what happened. Neither can he. I doubt he would have been able to forgive me then, and I know he can't forgive me now."

"You do not know that for certain." She closes her eyes and leans her head against the back of the chair. For a minute, I think she's fallen asleep. Then her eyes open.

"Tallulah Falls," she croaks, "is out of the question. In this life, anyway. For me. But you and Nigel—"

"Wait. You can still go to Tallulah Falls, Hazel. It's not too late. I could help get you there."

"No, Maggie. You do not understand. Mack's sister called today."

"And?"

"She and her husband are finally moving to California where their youngest has twins." She takes a deep breath, except she can't. She clutches her chest. I reach for her hand, but she waves me away. "It is where they belong."

"When are they moving? And what about the house?"

"That is not my point, my dear. My point is you still have time. To make things right. To help me make things right. With all of it."

I'm trying my best to follow the conversation, but everything blurs. "I don't understand. All of what?"

She's about to answer when a man walks into the room.

"Hello, Hazel."

Her eyes follow the voice. "Good morning, Mr. Dooley."

The man nods at me, but his eyes rest on Hazel. I've seen him pacing the hallways and sitting with Hazel's roommate whom I've all but forgotten until now.

"Mr. Dooley," she continues. "I believe the two of you have not been properly introduced. Maggie, my dear, this is ..." She coughs and sputters. "... Mr. Hugh Dooley. A fine, fine man."

"Well, now," he says. "I don't know about that."

"And Mr. Dooley, this is Maggie Prescott. April's ..." But this time, she doesn't finish. Her eyes close, her shoulders slump, and her head falls forward.

"Hazel?" I yelp.

"Pull the cord," Hugh instructs, pointing to the thin piece of rope hanging from the wall.

I do, and bells go off. Then all hell breaks loose.

# *Chapter 16: April*

Snow covers the patio. This time I'm dressed for the elements—black parka, multi-colored gloves that a resident's family gave me last year for Christmas, gray wool hat. I've bundled up Mom as well, who walks in circles in the fluffy snow, but her winter jacket appears loose on her small, shrunken frame. I hold a cigarette between my gloved fingers and am about to take another puff when a hand reaches in front of my face and pulls the butt from my lips.

"You said you shouldn't smoke." Hugh throws my cigarette to the ground. The tracks behind him reveal the path he took around the building.

"So did you." I swipe the cigar poking out of his breast pocket.

"Touché. But do me a favor? Don't throw it in the snow."

Before I can offer a comeback, Mom's laughter catches our attention, and we both watch as she scoops the white powder into her mittens and throws it in the air.

"Your mother?" he asks.

"Yep."

"I didn't realize she was so—"

"Active?" I shrug. "She seems to have this newfound energy. She's happier, too." I shiver and inch down into the collar of my coat. "So what do you do, Hugh, when the meddling family members are right? I mean, it seems maybe some of Maggie's potions and voodoo doctors are working after all."

He stares at Mom. "You thank them," he says.

"Is that what you do?"

He turns and looks at me. "Only if they're right."

"Is your daughter ever right?" I'm surprised at how strident my question is, but having him so close to me is unnerving, this man that I've been thinking about way too much in my spare time, and all because of his damned Christmas tree. "I'm sorry. I didn't mean to pry." I walk away from him and head towards Mom who's getting ready to put a fist full of snow in her mouth. I redirect her hand to the ground. She grins—it's a child's smile, full of wonder and enchantment at the first snow of winter, and I'm reminded of my little boy, my Jimmy. I lead her back to the patio where I've shoveled a spot down to bare slate, and she starts twirling, arms outstretched. "I'm just stressed, I guess."

"What's the latest on Hazel?" he asks.

Legally, I'm not supposed to discuss a patient's condition with anyone outside of Saint A's medical personnel, but Hugh is the husband of Hazel's roommate. Seems to me he deserves to know. Besides, I *want* to talk to him about it. Not a good sign.

"Pneumonia," I hear myself say. "She got it around this time last year and the year before that. Pneumonia is usually a death sentence in nursing homes, but Hazel's always bounced back. It's the fainting spell that surprised everyone this time. I even heard the words 'panic attack' bantered about. Have no idea what could've sparked that. Anyway, she should be back from the hospital in a few days." He doesn't say anything, but his face looks funny. "What?" I ask.

He shakes his head. "Nothing."

"Do you know what upset Hazel?"

He shrugs. "Not with any certainty. She and Maggie sounded as if they were having a serious conversation before I came in."

"Serious? Serious how?"

"I'm not sure. And I don't want to upset you."

But it's too late. I'm already upset. I'm tired of Maggie interfering. I don't care about her history with Hazel. She has no right to walk in here and upset a dying woman. *But she's not dying,* I remind myself. *Hazel will live forever.*

"Tell me," I demand. "If you're my friend, you'll tell me."

"I am your friend," he says quietly, but that's all he says.

"Hugh, please."

He sighs. "When I arrived, I heard voices coming from inside the room, so I waited outside the door. You know how thin the walls are. I overheard parts of their conversation. I couldn't make out everything, but both Maggie and Hazel sounded upset and then Hazel was apologizing for something. I don't know what."

"What a pain in the ass Maggie is! She's caused nothing but trouble since she arrived."

"Except," Hugh says, "your mother may be responding to some of the treatment Maggie has advocated."

"Whose side are you on?"

"Is that what it's about? Sides?"

We're both quiet, and I turn my attention to Mom, but I can feel his eyes on me.

"Oh. There was something else," he murmurs.

I face him. "Yeah? What?"

"Something about a house. About people moving from a house in—"

"Tallulah Falls?"

He snaps his fingers. "Yes. That's it. Tallulah Falls."

I let out a low whistle, and Mom covers her ears. So Mack's sister is finally selling the ol' homestead. Now Hazel will never have a chance to live in the house Mack built.

"Guess there was more of a reason for her to be upset than just Maggie," Hugh says.

"Yep. That would do it. This house is special. The love of her life built it, and she never got to live in it. She's never even seen it."

Hugh nods. "Perhaps that explains the panic attack."

The December sun has all but disappeared, and his words settle around us with the dusk. My head hurts, and I want to change the subject. Mom and I hold hands, and I swing our arms high in the air and back down again. She laughs.

"She never used to like winter," I say. "But look at her now."

"It's never been my favorite season, either."

When he says this, I realize how little I know about Hugh Dooley, how one-sided our friendship—if you could even call it that—has been.

"So what is your favorite?" I ask.

"Summer," he says without hesitation. "Of course, that might have something to do with the fact I've always had them off."

"What sort of work do you do? Or did you do?"

"Professor at the college in town. I'm on an extended sabbatical, pseudo medical leave right now, which will likely turn into an early retirement at this rate."

"Oh."

He smiles. "You weren't expecting that, were you?"

Mom crouches and attempts to create a snowball. I stoop to help. "I haven't had a chance to read Gloria's chart too thoroughly. Usually information on spouses is in there."

"Well, you have been otherwise occupied the last few months."

"I suppose," I say rolling the snowball into the base of a snowman. "What do you teach?"

"American history with a focus on the antebellum period, Civil War, and Reconstruction."

"A Lincoln scholar," I say.

"By default, yes, although early in my career I had much more interest in his so-called demented assassin."

"So-called?"

"That's right."

"You mean John Wilkes Booth wasn't crazy?"

"What I mean—and this is an entirely unoriginal concept, but it still holds true—is that there are two sides to every story. At least."

"So you're saying there's more than one side to the Lincoln assassination?"

He nods. "At least that's what my book purported."

"You wrote a book?"

"Yes. You probably have heard of the whole 'publish or perish' mentality in academia."

I know nothing of this mentality, but nod anyway and watch as Mom starts on the snowman's body, somehow remembering this basic childhood skill. "Do you like teaching?"

"I adore it." He pauses. "Of course, it's all I know. I've been doing it since I was twenty-five years old. It's where I met Gloria, you know."

I didn't know. "Oh, is she—"

"—a professor as well? Yes. English. Poetry is her first love. We actually named our daughter after her favorite poet, Adrienne Rich."

"Wow. That's cool."

He smiles sadly, as if it is cool on the one hand, but at the same time, it isn't.

"So," I say searching for a way to redirect the conversation, "Wilkes Booth."

"Yes?"

"Did he do it?"

"Let's just say he most likely didn't do it alone."

"Really?"

"Yes."

"Guess I'll have to check out this book."

"That would bring the total number of readers to five then," he laughs.

"I'm sure you had more readers than that."

He shrugs. "It was thirty years ago. At the time, the school wasn't too supportive of my efforts."

"How come?" I finish rolling a smaller snowball and place it on top of the snowman's torso. Mom claps. I look around for something to make eyes and a mouth, but Hugh beats me to it and plucks some holly berries from a nearby bush along with some rocks he has somehow unearthed.

"The dean was rather conservative and didn't appreciate my conspiracy theories," he continues while handing me the berries and rocks. "To be perfectly frank, he thought I was a left-wing nut job."

"Why didn't he get rid of you then? Push you out. Recommend you take a job somewhere clear across the country?" I form a wide smile out of the berries and hand Mom the rocks. She stares at them in her mittens.

"Easier said than done. Besides, I was married to his daughter."

"Ah," I say.

"He never did like me. He had someone else in mind for Gloria to marry, not some young whippersnapper nearly a decade younger than she was. He thought Gloria married me to spite him."

"I see."

"A complicated web we weave," he says. "Etcetera, etcetera, and so forth."

I direct Mom's hand to the snowman's face, where the eyes should be, but then need to pry the rocks loose from her grip. Hugh's cigar becomes the carrot nose we don't have, and finally, the face is done, albeit a little crooked.

"Nice work," Hugh says.

And it would be, if this were Jimmy's snowman. But as I survey our efforts and assess Mom's childlike wonderment at it all, I can't help but feel incredibly sad at this backwards progression she's making.

"Your mother would be proud," he continues. "Of you. Your patience. Everything."

I shake my head, unable to speak. *Not everything,* I think.

We're quiet for a while, watching Mom dance around the snowman, her arms stretched out wide like an airplane, and suddenly I'm aware of Hugh's hand, rubbing the length of my spine, up, down, and up again. His touch is barely discernible through my parka, but it's there nonetheless.

"It's so hard," I whisper. "And so unfair." These are the only words I can get out. Any more, and I'll cry. I wait for him to offer soothing platitudes, like the ones I've been offered before on the rare occasions I've opened up about Mom's illness, the well-meaning people trying to provide comfort in their words, yet failing every time. But Hugh says nothing, simply bearing witness to my pain.

I don't think I've ever felt so grateful for silence.

# Chapter 17: Nigel

Maggie and I met during a community protest in Harvard Square back in '73. Nine years prior, the Kennedy Library Corporation had selected I. M. Pei & Partners as architects of the John F. Kennedy Presidential Library, which was supposed to be housed on Bennett Street in Cambridge, a short jaunt from Harvard Yard. Two million people were expected to visit annually, pouring mind-boggling revenue into city coffers while the value of Cambridge property appreciated.

Enter the Neighborhood Ten Association, a group of concerned citizens opposing the development. Be it a prison or presidential library, no one likes such expansive structures in their own backyard. Eventually the "N10A," as Maggie dubbed them, got its way. After a court challenge in '75, the Kennedy Corporation decided to—on its own—move the library to Columbia Point.

As a law student at Harvard, I followed these community rumblings since public policy debates fascinated me. I also had a personal problem with the mighty—even if it came under the guise of a nonprofit organization— trying to smite the voices of the lowly; it reminded me too much of my father. Maggie filmed the protests and interviewed scores of store vendors, residents, and students like myself, all for the documentary on the N10A that she was working on for school. I'm not sure which came first—her capturing my image on film or her captivating my attention with her brilliance in body and mind.

Looking across the table at Trudie Collins, I can't imagine years from now thinking back to this Starbucks moment, which is like so many others in thousands of lives. Perhaps I'm feeling so sullen because Maggie was nowhere to be found this afternoon when Trudie showed up at Saint A's for our "coffee date," even though I dragged her throughout the building, hoping to bump into Maggie. We even stopped by Hazel's room—I'd heard about her illness—but when I poked my head inside, the old woman lay in bed, sleeping. We bumped into April, too, and I thought she might be my savior, running to tell her sister that she saw me with another woman. But then again, given the contentious relationship between the two, why would she?

"So," Trudie says.

"So," I repeat.

"Tell me about Nigel Hurst."

"Oh, him." I roll my eyes. "He's quite a boring old ass."

"Mm. That's not what I've heard."

"And what have you heard?"

"That he's this dashing fellow. Smart, too."

I raise my brow. "Well, the dashing I'll buy. But smart? Sounds like he's got everyone fooled."

She laughs. "Well, he would need some smarts to be a lawyer, right?"

"True, true. But that doesn't necessarily make him exciting. In fact, I suspect it would be more interesting to talk about someone else."

She smiles. "Really?"

"Yes."

"Like who?"

"Oh, I don't know." I stroke my chin, pretending to think. "How about Ms. Trudie Collins?"

"Oh, her," she whispers, while leaning into the table. "She's a wild one, you know."

"How so?"

She smacks her lips together. "Well, on the surface she seems nice and sweet and innocent."

"So I hear. Go on."

"But on the inside, the Trudie under the cover of night. *Well.*"

"Yes?" I find I'm almost breathless.

She smiles coyly, while rubbing the rim of her cup with her index finger. "I shouldn't say anymore. Wouldn't be right."

I lean back in my chair and sigh. "Guess I'll have to find out on my own then."

"Guess so." She takes a sip of coffee. "If you're lucky, that is."

She tries hard not to giggle, but it bubbles up in her throat, bursting from her mouth in an enchanting peal of mirth. I find myself archiving our playful conversation in my head, her laughter the soundtrack.

"Tell me more about radio," I ask. The numbers and letters I had been trying to read on her business card the other night were radio station call letters. The similarity between her career and Maggie's is not lost on me.

"What would you like to know?"

"Well, you're a—"

"DJ," she says. "Disc jockey."

"Right. Tell me about that. What does a DJ do? How'd you get started?"

"Well, I work for a music station, so basically I'm the accompaniment to the music. I talk about the artists, introduce songs, give away concert tickets and other prizes on the air, all the while sounding bright and happy, even if I don't feel like it."

"I can't imagine you not being bright and happy." The sentence slips out, and the pink rises to her cheeks.

"You'd be surprised."

"Do you like being a DJ?"

"Love it. It's kind of cool getting paid to play and talk about music—things I do anyway. I lucked out, landing in Boston and all. I'm from here originally, but after college, I had to go to East Oshkosh, Vermont, to work overnights for some little station that had more cows as listeners than people. Not fun."

"Did you go to school for broadcasting?"

"Yep."

"Where'd you go?"

"Emerson." When I don't respond, she tilts her head to the side and arches her left brow. "What's wrong?"

"Nothing," I say quickly, wondering if perhaps this is all a joke, or if Maggie has come back in a younger form. *Except Trudie isn't Maggie*, I remind myself. They have some things in common, yes, like their educational backgrounds and current jobs and the fact Trudie arches her left eyebrow the same way Maggie does. But they're not the same. Trudie Collins is not Maggie Prescott.

"You're thinking something," she presses. "What is it?"

"I'm thinking," I begin, struggling to put a cohesive thought together, "why radio and not television? You're a beautiful woman. You'd look fantastic on camera."

She blushes again and looks down at her coffee cup.

"I'm sorry. I don't mean to embarrass you. But let's face it, Trudie." She looks up expectantly, and I can't help but smile. "You're hot."

She laughs. "Well, I don't know about that. Have you ever heard the expression 'a perfect face for radio'? That's how I've always felt—that I had a perfect face and body for radio. Not TV. I was overweight as a kid. Something I've battled all my life."

I don't know what to say. The woman before me is so tall and slim. Even with another twenty pounds, she'd still be stunning.

"There's another Emerson grad who's made it big in television," she continues, obviously trying to change the subject. "And she's got connections to Saint A's, too."

"Oh?" My voice raises one full octave. I don't like where this conversation is going.

"Yep. Maggie Prescott."

"Ah, yes."

"Have you seen her?"

"On TV all the time."

"No, silly." She giggles. "I meant at the nursing home. She's there, like, every day. Word is she was adopted, and I guess her adoptive mother lives there but has Alzheimer's and doesn't even know who Maggie is. And get this—you know April, the activities director? Turns out she and Maggie Prescott are sisters."

"Half sisters," I murmur.

"What?"

I clear my throat. "Well. I heard that they share the same mother, yes. But—"

"Oh, I see." Trudie nods in understanding. "Right. Half sisters. So you've seen her, then?"

"Who?"

Trudie rolls her eyes and laughs. "Maggie Prescott."

"Oh, yes. Have you?"

"I interviewed her."

"You what?"

"On air. When she first came to Boston and was promoting *New England Journal*." She shrugs. "I'm sure she wouldn't remember me, though."

I think back to a story Maggie told me about how she learned the names of all the American presidents and vice presidents—and could recite this list from present to past, or past to present—at the age of six. How she never forgot all the elements in the periodic table, even though chemistry was her least favorite subject. How she could recite passages from Shakespeare that we English scholars always prided ourselves on knowing, but how Maggie could continue with the recitation long after my memory had conked out.

"Somehow I doubt that," I say.

Trudie looks at me curiously. "Why do you say that?"

"I've read that she has a photographic memory." This is true. I have.

She shrugs. "Maybe."

"So tell me about your Aunt Gertrude." I hope this suggestion effectively changes the Maggie Prescott subject.

"Good ol' Aunt Gert. I'm named after her, you know."

"I didn't know. Well, I hadn't thought about it. Makes sense. Gertrude, Trudie. I think I prefer Trudie."

"So do I! Do you know what it's like growing up as Gertrude?" She wrinkles her nose. It's a cute button nose with a splash of freckles across the bridge. "It's such an old fashioned name. And not one like Hannah or Olivia. It sounds so—"

"Matronly?"

"And then some. Old spinster-ish, which I guess I am."

"Oh, please," I say. "If you're a spinster, what does that make me? Jurassic?"

"I've always liked dinosaurs."

"Wonderful. I'm officially a fossil."

"No, but seriously. It's tough meeting men at my age."

I desperately want to know what age that is, but don't want to be rude by querying. I should have asked when she graduated school. She smiles now as if she can read my mind.

"I'm forty-two, for enquiring minds that want to know."

"Right. I'll be sure to pass that information along if I ever encounter one." I grin. "You don't look it. Besides, I dare say forty-two is far from spinsterhood."

"It would be in Victorian times."

"Well, I guess we're lucky that it's the twenty-first century. You still have a chance."

"What about you?"

"What about me? Is this your way of inquiring about my age?"

"Among other things."

"Let's see. I'm fifty-five, if that helps. Which would make me dead in Victorian times."

She laughs, and so do I.

"Have you noticed how easy this conversation is?" she asks shyly.

I nod, because it's true: I have. And this is dangerous. I should end things now before they go any further.

"I guess it would be safe to move on to item number two then," she muses.

"What?"

"I believe dinner was next on the list, remember? Right before Rio?"

As if I could forget. "Ms. Gertrude Trudie Collins, are you asking me out on a dinner date?" I feign shock.

"Welcome to the twenty-first century."

"Much better than those stuffy old Victorian times."

All serious now, she scrutinizes my face, her smile on hold. "Is that a yes?"

I try to say *No, Trudie. Let's just be friends,* but instead something else emerges from my lips. "Yes, Ms. Trudie Collins." I nod and then whisper, "That's an emphatic yes."

# Chapter 18: Maggie

The more time I spend with Kate, the more I think we're connecting. No, she's not talking to me or calling me by name or even showing a glint of recognition in her eyes. But there's something.

I've ditched the station's camera crew for my small, but expensive, personal hand-held camera. I've assured Serena that I'm documenting the time I spend with Kate, but the truth is I'm not doing this for her or *New England Journal*. I'm doing it for me so that I have a record. In the middle of the night, when the world sleeps, I play back my tapes, watching my mother—my *mother!* I do it to remind myself of what's real and maybe of what's important.

When my mum died, I was only ten years old. She fought hard. So hard, in fact, that when she was on her deathbed—after we'd said our goodbyes and our I-love-you declarations—she rallied for six more weeks. It appeared—in my memory, anyway—that she was getting better. I was young, my father was uneducated in the ways of medicine or cancer, and my mother allowed us to believe she was getting better because she so desperately wanted to believe it, too. We all did. But the cancer was still there, still ravaging beneath her skin, snaking through her organs, painting them black with poison. The next deathbed vigil was more painful than the first, more harrowing than anything I'd ever been through before or since. In many ways, I felt Mum died twice. I think it was then that I gave up on second chances.

Yet here I am filming Kate, a woman who rejected me for the first time fifty-two years ago and who certainly shows no sign of accepting me now, even though I feel some sort of something. Here I am taking a second chance with a friendship with Hazel, an old woman whose lungs struggle with every breath, whose decision to withhold that letter from Nigel may have altered history, or, at least, the history of two young lovers. Here I am fantasizing about a man and a relationship that was over decades ago and wondering if there's a possibility for forgiveness, for redemption, for another reel of film. What happened to my *id*, to my strong-willed subconscious that promised never to let me suffer two deaths at the same time again?

#

"My dear, what is it?" Hazel asks as I help her sit up in bed. "You are preoccupied."

"It's nothing."

"Is everything okay with Kate?"

"Yes."

"April?"

"Oh, just wonderful." My voice drips in sarcasm.

"Have you spoken with Nigel about—"

"Nope," I say, cutting her off. "And I'm not going to either."

She shakes her head.

"Listen, Hazel, are you sure you want me here for this?" I'm determined to change the subject. Enough with Nigel, April, and Kate.

"Yes. I am sure. I want Michael to know we have reconnected, and I want you here to bear witness to whatever he has to say."

"You know he's not my favorite person."

"Nor is he mine," she sighs. "But he is my only nephew, the only blood relation I have left." She pauses. "Despite everything, I do love him."

"Knock, knock," a voice calls out, and then Michael Cooke strides into the room. "How are we today, Aunty?" he says, and then stops in his tracks when he spots me. "Maggie!"

"Hello, Michael." I get up and extend my hand. "It's been a long time."

"I didn't know that you and Aunty were in touch."

"It's wild, isn't it?" I gush. "Hazel and I reconnecting after all these years."

"Ah, yes." He looks from me to Hazel and back to me. "How nice." He recovers quickly and grins. "You look even better in person than you do on TV."

"Thank you," I say, while trying not to gag. Wish I could say the same for him. Years ago, he was a skinny pimple-faced political panderer with a severe case of halitosis and an overabundance of confidence. He asked me out repeatedly, even after I started dating Nigel, and yet he never understood why I declined his offers. Today, his pockmarked face is bloated. He currently serves as a Massachusetts state rep while rumors abound about his drinking and womanizing on Beacon Hill. He's also the reason Hazel never returned to her home after her hip replacement surgery nearly a decade ago.

"So, Aunt Hazel. What did you want to see me about? One of the nurses giving you problems again?" He chuckles and then stops when he sees we don't find his comments amusing. "Perhaps we should talk in private?"

"Nonsense," Hazel says. "Maggie is practically family."

He takes a deep breath, like a bull prepared to fight. This is killing him, no doubt. Her home in Wellesley is probably worth a small fortune, and Michael is her only heir. Unless "family" like me shows up. I instantly understand why Hazel wants me here, and I'm more than happy to play along.

"Of course." Michael sits in the chair facing Hazel, while I take my place at the foot of her bed. "Well," he says. "Let's have it."

"Michael, I want to come home."

With his index finger, he pushes his wire-rimmed glasses up his greasy nose. "You mean for Christmas?"

"No. I mean forever. Until the end."

He blinks a couple of times and rubs the side of his pudgy pale cheek. "Aunt Hazel, I don't think that—"

She holds up her hand to stop him. It trembles in the air. "I want to come home to my house. I do not want to die here."

"Now, Aunt Hazel. You're not going to die."

She stares at him until he shifts uncomfortably in the rocking chair.

"Well, you're not," he says, sitting up straighter. "I won't allow it." He smiles, triumphant.

"My dear boy, I know you think you are important, but I can assure you of one thing: you are not, at least when it comes to that." He draws air into his chest to protest, but Hazel continues. "It is my house, after all. You have been merely watching it for me for the last decade while I recuperated here."

"That's right." He nods. "And you're still not healed, Aunt Hazel. Besides, it's a busy time of year. It's the week before Christmas, after all. I entertain quite a bit due to my position with the Commonwealth, which you may not believe is important, but I can assure you, it's a lot more so than you think."

"Is that a no then?"

"Not necessarily. I'll have you over for Christmas dinner, of course. But I'm also having a New Year's Eve party, in addition to Christmas parties. I can't imagine your wanting to be around for those. You need your rest after all."

"So after the first of the year—"

"We'll discuss it more then, but I honestly believe this is the best place for you."

She smiles. "Of course you do."

"I only have your best interests at heart."

"I understand."

He studies her face, and I can tell the wheels in his head are spinning, rusty though they may be.

"You know what?" he says slowly, carefully. "You're right, Aunt Hazel. It is your house. I'm merely a guest, so if you want to come back—"

"Perhaps in mid-January?" Hazel suggests.

He nods his head in agreement but then snaps his fingers as if he's remembered something. "I'll be skiing in Aspen for two weeks in January. I wouldn't feel right leaving you home alone. I should be there to care for you, if you were to come back." He tilts his head, pondering the dilemma. "Well, in any event, we'll discuss it again soon. Let's get through the holidays first." He glances at his watch. "I should get going. So nice seeing you, Aunty. You're looking so much better. Keep resting. I'll call later this week." He gets up and kisses her on the forehead before turning to me.

"And Maggie, so good to have you back in Boston."

"Thank you."

He pauses then smiles sheepishly. "Um. I don't suppose—"

"Yes?" I know where this is going, but I fake innocence.

"I don't suppose you'd be interested in having dinner sometime? I'm dining with the governor next Saturday." He pauses. "I'd love for you to join me."

"I'm afraid I can't."

"Ah, yes. Silly of me to assume you're single."

"I am single." I smile sweetly and wait for my words to sink into his thick skull. Hazel stifles a laugh with a cough.

"Right," he says quickly, his face reddening. "Well, so long, Aunty." He nods at me, and with that, he and his cheap aftershave are gone.

"What an ass," I mutter.

"Agreed," Hazel says. "But I needed to hear him deny me my house one final time. To be sure."

"Write him out of your will," I say, only half joking. "He doesn't deserve your house."

She clasps her hands together, a faraway look in her eyes. "Don't worry, my dear. My house will be safe." She pats what looks to be a business card on her nightstand. "I've consulted an attorney about it."

#

Seeing Michael Cooke brings me back to a time I'm trying harder and harder to forget: the time with Nigel. The time when everything went bad. I replay conversations in my head as I cruise past April's driveway for the third time.

It's late, around ten thirty. Tonight was the resident outing to a local shrine to see a holiday light display, and even though April and the residents would have returned on the early side—around eight o'clock—I know she lingers around Saint A's. One of the nurses recently told me that April stays with Kate every night until she falls asleep. For some reason, the image is comforting to me.

While looping around the neighborhood, I imagine what it would have been like to grow up in a real house rather than a two-bedroom apartment above our old family deli two towns away. It's a dangerous game I'm playing, the what-ifs. Usually I have better control, but it's gone to hell since I showed up here.

Spying April's car—finally—I pull in behind it and study the structure before me. It's a stately colonial with a farmer's porch, and I know for a fact it's on the list of historic homes in MetroWest, the label given to a group of cities and towns twenty-five miles west of Boston. The first time I saw the house, I drove right past without offering more than a mere glance, all the while adjectives like "bucolic" and "rustic" and "homey" popped into my head. The hedges surrounding the perimeter of the property, now covered in snow, are in dire need of upkeep. The white paint is peeling, a couple of black shutters need repair, and I suspect that the inside would conjure terms like "fixer-upper." Except this one would be worth restoring to its former grandeur from an era where roads weren't paved, people died before they got stowed away in nursing homes, and things—from my vantage point, anyway—were much less complicated.

I mount the four steps to the porch and rap on the front door. To my right, an old wicker rocking chair stands tired and worn, as if it's longing for someone to sit in it one last time but may be too fatigued to handle the weight. The only light comes from a Christmas tree in the front window.

The door opens, and April stands with one hand on the doorknob and the other behind her back. Her hair is mussed up, her cheeks flushed, her eyes without a lick of makeup. She glares at me. I wait for her to invite me inside, but she doesn't say anything. I think I smell smoke.

"Is something burning?" I ask.

April rolls her eyes and sighs, while producing a cigarette from behind her back.

"I didn't know you smoked."

She takes a drag, tilts her head to the wooden awning above us, and blows a perfect ring into the frigid night. "I don't." She throws the cigarette over my head where it lands in a snow bank. "What do you want?"

"May I come in?"

She thinks about it and shivers. She steps aside, and I have no doubt she's relented because she's cold. I move past her into the hallway leading into what looks to be the kitchen. To my right is the living room where the Christmas tree is on display. A fat calico cat lounges lazily beneath it.

"So," she begins, and I turn around to face her. She crosses her arms and leans against the door. "What do you want?"

I'm too overcome with emotion to say anything, and despite my best intentions, I find myself walking into the living room. My fingers touch the fabric on the olive paisley couch; my eyes photograph the worn places on the maroon throw rug; my ears record every creak and groan as I walk across the hardwood floor. The pictures on the mantel above the fireplace catch my attention—dust covers the frames, as if they haven't been touched in years, and perhaps they haven't.

There are dozens of shots of a baby boy, whom I assume is April's son since he has her green eyes, which are the same color as Kate's, the same color as mine. Except his are fringed in long dark lashes, with dark brown eyebrows and hair, no doubt inherited from his father's Italian heritage. The pictures capture first steps, first teeth, first day of pre-school, until the images stop abruptly—there's nothing beyond what looks to be a four-year-old at Christmas. Thinking of April's dead son right now is almost too much to bear, an ache forming deep in my gut. I desperately try to make conversation.

"Kate lived here all her life, right?" I ask while glancing back at April. She nods and my eyes return to the room, drinking in the details of the crown molding and trying to guess how old the dark mahogany paneling is.

"There isn't anything here," she says softly. "I've looked."

I face her again. She casts her eyes to the floor, shifting from one foot to the other. "It's only you and Kate, isn't it?" I say.

She looks up. "What do you mean?"

"I mean, there isn't anyone else. No aunts or uncles or cousins. On either Kate's side or your father's. No one who would know anything."

April shakes her head. "They were both the only children of only children. The family tree stops right here."

It's a line I imagine April has used hundreds of times when explaining her familial circumstances to anyone who asks, except it has new meaning now in my presence. Walking toward the window, I gently touch one of the glass balls hanging on the Christmas tree while peering into the night.

"What about neighbors?" I turn around again. "Would they remember anything?"

The cat emerges from beneath the tree branches, stretches, and walks to April in a lazy, drunken stupor before rubbing itself against her legs.

"Doubt it. Many of the people who were around when I was growing up have retired and moved away. There are lots of young families with little kids in the neighborhood now."

"That must be hard," I say. "To be around."

April stares at me, her face stony. "So, what did you want again?"

"It's about Christmas."

"What about it?"

"I was wondering what your plans are."

"I'm working."

"On Christmas?"

"Nursing homes operate 24/7. We can't close up the cash register like they do at Stop 'n Shop."

"I know that," I say, irritated. "The news doesn't take a break, either. But you worked Thanksgiving. Don't you get some sort of trade off?"

"I volunteer to work. That way the people with kids can be home with them."

I'm struck at how similar our thought processes are. "You can't be working for twenty-four hours straight. You must have some time off on Christmas Day."

She sighs. "Maggie, what's your point?"

"My point is I'd like to spend some of the day with you and Kate."

"Why?"

"Why do you think?"

She crosses her arms again and leans against the wall. She's shorter than I am and leaner, too, with no chest to speak of. I've always hated what I've referred to as my linebacker-sized shoulders and childbearing hips. April's waist is as slim as a man's, which reminds me that even though we share one bloodline, there are still two others at work—our fathers'.

I gesture towards the tree. "Seems to me, you need to get some presents under there."

"I don't have anyone I buy for anymore. We keep all the residents' presents in my office."

"I meant for you."

She walks towards me and reaches for one of the ornaments—a wooden sleigh—and for the first time all night, she smiles. "The tree is present enough."

"Someone gave you the Christmas tree?"

"So I'm working Christmas. You got your answer," she says, ignoring my other question.

"April, you need to eat. Kate needs to eat. Maybe we can get together. Donuts for breakfast. Pizza for lunch. Chinese food for dinner." I shrug. "It doesn't matter what or when it is."

"What? You're not going to offer to cook?"

"I assumed you value your life too much."

She laughs, deep and scornful. "Goes to show you should never assume anything."

"Seriously, April."

She stands up straight and looks me in the eye. "Sis, what makes you think I'm not serious?"

Before I can answer, she walks to the door and opens it, effectively dismissing me. The cat follows and leaps to freedom. "Look," she says. "I really do have to work on Christmas. But you're welcome to eat with her."

I follow her to the door and step out onto the porch. The cat has disappeared. "What if I bring Kate someplace?"

"She's not great in restaurants."

"What about here?"

"Here?"

"I promise not to touch anything, and who knows? It might even be good for her. Familiar surroundings."

April glances into the living room. When she turns to me, her face is red, and tears cling to her eyelashes. She shrinks into the shadows of the hallway. "Do what you want. Door'll be unlocked."

The conversation—if that's what you can even call it—is over. I back out onto the front step, while she slams the door in my face.

When I started out in television, I used to keep track of the number of times people slammed doors in my face or hung up the phone when I hounded them for quotes or information. One of the more popular contemporary documentary filmmakers—Michael Moore—is notorious for these moments. It's true that you develop a thick skin. It almost becomes a status symbol, a victory of sorts, especially when you catch someone on film, opening the door in greeting and then slamming it in disgust when he or she realizes it's you.

But I don't feel victorious tonight.

## Chapter 19: Nigel

If someone told me I could fall for a woman over an appetizer of prosciutto-wrapped mozzarella with vine ripe tomatoes, I would say he was crazy. A man like me would need to get to the main course, at least, before becoming smitten. But Trudie Collins appears to have poked a hole in this theory, or perhaps it's this steak-house restaurant nestled in the heart of Chestnut Hill. A mere hop-skip-and-jump from the city, the place twinkles in Christmas lights and emits a healthy round of holiday cheer.

When I first bumped into Maggie, I imagined the two of us enjoying a romantic interlude here, knowing that in her worldly travels she has become quite the connoisseur of fine cuisine. This restaurant offers that along with an ambience of dark leather, mahogany, and an impeccable wait staff, which perfectly complements a quixotic rendezvous. Except now, I'm here with another woman. It's odd how guilty a man can feel when betraying his own dream.

I know I should come clean about the relationship I had with Maggie Prescott—one that I hoped to rekindle. Still hope, perhaps. If Trudie knows the truth and still desires my company, then I can go about my business with a spotless conscience. The problem is that Maggie's my issue, not Trudie's. It seems highly unfair of me to put the onus on her. She has accepted all of my other confessions—two failed marriages, one beautiful son—with equal aplomb. Of course, I haven't mentioned the drinking, but I haven't touched a drop in practically a month. Hardly seems newsworthy anymore. Tonight,

Trudie accepted my I-better-not-because-I-have-an-early-meeting-in-the-morning excuse without batting an eyelash. Her half-filled glass of merlot barely has my attention. Her looks, however, are another matter. Her blonde hair cascades down her back. Her makeup is wonderfully light—I've always hated what people do to Maggie's face for television—and her pale skin looks absolutely luminescent against her black cocktail dress.

"So," I begin. *Is she going to drink her wine?* "It seems I've been nothing but the confessor all evening. Certainly Ms. Trudie Collins has some skeletons in her closet, yes?" I push her wine glass toward her.

"Trying to get me drunk?" She smiles, lowers her eyes, and then slowly raises them until they meet mine. "Not going to work."

"Ah. I see how it is. I'm going to have to find out for myself." *She won't mind if I have one sip. One sip won't hurt.* I reach for her glass, but she pulls it back while laughing.

"If you're lucky."

"Seems I've heard that line before." And I laugh, too. She pushes the glass in my direction, unaware of this gauntlet she's thrown down before me.

"Go ahead," she says.

Sweat forms on my brow. My tongue dries and curls. If I told her the truth—*but what is the truth? That I'm a drunk?*—she could support me in my efforts, right? No. That's not her job. It's not anyone's job.

Trudie rolls her eyes at my hesitation, takes the glass, lifts it to her lips, and swallows. "You snooze, you lose!" she giggles.

"Right," I say as nonchalantly as possible. "I'll remember that."

#

I drive her back to her condo in Newton, and we chat the whole time, until we're about a half-mile away when I imagine we both start to consider the inevitable goodbye. I pull into a visitor's spot in front of the brick building's entrance.

*This is it. I must explain things before I go any further. The drinking. Maggie.* "Well," I say.

"Well."

"Trudie, I had a lovely time. But I—"

Before I can say anything else, she reaches for my face, kissing me full throttle on the lips. Her touch is the perfect combination of firm, yet delicate. She pulls away gently, and we're both breathing hard. I'd kiss her again, but she's already begun her retreat, fingers on the door handle.

"If you call and ask me out again ..." She pauses and meets my gaze. "I'll say yes." She escapes from my Jeep, jumping to the pavement in her high heels and walking with a steady clip to the building. She puts the key in the lock, opens the door, and turns to wave as I back up.

I'm not sure what to think or how to feel anymore. The fact that I'm thinking of—and developing feelings for—Trudie Collins is troubling. Except maybe it's finally the good kind of trouble—the trouble you take to send a holiday card to an estranged friend; the trouble it takes to master a game, such as chess; the trouble it takes to unpack the baggage you've carried for thirty years; the trouble it takes to be done with old lovers once and for all.

# Chapter 20: Maggie

Christmas mornings were wonderful up until I was ten. My mum made sure of it with extra large stockings bursting at the seams, countless presents underneath the tree, a personal letter from Santa himself left next to the empty plate where we'd placed homemade chocolate chip cookies the night before. Even my father, who was always so sullen and serious, lightened up, at least for those early morning hours filled with my endless squeals of delight.

After Mum died, Christmas mornings became another reminder of the emptiness in our lives. Dad started opening the deli on Christmas day, even though he had few customers. I helped out at the cash register, because what else was there to do? Christmas was for families, and ours—imperfect though it had been—had all but disappeared with Mum's last breath.

It was during those sad Christmases that I first started thinking about them, my biological mother and father. I'm grateful my parents decided to be honest with me from the start about my adoption. Of course, as a child, I had a limited understanding of what adoption meant. Sure, I understood the science, but it wasn't until after I'd started college that I began to contemplate the emotional ramifications. Who was my real mother? Wasn't the woman who had awakened me in the morning with a different song for each day of the week, who tucked secret messages on my napkins in my lunch, who lovingly made my first-day-of-school dresses—wasn't she my "real" mom? Or is it impossible to break the connection between a woman and the child she carries in her womb, and would this connection trump the one I had with the person who had raised me for the first ten years of my life? I imagine this is what influenced my decision about finding my biological mother first, as opposed to searching for both biological parents at the same time. For me, I wanted—no, I needed—to find *her*, this woman who had carried me for nine months, labored during my birth, held me, but gave me away anyway. Why? Was she simply too young to face the responsibility? Was an overbearing adult controlling her actions? Had she been molested? Raped?

I shake away these thoughts and turn my attention to the one person who has the answers locked deep inside her failing mind. Kate and I have spent this Christmas morning in the quiet of her old house, April having escaped long before we arrived. I brought donuts and coffee, but Kate's java ended up all over the kitchen floor, the jelly from the munchkins on her shirt.

I try entertaining her with Christmas music and *Frosty the Snowman* on TV, but neither holds her interest. Instead, she wanders around the house, aimlessly. This is when I find the laundry basket atop the dryer, filled with clean sheets and towels. I carry the basket into the living room, sit Kate down on the old paisley couch, fold a towel, and then hand her one to fold. I've seen the therapists at Saint A's employ this "game," the repetitiveness and simplicity of the task perfect for dementia patients.

Kate sits and folds while I sit next to her and unfold everything she does, tossing the towels and washcloths back into the basket. She doesn't notice, and this breaks my heart. We do this for what feels like hours until she stands abruptly and dumps a pile of sheets to the floor. She walks to the fireplace, stops, and gazes at the photos on the mantel. I get up, stand beside her, and try to home in on the picture that has caught her attention, a shot of her and Jimmy. They're on a beach somewhere, windblown and squinty-eyed from the sun. They look so happy, so alive. Placing my hand on Kate's shoulder, I hold my breath waiting for her to flinch or lash out at me, but she remains perfectly still.

"That's you," I say, touching the glass covering the photo. "And Jimmy. Your grandson."

She faces me, and I search her eyes for some semblance of recognition or comprehension, but I can't tell either way. So instead, I gently turn her back to the photographs.

I don't know how long we stand there staring at them.

# *Chapter 21: Nigel*

Christmas afternoon, and the letdown from the holiday has already begun seeping into my weary bones. The last twenty-four hours have been a mad dash between the Christmas Eve party at Anne Marie's, church services with Mum at the crack of dawn this morning, and then back to Anne Marie's place to watch Max open his loot for five hours. When I finally said goodbye to my tired boy as he prepared to trek to his maternal grandparents' home in Wellesley, I was relieved to be returning to my mother's house. That was until I realized her buffet-style "drop in when you can" invitation to every person in eastern Massachusetts was not merely a rumor, but a reality.

#

"I'd like to dedicate a song," I say into my cell phone, while hiding out in my mother's laundry room, "to all the souls who've had enough of this bloody holiday cheer. Perhaps a little ditty by Nine Inch Nails." I have no idea what Nine Inch Nails sings, but I bet its version of "It's the Most Wonderful Time of the Year" would kick Andy Williams's ass.

"That wouldn't be a cheery thing for me to say on the air, now would it?" Trudie chides.

I hop on top of the washing machine. "Are you sure it's okay to chat right now? I don't want to get you in any trouble."

"We're three Christmas songs away from my next stop set."

"Your next what?"

"Commercial break," she says. "Sorry. Can't help but slip into radio jargon when I have a microphone in my face and four pages of Christmas music to play."

"Four pages of Christmas music? My dear woman, your job is harder than I thought."

"And don't you forget it! Hey, hold on while I press a button." Papers shuffle in the background. "Okay," she says. "I'm back. So, was Santa good to you?"

"Sadly, no. No sports car in the driveway, no deed to a Spanish villa in my stocking. Quite depressing, actually."

"Hmm. Sounds like someone's been naughty."

"I can't help it. I'm so much more entertaining naughty than nice."

"I'll keep that in mind."

"And what about you? Did Santa fulfill every single last wish and desire?"

She doesn't respond, and I strain to listen, thinking she may be hitting more buttons or getting ready to talk on the air. I can discern Madonna's rendition of Eartha Kitt's "Santa Baby" in the background.

"You still there Trudie?"

"Yes," she whispers. "Santa's done a real good job."

I can tell by the tone of her voice that my question—and specifically, her answer—has taken on new meaning. While a part of me rejoices, nagging doubts still exist in the back of my head and, perhaps, my heart. Why is it that a beautiful, intelligent, talented woman without any obvious baggage should enter my life and we immediately hit it off, yet I still found myself taking a detour to Saint A's on the way back to my mum's house this afternoon so I could see if Maggie's car were there?

"Trudie," I say. "Do me a favor?"

"Another crazy song request?"

"No. I want you to put in a good word for me with Santa. For next Christmas."

She sighs, and I can almost feel her smile through the phone. "It'd be my pleasure."

# *Chapter 22: April*

Christmas night, and all I want is to crawl into bed and sleep until June, which I might be able to do since, thankfully, the house is as I left it. There's no evidence of Maggie and Mom's earlier visit.

Sitting crossed legged on the floor, I reach under the Christmas tree and plug in the lights while Ming Toy, my old calico cat, spreads out in all her white, black, and brown furriness. That's when I notice she's sprawled on top of something. As I attempt to push her aside, she firmly stands her ground, or at least her small patch of the red skirt around the base of the tree. Finally, I'm able to grab hold of what looks to be a present and slide it out from underneath her.

It's a few inches thick, about the size of a book, and not too heavy. My heart jumps because I'm thinking it might be from Hugh until I spy the delicate handwriting on the tag that hangs from the festive red and gold paper.

*To: April*

*~~From:~~ Love, Maggie*

I stare at it for a long time. Ming Toy rolls over and finally decides my lap looks like a good place to hang out. As she makes herself comfortable on my knees, I pull the tag free, place it next to me on the floor, and tear away the wrapping, which reveals a simple forest green box. Inside, white tissue paper covers an antique pewter picture frame with scalloped edges. There's a photograph in it, too. I lean over and hold it under a white bulb from the tree.

It's a shot of Maggie, Mom, and me when Maggie was in full I'm-going-to-cure-Mom-of-this-disease mode. I remember when my assistant Heather took it about a month ago after a family had recently donated a digital camera to the activities department. I put Heather in charge of figuring out how to use it, which she did in five minutes since she's twenty-two and practically grew up with all things electronic. Maggie had brought Mom down to the activities room for the morning coffee social with the other residents, which for some reason annoyed the hell out of me, mainly because I didn't have it in me anymore to do it myself. Watching Mom while doing my job was no longer a challenge—it was impossible, and I had hated Maggie yet again for one-upping me.

"What are you bringing her down here for?" I crossed my arms and stood above Maggie as she sat next to Mom at the table.

"What do you mean? It's a coffee social for the residents, isn't it?"

I couldn't tell if she was being snide or serious. "Yeah. But in case you haven't noticed, she's not too good in social situations."

Maggie crossed her arms, mimicking my stance, and tilted her head. "Is that so?"

"Yeah. That's so."

"That's interesting, April, but let me ask you this. When's the last time you've seen her in an actual social situation? Most days she's so drugged up that she sits around upstairs staring out the window."

"And when's the last time you've seen her off her meds, Maggie? Because watching her jump out the window wouldn't be much fun either."

"Hey you two, I want to take a picture." Heather nudged me toward Mom. "You and Maggie lean into your mother. We'll see if this thing works."

I think Maggie was as surprised as I was with how easily "your mother" escaped from Heather's mouth.

"Heather," I said through clenched teeth. "This isn't a good time."

"You asked me to figure out the camera. It's time to test it. C'mon."

Grumbling, I bent down and leaned my right cheek into Mom's. Maggie leaned in from the left. Heather backed up, holding the camera straight out in front of her face.

"Say *happy family*," she'd said.

The result of this Kodak moment is now in my hand: Maggie beaming her best television smile, Mom staring at the table, and me glaring at everything. I tuck the frame under the Christmas tree's red skirt—out of sight, out of mind—and look up toward the ceiling. That's when I notice the mantel: the pictures are no longer in the right order.

Dumping the cat to the floor, I scramble to my feet. The last time Joelle was in the house, she suggested that I put the pictures of Jimmy and Vinny away because maybe they subconsciously added to my pain. But my biggest fear has never been the pain; my biggest fear has been forgetting them.

Dozens of fingerprints show up on the dusty frames, and I begin to imagine what went on this afternoon. Had Mom been looking at the pictures? Did she remember anything? Alzheimer's patients occasionally have lucid periods that can last anywhere from a nanosecond to a couple of minutes. I've seen it happen with other patients: Lucinda Raphael meeting her estranged son after twenty long years and whispering "Alejandro" over and over; Brenda Smith gaping at the television set in the dayroom when the Twin Towers fell on 9/11, fear registering in her eyes because she had worked in New York City for fifty years and the structures had been branded on the threads of memory she had left; Fred Castillo patting my face and calling me Anita—his wife's name—and not because he had forgotten her but rather because something about me made him remember.

I return to the tree, grope underneath the skirt until my hand feels the frame, take it, and place my new photo—my only Christmas gift—in the spot next to the picture of Mom and Jimmy from our vacation on Cape Cod almost twelve years ago. The fancy clean frame stands out against the others, but I don't care. It's a strange little family, but it's my family, my history.

Returning to my spot by the tree, I lie on my back, looking up through the branches like I had done a few weeks ago when I had my meltdown. Ming Toy sniffs my red Santa Claus sweater, kneading the material between her paws, before settling part of her body on my chest. I brace myself for the crying and tears, but this time, they don't come.

# *Chapter 23: Maggie*

New Year's Eve, and April still hasn't said anything about my gift. Maybe I'm going crazy. Maybe I thought I left it for her underneath the Christmas tree, but it's actually sitting in the bottom of my car. Maybe I should stop trying so hard. Maybe I should stop trying, period.

Despite my less than friendly mood, I know I need to be "on" tonight. I traded covering First Night in Boston for First Night at Saint A's. It's the annual New Year's Eve Ball, an event that April started her first holiday season here. She transforms the residents' dining area into a silver and gold ballroom, complete with champagne flutes filled with sparkling apple cider for toasting later in the evening, sherbet punch and eggnog, and endless hors d'oeuvres. The residents dress in their finest clothes, their families and friends wearing genuine smiles for once.

Kate sits at a table surrounded by some of the women from her floor. Her hair's been curled, and she wears a bright red sweater, gold earrings, and a hint of raspberry gloss. She looks healthy, alert even. Sipping my punch, I turn my attention to the entertainer at the front of the room.

"That's Jerome Mulberry. Mulberry's Magic," a nasally voice whispers behind me. I whip around and find Nigel standing practically on top of me. His nose is slightly red.

"Odd place to spend New Year's Eve, don't you think?" I say.

He shrugs, and I notice he's wearing a tuxedo, complete with black cowboy boots. I've always been a sucker for a guy in a tux, and I try not to gawk.

"It was Max's decision. He had a choice between here or Boston, and he chose here. Then again, Ruth talked it up quite a bit." He gestures toward Max and an old woman dressed in a black sequined blouse that can barely contain her droopy bosom.

"I see," I murmur and before I can stop myself, something else spills from my mouth. "I was wondering where you'd been."

He shoots me a quizzical look, and my face reddens. He's the only person who can do that. Blushing on camera—getting flustered for any reason no matter to whom you're speaking—is not acceptable, and it's never been a problem any other time in my life.

"Thought you and Ruth had a spat," I quickly add.

Nigel nods and coughs. "Been occupied."

"Not that it's any of my business anyway." He's so goddamn handsome, that I almost can't stand it. I turn around and focus my attention on Jerome Mulberry, a rotund man with a shaved head who sits before his keyboard and makes such a production of his white-gloved hands twirling through the air before touching the keys. Except "touch" is the operative word.

At first, I can't be sure, but as I inch closer and closer I notice that he's not touching at all but merely brushing the keys with his gloves, all the while preprogrammed music is piped through the two large speakers sitting on either side of him. With a microphone in front of his face, he does appear to be singing, but I'm not even sure of that.

"This guy's a fraud." I shake my head, knowing that the nursing home has to pay these so-called entertainers. "Can't April find someone better? Seems like a waste of money to me."

"Residents love him, though," Nigel says. "He gets the room jumping."

"Jumping?"

He grins. "You know what I mean."

"Mm."

"Cut him some slack, Maggie. The man is old. He was an aspiring jazz musician and now is—"

"—a mindless hack." I don't mean to sound so harsh, but the words come out before I can censor them. The air around us feels heavy.

"Well," he says quietly. "Not everyone can be you. You should take the time to find out his background before judging what you see. You never know. Might make a good story, which is what you're always after, isn't it?"

"Nigel, I didn't mean—" But it's too late. He's already retreated to Ruth's side, and my eyes fall on April, who's at Ruth's table and helping a resident drink from a champagne flute. She's dressed in a hunter green floor-length velvet dress, which is striking against her pale skin and red hair. She glances up, and I smile, but she looks right through me before returning to the old man who has juice dribbling down his chin.

Jerome takes a break from his singing and faux playing amidst applause from residents and family members alike. "Thank you very much," he bellows. "We'll be back in five." As if he has some sort of imaginary band that needs to take a break.

I walk over to him, and he wipes the sweat from his brow with a deep purple handkerchief that matches his purple bow tie. He smiles when he sees me studying his keyboard.

"This ain't really my instrument."

"No?" I feign shock.

"I'm a bass player." He peels off one white glove, revealing a severely gnarled and arthritic right hand that reminds me of the root system of a tree pulled from the earth. Then he tugs at the other glove. He has four missing digits, nothing but stumpy nubs in their place. "Well," he whispers. "Was. Before the War. And the arthritis." He swallows hard and peers at my face. "Yer that girl on the television, ain't ya?"

I feel so humbled I don't know what else to say. Except, suddenly, an idea occurs to me, and Nigel's words repeat in my head: "*Might make a good story.*" Over the last two months, I've seen my share of entertainers here at Saint A's—Rainbow with the voice of an angel who books these gigs to help pay for her tuition at Berklee College of Music; a mother-daughter team who apparently travel to nursing homes up and down the east coast; a magician who plays as many colleges as he does rest homes and assisted living facilities; a storyteller whose soothing voice tells tales to kids in libraries throughout Massachusetts as well as places like Saint A's. Having politely chatted with some of these people, I know that for many this is their sole source of income. It's a business, this nursing home circuit.

"Maggie Prescott," I say while taking his disease-riddled hand in my own.

"Jerome Mulberry. Nice to make your acquaintance, Ms. Prescott."

"Jerome, how'd you like to be interviewed?"

He gapes at me and says nothing, and I wonder if he's heard me. I glance back at Nigel, who's watching us.

"Fer the television?" Jerome finally says.

I turn around and nod, intending for my words to confirm his question, but instead something else comes out of my mouth. "For a documentary."

When he appears puzzled by the term, I quickly say, "A documentary film."

"Hot damn!" He slaps his knee, and his laugh is deep and rich. "I always wondered what it'd be like."

I tilt my head to the side and arch my brow. My kill cue, Nigel used to call it. "Wondered what *what* would be like?"

He studies my face before smiling broadly, revealing two gold-capped front teeth. "This."

# *Chapter 24: Nigel*

I walk away from Maggie for more than one reason. Yes, her reaction regarding old-man Mulberry was rather condescending, but I could forgive her for that. Yes, my cold has me feeling a little out of sorts. But the real reason I walk away is because of the electricity she generates in her pale gold gown.

I was surprised Max opted for Saint A's as opposed to the remote broadcasting booth in the station van that Trudie said he could be a part of if we attended First Night celebrations with her. The two of them met this past week, while Trudie was on the air. I figured the radio station would eliminate any discomfort, and indeed it did. Max's eyes bulged at the number of dials and buttons on the "board," as Trudie called it, and I thought the boy would do back flips when Trudie allowed him to press some buttons for her, going from one song into another. I also met a producer named Happy Byrd, a short, stocky man about Trudie's age with a balding crown and long blonde ponytail. His incessant lurking had suggested to me that his interest in Trudie went beyond professional camaraderie.

#

"What kind of name is 'Happy'?" I whispered to Trudie as we stood outside the man's production studio and watched as he recorded Max's voice for a radio commercial. Trudie's perfume filled the air between my lips and her ear. She wore pleasant fruit scents that seemed to change every time I saw her—one day it would be apples, another day strawberry, and still yet another, peach. It was like dating my very own living and breathing fruit salad.

"His real name is Felix, which means happy. He's been 'Happy Byrd' since he was a kid."

Through the glass window looking into Happy's studio, I watched him direct Max, whose head seemed so small beneath the black headphones.

"He's interested in you."

"Who is?" she asked innocently, but I didn't buy it.

"Mr. Felix 'Happy' Byrd."

"We're good friends, that's all. As a rule, I don't date co-workers. At least, not anymore. I had a bad experience a few years back."

"Ah, yes, but rules were made to be broken."

She glanced up at me and smiled. "Jealous?"

Dipping my head toward hers, I kissed her quickly on the lips, hoping that that would be answer enough, even though I wasn't sure what my answer would be if I had to verbalize it.

After Trudie and Max finished up, we went ice-skating at the Frog Pond in Back Bay. Max didn't seem bothered at all with my holding Trudie's hand as she glided effortlessly and I stumbled around the ice rink. So when I asked if he wanted to accept Ruth Frankenfeld's invitation to join her at the New Year's Eve Ball or accept Trudie's invite to First Night, I was more than a little shocked when he questioned me about Maggie.

"Will your friend be at Saint A's?"

"Trudie?"

"No. Maggie."

Perhaps television stars trumped radio disc jockeys in Max's world. "I don't know. What does that have to do with anything?"

He shrugged. "Just wondering."

"Well, what's it going to be then?"

"Let's go to Saint A's."

"Maxwell, don't feel you have to choose that for me. I imagine First Night in Boston will be more fun for someone your age. Mine, too."

"But it would be nice for us to go to Saint A's. For Mrs. Frankenfeld."

It was hard to argue with that, since I knew Ruth and her family were on the outs again after spending a miserable holiday together. *Well, fine,* I'd thought. It won't be a problem seeing Maggie if she's there. I've barely thought of her all week, and when I have, it's been a fleeting thought. Trudie occupies my mind, as she should.

Except now as one of the male residents named Rich Garrity and Maggie attempt to dance to "Baby, It's Cold Outside," I'm not so sure. Jerome Mulberry has found a duet partner in one of the aides, whose surprisingly beautiful voice is the perfect accompaniment to Jerome's bass-sounding refrain. I laugh as Old Man Garrity tries not to grimace when Maggie steps on his toes. She never could dance. As I start to walk toward them, a vision of Trudie flashes through my mind, but I ignore it.

"Such an amateur," I say while tapping Rich's shoulder in an attempt to cut in.

"That's not a very nice thing to say about Mr. Garrity, Nigel," Maggie hisses through a strained smile.

"I meant you, sweetheart." I lean into Rich's good ear. "My dear man, I hear Violet's dance card has your name all over it." I gesture toward a lovely, slim woman with long silvery locks who is twirling by herself, arms outstretched toward an invisible dance partner. Rich's eyes light up at my suggestion, and he shuffles over to her in old-man debonair flair.

I hold out my hands to Maggie, who looks at me as if I have three heads. I also notice that a crowd is beginning to form around us. All night, people have been approaching Maggie and asking for autographs. Lucky for them, her demeanor seems to have improved dramatically since my conversation with her earlier.

"Come on, old girl. Let's give it a whirl."

"You've got to be kidding."

I take her right hand in my left, and with my right arm, I grasp her lower back, pulling her close. "Not even a little bit," I whisper, and we dance one verse in silence.

Maggie stirs in my arms. "Nigel, this is—"

"Nice?" I interrupt. "Yes. I agree. Well, someone had to come to poor Mr. Garrity's rescue."

"Was I that bad?"

"Mugsy, my darling, yes. You were that bad. But it's the only evidence I have that you're human."

"Why do you do that?" she pouts.

"Do what?"

"Act as if I'm infallible."

"It was a joke."

"I'm not, you know."

I consider her eyes—a mixture of fear, guilt, and remorse. "I know."

"No. You don't."

"Why so serious, Mugsy? Can't we enjoy the evening? The chance at a new year?"

She peers into my face, searching. "Even if we haven't made peace with the old?"

I don't like the territory we're heading into, so I slide my hand up and down her back and lean my cheek into hers, hoping this will be answer enough, even though I'm not sure it is for either of us.

She leans into me, and I feel her sigh. I pull my head away slowly, so I can look into her face, into her eyes. As I do, she smiles, and I'm about to lean in and kiss her—to hell with my cold or what's right and wrong for my heart—when I spy someone lurking in the doorway. *Two* someones, actually: first April, who has turned around and walked away, and second, Trudie.

She clutches the handles to her Aunt Gert's wheelchair, and even from this distance, I can tell she's curious and concerned, all wrapped into one. Making eye contact with me, she smiles, pushes Aunt Gert next to Ruth, pats Max on the head, and walks toward us.

"Trudie." I let go of Maggie.

"Hi." She's breathless and wearing a long winter-white coat.

"This is a surprise," I say, noticing that Maggie has looked from me to Trudie and back to me.

Trudie smiles at Maggie. "Hi, Ms. Prescott. You probably don't remember me, but I interviewed you—"

"Trudie Collins, Magic 106.7," she rattles off, as I knew she would. She extends her hand. "Please, call me Maggie. Good to see you again."

"Thanks. You, too." Trudie turns to me. "I convinced the afternoon guy to cover for me tonight. Thought we could spend part of New Year's together after all."

Maggie coughs. "Well. I should be going."

"Oh, don't leave on my account," Trudie says.

"I need to get going anyway. Good seeing you again, Trudie." She glances in my direction and nods.

"Happy New Year," Trudie says.

"You as well." Retreating fast, she refuses to make eye contact with me. She heads for the door and disappears down the hall.

"Nigel? You okay?"

I turn back to Trudie, who is staring at me with such hope and fear.

"Should I go?" she whispers.

I shake my head, wrap my arms around her, and, once again, find myself hoping my nonverbal gestures are answer enough.

# *Chapter 25: April*

"Good party," Hugh says while leaning against my office door. "I think we're closing the joint."

Elbows on my desk, I massage the skin above the corners of my eyes. "I think the Brazilians spiked my eggnog."

Hugh glances at the three empty cups next to me. "You going home?"

"Uh huh."

"How 'bout I drive you home?"

"I'm fine."

He picks up one of the cups and sniffs it. "Not fine enough to drive."

"I'm just down the street. I can walk." I attempt to stand and stumble instead. Hugh catches me by the arm.

"Right," he says. "C'mon, party girl. Get your stuff."

"But my car—"

"Will be fine here. I'll pick you up and bring you into work tomorrow morning." He pauses and assesses my condition. "Or afternoon."

#

We don't talk on the short ride to the house, and I'm thankful since the motion of the car is making me a little woozy. Conversation would be a challenge.

I'm not sure why this party was so hard. New Year's is one of those holidays that I stopped feeling depressed about a long time ago. It's always been so overrated, wrought with so much pressure: what to do, where to be, who to kiss at midnight. Unless you're standing in the middle of Times Square or you've been invited to some exclusive party, seems anything else is inferior.

Other years, throwing this bash at Saint A's has been more of a relief than a burden. Besides, it's nice to bring a little bit of normalcy—a little bit of how life was like on the outside, long ago—to the residents. Their families appreciate it, too. It gives them some place to be, something to do, an excuse for not being wherever other people think they should be on December 31.

But so much has happened this year, at this party: Hazel relegated to her bed due to illness, Maggie creating a scene in her designer gown and celebrity essence—her very existence a reminder of how little I've done with my life, and her loving care of Mom reminding me how I failed there, too. On the cusp of a new year when I should be making resolutions and having hope, I struggle instead to know who I am or what to feel, especially when I'm near this man who now guides me up the porch steps and stands not even two feet away from me as I fumble with the doorknob.

"Come in." I'm not sure if it's a request or command, but regardless, Hugh follows me into the living room. I stoop to turn on the lights to the tree, and, exhausted by my efforts, I sink into the cushions of Mom's old paisley couch. That's when I notice Hugh is standing on the spot where it happened, and the memories from that night come flooding back. I shake my head and squeeze my eyes shut.

"April? You okay?"

*No,* I think. *I'm not okay.*

"April, do you want a glass of—"

"I hit her," I interrupt.

"What?"

"I hit her."

He tilts his head, confusion spreading over his face. "I don't understand. Whom did you hit?"

"My mother. I hit my own mother. In this very room. Right where you're standing."

He doesn't glance down, doesn't even shift from one foot to the other as my eyes move from the floor to his feet—I didn't even notice he was wearing shiny black shoes—to his charcoal gray dress pants, his long black winter coat, his festive green silk tie, his face. Except the face is no longer his. It's the face of God, of the universe, of Jimmy, maybe, and I wonder for the umpteenth time if I'll ever be able to forgive myself for that night two and a half years ago when I'd done the unthinkable, when I had fallen asleep on the couch without having locked the doors, without having known exactly where Mom was. I was tired, so very, very tired. The state inspectors had been at Saint A's all week, which meant longer hours and everyone on edge. That morning, the air conditioning had broken in my half of the building, and sweat pooled underneath my unshaven armpits, behind my knees, in the creases where my underwear met my skin.

Before picking up Mom from the senior daycare center where she spent three days a week—a place that had been warning me for the last two months they couldn't "handle" her anymore, that her care was beyond their capabilities—I dashed into Stop 'n Shop for some groceries. I'm not sure what it was about that day, but every aisle I turned down, I witnessed another reminder of the life I no longer had, would never have again: the thirty-something mom in cut-off jeans and the dad with his muscular tanned legs placing a watermelon in the back of the shopping cart with a little boy in a popsicle-stained T-shirt; an older couple, probably in their sixties, holding hands as they filled their basket with buns and turkey burgers for the grill on the deck back home where an evening of good food, drink, and memories awaited them; the teenager named Natasha who rang up my purchase—cat litter, bananas, milk, and three bottles of bleach, the only thing strong enough to get the stink of urine out of Mom's bed sheets—and the faraway look in Natasha's dark brown eyes as she thought about boys and makeup and the fact that her whole life was ahead of her, untouched like the virgin she probably still was.

When I finally arrived at the daycare center to retrieve Mom, she refused to get in the car.

"Leave me alone," she yelped. "Where are you taking me?"

She'd been diagnosed with Alzheimer's only nine months before but had declined rapidly, becoming a textbook case for the worst symptoms.

"I'm taking you home," I said through clenched teeth.

"But I don't know you! Stop!"

I ignored her as well as the hole in my heart, which grew every time she claimed she didn't know who I was. It was a common manifestation of the disease, yes, but that didn't make it any easier to bear.

"Help, help, police!" she cried as I struggled to strap her seat belt. But by the time I'd wiped my sweaty brow, cursed my sorry life, and slid into the driver's side, she had calmed down.

"Where are we going?" she asked.

"Home."

Five minutes later, she spoke again. "Where are we going?"

"I told you already. We're going home."

Ten minutes later, again: "Where are we going? Where are you taking me? I don't know you!"

Ignoring her, I gripped the steering wheel tighter and tighter so I wouldn't scream. I missed my mother and hated this cantankerous, combative, confused, all-consuming shell of a woman who had taken her place.

When Mom and I finally walked into the house, every last inch of my being ached for normal. I longed for my Vinny who'd say, "Looks like you had a long day, honey. Why don't you lie down and rest while I cook dinner and Jimmy sets the table?" I felt drugged, unsteady, and collapsed onto the couch, only to awake hours later to the sound of summer peepers making their nightly call in the thick August heat.

It was the only sound.

After spending twenty minutes racing through the house, our backyard, the park across the street, I found Mom wandering six houses down from our own. She had opened a neighbor's unlocked backyard gate where an in-ground pool waited to drown her. I looked up to the heavens, tears streaming down my cheeks, and not because I was almost too late but because I was too early.

"What the fuck are you doing?" I wanted to scream the words at the top of my lungs, but it was after midnight, so my voice was low and menacing. I walked toward her, and she fell to the ground because I shoved her there. Hard. I pulled her up quickly and dragged her home.

Inside our house, she scampered across the wooden floor of the living room like a wounded animal, but I caught her arm in my own, swung her around to face me.

Truth be told, she hit me first. But I hit her back, four bloody times.

Early the next morning, before the sun traded places with the moon, I called Joelle. "April, what is it? What happened?"

"I need you to come over." I stopped, because I wasn't sure who was talking. When did my voice sound so little? "Please," it continued. "Just come."

She did. When I pointed out the bruises on my mother's face, the red stain on her collar and shirt from her bloody nose, the blue and purple fingerprints embedded in the skin on her arms, Joelle whispered, "My God. Who did this?"

I said nothing until I was sure she understood what my silence meant.

"Report me," I finally choked.

"For what? Being human?"

"You know for what. It's abuse. It's a crime. We're bound to report this sort of shit when we see it at Saint A's."

"This is different."

For the first time all morning, I looked Joelle in the eye. "How's this different?"

"Because," she'd said while brushing away her tears, "it's you."

#

When I'm done confessing and I look up to see if Hugh's still standing there or if he's gone, he is gone from that spot. But he hasn't walked out. Instead, he sits next to me now, reaches for my hand, which I don't even realize is trembling, and lets me cry.

#

*Left eyelid. Right eyelid.* I don't know where I am, and I like the feeling. But then, the living room comes into focus: the lights twinkling on the tree, the photos above the fireplace, Hugh sitting next to me, chin to his chest, sleeping in his coat. I try to shift my position without disturbing him, but it doesn't work. He stirs and looks up.

"Hugh." I pause because I'm not sure what should come next. "Thank you. For listening."

He nods but says nothing, and I know he must hate me.

"You don't have to stay," I whisper. "I'm okay."

He nods again, gets up, and heads for the door. Then, he faces me one more time. "I don't, you know."

"Don't what?" I say, confused.

"Hate you."

I touch my throbbing head. "Hugh, did I just say—"

"It's what you were thinking, wasn't it? That I must hate you." He shakes his head. "I don't."

I try to smile, willing myself not to cry again. "Thank you."

"No. Thank you. For trusting me with the truth." Hand on the doorknob, he turns to go, but I'm off the couch like a shot, ignoring every warning bell that's going off in my head.

He turns around in time to see me coming toward him. I reach for him without hesitation, leaning my body into his, hugging him—feeling the strength of his arms around me, of my Daddy's arms, of Vinny's arms, of Javier's arms. I pull away slowly, without completely letting go.

Truth be told, he kisses me first.

*January 2007*

# *Chapter 26: Hugh*

When Adrienne was a little girl, I called her Princess Panacea.

"What's that, Daddy?" she had asked, as I pulled her onto my lap and breathed in her sweet little-girl fragrance.

"A long, long time ago, Panacea was the goddess of healing."

"What's 'goddess'?"

"A special, beautiful person. Like a princess."

"Oh." She nodded. "What's 'healing'?"

"Healing is when you make someone feel better."

"Like when I'm sick?"

"Right. Or when someone is sad, too."

"I make you feel better, right?"

"Yes."

"Mommy, too?"

I closed my eyes and pulled her close. "Yes. Mommy, too."

Soon after, I shortened it to plain "Pana," a nickname Adrienne apparently didn't mind adopting, at least for a little while. Buried in my bottom desk drawer is a box of her homemade birthday cards—every single one, up until my fortieth birthday. All are signed, "Love, Pana."

Only problem with the moniker is that it's inaccurate. Children are gifts, not cures. I have no doubt that the breakdown between Adrienne and me happened long before she turned thirteen; it began when I allowed myself to believe that her mere existence was enough to restore my marriage or, at the very least, enough to allow me to survive in spite of it.

#

That first morning I woke up next to April, on New Year's Day, I cursed myself. As I slipped out of her bed, careful not to disturb her, my brain repeated its logic that April had been tipsy—if not drunk—and would certainly want to forget this indiscretion, as did I. All I'd need to do was leave, and it would be over. I imagined we would never speak of it.

I got all the way to her front door, hand on the doorknob, but couldn't open it. Instead, I turned around and faced the hallway that led to the kitchen where directly in front of me on the counter sat a coffeemaker. The least I could do, I reasoned, was start a pot of coffee for her. Judging by the piles of empty Styrofoam cups she had on her desk at Saint A's, she drank endless amounts. Besides, her head could probably use it, too.

"So what are the chances she keeps her coffee in the freezer like I do?" I asked a pile of fur, which stretched and rolled over on the kitchen floor. Discovering a coffee can in the freezer door, I began my task. Soon the aroma filled the kitchen amidst the sputtering and spurting of the old percolator. As I gazed out the kitchen window onto the untouched snow in the backyard, I was reminded of the name Adrienne had given to her first cat: *Snowblink*. Then, a sleepy voice interrupted my thoughts.

"Mornin'."

I turned and found April leaning against the wall. She wore a blue terrycloth robe, tied loosely across her middle. It was all she was wearing. Her feet were bare, and her short red hair looked soft and rumpled, with tufts poking up here and there.

"I made coffee."

"So I see." She walked to the dish strainer by the sink, pulled out two mugs and two spoons, and set them on the counter.

I walked toward the fridge to get away from her, the musky scent from our night together having followed her down the stairs. Opening the door, I searched for cream, and, finding a carton, I opened it and took a whiff.

"Don't worry," she said, while pouring the coffee. "It's fresh. It's the one thing I buy regularly." Carrying the two cups, she moved to the kitchen table and motioned for me to join her.

"Sugar's in there," she said, jutting her chin toward a black-and-white marble sugar bowl, as if I were an ordinary houseguest making myself at home.

"I was going to leave," I said as I stirred the spoon in my coffee. "Before you got up." I placed the spoon on the table and looked at her. "I still will. If you want."

She held the mug to her lips and stared straight ahead. "Is that what you want?"

I closed my eyes. "I don't know." When I opened them, she was watching me. "What do you want me to do, April?"

I'm not sure what I expected her to say or do. Perhaps I expected her to remain quiet, her silence the only answer. Perhaps I expected her to cry. Maybe I thought she'd ask me to leave. Instead, she simply got up and stood before me. I leaned back in my chair, waiting, wondering what she was going to do, and that's when she fell into my lap, looping her arms around my neck, and sighing with contentment when I cradled her body to mine.

"You going in today?" I whispered in her hair. I felt her nod against my shoulder.

"You?" she asked.

"Yes," I sighed.

But we never did.

#

Today, I go for my early morning walk, as I've done almost every day
for the last thirty years, as I've been doing every morning since that first one
with April almost two weeks ago. She hasn't questioned my ritual, nor have I
explained, and it feels good, this understanding we seem to have of letting
things be.

On the street parallel to April's house, I stop and gaze at the swamp,
marveling at Mother Nature's ability to impress and surprise me with her
vast color palette, her canvas so different from one winter day to the next. I
never knew there were so many shades of gray, black, and white. For a
moment, I am happy.

Still, as I trudge along the snow-covered road on my way back to
April's, doubt wreaks havoc with my brain, and I decide that today will be
the day I return to my own home for good and end this affair once and for all.
It's been twelve days, and I'm beginning to forget what the inside of my own
house looks like, having stopped for only a supply of clothes over a week
ago. Certainly the mail must be piling up, the newspapers, too. The neighbors
are probably curious, worried even. What if they call the police? Or
Adrienne? Not that she would care if I went missing or fell down the stairs,
breaking a hip, or had a heart attack while sleeping in bed, but it would force
me to answer her questions: *"Where have you been? What have you been up
to, Daddy?"* Her accusations have haunted me for almost two decades. I'll be
damned if I give her more reason to hate me.

But as I mount April's front steps, my resolve melts away along with the
rest of me as I stand in the hallway shaking the snow from my boots and the
newspaper I rescued from the bushes. I rub my hands together and watch as
she moves about the kitchen, a hot pot of coffee waiting for us both.

The last two weeks feel like forever only in that I wish they could be. I
believe I could live the remainder of my days doing these simple things:
waking, walking, sipping coffee, reading the newspaper, talking, laughing,

making love to this woman, and falling asleep to the steady rhythm of her breathing.

The wish isn't new; it's the same one I had over three decades ago, when I married Gloria. If only she had wished it as well, but she didn't. At least, not with me. Too bad the people who first introduce you to wishes don't tell you how fragile they are. Because when you hold onto one too tight, it cracks.

# Chapter 27: Nigel

I didn't mean to sleep with her.

I know this sounds like the protest of a ribald teenager, but it's true. I never meant to get this involved with Trudie Collins. But here I am in her bed, my legs tangled in the sheets. As I open my eyes, her sweet face gazes down on me. Her hair is still wet from the shower.

"Mornin', sleepy head," she says.

"What time is it?"

"Eight o'clock."

"That's not late."

She smiles, dips her head, and kisses me. "Whatever you say."

"Whatever I say, eh?" Before she can respond, I push her onto her back, pinning her to the bed. She giggles the whole time.

"You're getting my pillows wet."

I tug at the front of her bathrobe until my hands can move freely over her damp skin. Today, she smells like strawberries and watermelon. "Goes to show you should have waited to take your shower."

"Why's that?"

"Because what I'm about to do here would have been fun to try in there."

\#

I lock up Trudie's condo with the key she presented me at breakfast and head to my Jeep. I fiddle with the radio dial and check my voicemail. There's a reminder from Maxwell about basketball practice tonight, one from Ruth Frankenfeld requesting yet another meeting to go over "important documents," and a hang up. I hit the phone options to see if I recognize the number, and my heart races when I hear it recited back. It's Maggie's. She called at 10:32 last night, long after I had taken Trudie to bed.

Why is she calling me now? Why should I care one way or the other? I'm so caught up in my thoughts, that I don't even hear Trudie's voice emanating from the radio until she's halfway done with her on-air break.

"… and this next song is for the handsome man who made my morning today."

I smile at the dedication as the first few notes of Marvin Gaye's "Let's Get it On" fill up my Jeep and push away my questions and nagging doubts, concentrating instead on this beautiful gift—this second chance at true love—God, the universe, you-name-it has given me.

*Aw, shit,* my inner voice says. *If only you believed it.*

# *Chapter 28: Maggie*

"What the hell, Maggie? Did you sleep here?"

I awake to Serena's face looming over my own. "What time is it?" I murmur.

Serena looks at me as if I'm crazy. "Ten. In the morning. Like, twelve hours after I left you last night."

I rub my head and struggle to sit up. As I do, a pile of folders and the book that had been resting on my chest crash to the floor.

"Please tell me you'll stop," Serena sighs as she stoops to pick up everything.

"Stop what?" I yawn.

"This obsession with all things Alzheim—" She pauses mid-word and looks at the book title. "*Writing, Directing, and Producing Documentary Films and Videos* by Alan Rosenthal?"

"Excellent," I say, grabbing the book from her clutches. "Your reading skills are improving, Serena."

"Ha ha. Very funny." She drops everything on my lap. "Seriously, though. What's up with this?"

"Nothing's up with this."

Serena rolls her eyes. "Riiiight. Nothing going on here. Perfectly normal for a television celebrity to fall asleep in her producer's office reading books on making documentaries. Yep. I get it. Sorry for asking."

"Did it ever occur to you that maybe I don't want to talk about it?"

"Oh, for chrissake, Maggie. If you didn't want to talk about it, then you would have done a better job hiding it. After all, this is my office."

"You have the comfortable couch."

"Uh huh." Shaking her head, she unfurls her newly knitted pastel scarf—the color reminds me of bubblegum ice cream—and throws her apple-green wool pea coat over the back of her chair. Ignoring me, she sits down, turns on her computer, and picks up the phone to check her messages. She jots down a few notes on her yellow legal pad. I can't take the silence any longer.

"Okay," I say to her back. "*If* you must know."

"Know what?" she asks innocently.

"About this book. And stuff."

"Wouldn't want to pry."

"I was planning on telling you about my project. Just not this soon."

"Whatever, Maggie."

"I went to school for film."

"Yeah, I know. I wrote your bio for the station's website, remember?"

"Specifically, film documentary. At least, that's what I always planned on doing until—"

"Yeah, yeah, yeah. Until some poor woozy chick vomited all over the set thirty some odd years ago, and you had to step from behind the camera to in front of it."

"She didn't vomit. She fainted."

"Whatever. Fast forward to what I don't know."

Serena probably knows me better than most people, and yet there's so much she doesn't know. "What you don't know is how much I wanted to make film documentaries. Practically my whole life. My whole career."

"Why didn't you then? I mean, lots of people in our industry dabble in other ventures. You have the name. Money. Means."

"Right."

"Sounds like you have the desire."

"Yes."

"So what's stopped you?"

I sigh. "You've heard the expression about life getting in the way while you're busy making other plans?"

"But how'd your life get in the way? I would think it would have inspired you. All the oddball stories you—we've—stumbled on over the years? Plus you know more about cameras and filming than some of the camera people we've worked with. I'm not buying that excuse, as poetic as it sounds."

Leaning back into the couch, I stare at the ceiling. Again. Last night, after I couldn't read anymore, I stared at the dots on the ceiling tiles, mentally connecting them until they formed a number that I had recently memorized: Nigel's cell phone.

Serena gets up and sits next to me. "C'mon," she says gently. "What's the real reason?"

"I don't know, Serena." I shrug. "Maybe up until now I've been missing my muse."

"And you found it? Here?"

"I don't know. Maybe."

"Who is it? Your mother?"

"No."

"April?"

I shake my head. "Nope."

Serena stretches her arms toward the ceiling before bringing them down and lacing her fingers behind her head. "Well. I'd love to think it was me. But you know I'd charge extra for that service."

I chuckle.

"Which means," she says slowly, "That it must be—"

"Don't say it."

"Why not?"

A picture of Nigel wrapping his arms around Trudie Collins on New Year's Eve flashes through my mind. "Because it's too late."

"How can it be too late?"

Another image quickly chases Nigel and Trudie away. It's an image of a young, naive me on a lonely journey to a Florida clinic. "It was too late a long time ago," I sigh.

"You only get one shot at capturing your muse?"

"No. But I've had two shots, Serena. And I blew 'em both times." The tears form with my words, and I let them fall without wiping or explaining them away. This whole situation has turned me into a sentimental schmuck, a trait I've always loathed in others.

We sit for a while in silence, and I'm thankful Serena doesn't push me, even though she's got to know I'm crying. Finally, she reaches for the papers and book on my lap. "Tell you what," she says softly. "I guess I can afford to give you a discount."

I turn to her. "On what?"

"Being your replacement muse. I mean it's a dirty job, I'm sure. But someone's got to do it."

Impulsively, I reach for her hand and squeeze. Neither of us is a particularly touchy-feely person, but she squeezes back anyway.

"You're a good friend, Serena."

She lets go of my hand and gets up. "Yeah, yeah, yeah. And because I'm so good, I'm going to make a Starbucks run. You want your usual?"

"Sure."

She slips into her coat and scarf, heads for the door, but stops when she gets there. "Maybe it's like baseball," she mumbles.

"What is?"

She tilts her head. "Muses. Maybe you still have another chance. Three-strikes-and-you're-out sort of deal."

"Leave it to you to come up with a sports analogy."

"Well?"

"Maybe."

"Which means?" she prompts.

"I still have another shot."

She smiles. "Just a thought."

A good thought indeed, I think, as she disappears down the hall. But, sadly, not likely.

#

Is it possible to make peace with your past by simply laying it to rest the way you do a corpse? I desperately want to, but memories from thirty years ago keep resurfacing, refusing to be ignored.

"I'm not going to beg you to stay," Nigel had said after I announced I was taking a job in Florida. I thought he sounded so stuffy and pompous for someone in his mid-twenties. "But what about your films, Mugsy?"

"What about them?"

"Ever since you were a little girl, it's what you wanted to do. Make documentaries."

"So?"

"So you won't be, if you take this job. And you'll disappoint your faculty advisor by reneging on your deal to go on location with him and film—"

"Nigel. What's your point?"

"My point is your passion. Why are you turning your back on your passion?"

"Who said anything about turning my back?" But even as I said the words, I turned away from him so he couldn't see the look on my face, revealing he was right.

"Fine," he continued. "But what about us? Why turn your back on what we have?"

"Can't there be an us even if I go to Florida?"

He didn't answer, and even I knew then that a long-distance romance wouldn't be easy simply because I wanted it to be.

We were okay, actually. In the beginning. We managed somehow to stay together for six months, Nigel being the one who'd fly down—and even drive—to Port Saint Joe to see me. He made the effort. He worked at it. I let him do the heavy lifting for both of us while I worked and learned and felt a whole new world opening up to me as wide as the Gulf of Mexico. Of course, that's not the worst of it. In the process of forcing him to do, well, everything when it came to us, I deceived him.

#

"So. You and this Oscar fellow," Nigel began one hot and sticky morning as we lay in my studio-apartment bed. The fan whirred by our heads as it attempted to circulate the thick furry air. Oscar was one of the station producers who had befriended me right away.

"Yeah?"

"Methinks he fancies you."

I threw off the thin white cotton sheet, revealing our naked bodies underneath. "Don't fucking start."

"Don't fucking start what, Maggie? I was merely making an observation."

I stood, picked up my T-shirt off the floor, and pulled it over my head. "More like an accusation."

Nigel sat up, pulling the sheet to his waist. "No. An accusation would sound like this: I think you might fancy him right back."

I glared, said nothing, and walked to the balcony, knowing he would take my silence as an admission.

"Right," he murmured. "I see how it is."

I stared out over the green-blue water in the pool. It was early yet—barely six o'clock, but already an older man with navy blue trunks, golden skin, and white hair was taking a morning dip. I listened to the water splash as he crawled the length of the pool and then back, the sounds punctuated by the slamming of closet doors and dresser drawers as Nigel packed his stuff and left.

That night, out of spite, stupidity, whatever you want to call it, I went out with Oscar. We kissed while sitting in a barroom booth, a jukebox blaring in the background. He tried more. I pushed him away and said no.

But it was too late.

Apparently, old softie that he was, Nigel had forgiven my rotten behavior from the morning and had come looking for me that night. When he didn't find me at home, he went to the local bar where we always hung out when he was in town. He found me there, sitting in a booth, lip-to-lip with Oscar, confirming his suspicions.

When I called Nigel a few days later, surprised that he had been silent for so long and that he had never come back to the apartment, he confronted me with his evidence.

I cried.

I cried and told him that what he saw wasn't *really* what he saw, that I had pushed Oscar away, that I hadn't slept with him.

He didn't believe me.

And if he hadn't believed that, I'd reasoned, how would he ever believe the baby I discovered I was carrying three weeks later was his?

#

*Only one way to find out*, I think as I stand up, pull on my coat, and leave a note for Serena. *Time for my last at-bat.*

# *Chapter 29: April*

"*Mujer bonita*," Inácio says as I mount the steps to the landing by the employee entrance. "Guess who's coming back?"

I shiver in the cold, impatient because I'm late. Ever since Hugh and I have been doing whatever it is we've been doing, I've been late four days out of twelve. And that's not counting New Year's Day when I didn't show up at all. Inácio flicks his cigarette to the snow-covered cement.

"Who?" I ask, even though I can guess the answer.

"You know, *bonita*. Your man. Or your other man, I should say. Seems you have many."

*Don't blink. Don't blink. How could he possibly know about Hugh?* "I don't have a man, Inácio." I stare him squarely in the eyes. "You know that."

Snickering, he leans back against the brick building, his thin pale blue scrubs barely providing protection from the frigid January air. "Javier would not be pleased to hear you say such a thing."

"Well, maybe Javier should worry about pleasing the other woman in his life. Like his *esposa*. You know, the one he forgot to tell me about?"

Inácio laughs, nods, and lights another cigarette, while I open the door and leave him outside. As I make my way down the hallway by the kitchen, I can still feel his eyes on my ass. So Javier is coming back from Brazil. How long has it been now? Almost two years? He always said he was going to come back, and I figured he might. Many of the foreign workers come and go—I can barely keep track sometimes. They work and make money and bring it home to their families, exporting the American dream as efficiently as the government does cars and clothes.

"Well, whatever," I mutter as I swipe my credit-card-like badge through the digital time clock and Joelle bursts through the double doors.

"April! I've been looking all over for you. Come with me."

"What's wrong?"

She grabs my arm, pulls me through the doors, and drags me down the hall. "Hazel."

"What? Joelle—"

Joelle stops and takes my shoulders in her hands and looks me in the eye. "April, she's okay. She's okay, do you hear me?"

I swallow and nod. "What is it then?"

"It's her nephew."

"Michael?"

"Yes. He was in some sort of accident." She shakes her head. "He didn't make it."

#

I find Hazel sitting in her chair, still in her pearl white nightgown. The room is dark, the blinds drawn, Gloria looking lifeless as usual. Hugh isn't here yet, probably still showering at my place. My stomach turns with guilt.

"Hazel," I say, as I drop to my knees, wrapping my arms around her. "Joelle told me about—"

"Michael," she whispers.

"What happened?"

She shakes her heads and sighs. "His life is what happened, my dear. He lived too fast. Played too hard. I always knew it would get him in the end." She turns over the pink rosary beads she has threaded through her fingers. "I never thought I would be here to see it."

"Morning, Hazel," Maggie's voice calls out. "Sorry I'm here so early, but I have this idea that I'm working on and I wanted to run it by—" Maggie stops when she sees our faces. She looks from me to Hazel and then back to me. "What's wrong?"

I can't get my mouth to work, can't breathe, can't even move my arms from around Hazel's fragile body. It's Hazel who speaks in the same dignified, lady-like tone she's used all her life.

"It's Michael. He was in a skiing accident. He hit a tree. They say he died instantly." Tears cling to her lower eyelids.

"Oh, Hazel." Maggie deposits her Starbucks cup on the bureau and swoops down next to us. "I'm so sorry."

I lock eyes with Maggie as another form materializes in the doorway.

"Good morning, Haz—" Hugh takes one look at the three of us before hurrying across the floor to Gloria's side of the room. To Gloria—his wife. *His dying wife.*

"Miss Cooke, I'm sorry but my secretary didn't forward your message to my cell phone until—" Now Nigel stands before us, and I'm convinced that this is all a dream, that in a moment, I'll wake up. "I ..." Nigel pauses, coughs, and continues. "I heard the news. I'm sorry, Miss Cooke. I'll come by to talk to you later." He backs out of the door but stops abruptly. "Oh," he says. "My apologies, miss."

Nigel reenters and allows the person he bumped into access to the room. A tall, model-thin woman with long flowing black hair stands in the doorway. *Where have I seen her?* But then, she looks at me, and I know. She has Hugh's eyes. It's Adrienne, his daughter.

The heat rises to my face. My stomach back flips into my throat. My limbs weigh five hundred million pounds. I struggle to my feet, push past Nigel and Adrienne, and hope that I've grunted some sort of "If you'll excuse me" utterance before I lumber out of the room.

*Breathe, breathe, breathe.*

I'm sleeping with a married man whose daughter is probably the same age as I am. And not any married man, but a man whose wife lay dying, a woman who is in my care. Maybe the so-called bad luck I've had in this life hasn't had anything to do with luck. Maybe it has to do with the choices I've made. Maybe I've brought on all this misery myself.

Down the hall, I push open the community bathroom door, shutting it behind me, wishing that it locked, but it doesn't for safety reasons. I hang my head over the toilet, willing myself to throw up, half expecting that Maggie or Hugh or even Nigel might come through the door at any time to check on me. No one does. I dry heave and wretch. Sweat trickles down the side of my face. I lean against the wall, waiting for the nausea to pass, even though I know it's only a symptom of the real affliction: guilt.

Guilt, I've discovered, is like quicksand. The more you fight it, the more it sucks you into its thick gray abyss. If you allow yourself to sit in it and accept it, you eventually float to the top. Problem is it doesn't end there: you still need help getting out.

# Chapter 30: Maggie

Nigel follows April out of the room, and I get up and follow them both.

"Nigel. Wait."

He turns and faces me, and I'm about to speak, but stop short when I see the look in his eyes. For the last two months, his eyes have appeared the same as they had thirty years ago—inquisitive, supportive, loving. But something has changed. A black muddy darkness has spread over the brown of his irises. In that mud, I know what's there: anger, sadness, disappointment. I look for evidence of Trudie—a spark of sunlight, perhaps, but I don't see that either. Maybe because I don't want to.

"Yes?" he asks impatiently, while checking his watch. "What is it, Maggie?"

"I wanted to tell you about a project I'm working on—"

"What?" He shakes his head. "Hazel Cooke—probably the oldest friend you have on this planet—just lost her nephew. Your sister ran out of the room, obviously upset. And yet you want to talk about you. It's always been about Maggie, hasn't it? What Maggie wants, what will make Maggie happy. Poor Maggie has had it tough, losing her adopted mother and father at such a young age." He sighs and drops his eyes to the floor.

"Nigel. I—"

He looks up. "Don't."

"I want to—"

"You want to interfere with something I've got going on."

"What are you talking about?"

"Maggie, let's revisit Florida, shall we? I wanted you. You didn't want me. Then I got angry and left, and, suddenly, you wanted me. But you were too impatient to wait for me to get from Massachusetts back down to Florida, so by the time I got to you, you didn't want me anymore."

He waits for me to say something, but when I don't, he continues. "Fast forward to now. I bump into you, and all the old feelings come back. I go after you. Still, you don't want me. I meet someone else. And now you can't wait to get all cozy, talking about some project, even though I know it's a matter of time before you ..." He shakes his head and walks toward the elevators, unable to finish his thought. Finally, he stops and faces me again. "Maybe your coming back was what I needed."

"For what?"

"To get me over you, once and for all."

I hold his gaze, determined not to cry. I deserve every last ounce of his fury, and I know it. *Take it*, I tell myself. *Let him go.* But as I struggle to keep it together, the mud in his eyes vanishes, and the old Nigel—the one who never stopped loving me—is back. He reaches for me. I pull away.

"Maggie, why do you keep doing this?"

My brain implores my vocal cords to move, for my mouth to form words. Nothing comes out.

Shaking his head, he pushes the up button and the elevator arrives in seconds. He gets on and disappears behind the sliding doors.

"Strike three," I whisper, even though I know I struck out a long time ago.

# Chapter 31: Hugh

When Adrienne was a child, I often mused that she had gotten the best from Gloria and me. She inherited her mother's expansive mind and my dogged dedication to studying and learning. For all her mother's whimsy, she retained my grounding. She had her mother's luminescent skin and my height, and her eyes were the right combination of my blue and Gloria's gray. I believed she was perfect.

As she grew up, it was such a joy—and perhaps an escape—to rediscover the world through her eyes, a child's eyes. Walks around the neighborhood transformed into worlds of castles and kings and unicorns. Picking up furry black-and-white caterpillars became lessons in science. Bedtime stories ranged from Greek mythology to Shakespeare to her mother's poetry, the same poetry I had fallen in love with years before.

"My two lovely ladies," I'd sing whenever I saw them together. Adrienne would smile, Gloria would look away, and I would stand in the middle, holding firmly to the memory of the former and ignoring the reality of the latter.

Even after all this time, I don't know what else I could have done differently.

#

April's house is in darkness, and I debate about whether I should go in. It's late, past midnight, my driving around for the last six hours having failed to clear my head. I pull into her driveway anyway.

She doesn't keep the door locked, as if she expects bad news to work its way in regardless of a deadbolt. As my eyes adjust to the darkness, I feel the comforting stroke of Ming Toy against my legs. That's when I spy a form, straight ahead, sitting at the breakfast table.

"April?"

She makes no sound as I enter the kitchen, doesn't even look up as I flick on the light. She wraps her hands tighter around her mug, and I notice tearstains on her cheeks, the paleness of her face. I sit on the chair next to her, loosen my tie, and wait.

"What are we doing?" she finally asks.

"I don't know."

"It's wrong."

"You're right."

"So why are we doing it?"

"I don't know."

"Does your daughter ..."

I shake my head. "Adrienne doesn't know."

"How do you know?"

"I just do."

"What did she want?"

"Who? Adrienne?"

"Yes."

"I'm not sure. Checking in, I guess."

"You didn't talk to her?"

"We don't talk anymore."

April looks at me. "What did you do, Hugh?" she whispers.

"What makes you think I did anything?"

She casts her eyes downward, and I pray she doesn't cry.

"You don't want to know, April."

She nods, continues staring at her mug, and says nothing.

I sigh. "I had an affair. A long, long time ago."

"With who?"

"A grad student. At the college. Unfortunately, Adrienne found out. She was only thirteen." I pause. "She never forgave me."

"Just that one?"

"One person over the course of five months. But it was only one affair, if that's what you're asking."

"And Gloria? She knew, too?"

"Yes."

"And she ..."

"Forgave me."

April looks up again, questioning. "But Adrienne never did?"

"No."

"Why not?"

"That's a question you'd have to ask her."

"And that's it? That's all you did?"

*No. That's the beginning.* "Yes. That's all I did."

"But why does she refuse to sign the DNR?"

"She wants to hurt me."

"But she's hurting both of you. You and her mother."

I shrug. "Who said there's any logic to revenge?"

"Is that what it is? Revenge?"

"I don't know how else to label it."

She studies my face, and I almost falter and tell her everything. *It's my burden,* I remind myself. *Mine. Not April's.*

"I can't do this," she whispers.

"Do what?" I ask dumbly, even though I know.

"This."

I nod.

"You're married, Hugh. Your wife is ..." She pauses and wipes her nose with the back of her hand. "It violates every bit of ethics in health care. Not to mention you're old enough to be my ..." Her cheeks balloon out as she emits a long puff of air. I wait for her to finish, but she doesn't.

"Well," I say. "That pretty much sums it up."

"So why is it," she whispers, and this time she looks up at me, not caring about tears or snot or anything else. "That despite all this, I still don't want you to go?"

As I try to find the right words, she gets up and stands before me as she did on that first morning we were together. Except this time, before she can fall into my lap, I pull her down on top of me.

"Maybe," I say into her ear, "for the same reason I want to stay."

#

The chickadees, juncos, and nuthatches flitter about the trees and swamp stumps as I loop around the side streets on my walk the next morning. Occasionally, a male cardinal alights on a branch, adding a red splash to winter's canvas. It's a mild morning, early still, and the sun begins to rise as last night's conversation with April replays in my head. I haven't thought of Kendra Jackson in years—perhaps decades. It's funny how your mind files things away to the point you can almost forget about them. Survival mechanism, I suppose.

I didn't love Kendra, although I was fond of her. She loved me, or so she said, and I have no reason not to believe it except she was young—only twenty-three—and I'm not sure she knew the meaning of the word. But then again, who among us does?

I don't want to be thinking about this, but my mind refuses to cooperate and instead calls up the memories anyway.

#

"Professor, I have some bad news about one of your advisees," Dr. Karol Borowski had said. He was the dean of students. He was also my father-in-law.

"Who?"

"Kend-ra Jack-son." He watched my face as he carefully enunciated her name. I didn't blink. I didn't twitch. But it didn't matter. I knew he knew.

"Oh? And what's the bad news?" I managed to say.

"Academic misconduct."

"What? How?"

He threw a sheaf of papers on my desk. "Plagiarism."

"*What*? But how did you—"

"Doesn't matter how I found out. What matters is I did." His glasses sat halfway down the bridge of his skinny nose, but they hadn't slipped; it's how he wore them. "We have standards, Professor Dooley. A name to protect. I have no patience for scandal."

I stared at the papers on my desk. "Are we talking about plagiarism here?" I stopped and looked up. "Or something else?"

A smirk dripped from his crooked lips. "What else would we be talking about, Professor Dooley, but the wayward actions of your advisee?"

I paged through the papers, skimming the text. "This is not her work—"

"Precisely."

"No. I mean, this isn't what she's been working on. Look, the notes in the margin aren't even her handwriting. There's been a mistake."

"Make no mistake about it. She is guilty. Admitted as much to me."

"But she didn't do anything wrong!" I jumped to my feet, but he stared me back down. "Her career," I whispered. "What about her future?"

"Ah, the indiscretion of youth. I suppose even though we can't tolerate it here, it's not up to me to subject her to eternal damnation. She is responsible for her own soul. I told the young lady that she had two options: she could withdraw, citing whatever reason she deemed appropriate—sick parent, wanderlust—and the school would not make an issue of her egregious acts, wouldn't even note it in her file."

My stomach churned acid all the way to my throat. "And the second option?"

"Disciplinary hearing, with possible expulsion—which would be likely, given the circumstances—and notation of academic misconduct on her file and transcript. And an investigation into anyone she claimed aided and abetted her." He paused. "She, of course, is a bright young woman and chose wisely."

His smile disappeared, and in its place was hell. He leaned over the desk, into my face, and spat, "I spent too long building this school. And I'll be damned if I see its name or mine tarnished."

I pulled back, rubbed my hand over my mouth. "Who knows?" I knew we both knew my question had nothing to do with alleged plagiarism.

He withdrew, straightened his jacket, and adjusted his red bowtie. "The people who need to know, know."

By the time I arrived home that evening it was obvious what that statement meant: Gloria knew. And so did Adrienne. At the dinner table, Pana pushed her food around her plate, excused herself, and escaped to her bedroom. Gloria and I sat there for the longest time without saying anything.

"Maybe I should leave," I finally whispered.

"If you leave, you'll never see Adrienne again."

I couldn't recall the last time I had heard such urgency—such passion—in Gloria's voice.

She placed her hand atop mine. "My father will make sure of it. You know that."

"What about Adrienne?"

"She'll get over it. Some kids were teasing her today, that's all."

Three of us professors—all "close" to Dr. Borowski—sent our children to the same prestigious private school; it sounded as if he had carefully considered his strategy.

Gloria squeezed my hand. "You've always been her hero. She's disappointed, but it would have happened sooner or later. She is thirteen after all. This is the age she's supposed to begin hating us."

I winced. I couldn't stand the thought of Adrienne hating me. "And what about you?" I said. "Don't you hate me? How could you not?"

She removed her hand, sipped the last of her wine—how many glasses had it been that night?—got up, and began to clear the table. "I don't hate you."

"Maybe you should leave *me*," I pressed, not understanding why she was so calm regarding my infidelity.

"Is that what you want, Hugh? For me to leave?"

"It's never been what I wanted." Gloria had left me a long time ago, if she were ever truly there in the first place. "What do *you* want?" I whispered.

She shrugged, never answered. Years later, I realized that in her silence was an admission: *I've tried leaving. But he won't let me go either.*

There was a time when I admired Dr. Borowski, considered him a father figure, mine having never forgiven me for developing brains over brawn and a desire to learn over a desire to fix johns for the rest of my life. Dr. Borowski made me feel special. *"We have high hopes for you, Professor Dooley. High hopes."* But his enthusiasm for me and my career waned when he realized how liberal my philosophies were, which conflicted with his conservative, traditionalist nature. And then there was Gloria. He had all but married her off to some old boorish academic, the next heir apparent of the college. But then Gloria set her sights on me. Perhaps that should have been a clue—the fact that this intelligent, beautiful thirty-one-year-old woman was single and expressed sudden interest in a twenty-five-year-old man who was still so green in the ways of the world. But what can I say? I was smitten. We dated for six months before marrying on June 26, 1974, the most impulsive, impetuous, and, implosive day of my life.

#

As I finish my walk and mount the porch steps to April's house, I'm so wrapped up in this memory that I don't notice the car on the street or the woman at the front door until I'm standing next to her.

"Hello," Maggie Prescott says, startled. "It's Hugh, right?" She's tall, and her gaze is even with mine. "Your wife is Hazel's roommate."

"Ms. Prescott," I say, wondering what this is all about and if April is expecting her."Oh, please call me Maggie." She pauses and watches me with a puzzled expression. "I just got here. Haven't even knocked."

"Well, then," I say. "Come on in." I open the door and hear the water running from the shower upstairs. I walk toward the kitchen. When I don't hear Maggie's footsteps behind me, I turn around. "Coffee?" I call out. "I brewed it before my walk."

"Um." She squints. "Sure."

She follows me into the kitchen, and I pour two cups. "Cream and sugar?"

"Thanks."

I motion to the chairs. "Please. Sit."

She does and sips her coffee for what feels like three hours even though it's probably more like two minutes. Finally, the water turns off above our heads, and I pray that April doesn't come down the stairs naked.

"Hey, Hugh?" April's muffled voice calls out.

I smile at Maggie and can't decide if she looks more curious than shocked or the other way around. "I'll go get April." I head to the stairway and stand on the bottom step. "April! Maggie is here."

"*What?*"

"Maggie is here," I yell again.

April practically tumbles down the stairs, while tying her robe, her hair covered in a green-towel turban. She races for the kitchen, and I'm right behind her.

"Maggie!"

"April. Hi. I'm sorry to … I wanted to …" Maggie pauses, looks from me to April, and begins again. "I wanted to see if you wanted to go to Michael's wake together. I'm assuming you're going."

"I'm taking Hazel."

Maggie nods. "Right. Well, maybe I could help with that."

April says nothing, and I notice the floor is still wet from her footprints. "Okay," she finally says.

"Okay? So we'll go together?"

"Yeah."

"Good. Well—"

"Yes. Well, I'll walk you out." April looks down at her robe. "To the door anyway."

"Of course," Maggie says, getting to her feet. "Thanks for the coffee, Hugh."

"No problem."

While Maggie reaches for the purse she's dropped to the floor, April shoots me an "are you crazy" look. I shrug and mouth, "I'm sorry." She leads Maggie to the door, and I watch from the kitchen.

"Okay, so I'll see you tomorrow afternoon," Maggie says.

"Wait. Don't you have to work?" April asks.

"Got the day off. For this."

"Oh." April's back is to me, but I can still hear every word. "Maggie," she whispers, "No one knows about—"

"Don't worry. I won't say anything. It's none of my business anyway."

The door closes, April leans her face against it, and I come up from behind, wrapping my arms around her middle. "This is crazy," she murmurs. As usual, I don't say anything and simply hug her tight.

# Chapter 32: Maggie

It has been a week of black: black hosiery, black dresses, black moods. Michael's service was full of pomp and circumstance, just like his life. April barely said two words to me. Not sure if it's embarrassment about Hugh Dooley or her distaste for me.

"Maggie, my dear?"

I turn to Hazel, who's wrapped in blankets on top of her bed. "Hmm?"

"Have you talked to Nigel yet?" She speaks loudly, as if she can't hear herself. The effort exhausts her. She leans against the pillows and closes her eyes.

"No," I whisper.

"Why not?"

"He hates me Hazel. He finally hates me. Why should I tell him the truth? So he can hate me more?"

"He would not hate you if he knew the truth. The whole truth."

"Nigel lives in a black and white world. No shades of gray. He would never be able to forgive me."

She opens her eyes and fixes them on me with such urgency, such passion. "Perhaps the person who needs to forgive is not Nigel."

"What do you mean?"

"Sounds to me that the person who needs to forgive you is *you.*" Her eyelids drop again.

I say nothing because, honestly, what can I say? Maybe she's right. I wonder if Kate suffered guilt after giving me up. There's so much I'd like to ask her, so much I want to know. Sighing, I adjust my position in the chair and allow my eyes to wander Hazel's room: the sterile white walls, Gloria's lifeless body in the bed next to Hazel's, the empty chair where Hugh usually sits.

"Hazel?"

"Yes, dear?"

"What do you know about Hugh Dooley?"

Her eyes flutter open. "Why do you ask?"

*Should I tell her?* "Let's just say I'm not the only one with secrets."

"Would this secret have something to do with April?"

"So you know. About the two of them," I say.

"Suspected. I have not discussed it with either of them."

"What do you think?"

"My dear, I am the last person on this earth who should pass judgment."

"But don't you think it's wrong?" I gesture toward Gloria.

"Perhaps," Hazel says. "But who are we—you and I—to know what is and what is not meant to be?"

"I care about her."

"As sisters should."

"I don't want to see her get hurt again. She's been through so much already."

"My dear, it is beyond your control."

"But—"

"The one thing you do have control over is your situation. Maggie, my dear, talk to Nigel. Tell him what really happened to you in Florida."

# *Chapter 33: Nigel*

I don't make a habit of eavesdropping. Honest to God, I don't.

I can't help that I was going about my business, dropping off some papers in Hazel's room for her to sign. I can't help that my hearing is good. I can't help that Hazel's ninety-three-year-old ears are not, forcing her to speak extra loud so that she can hear what she's saying. I can't help that the words, *"Talk to Nigel. Tell him what really happened to you in Florida,"* are emblazoned in my brain in big orange letters like a branding iron to a heifer.

#

My cell phone rings, and I realize I've driven past the street to Anne Marie's house, where Max is waiting for me to pick him up. I put the device to my ear without even looking at the caller ID.

"Nigel Hurst speaking."

"Hey, you!" Trudie sings.

"Hey there."

"Where are you?"

"On my way to pick up Max," I say, while turning down a side street and navigating back into traffic. "For basketball practice."

"Guess what?" she bubbles.

"What?"

"It's time for that third part."

"Third part?"

"You know," she says. "Rio at sunset. You're not going to believe this, but there's a station promotion for one of the airlines. They're sending us to Rio—first class. I'll be doing a 'Postcards from Rio' sort of thing where I call in and record my experiences for playback on the air."

"Us?"

"Yeah! I get to bring a guest."

"Oh."

There's a long pause, and I silently curse myself for not sounding more enthusiastic.

"You don't sound too excited," she murmurs. "I assumed you'd want to go."

"I'm shocked, that's all. It's not every day a beautiful woman calls me and tells me we're flying first class to Rio. When are we supposed to go?"

"Next month."

"Brilliant." I pull into Anne Marie's driveway, and Max jumps down the steps. "Trudie, I'm at the house—"

"Oh, okay. I won't keep you. We'll talk more tonight?"

"Yes."

"You want to go, right?"

I pause, caught for the first time with a direct question where I can't use a nonverbal gesture in response. "Of course," I say. But in my heart, I don't believe it.

#

Sitting in the gym's bleachers, I notice my hands trembling. Nerves, I tell myself, but my inner voice laughs derisively.

*What?* I say back. *Trudie has me feeling all discombobulated. How can I possibly go on this trip? How can I possibly not go? What about the information Maggie's withholding? I've got a lot on my plate, you know.*

*You have bigger worries than all that,* the voice retorts.

*Listen. I haven't had a drink in—*

*Doesn't matter,* the voice interrupts. *Have you said it? Out loud?*

*Said what?* But, of course, I know what.

#

Sitting in the back of the church basement, I wrap my hands on the steel chair's base. The room smells of burnt coffee and cigarette smoke. I attempt to make out the speaker's words, the same old coot I saw a few months ago who told me the only way this will work is if I come on down. But it's as if he's speaking a foreign language.

*See?* I tell myself. *I'm here.*

*Say it,* my inner voice commands. *Stand up and say it.*

*Why? I'm here, aren't I? I've stopped drinking. I'm sober.*

*Dry drunk,* the voice says.

*Sober,* I say.

*Fine,* the voice demurs. *Then get up and say that. Say you're an alcoholic and that you're finally sober.*

I hold my breath, grip the seat tighter, and will myself to stand. I can't.

*As I thought,* the voice says. *As I thought.*

*February*

# *Chapter 34: April*

"Oh, Mom. I wish I could talk to you."

She stirs at the sound of my voice but doesn't wake. I push back her hair, kiss her forehead, and swallow hard. When I've composed myself, I walk to the door, but not before locking eyes with Esther Higgins, my mother's roommate.

Esther's a kind old woman, but as frail as eighty-year-olds come. She's also the first roommate who hasn't complained about Mom's habit of going through dresser drawers and closets. Mom often appears in a doorway with someone's underwear or socks wrapped around her wrist like a bracelet. "That's good, Kate," Esther will say. "You found my favorite panties. Now put them back and find my favorite shoes." Mom doesn't understand the command, not that it matters. Esther's voice is soft and soothing, not angry or frustrated like the nurses and aides who must rescue residents' belongings from Mom's surprisingly strong grip.

"Between the two of us," Esther whispers as her eyes move from me to my mother, "we're almost a whole person."

I don't know what to say, don't even know if she wants me to say anything. Maybe she says it because she needs to share the observation with someone who'll listen, someone who can understand. I attempt a smile.

"Good night, Esther."

"Good night, April."

#

Back on the first floor, I head toward Hazel's room. Usually, she's up, and we chat for a bit in private since Hugh leaves after the aides get Gloria cleaned up and repositioned for the night, but Hazel's been going to bed earlier and earlier, as if her body can't get enough sleep. I peek in the room anyway. Once my eyes adjust to the dark, I wait until her chest rises beneath the thick blue quilt before I leave.

Sad shadows fill the hallway on the way back to my office. During the day, sunlight pours from the windows, and it's okay—cheery almost. As the day wears on, however, especially when the seasons change from fall to winter, the darkness seeps in faster and faster, like water rushing onto a sinking ship.

Hugh will be waiting for me when I get home, and the excitement in my mind and heart wrestles with the guilt rising in my belly. In my office, I sit in my swivel chair for a while and hold some of the photographs of Jimmy and Vinny. I polished their frames yesterday, the twelfth anniversary of their deaths. Five years after they died, Joelle asked me if I would consider dating again.

"How can you ask me that?"

"I can ask you because it's been five years, April. And because you're young. And because Vinny and Jimmy wouldn't want you to spend the rest of your life alone."

Even though I appeared outwardly annoyed by Joelle's question, the truth was I found it a relief, liberating almost. Right before she asked me, I had been catching glimpses of my future self in dreams and daytime reveries, and this person—this truly grown-up me—was not alone. I felt guilty about that, like I was cheating on Jimmy or Vinny. Yet Joelle's query gave me permission to consider it, even though as the years passed, as Mom grew sicker, as Javier came and went, as I became older and more resentful, it appeared less and less likely that this person would ever emerge from the shadows of my sadness.

But today, everything is different, thanks to one tipsy New Year's Eve kiss that led to so much more. Now, there's Hugh. Despite the fact he's twenty-three years my senior and is married and his wife lay dying, my future self has blossomed like tulips in the spring, and I find myself lingering on her reflection in the mirror, liking the way she looks and the way she smiles. Problem is if I look too long, I see something else. Deep inside, near the core of her being, is a glow. I know it's the seeds of unborn children still wanting a chance at life.

# Chapter 35: Hugh

When Adrienne was eight years old, I bought her a folding artist easel, oil paints, an assortment of brushes, two brand new canvases, and a palette. It wasn't an impulse buy; Pana had shown an affinity for art since she was old enough to hold a crayon. Her teacher had been giving her lessons on the side, schooling her in form and technique. "Your Adrienne's gifted," he'd tell me, but I already knew that she was.

Still is.

Now when she sits at her potter's wheel or before her easel, I wonder if she ever thinks of me, if she ever thinks back to the time when all I did was encourage her and cheer her on. I pray she does. A piece of me believes she must. It's comforting for me to think that.

#

As parents, we tend to stockpile happy memories, remembering where we've hidden our cache the same way hungry squirrels remember where they've buried acorns for winter. And I, too, have my share—first steps at the beach on the Cape; first words, such as "Daddy" and "book"; first time watching her ride her bike without training wheels or any assistance from me; first day of school, when she looked at me, so determined not to cry, as she boarded the school bus. But there is a standout memory—one so perfect and pristine that I sometimes wonder if I lived it or conjured it.

It was early August. Gloria, Adrienne, and I spent our summers on the Cape, in my father-in-law's second home, which was on a private part of

Nauset Beach in Orleans. The summer had been especially hot, even on Cape Cod where sea breezes usually kept things comfortable. It hadn't rained in seventeen days, and it showed. Lawns were turning brown, water bans were in effect, and the dirt road leading to our summer retreat lay dry, cracked, and parched.

One afternoon, Pana and I—desperate to escape the brutal heat outside—played cards in the kitchen, two fans mounted on the countertops and directed at our faces. Gloria napped on the couch in the next room, an empty bottle of white zinfandel at her side. Pana was trying to remember a game some of the children in the area had taught her, but she couldn't remember all the rules and was making them up, mostly in her favor, and giggling the whole time at the feigned look of shock on my face every time she won. She couldn't have been more than ten or eleven, still sweet and innocent. Still my little girl.

"Hey, look!" I said, pointing out the kitchen window. Low-lying gray and black clouds had obliterated the sun.

"Is it supposed to rain?" she asked. "Finally?"

I shook my head. "No. At least, that's not what the weatherman said this morning."

She nodded, we stared at each other, and then as if the thought passed from my mind to hers, we got up without a word and raced to the screened-in porch where we could get a better view of the sky. The wind had picked up and the leaves on the trees flipped over, revealing their pale green undersides.

"Listen," I said.

Pana tilted her head. "What?"

"No birds."

Thunder rumbled.

"There!" she said. "Did you hear it?" She leaned her body into mine. Not out of fear or concern—she wasn't a timid child—but out of the human need to share moments, no matter how grand or small. The rain came, and I could tell by the movement of the clouds that this was a teaser, not a full-blown storm.

"C'mon," I yelled, as I pushed open the screen door and ran into the yard.

"Daddy! What are you doing?"

I glanced over my shoulder, and she stood in the doorway, one hand holding open the door. Her legs were toothpick-skinny and knobby-kneed beneath her pink shorts, her torso flat and boyish in her white tank top. She wore her black hair in a ponytail pulled high atop the crown of her head, and even then it flowed down her back, almost touching the tip of her tailbone.

I twirled, staring at the sky, letting the rain pelt my face, opening my mouth and drinking it in. I could tell Adrienne wanted to follow, but didn't know if she should because she'd get wet and, well, you didn't do things like run out in the pouring rain. I breathed deeply and sighed.

"Pana! Come smell the petrichor!"

"The what?"

"The petrichor," I yelled and laughed at the same time.

Curiosity got the better of her. She peeked over her shoulder to make sure her mother wasn't standing there waiting to tell her that her father was crazy. She chewed on her lower lip while smiling—the way she always did when she was trying to tell a joke and not laugh—and she ran out into the rain, toward me, squinting her eyes as the drops hit her face.

"Okay. Smell what?" she asked as she stood next to me.

I squatted next to her, my arm draped over her shoulders. The rain was already beginning to taper off, and sunshine kaleidoscoped through the clouds. "Take a deep breath. Through your nose."

She closed her eyes and did as she was told. When she opened them, I knew she had smelled it.

"Wow! It smells so good! It smells ..."

"Fresh?"

"And clean! And green!" She took a deep whiff, her whole body rising from the ground. "What's it called again?"

I leaned my mouth into her ear. "Petrichor," I whispered. "It's called petrichor."

Petrichor was my favorite word. I had learned it when I was sixteen, from the magazine *Nature*, a subscription I paid for myself from the paper route I had had since I was nine years old. I think my father secretly wished I was addicted to comic books or even dirty magazines instead of science journals, but I was hooked.

Petrichor comes from the Greek word *petros*—meaning stone—and *ichor*, which was, in Greek mythology, what filled the veins of the gods, keeping them immortal. Two Australian researchers coined the term *petrichor*, which they said was the refreshing scent produced after a replenishing rain. Specifically, the researchers identified the oil from the plants that released the fragrance.

"Petrichor," she repeated slowly, after I explained the word's origin. She closed her eyes, breathed in deeply, opened them, looked at me, and smiled. Raindrops clung to her lashes, and I could tell she loved the word as much as I did.

Early the next morning when I went into the kitchen to make coffee, I found Pana asleep at the table. Her easel was behind her, and on it, a painting. Watercolor was her medium that summer, and she had painted a picture of us—a man and a little girl twirling in the rain amidst trees and flowers and scorched earth. But she had done something interesting; the colors became brighter from the perimeter to the middle, until the man and little girl were standing on a patch of glorious green earth surrounded by brilliant red, pink, purple, and yellow flowers, the leaves of the trees overhead brighter than the trees on the side. It was as if the rain had not only revived the earth, but also the man and girl and the world in which they stood. Pana had called her painting "My Petrichor," and I swear I could detect the sweet scent every time I gazed upon it.

#

"Hey, you."

I look up from the fire. "Hey, you, too." I stand, and my legs are stiff. I take April's hand in my own and lead her to the couch. She tugs off her jacket and scarf, kicks off her boots, and curls up next to me. I rest my cheek atop her head. The flames mesmerize us for a while, but then my eyes wander to the mantel with all the photographs of Jimmy and Vinny and the new one in the middle of Maggie, April, and Kate. On the far end is an old Polaroid tucked into a frame—a shot of a man and a little girl, a little miniature version of April.

"April?"

"Hmm?"

"How did your father die?"

She sighs. "Which version do you want to hear?"

"What do you mean?"

"I mean," she says, while righting herself and looking at me, "there's the version my mother told me when I was a little girl. And then, there's the truth."

"Tell me both."

She gazes at the fire. "He died when I was five years old. Car accident. At least, that's what my mother told me."

"But it wasn't a car accident?"

"He died in a car. That part's true. But it was no accident."

I don't like where this conversation is headed, and I can feel my heart transition from a steady beat to a trot.

"He committed suicide," she whispers. "Shot himself."

The trot turns into a gallop, and I labor to breathe.

"I didn't find out," she continues, "until my senior year in high school. I was in the attic, going through old photo albums because I needed a baby picture for my yearbook. That's when I found it. His note. The one he left behind to my mom and me." She pauses, her eyes open wide, lost in a memory from long ago. "It was in the seam of one of the albums, along with his obituary. I had seen the obituary years before. All it said was that he had died suddenly. I was too young to know that 'died suddenly' was a code for things you didn't want people to know. Like drug overdoses. Or embarrassing things like having a heart attack in a mistress's bed. Or suicide."

"My God." I cough, gasping for air.

"Hugh? You okay?"

*Breathe*, I tell myself. *Breathe*. Concern spreads across her face. She reaches for my hand, holds it, and waits. "I'm okay," I finally manage. "I can't imagine what that must have been like for you."

"I don't know what was worse—knowing my father had committed suicide, or knowing my mother had lied to me about it for all those years. I mean, I know she couldn't have told me when I was a little kid. But when I was older, especially in high school, I asked many questions about him. She had the opportunity. Made me wonder what else she lied about. I asked her that, too, and she said there was nothing else to tell." She turns back to the fire now, shaking her head. "That was a lie, too, apparently."

*Don't ask. Don't ask. Don't ask.* "What did the note say?"

She doesn't respond, and I begin to think that maybe the words never left my lips.

"It said, 'I'm sorry.'" Her voice trembles when she speaks. "'I'm sorry. It's not your fault. Please know it's not your fault. But I can't live with the pain anymore. I'm sorry. I love you both. Please forgive me.'"

I squeeze her tight, muffling her words into my chest, because I can't stand to hear anymore, even though I want to tell her everything, to let her know I understand all too well about suicide and lies and shams. "April, I—"

Pulling her face up to meet mine, she kisses me before I can speak. "No," she says, against my mouth. "It's okay. There's nothing you can say. Just kiss me. Love me." She stops, looks me in the eyes, surprised at her own request. "I mean," she says quickly, "I'm sorry. Don't think—"

I rub my finger along her wet lips. "Too late to take it back," I whisper as I kiss her. "Too late, because I already do."

# Chapter 36: Nigel

I have never been so happy about basketball playoffs in all my life, even though I can't stand the bloody game.

"You're coming, right, Dad?" Max had asked that afternoon.

"Max, I wouldn't miss it for the world." *Or Rio,* I'd thought.

#

"So," Trudie begins after we place our order. "What's up?"

"What makes you think anything is up?" I eye her pina colada.

She arches her brow. "I can tell."

"Well, I have good news and bad news."

"Okay. Give me the bad news first."

"I'd like to start with the good news because it will help explain the bad." I pause while the waitress places our salads before us. "Maxwell's basketball team made the playoffs."

"That's great! He must be excited. I'll have to ..." She stops and tilts her head to the side. "What can I get for a twelve-year-old boy to celebrate basketball playoffs?"

"I don't know," I say quickly because I don't want the conversation to derail. "But this leads to the bad news." She smiles and pops a cherry tomato into her mouth. I clear my throat. "The playoffs begin in a couple weeks."

The smile disappears once she does the math. "As in—"

"Yes. As in our week in Rio."

She licks her lips, nods her head, and waits. Finally, she takes her napkin and wipes her mouth.

"I promised him I'd be there." I pause, hoping she'll say something, but she doesn't. "Besides—"

"Besides what?"

I shrug.

"What were you going to say?"

"I don't know."

"Yes, Nigel. You do. Say it." She looks at me, her eyes filled with tears.

*I'm an alcoholic who's in love with another woman. Sorry.* "I was going to say that a week's vacation together in another country is moving things a little too fast. For me."

She curls her chin to her chest as a tear rolls down her cheek. I reach for her hand, which is on the table, and she lets me touch her. "Trudie, I'm sorry. I should have told you sooner—"

"No," she interrupts, looking up. "I knew I was rushing things. I knew you weren't ready for this. I knew from your reaction when I first told you."

"Listen, we haven't been together all that long. And, well, you have to admit, I don't have the best track record when it comes to relationships. I rushed into both of my marriages. I need to take this slow so I don't screw it up." *So I can finally admit to what I am. So I can find out what's going on with Maggie, what went on with Maggie thirty years ago. So I can stay sober—okay, at least dry—when I do find out the truth. Whatever it is.*

"We'll have other chances at Rio," I continue, but even as I say it, I don't believe it. I glance at her, to see if I can gauge what she's thinking. "Will you be able to find someone to take my place? A girlfriend maybe? Perhaps your sister?"

She sighs, shakes her head, and reaches for her fork. "No. Yes. I'm sure I could, but it's no big deal. Happy and I will be working a lot anyway. Maybe it's all for the best."

I forgot about Happy Byrd, her producer, the one who'd be tagging along with us. I'm sure he was as thrilled with the idea of me going on this trip as I was with the thought of him.

"That's right," I say. "Happy is going with you." I'm surprised at the jealousy in my voice, and Trudie must be, too, because she smiles a relieved smile.

"Jealous, counselor?" she says. "Well, you had your chance."

I grin, once again allowing her to interpret my nonverbal gesture however she wants, even if her interpretation is inaccurate. Jealous? Maybe. Had my chance? Deep down the only chance I've ever wanted was to be with Maggie. But I had that already, a long time ago. Didn't I? *Talk to Nigel. Tell him what really happened to you in Florida.*" Hazel's words repeat in my head like annoying lyrics to bad songs you can't escape. I guess that's what it comes down to—I won't be able to escape, or move on, as in with Trudie, until I find out what Maggie isn't telling me.

"Florida," I whisper.

"Florida?" Trudie blinks. "What about Florida?"

"Maybe," I say, trying hard to recover, "We can plan a trip to Florida."

"When?"

I shrug and smile. She studies my face, and I wonder if she's on to me.

"Ha!" she exclaims as her mouth spreads into a grin. "If you're lucky."

# Chapter 37: Maggie

When Nigel and I broke up for good and I knew there was no way he was going to come back, I did what I have done all my life: I threw myself into my work.

I'm lucky, I suppose, that I like what I do and that it has meaning. To me, anyway. Still, Nigel has always been right about one thing: broadcast journalism isn't documentary film. Even though I've enjoyed my career, it has effectively kept me at arm's length from my real passion. Except now I'm wondering if it isn't perhaps the other way around. Maybe I've kept myself away by using my job—a very good and rewarding job—as an excuse.

#

Serena and I sit on my living room floor in front of the electric fireplace. She keeps flicking it on and off with the remote control wand, as if she can't believe her eyes, even though we did a segment a month ago called "Fire Starters" on all the different options in fireplace technology, from gas to electric to pellet stoves.

The condo I've been renting is far from homey—the fireplace is the closest it comes, which isn't saying much. Serena keeps bugging me to start shopping for something permanent, but that word has never been a part of a broadcast journalist's vocabulary. I've lived this way for the last thirty years—a nomadic lifestyle of sorts, never investing much in my apartments or condos even though, to the casual observer, my abodes have always appeared expensive and luxurious. I've had home bases in many cities around the world: Chicago, London, Paris, New York—even Sydney for nine months—and, now, Boston.

For the last two hours, we've been drinking wine and brainstorming ideas for our project that we've tentatively dubbed "Entertaining Grandma Moses."

"There's this guy who juggles cats," Serena says. "In Salt Lake City."

"What?"

"Yeah. I talked to the activities director of the Salt Lake City Rehabilitation Center. Also known as 'Salt Lake Seniors.'" Serena shuffles through the papers on her lap. "Her name was Liz Sheldon. She said the guy is their most popular act. He travels throughout the state and has even made it to Vegas."

"Vegas? Really?"

Serena laughs. "Well, not the Vegas you and I think of. A nursing home on the outskirts of town."

"Hmm." I stare at the flames, and the neon orange reminds me of the psychedelic colors of hotel signs on "The Strip," the official nickname for Las Vegas Boulevard South, a three-and-a-half-mile stretch of highway and home to some of the most famous and ostentatious hotels and casinos in the world. "I'm surprised PETA hasn't been called in."

Serena shrugs. "The woman told me the cats love it. Here's the kicker, though. After he's done entertaining them with his act, he turns it into a pet therapy session with the cats. And the Rottweilers."

"Rottweilers?"

Serena hands me a copy of a magazine article. "Apparently, Rotties make good therapy dogs."

"Yeah, right. Only when Cujo isn't available."

She snorts, and our combined creative energy charges the air. We're still in the pipe-dream stage, letting our ideas flow freely. We don't know what slant we're going to take, but Serena sees what I see—the possibility. Nursing home entertainment, a weird sub-culture rivaling traveling carnivals. Whoda thunk it?

The doorbell chimes, and Serena shoots me a quizzical look as I glance at the funky chrome clock on the wall: 11:26.

"You expecting anyone?" she asks.

I shake my head, hoist myself from the Lotus position, and walk stiffly to the door. I peer through the peephole and pull back in shock.

"Who is it?" Serena asks.

The doorbell rings again. I hold my breath and open the door.

"Hello, Maggie."

I'm unable to speak. Nigel looks past me and into the living room where Serena sits and then scrambles to her feet.

"I'm sorry," he says. "I should have called first. I was in the neighborhood. I saw your lights on from the street. I'll go—"

"Wait!" Serena interrupts, while throwing her backpack over her shoulder. "She could use the company. I was just leaving."

"Serena," I hiss.

Ignoring me, she smiles at Nigel and holds out her hand. "Serena Flores."

He grasps her hand in his own. "Nigel Hurst. Pleasure to meet you, Serena. We've talked before on the phone."

"I know. I remember," she says while smirking at me. "See you tomorrow, Maggie."

"Serena!" I yelp, but she's out the door and closing it behind her before I can say anything else.

Nigel and I look at each other for what feels like forever. "So," I say. *Do I smell cigarettes?* "What did you want?"

"The truth."

I'm not expecting this response, and the surprise must show on my face. "I don't know what you're talking about—"

"Maggie, stop. I overheard you and Hazel talking the other day—"

"You were eavesdropping?" My mind rewinds the conversation. *What did we say?*

"No. I said I overheard."

"Same thing."

"No," he sighs. "They're not. Eavesdropping is intentional. Overhearing is accidental."

"Typical lawyer. Spinning everything to your advantage."

"Maggie, I didn't come here to quarrel."

We stare at each other again. Finally, he breaks my gaze and allows his eyes to wander around the room. "Nice place."

I shrug. "It's okay, I guess." I pause again. *Yes, that's definitely cigarette smoke.* "Have you been smoking?"

"What?" he asks.

"You smell like cigarettes."

"I do?" He sniffs his jacket. "Blech. You're right."

"So you smoke now?"

"No," he says. "Just came from a meeting."

"At eleven o'clock at night?"

"Yeah, well. You know me. Maybe we should sit down."

I shrug and lead him to the white leather couch in the living room.

"Look," he says. "I'm sorry I was so harsh a couple of weeks ago. I don't entirely know why I'm here now. But as I said, I overheard Hazel suggest that you should tell me what really happened in Florida."

"You know what happened in Florida," I whisper, while folding and unfolding my hands in my lap.

"Do I, Maggie?"

I lift my eyes until they meet his. "Did it ever occur to you that maybe you don't want to know?"

"Yes. It did. But not knowing is worse than knowing. Tell me, Maggie. For both our sakes. Tell me."

His words, of course, make perfect sense. What Nigel wants is the answer to why. Hasn't that been my mantra my whole career? My whole life?

"I was pregnant," I hear myself say.

Nigel gapes at me, jaw open. "What? Was it—"

"Yes. It was yours."

"But I don't understand. What about—"

"Oscar?" I interrupt. "Nigel. I told you then, and I'm telling you now. Nothing happened with Oscar."

"I saw you, though. I saw both of you. Kissing. The day I left."

"That's all you saw. That's all that happened."

"Why should I believe that?"

"Because what I'm about to say would be easier if I lied to you about Oscar. I'm not lying, Nigel. Oscar was a friend. Nothing more. The baby was yours."

"What happened?" His face is ashen, his eyes are dim, and I can't fathom how I'll get through this. "I mean," he continues before I can start, "there was the car accident."

"Right."

"And, oh no. Christ, no. You lost the baby?"

I nod because he's right, but that's not all of it. He reaches for me, and I shrink back into the couch.

"What is it?" he whispers. "Maggie, please. Let me in."

"Let you in," I murmur. "Well. We'll see if that's what you want once you hear the rest."

"What more is there?"

"Nigel, you surprise me. You're usually good with logic. And questions."

"What do you mean?"

"Think about it."

He shakes his head. "You were in a car accident in Florida. Hazel called me. I flew down and got to you within forty-eight hours."

"Right."

He furrows his brow while putting the facts together. "Two cars. You were hit as you made a left-hand turn onto a main drag, as I recall. It was a teenage driver. Right?"

"Yes."

"So the accident wasn't your fault." He leans back into the couch. "I remember when I got to the hospital, he was there. Oscar. I thought I was too late. That you had moved on for real." He sighs and looks at me. "That's it, right?"

"You never asked where I was going that morning. Which is what I explained in that letter Hazel never ended up giving you."

He shoots me a quizzical look. "Well. Where were you going? You were in St. Petersburg. I figured you and Oscar were on vacation or something."

"No," I say. "We weren't. It was only me."

"St. Petersburg has to be a five-hour trip from Port Saint Joe at least."

"Six hours." *Six very long hours.* "I was going to a women's health clinic." I glance at Nigel who is sitting up straight, alert, and in trial lawyer mode.

"Maggie, no. Was it a—?"

"It still is." The particular clinic I went to in St. Petersburg had opened in '75, two years after *Roe v. Wade.* In theory, I could have been done with everything in less than twenty-four hours: six hours down, six hours for pre-op and the actual procedure, and six hours back, although I had booked a room at a local motel, figuring the last thing I'd be up for doing was driving after having an abortion.

#

"Are you sure about this, Maggie?" Hazel had asked on the phone when I explained my intentions.

"Yes."

"I will come down. I will be there with you."

"No. I'll be okay. You have school."

"You cannot do this alone."

"I'll be fine."

And for five-and-three-quarter hours, until I entered St. Petersburg, I was. But as I peered at the directions I had scrawled on the back of an envelope and counted the numbers on the street to the clinic, my heart raced. *Nerves,* I told myself. *You're doing the right thing.*

I drove past it the first time, caught off guard by the throng of protesters outside the building. I turned down a side street, pulled into a driveway, and placed my head on the steering wheel. The protesters' signs flashed before me in bold blacks and reds, the words swimming together and making no sense except for one: *Thank God Your Mother Was Pro-Life.*

All I could think of was Kathleen Keegan, the name on my birth certificate, the only information I had on my biological mother. Nigel had once said he thanked God every day that my biological mother had had me. Kathleen Keegan, a woman who had no choice in 1954 but to keep me or give me up. What would she have chosen had she had this option?

I backed out of the driveway, retraced my steps, turned on my left-hand blinker, and pulled out into traffic in the direction of the clinic. I believe in my heart I would have driven past the building and protesters, gotten back on the highway, and headed home. But I have no way of proving this, no way of knowing for sure that's what I would have done. The one thing I do know is this: if I hadn't been in St. Petersburg that morning, I wouldn't have been in that accident. No matter how you looked at it, the loss of the baby was my fault.

#

"My God," Nigel says as he puts the puzzle together. "You were going to get an abortion? You were going to abort our child? And not even tell me about it? Not even give me—us—a chance?"

Horror sweeps his face, contorting his handsome features into the ugliness of my nightmares. I don't look away, knowing I deserve every ounce of hatred he can muster.

"I'm sorry."

"Is that all you can say?" he spits as he stands. "You're sorry?" He shakes his head in disgust, walks to the door, and turns around. "I'm sorry, too. Sorry I ever cared. That I spent nights awake dreaming of you and a family together. Of us. No more, though. At least now I know."

"Does that make it easier?"

"What?"

"To hate me?"

"I don't hate you, Maggie." He pauses and then adds, "I don't anything you."

When he realizes I'm not going to respond, he nods, opens the door, and slams it shut behind him. I stare at the fireplace. The problem with these electric versions is that they don't emit any heat; they're all for show. Somehow, I can't help but see myself.

# *Chapter 38: Nigel*

When Maxwell was born and I held him for the first time, I experienced a love like no other. No one had warned me that an eight-pound pooping pile of flesh could lasso my heart forever. In fact, the nine months of pregnancy had centered on what Anne Marie would go through: the hormones, the potential baby blues, the transformation of her whole world. I didn't mind playing second fiddle. After all, Anne Marie was the one who was pregnant. All those baby and pregnancy books knew what they were talking about, right?

Anne Marie was jealous, at first, with how well and how fast I bonded with Max.

"He stops crying for you," she'd say. "What's wrong with me?"

"Nothing's wrong with you, my love. You're a wonderful mother."

This I believed. Secretly, though, I liked to think that perhaps I had a special bond with my child. I promised myself that I would avoid all the mistakes that my own emotionally unavailable father had made with me. I'd take the time with Max. I'd be there. I'd always be there.

I didn't think much of Maggie during that time. Sleep deprivation had something to do with it, I'm sure, since I got up every two to three hours in the middle of the night with Anne Marie, even though she said I didn't need to. The truth is I didn't think of anyone or anything besides Max. I didn't consider my wife, or my mother, or my colleagues, or Maggie Prescott. I had become lost in this child, and, for a long time, I didn't see anything wrong with that.

"We don't spend any time together," Anne Marie would say, and I'd look at her, completely dumbfounded, because I couldn't understand her claim: we were sleeping in the same bed every night, sharing meals, raising a child.

"That's not Nigel and Anne Marie, the couple," she'd argue. "That's Anne Marie and Nigel, the parents. The homeowners. What happened to Nigel and Anne Marie, the lovers?"

I never could answer her, mainly because I didn't know how. I never thought of Anne Marie in that way—as my lover. We worked at the same law firm, the same one that hired me after I graduated from law school. I'm not sure when we started dating, not even sure how it evolved into marriage. Anne Marie asked me to marry her. To this day, I don't believe I said yes. I merely grinned and kissed her, allowing her to interpret my gestures as an affirmative, which she did.

When the fights with Anne Marie became more constant, which coincided with my increased alcohol consumption, my mind created a fantasy world to which I escaped—Maggie, Max, and me living together as a family. It's not that I wanted Anne Marie out of my life; I would never in a million years take Max away from his mother. I suppose what I wanted was what so many of us dream of—a chance to relive the past the way we had always intended.

#

"Mr. Hurst?"

"Yes, Miss Cooke?" The words come out automatically as I look at Hazel's tired face. She's propped up in bed, and I sit in the chair by her side, trying my damndest not to shake. We've resorted to surnames for the sake of our client-attorney relationship, even though we've both more than once slipped up and used one another's first name.

"I am done signing these." She leans into her pillow and closes her eyes.

"Right. Excellent." I gather the papers off her lap, glancing at the three places where she was supposed to insert her signature.

"She told you, didn't she?" Hazel murmurs.

"I beg your pardon?"

Her eyes open. "Maggie told you what happened in Florida."

"Miss Cooke," I say in my most professional voice, "I imagine your roommate's husband will be arriving soon, and I know you don't want Ms. Sullivan-LaMonica or Ms. Prescott to see us together." I point to my watch. "It's almost eight o'clock. Your breakfast will be arriving shortly, and besides." I pause and sigh. "We shouldn't be talking about what Maggie told me."

"What did she tell you?"

"Hazel—"

The old woman holds up her hand. "Tell me."

"C'mon. You already know." The vain in my forehead pulses with my words.

"What I know should explain what happened in Florida and change the way you feel about Maggie."

"You're right. It does."

"For the better," Hazel insists.

My head hurts trying to follow the conversation. "Are we talking about the same thing?" I lean into her bed. "Why would Maggie's aborting our child make me feel better?"

Hazel shakes her head. "She didn't do it."

"No. An accident got to her before the doctor's knife could."

"But she was turning around—"

"What?"

"Maggie drove *past* the facility. The protesters surprised her. She pulled down a side street and was turning around when she was hit."

My mind races as I try to process this information. "Was she turning around to go back to the clinic?"

Her chin trembles. "She was turning around to go back home. She blames herself, you see. She says that if she hadn't been down there in the first place, the accident would never have happened, but—"

I rub my eyes. "But what, Hazel?"

"My dear man I have been on this earth a long, long time. I have read—and followed—different philosophies to get me through my life. The one that has endured is this: if it is meant to be, it will be."

My hands shake, my head hurts, and my tongue feels thick and leathery. If I didn't know better I'd say I was hung over. It's taken every ounce of strength in my body not to drink after the conversation with Maggie, which was—what?—two weeks ago now. Two very long weeks.

"I'm not a fatalist," I hear myself say. *But you are an alcoholic. A dry drunk who doesn't have the courage to say it out loud,* the voice admonishes.

"Aren't you, though? Haven't you always believed that you and Maggie were meant to be together?"

"But—in case you haven't noticed—we're not. So much for fate."

"It's not over yet."

"It's not that simple."

"Yes," she says as she shifts her position. "Yes, my dear Mr. Hurst, it is."

I'm about to protest further when a man strolls into the room—the husband of Hazel's roommate—and nods in our direction, before bending over his wife, kissing her on the forehead, and settling into the rocking chair.

Before I can say hello, or offer a kind word, or extricate myself from this ridiculous situation, Hazel speaks again, two ticks louder than before.

"When you love someone, it *is* that simple."

From the corner of my eye, I see the man's head jerk up at the sound of her voice. Hazel glances in his direction. That comment, apparently, wasn't meant for my ears only.

"That is all, Mr. Hurst," she sighs while closing her eyes. "For now."

#

Hazel's dismissal reminds me that I should probably check on Ruth Frankenfeld, even though I feel like shit, I'm still trembling, and now I'm sweating like a pig. As I emerge from Hazel's room and turn the corner, I walk directly into Trudie.

"Trudie!" *Jesus!* "What are you doing here?" My goal this morning had been to avoid April and Maggie. Trudie never crossed my mind. We hadn't talked in a week. She had been leaving me messages, and I finally returned them four days ago on my way to the office. I listened to the radio, waited for her to start speaking over the airwaves, and then I dialed her cell phone and left a message. She should be in Rio now.

"It's Aunt Gert. She's—" Trudie sniffles. "—Not doing well."

"I'm so sorry."

"I wanted to stop in before work. In case—"

"Of course, of course," I say, taking her elbow and directing her down the hall. "What about Rio?"

She shakes her head. "The afternoon guy went. I couldn't go. Not now." Her chest heaves, and I pray she doesn't cry. She composes herself and looks up at me. "What are you doing here so early?"

"Finishing up a new client meeting. I thought I'd stop in and see Ruth while I was at it."

We continue walking and soon arrive at room with a placard on the door that reads: "Gertrude Collins" and "Jane Woodstock."

"I've been calling," she whispers, leaning into me.

"Yes. I know. Didn't you receive my message?" I try to avoid looking at her face, but it's hard to do when she's a mere foot away and staring at me intently. Death ray vision, I think, since I can feel her eyes boring into my skull, searching for an explanation for my sudden radio silence.

"Nigel. What's going on?"

This time, I meet her gaze, which is bordering on anger, an emotion I've never seen in her eyes before.

*I'm an alcoholic, Trudie. And I still have feelings for Maggie. I want to have feelings for you, but I don't.*

"Nigel?"

"Nothing is going on."

"Then why the sudden silence? Did I do something wrong? Are you angry with me?"

I gather Trudie in my arms and kiss the top of her head. "No, Trudie. You've done nothing wrong." *Pause.* "Listen. I'll come over tonight."

"Promise?" she asks.

"Promise," I whisper.

She leans into me, not all the way, and I can tell she wants to believe me but doesn't.

#

I finally escape, using Ruth as an excuse, and leave Trudie to her Aunt Gert. It takes forever to get to Ruth's room. When I enter, she looks up, surprised, still eating her breakfast. She wears a purple housecoat that's buttoned up to her throat. She's always complaining of the cold, even when it's eighty degrees out.

"Mr. Hurst," she murmurs while peering at my face. "You look like death warmed over."

"Thanks." I loosen my tie and fall into the chair across from her.

"Well?" she asks. "Did we have an appointment?"

I shake my head, unable to speak. I want her to shut up. Her voice is so goddamn loud. I want a bed. I want to sleep for ten years. I want a drink.

"My dear man. What is wrong with you?"

*I'm an alcoholic. I'm an alcoholic. I'm an alcoholic.*

"I'm ..." I begin.

"Yes?" she asks when I stop.

*What the hell are you doing?* the voice spits. *This is your client!*

Ruth pushes her tray table aside and uses her legs to propel her wheelchair forward, like so many of the residents do. She comes up to me, and her normally stern features morph into puzzlement.

"Are you ill?" she says.

"You could say that."

"Do you need me to call a nurse? An ambulance?"

"Don't think it would do much good."

She leans back in her chair. "Well, what do you want me to do then?"

*There's nothing she can do, man,* the voice sighs.

"There's nothing you can do," I say. "Just something I need to do."

"Hmph." She wheels her chair backwards to its original spot. "Well what are you waiting for? Go do it. And leave me in peace."

What am I waiting for? What am I waiting for?

"Yes, ma'am," I whisper while dragging myself to the door. "I'll do that."

# Chapter 39: April

"Do you get these prickly hairs, too?" Dusty Dubois asks.

I bend over her chin, tweezers in hand, ready to pluck the stiff, gray whiskers growing out of her face and neck. Dusty is eighty-seven years old, always wins the monthly Scrabble tournament, cries herself to sleep at night because the arthritis in her hands and feet hurts so much, and is one of my favorite residents because of her dogged determination to never give up. She has more hair on her chin than her head, and her left eyeball points in an odd direction, forcing me to alternate my focus from one eye to the other. An oxygen tank hangs from the back of her wheelchair, and two thin plastic tubes snake over her earlobes and across her cheeks so they can deliver the life-saving gas to her nostrils.

"Yep," I say. "I have two or three regulars. No matter how many times I pluck them, they always grow back."

"I used to be able to do this myself," she wheezes. Dusty used to smoke two packs of Marlboro Lights a day, too.

"You've earned the right to have someone do it for you. Movie stars in Hollywood pay big bucks to have someone do what I'm doing." I stand and hand her a mirror. "There. I think I got 'em all."

She rubs her fingertips up and down her throat and places the mirror in her lap without even so much as a glance. Instead, she fixes her eyes—well, *eye*—on me. "You're wearing makeup."

"I am."

"Special occasion?"

"Not really. Just trying something different. You're the first person to notice."

"I suspect there's a man behind this."

I blush my answer.

"May I offer a piece of advice?"

"Sure."

"Don't settle for anything less than magic."

I'm not sure what I expected her to say, but this isn't it. "Dusty, how do you know when the magic is real and not some illusion?"

She lifts her hand and crooks a gnarled finger in my direction until I bend down into her face again. I notice a whisker I missed on her jawbone. "When you feel it in here," she rasps, while tapping my forehead, "as well as in here," and this time, she touches my chest, right above my heart.

Over the years, I've often wanted to trade places with the men and women in my care. They were almost done living their lives, for better or worse, and were on the threshold to somewhere else, and that somewhere else—heaven, sleep, nothing—held more allure and promise than the someplace I was stuck in. But today is different. Today, there's a man who loves me and who I love. The magic is real.

I haven't told anyone this. Not even Hugh. He must know how I feel by how I respond to him. Actions are more powerful than words, right? It's not that I don't want to tell him. I'm afraid once I allow the words to escape my lips and float into the universe the inevitable will happen. I'll lose him. That's what happened with the other men I've loved: my father, Jimmy, Vinny, Javier.

I know it's silly to think that my uttering one simple phrase will open a Pandora's box of sorts and bad luck will fall in my midst. I can't take the chance. I'll show it. I'll feel it. I'll do whatever it takes to convince him that I love him. But I won't say it.

It's not as if Hugh has actually said the words to me either. That night when I asked him to love me, I tried to backpedal, but he kissed me before I could and said that it was too late to take back my request because he already did. "Did *what?*" I could have asked, except we both knew what he meant. The word love wasn't necessary. It's better that way. Safer. For both of us.

I give Dusty a kiss on the cheek and wave goodbye as the dinner cart stops in front of her door. Sylvester, one of the aides, smiles as he passes me with a tray of food, and I think of Javier, who used to serenade the residents as he delivered their nightly meals.

Javier's been back for two weeks, working the eleven o'clock to seven a.m. shift, although I'm sure he's waiting for an opening on days or evenings. It'll be only a matter of time before I bump into him. I suspect he must know about Hugh and me since we've become lax in what we say or do at Saint A's, especially in the presence of the aides, many of whom have healthy grapevines. It's not as if Hugh and I make out in the back stairwell or feel each other up in my office, but we are, well, different around each other. Don't human beings release a scent when they're in love? Isn't it true that a person's intuition can tell when mutual attraction is taking place? When I pass the housekeeping crew in the hall, giggles and whispers follow me. Whenever I enter the employee break room, a hush seems to fall over the workers. Even the residents—like Dusty—have noticed a change in me.

Of course, I might be paranoid.

My old friend, guilt, accompanies me on the drive home. I can't remember the last time I left Saint A's without making sure Mom was safely tucked in bed, sleeping. Hugh said he had a surprise for me and that I should come home early, but when I arrive, his car isn't there, and my heart sinks along with the setting sun. Ming Toy greets me as I climb the porch steps and push open the door. The phone rings, and I race to the kitchen to answer it.

"Hello?"

"April, it's me."

"Hi, me." I find myself smiling into the receiver at the sound of his voice.

"There's been a change in plans. I'll be by later."

"Is everything okay?"

"Yes. Everything's fine."

I wait for him to continue, but he doesn't. "Well—" I begin.

"Well," he interjects. "I'll let you go."

I'm sure he doesn't mean it like that, but hearing him say the words *I'll let you go* makes my legs feel amusement-park-ride wobbly. I grip the counter top for support.

"April?"

"Yeah?"

"I'll see you soon, okay?"

"Okay."

"And ..."

"Yes?"

There's a long pause. "I love you."

Doubt slips away with the sound of that one simple sentence. Problem is that he's expecting me to say it back, and I can't. My brain commands my mouth to speak, but my heart won't let my lips move. His disappointment is palpable—alive, even—and I picture it reaching through the phone line and tugging on my tongue.

"Goodbye, April," he whispers.

"Bye," I say as he hangs up.

"You can blame me," Maggie's voice calls out.

I drop the phone, and it hits the tile floor with a thud, as Maggie stands before me.

"You should lock your door," she continues, while placing a brown paper bag on the kitchen table. The smell of Chinese food fills the air.

"What are you doing here? And what do you mean I can blame you?"

"That was Hugh, right?"

"How'd you know that?"

"I asked him to get you here tonight."

"You what? Why would you do that?"

"April, you don't usually embrace seeing me. And the conversation I want to have isn't the kind we can conduct at Saint A's or on the way to a wake."

"So you had Hugh make plans with me and then ..." I shake my head as the pieces fall into place. "So he didn't even have a surprise for me."

"Well, I guess that depends on what you consider me to be."

"You're right. What was I thinking? You certainly are a surprise, Maggie."

She ignores my sarcasm and pulls out the white containers. "You a chopstick girl or do you want a fork?"

"I don't want any of this."

"C'mon, now. I have scallion pancakes. I hear they're your favorite."

"Maggie. Why are you doing this?"

She stops, closes her eyes, and drops her chin to her chest. "Please. Can't we have dinner together and talk?"

Shaking my head but unable to say, "Get the fuck out of my house," I open the silverware drawer and retrieve spoons, forks, and knives. "Don't you ever work?"

"February sweeps is over tomorrow," she says as she reaches for two plates from the cabinet over the sink and sets them on the table. "But we pre-recorded my segment for tonight's show so I could have the evening off."

"Lucky me," I murmur as if I'm supposed to understand what February sweeps means.

She ignores my comment and surveys the table. "There. *Mangia.*"

"Isn't that Italian?" I say, crossing my arms, refusing to sit.

"My Chinese is rusty." She copies my movements, and I can picture Hugh walking in, hours later, finding us in this standoff position. The aroma gets the better of me. I shrug, pull out a chair, and sit. Maggie does the same.

"So what did you want to talk about?" I scoop some fried rice onto my plate and stuff a scallion pancake into my mouth, manners be damned. She sighs, and I suddenly feel sorry for her because I can sense a lifetime of questions in word balloons above her head.

"I don't know."

"You don't know? I thought you had our dinner conversation all planned out."

"But now that I'm here ..." Her eyes wander around the kitchen, and I wonder what she sees—if we see the same things. "What was it like? Growing up in this house?"

"What was it like?" I consider the question. "It was great at times. Sad at others. Like most people's lives, I guess."

"Did you ever wish for a sister or brother?"

"I dunno," I lie. "Maybe."

Finished with her visual tour of the room, she rests her eyes on mine. "Have you had a chance to search through any more stuff or to remember anything? Anything at all that might be a clue as to what happened to Kate when she had me?"

"Why is that so important to you?"

"You just said it."

"What?"

"Why. I need to know why. It's a very basic human need. The questions we can't answer are the ones that haunt us." She leans into the table, picks up her fork, and twirls a lo mein noodle around the shiny silver tines. "Maybe I'm tired of being haunted."

She's right about the haunting, even though I'd never thought of it that way. *Why* did Jimmy and Vinny have to die? *Why* didn't Mom tell me about Maggie? *Why* did Javier lie to me? *Why* is it so hard to say "I love you" to Hugh?

"So," Maggie presses. "Have you remembered anything? Found anything?"

The answer is I hadn't until I told Hugh about how I found Dad's suicide note. Maybe there's an answer to another "why" still hidden up in the attic.

"If you want," I hear myself say, "we can go in the attic and look through some of the photo albums and stuff up there."

Maggie nods. "Yeah?"

"Sure."

We bring the Chinese food containers with us, and I uncork a bottle of red wine that a resident's family gave me a long time ago. I'm not sure how long we pore over the albums. Most of them document my life—baby pictures, Halloween costumes, my childhood bedroom that looks as if someone had thrown up red and pink all over the place when in reality it was supposed to represent all things Strawberry Shortcake, which was *the* doll to have during the late '70s and early '80s.

Maggie asks questions, and I answer them all in more detail than I thought possible. I don't know if it's the wine or the fact I'm talking about something I know so well—my life—or if Maggie has a special talent for making her interview subjects feel comfortable. I tell her about Dad's suicide note, and we carefully tear back the covers of each album, but find nothing.

"What time is it?" I finally yawn.

Maggie squints at her watch under the lone light bulb above our heads.

"Almost midnight." She yawns, too. "I probably should get going. Thanks, April, for sharing these pictures with me. I feel like I know you better. Kate, too."

"I did all the talking. You might know me, but I don't know much about you."

"Well, then," she says. "I guess we'll have to do this again. At my place. Look at my pictures."

With her words, I feel something indescribable—a charge. Maybe even a connection. We descend the stairs in silence and gather her things, and I lead her to the front door, wish her good night, and watch her drive away just as the phone rings. I run to the kitchen to answer it.

"Hello?"

"April. It's me."

"Hugh, where are you?"

"Home."

I nod to the receiver. "Oh."

"I drove by your place a few times, but I saw Maggie's car in the driveway. I wanted to give you both time together." When I don't say anything, he continues. "Are you angry with me for setting this up?"

I shake my head. "No. I'm not angry."

"Maybe it would be best—"

"Yes?"

"—if I stayed here tonight. I need to go through the mail anyway. Tomorrow's the first of the month. I should pay bills. Take care of some things."

I cover my mouth, trying to stifle the cry lodged in my throat. "Okay, no problem," I try to say, but it sounds more like a one-syllable squeak: "—*kay*."

"April," he breathes. "I'll see you tomorrow. Right?"

"Right."

"Good night."

"Night."

We hang up, and I try not to focus on the unsaid. Maybe it doesn't matter whether I think the word, say it, or scream it from the rooftops. Maybe what matters is that when I feel it, I shouldn't. Maybe I should grow up, get a grip, and leave Hugh Dooley alone to be with his dying wife. Maybe this is all for the best.

But as I sink to the floor in sobs, I know that I don't believe it.

# *March*

# *Chapter 40: Hugh*

When Adrienne married, her grandfather gave her away. No one thought this especially unusual since Dr. Borowski was much admired in the community, adored Adrienne, and was in failing health. Still, a piece of me died when I watched my Pana walk down the aisle in her ivory dress, while holding onto an arm that should have been mine.

That day, my body felt like one large pus-filled wound. Alcohol became the salve. Most people knew about Gloria's "problem" with liquor, even though she believed she hid it well. I, however, had witnessed our friends' eyes looking away, embarrassed, when this brilliant professor would slur her words at two o'clock in the afternoon. I heard the understanding in their voices when I would call to cancel plans—birthday parties, cookouts, weddings—because Gloria "was not feeling well." I was the one who cleaned her up, sobered her up, only to go through it all over again. In the early years, I tried to shield Pana from Gloria's excesses, but you can only hide so much from a smart, intuitive little girl. You would think Adrienne would remember this, but her memory, sadly, begins when she's thirteen, after discovering my affair with Kendra Jackson. She blamed me for her mother's increased drinking then, and again two summers later when everything went to hell.

Ideals, such as Truth, are useless in reality. The Truth would not have saved me; it would not have set me free. Instead, it would have caused a young girl to hate her father *and* her mother. I didn't see the sense in that. Still don't.

Gloria, of course, held her liquor better than I did, and she did her best to take care of me on Adrienne's wedding day, shadowing me, running interference with people—like her father—who might trigger something inside of me, and making sure my wine or champagne glass was never empty.

We made love that night—I'm still not able to think of it as merely intercourse—although all I remember of the event is waking up next to Gloria in the early morning sunlight, a soft summer breeze billowing the white curtains toward our bed, where we lay naked. Even then I knew it would be the last time. Despite the crushing pain in my head, I forced myself to focus on her body—the rounded curve of her hip, the birthmark above her navel, the mounds of flesh on her chest, ample and ripe, though not as firm as they had been over two decades ago. Whose body was this? I didn't know. It had never belonged to me.

We didn't discuss my move later that day into the guest room on the first floor, but something odd happened after I entered my new quarters: everything improved. We had stimulating conversations over breakfast, dinner, afternoon coffee, and tea, much like the ones we had when I first met her on campus, a quarter century earlier. She drank less, or so it seemed, or maybe my sleeping in a different bed gave my nostrils a break from the stale boozy smell that emanated from her pores. We hosted dinners, attended others, took in plays in town and films at the local art house. We were what we had always been, even during the worst years of our marriage: best friends.

I didn't see Pana much during that time. She visited when she knew I was in class, and she invited us over to the house as a pair only when she knew she wouldn't be able to explain our absence at important events, such as my grandson CJ's christening. I sensed that she didn't tell anyone our secret except to Chris, her husband, who avoided talking to me and always redirected little Christopher Junior away from my grasp. Gloria would hold my hand tight during those times—showing her solidarity to me, which drove Adrienne insane. It was Gloria's own way of telling me thank you. I always squeezed her hand back because I needed that. She was the only family I had left.

I never expected in Gloria's final days on this earth that I would fall in love with another woman—a woman twenty-three years my junior and only a couple years older than Adrienne. I never expected how hard it would be to fall asleep alone again when I had been sleeping with April for only two months. I never expected how frightened I'd be at the thought of losing her, but then it occurred to me that this experience was new; I had never lost before because Gloria was never mine to begin with.

#

I drive to April's house the next morning at a quarter to eight, but her car is gone. My heart beats with worry, but my brain reasons that she must already be at work because where else could she be. Who knows? Maybe she couldn't sleep either.

My muscles relax when I spot her car in the parking lot at Saint A's. I strum the steering wheel impatiently, knowing the lobby doors are locked until eight a.m., and I stare at the orange digital numbers on the dashboard, willing them to speed up. The morning receptionist lumbers across the pavement on her bad knee, and I jump out of the car and dash across the lot, causing the poor old woman to jump.

"Mr. Dooley!"

"Sorry. Didn't mean to scare you. Thought you could let me in."

"Everything okay?"

"Oh, yes, fine. Couldn't sleep, that's all. Got an early start to the day."

She swipes a card in front of a keypad on the brick wall, and the electronic doors to the building slide open. I head down the hall and turn the corner to the activities room, where I hear voices—April's and someone else, a man, I think. I listen outside the main door to the large cafeteria-sized room, her office on the far end. But the voices stop, so I look, and then I see why: a man—one of the aides, I assume, by the way he's dressed in blue scrubs—has his hands on her face, pressing his lips to hers.

I don't watch, but it doesn't matter because it's all I can picture as I turn around, nearly knocking over a bookcase filled with paperback romances, and gallop down the hall and out of the building, get in my car, and drive off.

I don't know where I'm going. The truth is I never have.

# *Chapter 41: April*

Pink assessment sheets for five new residents cover my desk, but instead of doing my work, I turn to the list I've made of reasons why my little affair with Hugh should end. I've decided to keep it in my back pocket, hoping the logic will seep into my skin, my bloodstream, and, eventually, my heart.

*He's married.*

*His wife is dying.*

*He's twenty-three years older than me.*

*I still want children.*

*He had an affair.*

*I could lose my job.*

*It could cause problems for Saint A's.*

Somehow, though, none of these reasons appears strong enough to counteract what I feel for him. How did I let this happen? How did I get into an impossible situation yet again?

"Good morning, *namorada*."

I jump at his voice, a voice I haven't heard in almost two years. "Javier!"

"You work early today. Or maybe you come to see me?" He looks thinner than I remember but is still just as handsome, with strong arms and smooth caramel skin.

"No. I'm working early. What are you doing here?"

"I walk by and see light. I come to see if you are here."

I fold my list and slip it into my pocket. "I'm busy. Lots of paper work."

He smiles that sexy lopsided smile that won me over so long ago. His five o'clock shadow is showing, even though I remember the stubble would seemingly appear within hours after he shaved, leaving my face wonderfully raw and red whenever we kissed.

"*Namorada*, no hug? No kiss? It has been a long time."

I look past the thick wavy black hair, the bedroom eyes, and the mouth that whispers *sweetheart* in Portuguese to the little shit of a man who lied to me about the wife and children he had back home. At least Hugh's been straight with me.

"And why has it been such a long time, Javier?" I get up, gather the assessments in my hand, and tuck a pen behind my ear. "Because you had to go home. To. Your. Wife."

"No more," he whispers.

I shake my head, reach for his left hand, and lift it up to his face. "Do you really think I'm that blind?" My finger circles the almost indiscernible tan line around his ring finger where his wedding band was, no doubt, for the last twenty months. I'm proud of my chutzpah, wishing there was someone around to witness me being so strong and witty. I'm so caught up in my proud moment, that I don't react in time when he shakes off my hand, grabs my face, and kisses me—hard—on the lips, trying to force his tongue into my mouth.

I push him away. "What the fuck was that?"

"A kiss. For my *namorada*."

"No. That noise. I heard something." I push him away, walk into the activities room, and look toward the door that leads to the hallway. It's empty. Javier comes up behind me and loops his arms around my waist.

"No, no, no!" I wriggle free and face him. "Javier, it's over. Do you understand? *Oh-ver*. It was over a long time ago when you lied about your wife and kids. What do you think? You can walk back into my life after all that's happened? That's not the way it works here. That's not the way it works anywhere."

He scowls, nods, and shoves his hands in his pockets. When he looks up, I'm not sure what I see in his eyes.

"I am sorry."

"That's fine," I say. "But it doesn't change the way things are."

#

*The way things are,* I think after he leaves. *The way things are.* I pull the list from my back pocket. Despite the way things are, all I can think about is being with Hugh. Crumpling the paper, I toss it into the wastebasket, gather the assessment sheets, walk across the room toward the hall, and pray with every ounce of my being that's what he wants, too.

# Chapter 42: Maggie

"You're early," Serena says when she finds me sitting on her office couch with my coat still on. "Or you spent the night here again. Which is it?"

"Just got here. Couldn't sleep."

"Everything okay?"

"Yep."

"That the truth?"

"Nope."

"Want to talk about it?"

"Nope."

Serena shrugs out of her coat and flops into her chair. "Okay, then." She begins her morning routine of checking e-mail and voice messages.

"I had dinner with April last night."

"And?"

"And ..." I stop because the damn tears surprise me. "It was great," I whisper and sniffle.

Serena swivels and looks at me. "Um, yeah. That sounds convincing."

"No, really. It was. I don't know why I'm getting so emotional about it." I wipe away a tear. "I guess I wasn't sure we'd ever get to this point."

"What point is that?"

"Where we could sit and talk about things. Laugh even. We practically spent the whole night in her attic looking at old photo albums." I shake my head. "She's finally letting me in, Serena."

"I told you it would happen. I knew your charming ways would win her over eventually."

"Charming ways? That's not how you normally refer to them."

Serena grins. "Hey, you never told me what happened with you and your British muse."

I take a deep breath. "Nothing happened."

"Nothing?"

"Nope."

"Did you tell him about the project that night he came over?"

"No."

"Why not?"

"It's not what he came over to talk about."

"Well, what did he come over to talk about?"

"That's not for discussing either."

"But he's your muse. What happened to your last at-bat?"

"I struck out."

"How? I mean, he came to see you. He must be interested."

"Serena, it's not that simple. Nigel and I were very young when we were together. He's still interested in that person. Not the person I am today. The woman I've become."

Serena wrinkles her nose. "Which version do you like better?"

"What?"

"Which version of yourself do you like better?"

I gaze up at the ceiling tiles that I've come to know so well over the last several months. "This one. I guess."

"Why?"

"The young me was naïve. Idealistic as well but too naïve. This version of me has lived. Has seen the world. Has recently come clean about everything. She's not hiding from herself anymore. She accepts herself, mostly. Warts and all."

"Eww. Too much information. Didn't know you had any warts."

We both laugh, and Serena returns to her keyboard while I commune with the ceiling.

"Only problem is ..." I begin.

"Yeah?"

"Both versions still love Nigel Hurst."

She swivels slowly in her chair and faces me. "But are you in love with the man you remember or the person he is today?"

I think about this. I think about his smile and the way he looks at Max—his love for children even more apparent than it was decades ago. His sense of humor is just as witty, and his love for me—well, up until a few days ago—was just as simple and pure. Has he changed? Grown? Of course. Is he the same man that he was when I was in college and he was in law school? Of course not. I loved the man back then, but I could love today's version even better, if given the chance, I think. A chance, I remind myself, that is clearly not going to happen.

I've never been an overly religious person, but I've lived long enough to note the giving and taking that God does is seldom arbitrary when examined closely. I might not have Nigel, but it's not because of secrets anymore. It's because of the truth. Instead, I have a sister and the chance for a relationship so rich and deep that I can't wait to see April again and continue on this journey. I have my documentary—this baby of sorts—that has been germinating in my womb since I was ten years old, from the time I held my first movie camera. What is it that Hazel always says? "*What will be, will be.*" Maybe she's right.

"I love both," I murmur.

"Well, if you can love both, there's no reason why he can't learn to do the same. Someday, maybe."

*Someday, maybe. Someday, maybe.*

"Serena?" I say while grabbing my project folder from my briefcase and scribbling down the phrase.

"Yeah?"

"I think you just came up with the working title for our documentary."

# Chapter 43: Nigel

As an attorney—especially one who handles estate planning—I've become privy to my clients' secrets. Due to ethics and attorney-client privileges, I'm required by my profession to keep these secrets and revelations confidential. This has never been difficult for me, but I have found on more than one occasion that when a client reveals a secret to me a change occurs. Sometimes it's an obvious physical reaction—worry lines disappear, shoulder tension dissipates, smiles come more easily. Other times, it's as if peace settles over the person like mist—gentle, almost imperceptible.

Theories exist that the most debilitating part of having a secret is that people so often feel alone in their burden. Often the sheer act of simply sharing it with another human soul is enough to trigger the healing process, to make what might have felt like the most miserable guilt in the universe nothing more than a blip on life's radar.

Last night as I stood shaking at the podium, convinced there was no way in hell I could utter the phrase that I had come to say, I thought of Maggie and her secret from so long ago about losing our child. Had she finally found some peace in her admission to me, despite my harsh response? Did I want her to have peace? As I looked out at the men and women in the crowd, their eyes fixed on me with understanding and encouragement, I realized that I wanted Maggie to have peace. That *I* wanted peace and the chance to begin healing, finally.

#

"So," Trudie begins.

"So," I say while looking up from the newspaper I've been staring at for the last fifteen minutes.

"You were late last night."

"I know." Pause. "I'm sorry." *Tell her,* the voice urges. *You finally told a room full of strangers "Hello, my name is Nigel, and I'm an alcoholic." So tell her where you were.*

"Why'd you even bother coming over?"

"Because I said I would." I think back to our encounter at Saint A's yesterday morning even though it feels like a lifetime ago. "I didn't want to break my promise."

"I see. So where were you?"

"I was at a meeting."

"Until midnight?"

I swallow. "It was a long meeting."

She nibbles on half a bagel and points the other half at the bowl in front of me. "Cereal's getting soggy."

"Right." I shove a spoonful of granola-crunchy flakes into my mouth.

"So anyone I know at this meeting?"

"Pardon?" I say with my mouth full.

"Was there anyone I would know at this meeting?" Her normally happy voice has an obvious edge to it.

"I don't think so. Why do you ask?"

"Because you called out another woman's name in your sleep last night."

"I did?" *What did I say?* "How do you know you weren't the one dreaming?"

"Could be, could be." She tries to chuckle, but I can tell she's faking it. "Funny, though, the name you said is a name we both know."

"Oh?"

"Yep. It was Maggie."

"Maggie?"

"And the only Maggie I know who I know *you* somehow know is Maggie Prescott."

I spoon more cereal in my mouth and watch as she continues to spread what looks to be three inches of cream cheese onto her bagel. Her hand shakes, and she throws down the knife. It makes a clanking sound against her plate.

"Dammit, Nigel, tell me the truth. Please. Tell me."

I raise my eyebrows, hoping to look innocent. "About what?"

She shakes her head and considers my face as if it's the first time she's ever looked at it. "About whatever is going on."

"Nothing," I say quite confidently because it's the truth, "is going on."

"Then tell me what went on. Because there's something you're not telling me. If my gut is right—and it usually is—something is going on. And that something has to do with Maggie Prescott."

"Why do you say that?"

"Why? You want to know why? I'll tell you why. Any time her name comes up, you act strange. Like the first time I mentioned the two of us went to the same college. Or how 'bout when I go to surprise you on New Year's Eve and I find you dancing with her? *Oh, no*, I tried telling myself, *they're only trying to entertain the crowd. Two friendly people, that's all.*" Trudie stops, wipes her right eye, and catches her breath. "And then you're crying out the name 'Maggie' in your sleep. You know, I might not be as smart as you. I might be some dumb radio girl, but even I can see that there's a connection. And then there's the way you've been acting. Backing out on our trip. Not calling me. Coming in late from a so-called 'meeting' smelling like cigarettes and God knows what else. Nigel, we're adults, not kids. One of the reasons why I'm single is because of the games that men insist on playing. I love you, Nigel. I really do. But I'm forty-two, and I'm too old for this shit."

"You're not old," I try to joke as I reach for her hand, but she leans back in the chair and crosses her arms. "Right," I sigh.

"Right, what?"

"You're right." When I notice her chin begin to quiver, I quickly continue. "I knew Maggie. A long time ago."

"Knew?"

"We were lovers."

"Were?"

"Yes, were. We're not now. Haven't been in a long time. Since law school."

She uncrosses her arms and leans into the table. I can see down the front of her scarlet silk bathrobe to the bare skin above her breasts. "Why didn't you tell me?"

"I don't know. I tried. Not very hard, but I did."

I feel her eyes on me, but I don't have the heart to look into them. Instead, I watch the remaining flakes drown in the pool of milk.

"Nigel. What I said a minute ago. I meant it. I've fallen in love with you."

"I know it, Trudie. And the truth is I want ..." I stop, unable to go on.

"Yes?"

"The meeting last night ..." *God, why can't I tell her? Isn't sharing the ugliest part of yourself something that you should be able to do with someone who loves you? Who can forgive you and understand your secrets?* I look up but can't seem to focus.

"Do you love me?" she whispers.

"Trudie ..." I reach for her hand, but she pulls away.

"It's a simple question."

"I want to love you, Trudie. But—"

"But," she finishes for me. "You don't."

My silence is confirmation, broken only by the sound of her sobs. I again reach across the table for her hand.

"No. Please go. Leave me alone."

"Trudie. I—"

"Go," she wails. "I'm fine. I'll be fine." Her face crumples as she whispers, "I've always been just fine."

# Chapter 44: April

Joelle pushes open my office door where I've been hiding all morning trying to catch up on paperwork and trying to forget what happened with Javier earlier. Joelle and I have been avoiding each other lately. I suspect she knows about Hugh and me and doesn't approve.

"April," she says. "Just wanted to check on you. Figured you might be upset."

*Had she seen Javier and me? Is that the noise I heard?* "About what?"

"Hazel."

My stomach drops. "What about Hazel?"

"They took her out early last night."

"Is she okay?" I shuffle through papers on my desk, looking for the daily census that would have alerted me to this fact.

"She's stable. She's coming back later this morning."

"Thank God."

Joelle casts her eyes downward and shifts from one black three-inch pump to the other. I know she has something else on her mind. Hugh, Javier, something.

"What is it, Joelle? Spill it."

She raises her eyes until they meet mine, and in them is what I've seen a million times before when she's comforting the families of dying residents. "April. Her organs are failing. She doesn't have much time left. You need to prepare yourself."

"What are you talking about? I saw her yesterday. The day before that. She's fine. She looks fine."

"No, April, she doesn't. And you know it. Although you've been wrapped up in other things lately, haven't you?" Joelle shakes her head and holds up her hands. "I'm sorry. That was uncalled for. At some point we'll need to discuss *that,* but I'm not prepared to go there right now because the less I know, the less I'll ever have to deny. But you need to face the truth about Hazel. She's an old woman, and she's dying. They're sending her home to die."

I gulp air into my lungs and muffle a cry. The tears come anyway.

Joelle's face softens. "April, everyone agrees that she's not going to bounce back this time. Even Hazel."

"No one knows that for sure. You don't. I don't—"

"Don't you, though?" Joelle reaches out and places her hand on my arm. "And doesn't she?"

#

I race to Hazel's room, desperately hoping I'll find Hugh, but the only person there is Gloria in all her lifeless splendor. I lean over the cool metal bars of Gloria's bed. I know her outer shell has suffered—bruised by disease and alcohol and the general wear and tear of life—and masks the beautiful woman I have no doubt she once was. I want to see her eyes. No, I need to see them. To look into them. I need her to know I'm so sorry for everything. I reach out my hand to her face, and my fingertips graze her eyelid.

"Hello."

I jump, draw back my hand, and turn my head. It's Adrienne. "Just pushing the hair back from her face," I say.

Adrienne considers my statement, and I can't decide if she looks concerned or suspicious. *It's all in your imagination,* I tell myself. *How could she know?* I try not to stare at her, but it's hard because she is a stunning woman. Her black hair is pulled back in a long glossy ponytail and a few wispy bangs frame her porcelain skin. Her eyes, which are fringed in the longest black lashes I've ever seen, look bluer than I remember, but that might have something to do with the deep indigo sweater poking out of the top of her floor-length black coat. Next to her, I look like a child—she has to be at least six inches taller than me. Willowy. That's how I'd describe her. Willowy.

"It's April, right?" she says.

"Yes."

"Well, April, I don't suppose you've seen my father, have you?"

"Not today."

"I see."

"Is there a message or something I can tell him?"

She walks to the other side of the bed and waves her hand in my direction as if to say, "Be gone!" I don't know if it's fatigue or angst or what, but her dismissive gesture pisses me off. She bends over her mother and inspects her face. My anger flares. Why does she insist on causing Hugh so much pain?

"You know," I begin slowly, "your dad really cares about you. Loves you." At first, I don't think she's heard me, since she doesn't move, doesn't even twitch. Finally, she raises her eyes and smiles a smile that tells me she knows something.

"Seems to me a person shouldn't speak about something she doesn't know."

"But I do know. He told me."

The smile disappears and in its place is confusion. "He told you what?"

"You know."

"No," she says. "I don't know. Why don't you tell me?"

"He told me about what happened," I mumble. "When you were a kid."

"Sorry. I'll need more than that."

I roll my eyes. "About the grad student."

"The who?"

"The grad student," I say louder.

She smiles triumphantly. "Oh, you mean Kendra Jackson?"

"Yes."

"Of course, he told you about Kendra!" She drops her head back and laughs. "Well," she says while holding my gaze. "Next time you see him, have him tell you about Winnie."

"Winnie?" I think I might vomit.

"My best friend." She watches me. "I stopped counting after that."

I hear the EMTs and the clank of the stretcher before they even enter the door. Two men cloaked in navy uniforms transfer Hazel to her bed. The whole time, I feel Adrienne's eyes on my back.

"April, my dear," Hazel whispers, holding out a gaunt, trembling arm. "I made them bring me back."

"Hazel," I say, trying hard to compose myself for her sake. "Who do you think you are, going to the hospital on the one night I leave early?" I smile wide, the sort of fake smile you wear when someone tells you to be in a picture and you don't want to do it. As I pull up the rocking chair to Hazel's bed and grip her bony hand in mine, Adrienne slips out of the room without so much as a hello to Hazel or goodbye to me.

"I know, my dear, and I am sorry. But enough of that. Tell me. How was your evening with Maggie?"

I raise an eyebrow. "You were in on that?"

She smiles and attempts to squeeze my fingers. "It was my idea."

"I should have known."

"Well, how was it?"

I think back to last night, which seems so long ago, even though it was a mere twelve hours. "It was fine. I wasn't too happy about her barging in on me at first, but then we started talking and drinking some wine—"

"Ah, yes." Hazel smiles and closes her eyes.

"And it was good."

"I am glad." She lets go of my hand and places it on her chest. I watch her breathe for a while, thinking she's fallen asleep, when she opens her eyes. "Where is Mr. Dooley?"

"I don't know."

She turns her head so she's facing me. Her face appears so small and pale next to the blue pillowcase. "Is everything okay?"

"I don't know," I whisper.

"He is a good man, my dear."

"Is he? How do you know for sure? How do we know for sure about anyone?"

She smiles again, searches for my hand that is hidden in the folds of her blanket and pats it. "Trust me. And trust your heart."

I try to smile as convincing a smile as I can manage. The last thing Hazel needs in her last days, last hours, is to worry about me.

"April, my dear?"

"Yes?"

"When the time comes—"

"Hazel, don't talk like that. You're going to be—"

"Hush, hush, my dear. Listen."

I turn over the palm of my right hand so it's hugging hers, and we lace our fingers together.

"When the time comes," she continues, "you will need to do a few things for me."

"Anything. You name it. Tell me, and I'll take care of anything you want."

"The house in Wellesley is on the market. When it is sold, whatever is left after taxes and attorney fees and whatnot will go here."

"*Here*?"

"Yes. To the activities department of Saint Anthony of Padua Healthcare Center."

"Hazel! I don't know what to say. Why?"

"Because, my dear, you have been so good to me. You are the shining star in this place. You are the one who has put it on the map. With your love and thoughtfulness and effort. Everything you do, and not only for me, but for everyone."

"C'mon. I'm not—"

She releases my hand and holds up her own. "You will be able to do all the things you have talked about over the years. More outings. New handicap vehicles. A new patio—"

"With a hot tub, of course," Maggie's voice interrupts. "That's what we were talking about last night. Right, April?"

Maggie is at my side, awaiting an answer to her question. I clear my throat and pick up on her line. "That's right. We'll call it the Hazel Hot Tub."

"Hmm," Maggie says. "That could make an interesting feature on *New England Journal*."

I glance up at Maggie and she gives me a comforting "everything's going to be okay" smile. "Well," I say. "I'll leave you two to talk."

"April," Hazel whispers as I get up.

"Yes?"

"Remember what I said before."

"I will." I bend over her body and kiss her on the forehead, not knowing if this will be the last time.

"Go now," she says. "All will be okay."

\#

I manage to make it through the crowded hallway with the lunch carts and the residents heading into the dining room and the lingering residents in the activities room fighting over who gets to name the most recent addition to the fish tank Heather has set up. I enter my office, close the door, and silently pray I can avoid a complete meltdown at work when someone—or something—bangs at my door.

"Yes?" I ask impatiently. "What is it?"

The door nudges open, and there stands Mom in a bright red sweat suit with a coffee stain down the middle. Heather must have brought her down for morning coffee social again, or maybe Maggie did before she stopped by Hazel's room. It's all I can do not to scream because this is exactly what I need right now: my mother. And here she is. Except she's not.

"Mom," I whisper and I hold out my arms. She looks at them tentatively, and it almost seems as if she's trying hard to remember what she's supposed to do, when she finally takes the three short steps toward me. I loop my arms around her waist, pull her close, and rest my head on her belly. Her body is stiff and unsure, and she keeps her arms by her side, but it doesn't matter; I hug her enough for both of us and pretend she's really there.

# *Chapter 45: Hugh*

When Adrienne announced she had selected Saint Anthony of Padua Healthcare Center as Gloria's rehab facility even though everyone, including Gloria's doctors, knew there was no hope for rehabilitation, I realized how out of touch with reality Pana had become.

"You did this to her," she'd said after we moved Gloria into her room and we stood over the hospital bed staring at Gloria's lifeless body. I didn't bother responding or objecting or screaming or yelling. There was no point. Still, it hurts. It hurts every time she looks at me with such suspicion and hatred. It hurts to know how strong our bond once was—father and daughter—and to have watched it disintegrate into nothing but colorless fraying threads.

#

I sit on April's front steps, the front door locked, the porch light on, shivering as night falls. I have no idea when she'll be home, if she'll be home, or if she'll even be alone, but I have nowhere else to go. Everything is in Adrienne's name now—or will be, once Gloria dies: the small condo that Gloria and I bought eight years ago after we sold the house, the summer home on the Cape, even the car that I drive. Years ago, when I realized what Adrienne was doing and the pull she had on her mother, I decided to be proactive rather than reactive. Slowly, I started funneling money to a separate bank account that no one knew about. Not much at first and nothing that would arouse suspicion. Gloria must have known about it at some point, but she never questioned me, and I can only assume she covered for me if Adrienne ever questioned her. Today, there's a healthy amount—not enough to live on forever, but enough to get my own car and place until retirement savings kick in. I can still teach. I have colleagues throughout the country and offers to teach, even as an adjunct. The one thing Adrienne was never able to destroy was my reputation as a professor. Late at night, I hold onto that. *If she hated me to the core of her being,* I reason, *she would have tried to take that away, too.* Funny what form hope takes in the nighttime shadows.

#

April pulls into the driveway, gets out of the car, and slams the door. She marches up the steps to where I stand, pushes past me, and fumbles with her keys.

"You locked your door," I say.

"Yeah. My sister said it would be a good idea." Her eyes meet mine. "I think she's right. Keeps the trouble out."

I reach for her arm. "April, I saw you this morning—"

"Tell me, Hugh. Has everything been a lie?"

"What?"

"Or only certain parts?"

"April, what are you talking about?"

"You must think I'm stupid. And you know, you're probably right. But just because I'm not the brightest bulb on the tree doesn't mean you have the right to lie to me."

"I didn't lie to you."

"Oh, we're going to get technical now, are we? Okay. Maybe lie is the wrong word. But leaving out big chunks of the truth is just as bad as lying in my book." She gives up on finding the key and crosses her arms.

"Maybe we should go inside."

"Why? So you can avoid telling me the truth some more?"

"Dammit, April, you know the truth."

"Why'd you come back here?"

"What?"

"Why bother? Why not move on to the next one."

"The next one *what*? April, you're not making any sense."

"You told me that you had one affair. One."

"That's right."

"Not according to your daughter."

"Oh," I say as everything starts to make sense. "You spoke with Adrienne."

"Yeah, I spoke with Adrienne. She told me to ask you about someone. Winnie, I think it was. You know, her best friend."

Hearing Winnie's name knocks me off balance, and I grab the porch railing to right myself. Concern washes over April's face. At least the hate hasn't taken root in her. Yet.

"How many have there been, Hugh?" Tears spring to her eyes. "Why didn't you tell me?"

I turn away from her, sit on the top step, and blow into my cold hands. "I did tell you. There's only been one."

"Then who is Winnie?"

The answer to that question should begin like this: *Winnie is* ... The problem occurs with what follows the word "is." Winnie is so many things. Winnie is symbolic, forever a reminder of my sham of a marriage. Winnie is the source of Adrienne's hatred. Winnie is dead.

April sits next to me, drawing her legs to her chest and wrapping her arms around her knees. "Tell me the truth. I want to know. I deserve to know."

"The truth is that I've come close to telling you several times."

"Okay. Tell me now. Adrienne said Winnie was her best friend."

"She was. At least, during the summer months. We summered on the Cape in my father-in-law's home. Winnie and her family summered there, too, in a house down the street. They met when Adrienne was eight or nine. Winnie was a year older, and probably five years wiser on top of that, something Adrienne loved." I pause and blow into my hands again. "I was never thrilled with the friendship, but Gloria reminded me that it would be okay since it was only for two months out of the year. Winnie lived in California, and even with regular pen-pal correspondence there was only so much influence Winnie could have from three thousand miles away."

April shivers next to me, and all I want to do is wrap my arms around her. I resist the temptation.

"Hugh, you and Winnie? You didn't. Did you?"

I ignore her question and continue with the story. "It happened when Adrienne was fifteen. That summer when Winnie arrived, she had changed. She was nearly six feet tall, track-star skinny, and had a buzz cut, which was quite a shock considering she and Adrienne had been so proud of their long hair that they had only twelve months earlier. Winnie didn't look sixteen, nor did she act it. I know they did drugs that summer—pot and who knows what else—and they started hanging around with a crowd that discussed topics Adrienne found alluring, such as poetry and philosophy and sexuality. 'It's a phase,' Gloria had said when I voiced my concerns to her. 'Only a phase. Remember how we were when we were young? All the late-night discussions?' I did remember, although I remembered that happening in college, not high school."

"So what happened?"

"What happened is it all got out of hand. All of it. The drugs. The subjects of their conversations. The sex." I take a deep breath. "Winnie committed suicide in our basement in August, right before we were getting ready to go back home."

April gasps. "She killed herself? Over you?"

"No, April," I say, shaking my head because, like Adrienne, she has it all wrong. "Winnie killed herself over Gloria."

My eyes meet hers, and her anger morphs into confusion. "What?" she whispers in a voice so low I have to strain to hear it. "Hugh. What are you saying? That Gloria is—"

"Yes. That's precisely what I'm saying."

"I don't understand. Gloria and Winnie had an affair? But you're married. You have Adrienne."

"April, I'm not the first person in the world to have a closeted gay spouse. And, unfortunately, I doubt I'll be the last."

"I still don't understand. Why does Adrienne hate you? Wouldn't she hate Gloria?"

I have often wondered what it would be like to tell someone the truth about what happened, the choices I've made, how I've lived my life. Would it be a relief? Would I feel vindicated? Would it fix everything?

"Adrienne doesn't know."

"How can she not know? You just told me that Winnie killed herself over Gloria and—"

"She doesn't know because I didn't want her to know. April, she never forgave me for Kendra. Our relationship had been strained for two years already. I couldn't stand the thought of collapsing her world even further."

"What about—"

"Besides," I interrupt, as the memories flood my brain, "I didn't have much choice."

#

Adrienne's screams had propelled me down the basement steps, two at a time, three at a time. I found her cradling Winnie in her arms, blood everywhere, Winnie's wrists limp on the floor, a razor blade by her side. I pawed Winnie's neck, searching for a pulse, a small throbbing bead signifying life, but I knew I wouldn't find it no matter how long I searched. By now, Gloria had roused herself from the bed on the second floor, coming to investigate Adrienne's screams.

"What is it? Hugh? Adrienne?" With each word, I could hear her sobering up. Gloria stumbled down the basement steps. "My God!" she cried. "No! Oh my God, no!"

I locked eyes with hers and shook my head, that one simple gesture a silent death announcement for a sixteen-year-old girl. I hadn't noticed Adrienne's movements until I heard the rustle of paper. I turned and saw my Pana, her face paler than it had been a millisecond before, holding a simple sheet of notebook paper. Her mouth slightly open, tears streaming down her cheeks, she read the words and shot me an accusatory look that I would come to know so well for the next fifteen years. The letter dropped from her hands, almost falling into a pool of blood. I snatched it up before it hit the floor and read it. It began, "You said you loved me, but now you leave. After I gave everything to you." By this time, Gloria was at my side, peering over my shoulder. Her hand flew up to her mouth. "My God," she murmured. "No."

Adrienne was on her feet, walking backwards toward the stairs.

"Adrienne," I said. "Wait! This is not what you think. I didn't. It's not me. It's got to be some mistake. I—" It wasn't a word that interrupted me, but rather a movement: Gloria's hand on my arm, digging her nails in so deep she broke the skin.

"Adrienne," she whispered. "It's okay. Come here, baby. It's okay." Gloria pushed past me and gathered Pana into her arms and the two of them fell to the floor, Adrienne convulsing in sobs.

"How could he? How could he? She was my friend. My *best* friend. She killed herself. Over him."

Gloria shushed her and pushed Adrienne's face into her chest. She leaned down and kissed the top of Pana's head, her eyes lifting slowly, focusing on me. I stood there, confused, paralyzed.

"Darling," she said, and I wasn't sure whom she was addressing. "We need to call the police, but before we do that, we need to do something else. I need you to agree to something else."

Adrienne stifled a sob, while pulling away from her mother. "What?"

"We need to destroy that letter."

"What?" Adrienne barely got the word out. I said nothing, convinced this was a nightmare and that I'd be waking up soon.

"That letter will ruin our lives."

Adrienne snapped free from her mother's grasp and scrambled to her feet. "How can you defend him? You always defend him. Like two years ago when he was fucking one of his students."

Gloria was on her feet. I couldn't remember the last time she moved so quickly without falling over. She took Adrienne by the shoulders, shaking her.

"Adrienne, listen to me," she hissed. "We can't bring Winnie back. This letter will do nothing but hurt you more in the long run. And me. And Daddy."

"But why? People should know the truth. The reason why. They should know why she did it."

"She's under age, don't you see? There could be trouble. Lots of trouble."

"Gloria!" I bellowed, realizing that even in a nightmare I couldn't let her go on like this.

"Shut up!" Adrienne exploded. She pointed an accusatory finger in my direction. "You don't have the right to say anything."

Gloria gently took Pana's face in her hands, directing it toward her own. "Listen to me. It's awful now, but it will get better. I promise. But we need to do this. If you love me, if you love Winnie, we need to do this. She wouldn't want to be remembered for this. You know that."

Adrienne wasn't listening to anything at this point. She had broken free from her mother's hands and fallen onto the stairs sobbing. Gloria got up and walked calmly to me. I hadn't realized I was still holding the letter until I felt Gloria prying it loose from my grip. I watched her, but it wasn't from my own body. It was as if I were floating above, touching the ceiling. Yes, a nightmare. That's what this was.

Somewhere, somehow there was a flicker of light. A match. I felt myself drop from the ceiling and reenter my body as Gloria lit the letter on fire, letting it fall into an empty wastepaper basket.

Adrienne was silent now, staring at Winnie's lifeless body in a pool of blood.

"Go call the police, Hugh."

We stared at each other and a lifetime of questions finally had answers. Winnie had been having an affair. Winnie had killed herself over a lover. Except the lover wasn't me. It was Gloria. Everything made sense. The way she had responded to my affair with Kendra. The endless nights when I would try to touch her, and she wouldn't allow me in, or, worse, when she would, but only when she had been drinking, and each time she had to increase the amount.

\#

"Hugh," April says. "Why should I believe this?"

"You probably shouldn't. It does sound like a fantastic tale."

"But—"

"It's not. It's the truth."

"I'm supposed to believe that your wife was having an affair with your daughter's sixteen-year-old best friend?"

"As unbelievable as it sounds, yes. And the truth is, I don't know for certain, and will never know for certain, what constituted their affair. Was it merely emotional? Partly physical? Full-blown physical? Had Winnie allowed it to get out of hand in her own mind?" I shrug. "Any of it is possible."

April rubs her face. "Why did you stay? How could you stay?"

"I know it doesn't make any sense, but you have to understand something. I loved Gloria. Still do. And I loved Adrienne. I loved the life we had, imperfect as it may have been. My own family was gone. I had nowhere else to go."

"And now?"

I reach for her hand and squeeze it. She gazes up at me, and in the dim porch light, I can make out the green of her eyes. "And now I do."

"Then why didn't you come back last night?"

I sigh. "Because I wasn't sure how you felt."

"What do you mean?"

"April, when a man tells a woman that he loves her, and she doesn't respond, well, it doesn't do much for his self-esteem."

"But I do, Hugh. I just can't say it."

"Why not?"

She releases my hand and shakes her head. "It's stupid, I know, but any time I've ever said it, I feel I end up losing those people. I mean, look at my life. My father. Vinny and Jimmy. Javier. Even Mom."

*Javier. That's who that must have been this morning.* "April. I saw you. This morning, I saw you in your office."

She jerks her head. "What? When?"

"I saw you kissing—"

"But I wasn't *kissing*. Well, I guess technically I was, but I pushed him away the moment he came at me."

"Was that Javier?"

"Yes. Coming back to see if he could get it on with me for old time's sake."

"And?"

"And what?"

"Is that what you want?"

"Of course not."

"Why not?"

She tilts her head in a thoughtful pose. "You want to know why not?"

I nod.

"Because I don't love Javier." This time, she takes my hand and squeezes.

"No?"

"No."

"Whom do you love?"

"You." She sighs. "I love *you*."

"And why on earth should I believe that?"

"Because," she says, while rolling her eyes at my point. "It's the truth."

I kiss her hand, and she smiles, but then it quickly fades.

"Hugh, I think Adrienne knows about us."

"Why do you think that?"

She shrugs. "Just a feeling. When I saw her today."

I sigh and shake my head.

"I know it's not ideal," she says, the alarm in her voice apparent. "But what can she do?"

"April, you'd be surprised. Did I tell you about her husband?"

"No."

"He works for the state. For the Massachusetts Department of Public Health. The Division of Healthcare Quality."

April's eyes widen. "You're kidding, right?"

"I wouldn't kid about this. Why do you think the administration and doctors don't press Adrienne a little harder for the DNR?"

"But even though she would think what you and I are doing is wrong, what could she do? Legally, I mean."

"I don't know. It could affect many more people than just you and me. Too many people here do good work. We can't jeopardize their jobs."

She shakes her head. "So what do we do?"

The words come out of my mouth before I can stop them. "We wait and see." I hate myself for saying it because this is how I've lived my life for too long, and April deserves more than that. *Wait and see—maybe things will improve. Wait and see—things are bound to level out.*

"Okay," she says. "We'll wait and see. I'm not going anywhere anyway."

"Good," I say as I envelop her in my arms. "Because neither am I."

# *Chapter 46: Nigel*

I do my best to avoid sounding moody in front of Max, but the boy is perceptive and has asked no fewer than seven times between dinner and bed if everything is okay.

"Everything's fine, Max. I'm a little preoccupied with work, that's all."

"Where's Trudie?"

"Her aunt is sick. She's been spending a lot of time at Saint A's with her."

"What about Maggie?"

"What *about* Maggie?"

He shrugs. "I dunno. You're friends with her, too, right?"

"Maggie's very busy."

"Dad, are you sure everything's okay?"

"Yes, Max. I promise you everything is fine."

Funny how we lie to our kids to protect them. In this case, everything is fine in Max's world. He's too young to have to worry about me. Besides, there's no need to anyway. That's what I keep telling myself at least. I've finally admitted to my own demons, albeit to a room full of strangers. Trudie knows the truth about Maggie and me, and I know the truth about Maggie. The fact that I still can't get her out of my head is irrelevant. It takes time to purge disturbing images from our subconscious. I imagine it'll happen sometime before the next century.

#

The doorbell startles me, and I jog across the floor before the idiot late-night caller wakes Max. I'm prepared to lambaste whoever is on the other side, when I see Maggie. She's bundled up in her long black coat and hunter green scarf, which brings out the color of her eyes. She's still in full makeup from the show tonight. She looks gorgeous, but I quickly remind myself that underneath the glamour is the woman who decided to abort our child. Or did she? Was Hazel right? Was she turning around and coming home? Can I forgive her either way? I open the door.

"Hi, Nigel."

"Hello, Maggie."

"I didn't wake you, did I?"

"Uh, no." I glance over my shoulder to see if I can catch any spying eyes. "I don't think you woke Max either."

"Oh! Sorry. I wasn't even thinking about Max."

"To what do I owe the pleasure?" I'm hoping she hears the annoyance in my voice and decides to leave.

"May I come in? It'll only be for a minute. I promise."

Curiosity wins over good judgment as I stand aside and let Maggie enter. Her eyes scan the loft.

"Nice place," she says.

"Thanks."

She smiles at me and says nothing.

"So," I begin. "What do you want?"

"Oh, right. Well. You're going to find this strange, but since I know you hate me, I feel you're the one person I can trust."

"Isn't that a line from some film?"

She tilts her head and ponders this. "*Casablanca*, I think. And speaking of film, well, here." She holds out an oversized envelope.

"What's this?"

"A proposal. For a documentary."

I stare at it, confused. "Why are you giving it to me?"

"Two reasons. First, I'd love your feedback. You knew me when this was all I ever wanted to do. I want to see if it lives up to the vision you had in mind for me."

I'm not sure how to respond to this, so I don't. "And second?"

"Second, I'd like you to consider producing it."

"What?"

"Listen, I need someone with business and legal savvy. Someone who can help keep the project on track. Someone who has the balls to tell me when something isn't working."

"And I came to mind?"

"Yes. Just because you hate me personally doesn't mean we can't have a business relationship. Some of the most successful business relationships are built on similar foundations."

"I don't hate you, Maggie."

"Oh, that's right," she says, nodding. "You don't 'anything' me. That'll work, too."

"I don't know what to say."

"Don't say anything. Read it first."

"Now?"

She laughs. "No, not this very minute. Sometime soon."

I tear open the envelope flap, pull out a sheaf of papers, and read the title aloud. *"Someday, Maybe—The Underground World of Nursing Home Entertainers."*

"It's a working title," she says.

"What made you decide to focus on this?"

"You."

"*Me?*"

"Remember New Year's Eve and Jerome Mulberry? You told me that I shouldn't judge him, that there might be a story there." She shrugs. "You were right."

"Are you saying I inspired you?"

"I guess that's what I'm saying." She pauses. "Is that a bad thing?"

"I suppose not."

"So you'll read it? Consider it?"

I catch the hopeful tone in her voice and feel a surge of something inside of me as well. "Oh, all right. I'll consider it."

"Great," she says while breathing a sigh of relief. "I appreciate it."

We walk back to the door in silence. Before she opens it, she glances back at me. "I am sorry, Nigel. About everything."

I swallow, nod, but say nothing. She gives a cursory nod back and leaves. I'm not sure how long I've been standing there staring at the door when Max stirs overhead.

"Dad?" His voice sounds sleepy.

"Yes, Max?"

"Who was that?"

"Maggie."

"What'd she want?"

"To give me something."

"What?"

I sigh, knowing that it will be faster to say it rather than play twenty questions with him. "A proposal for a documentary film she's working on."

"A documentary film?"

"Yep."

"Like a movie?"

"Yes," I say. "Like a movie. Now go back to sleep."

"Dad?"

I sigh again. "Yes, Max?"

"Why do you hate her?"

"Who?"

"Maggie. She said that you hated her."

"I don't hate her."

"Why does she think you do?"

"I don't know. But I don't hate her, okay?"

"Good."

"Why 'good'?"

"Because I like her."

"Who?"

"Maggie."

"You like her?"

"Uh huh."

"Why?"

"Because she makes you act all funny."

I jerk my head and watch as he hangs over the railing. "What do you mean 'act all funny'?"

He grins, and for the first time, there's a flash of the young man he's going to become, my boy disappearing before my eyes. "You *know*."

I roll my eyes. "Well, sport. I might not seem so funny when I come up there and put you back to bed."

He laughs, shakes his head at what he knows are his old pop's idle threats, and slips into the shadows. "G'night," he calls out.

"Night, son."

*Act all funny.*

Thing is, the more I think about it, I realize it's not an act. Never has been. Maggie has always had that effect on me, and, apparently—according to Maxwell anyway—she still does. Despite everything.

My eyes fall on the first page of Maggie's proposal that I hold in my hand: *Someday, Maybe.*

Maybe someday has finally arrived.

# Chapter 47: Hugh

As I descend April's porch steps for my morning walk, I notice Pana standing across the street by her car. It's early, barely six thirty, and I wonder how long she's been waiting there. Our eyes connect, and she shakes her head in disgust before turning away.

"Adrienne!" I yell as I race to the car before she can get in. She opens the door, but I close it shut. She spins around and glares at me.

Trembling, she brushes tears from her eyes. "What the fuck is wrong with you?"

"Adrienne," I whisper. "Let's talk about this somewhere else."

"Where?" she screams. "Where should we talk about your having an affair while your wife—my mother—lay dying? Inside there? Your mistress's house? Shall we make tea, Daddy?"

"Adrienne, calm down—"

"Calm down? Calm *down*?"

She brings her hands to her eyes and rubs them. Her fingernails are short and clipped with hints of dirt beneath them from the clay she uses to make— what? I don't even know anymore.

"It's not what it seems," I murmur.

"The fuck it isn't."

"Adrienne—"

"Shut up. Just shut up. You know what? I couldn't care less who you fuck. But have you ever thought of all the people you're hurting? And not just me or Mom but even them?" She points to the house. "How old is she? This April? She's got to be my age."

"She's thirty-four."

"Exactly. You're screwing someone who's young enough to be your daughter. Don't you see how fucked up that is?"

"Pana, I—"

She holds up her right hand. "Don't call me that."

Her tone goes from despair to hatred in one simple sentence, and I know enough not to push.

"What do you want me to do?" I whisper. I'm not sure why I'm asking her this, or what I'm expecting her to say. However, when I sense she recognizes the power she holds, I regret having asked.

"What do *I* want *you* to do?" She tastes the question like a lioness lapping her first bite of prey. "I want you to leave. For good."

"Fine," I say turning around.

"No," she says, gripping my arm. Despite the fact she has no real fingernails to speak of, she still somehow manages to dig into my skin. "Not just here. Leave your whore. Leave Mom. Leave this town and don't ever— *ever*—come back."

"What?"

"You heard me."

"And if I don't, what'll you do? Make my life a living hell? Too late for that, kiddo, in case you haven't noticed."

She shakes her head and smiles. "No, Daddy. I'll make *her* life a living hell. I'll make sure every newspaper between here and Boston covers this bitch who sleeps with her patients' husbands. I'll bring up your past. I'll bring up everything."

"Adrienne. I can't leave your mother. Not now."

She throws her head back and laughs. "It keeps getting more and more absurd. You can't leave my mother? Of course you can. Like you were ever there for her to begin with."

"Don't ask me to do that." My voice is hoarse, and I labor to breathe, but she doesn't notice, or doesn't care.

"I'm not asking you, Daddy. I'm telling you." She pauses and puts her hand on the door handle. "I'm going to let the administration know that you are no longer allowed in the building."

"Adrienne—"

"Don't worry, I won't tell them why. Not now, anyway."

"You can't—"

"Oh, yes, I can. Daddy, when I was a little girl, you told me I had it within my power to do anything I wanted, and well, good golly, at least there was one thing you didn't lie about."

I nod now, because I don't know what else to do. "Please let me say goodbye to her," I plead.

"Send her a letter and tell her the truth."

"I was talking about your mother."

Her lower lip quivers, and this time she doesn't brush the tears streaming down her cheek. "So was I. She can read it when she wakes up."

#

When Adrienne was in kindergarten, her teacher had the class draw pictures for words—whatever images the child wanted. On the afternoon of this exercise, I picked Pana up from school. As she donned her coat, boots, and mittens, I walked around the room, studying the artwork. Pana's symbols—yellow smiley faces, blue teardrops—matched her classmates' drawings except for one: at the end of the picture list, all the other students had drawn big red hearts. Pana's paper, however, had a person.

"What was the word for this one?" I asked.

The fluffy white trim of Pana's hood dipped into her eyes as she looked up at me. "Love."

I carefully constructed my next question—I didn't understand what or who the person was, but I didn't want her to know that. "Pana, you have the most creative mind out of all your classmates. The rest of them made hearts for the word love, but you made a picture of..."

"You," she'd grinned.

#

I watch her now as she speeds away and wish she would remember this, or that I could somehow remind her.

# *Chapter 48: April*

I sit next to Hazel's bed, watching her labored breaths. My back is to Gloria, but that does me little good since I feel her presence anyway. For the last half hour, I've been glancing at the clock on Hazel's nightstand every three minutes. It's almost ten, and Hugh still hasn't arrived. He was quiet when he came in from his walk this morning, pensive even. I kept asking him if anything was wrong, but he said nothing, just hugged me, which I realize now didn't answer my question.

Sighing, I eye the two-foot tall stack of paperwork I brought with me, figuring this is as good a place as any to get caught up. I pluck the top sheet—the daily census—and turn it over to find the list of new, discharged, transferred, and expired residents. I've always hated the term "expired," as if a person is nothing more than a carton of milk, having lived past the sell-by date. It's been a few weeks since anyone has died, but today a name is carefully printed in block letters: GERTRUDE COLLINS.

I suck in my breath and not because of Gert's death, which is sad, or even because I imagine Trudie Collins's devastation, but rather because I'm worried about who'll be next.

Joelle appears in the doorway. "April?" she says. "I need to speak to you."

"Right now?"

"Yes."

I pat Hazel's hand and follow Joelle. "Where are we going?" I ask.

She says nothing and continues walking brusquely down the hall, through the activities room, and out the patio door, which maintenance has finally unlocked in preparation for spring. The thermometer hanging from the Japanese maple reads fifty-four degrees, and it's not even noon.

"Hey, look." I point to the side of the building. "The crocuses are coming up."

"Cut the crap, April."

"Um, did I miss something? Or do you have something against crocuses?"

"I told you to be careful with Hugh."

"What are you talking about?"

She sighs, grabs my arm, and links it to her own. "Let's pretend we're looking at the garden shall we?" she says, while jutting her chin toward the automatic door, where a resident named Lucy is waving to us.

"Joelle, what's going on?"

"Adrienne Dooley-Whitmore is what's going on. I just got off a conference call with her and some of the other staff."

"And?"

"She's having her father banned from the building."

"What?" I try to pull away, but Joelle tightens her grip.

"Act cool, April. Act cool."

"Does Lance know why?" I whisper, referring to Saint A's administrator.

She shakes her head. "Luckily, Corporate has been riding his ass about other things. He doesn't have time to listen to rumors, most of which he can't understand anyway since his Spanish and Portuguese aren't that good."

"So what reason did Adrienne give?"

"She didn't."

"And that's it? Hugh's banned from the building because his daughter says so?"

Joelle stops and faces me. "She's in charge of her mother's care, and she has connections, April. Her husband for one. Besides, what did you want me to do? Press her for a reason? How the hell was I supposed to know that wasn't exactly what she wanted me to do? I was thinking of you at that point. Not Hugh."

"I have to find him."

"No, you don't. People are already talking. Lance had me put fliers in the employee break room, by the punch clock, and with the nurses' stations on both floors stating that Hugh Dooley is not allowed in the building and any violation of this policy by anyone could result in termination. Promise me you won't do anything. Promise you won't try to sneak Hugh in to see Gloria."

"What can they do? Legally, I mean? If, you know, Hugh and I are out in the open?"

"I don't know." She wears the worried look of a mother. "But I don't want to find out."

"This is crazy," I say, but in the back of my mind, the conversation I had with Adrienne rewinds and replays. *How did she know? Was it something I said?* I shake off the thought and muster anger instead. "She can't keep him from seeing his own wife," I announce stubbornly.

"April." Joelle stops and gazes at the side of the building where I pointed out the blooming crocus. "She just did."

# Chapter 49: Hugh

The mild day turns into a raw rainy night, although I'm not sure when it happens. The last eighteen hours are a blur. It's two a.m., and I've been keeping watch for forty-five minutes on the side entrance of the building, where the employees come out for a smoke. Finally, two aides emerge, and one is Mickey Lopes. Mickey works the eleven to seven a.m. shift, but he's often still here when I arrive in the morning because that's the way he is. He enjoys his job and the residents, and he often fills in when others call out sick. If anyone will help me, it's Mickey.

The flicker from his lighter illuminates their faces, but I don't recognize the other aide. I walk over anyway. They look up as I mount the steps, and Mickey's eyes dart from me, to the other aide, and back to me.

"Mr. Dooley," Mickey says, while exhaling smoke. The other aide startles and stares at me.

*So, they all know. Adrienne was true to her word.* "Mickey, I need your help. I need to see my wife."

Mickey coughs. "They have your picture, Mr. Dooley," he says, "in the break room along with a letter saying you're no longer allowed into the building. That you are no longer allowed to see your wife. Anyone who helps you could lose his job."

"Mickey, please understand. I need to say goodbye one last time. That's all I ask. I wasn't allowed to say goodbye before this happened. I know I'm putting your job at risk, but—"

Mickey holds up his hand and blows a ring of smoke in the air. "They need us," he says, gesturing to the building behind him. "They are idiots for posting such a stupid rule. Wait here."

Mickey stamps out his cigarette and disappears through the door. I feel the eyes of the other aide on me. Glancing at him, I spy the nametag adorned on his chest: *Javier.*

Good lord. What is it that Hazel always says about fate playing a role in everyone's life? How had I arrived on the steps of a nursing home standing next to my lover's former lover as he waits to sneak me in to see my dying wife?

I extend my hand. "Hugh Dooley."

Surprised, Javier tilts his head and slowly reaches for my outstretched arm. "Javier Gutierrez. But you know that, yes?"

"Yes."

We stare at each other without saying a word. Finally, Javier nods. I'm not sure what the gesture means or if it means anything. The door opens.

"Okay," Mickey says. "Come. We walk ahead. You follow right behind."

Mickey and Javier lead me down a dark hallway that deposits us on the opposite end of Gloria's room. I pretend I'm invisible as I crouch and walk behind the two tall, muscular men. In the small space between their bare arms, I can make out the nurse's station, which—for the moment—appears unoccupied. Pausing in front of Gloria's room, Mickey noiselessly opens the door.

"We don't have long," he whispers. "My break is over in less than ten minutes. I'll be back in five to take you out."

I mouth the words "thank you," enter the room, and allow my eyes to adjust to the dimly lit surroundings before making my way to Gloria's bed, careful not to wake Hazel.

Bending down close, I'm almost able to make out the details of her face, the little things that you come to know in a person you've been with for thirty-two years, like the mole on her upper right cheek and the way one nostril appears smaller than the other. Except, how well did I know her?

Gloria and I never discussed Winnie.

I regret that now. Isn't that the thing everyone warns you about in life? You regret the things left unsaid rather than the words spoken. So much was left unsaid between us—unsaid, but not misunderstood. I suppose we stayed—I stayed, she stayed—for Adrienne, a plan that has backfired and then some, but if I had it to do all over again, I imagine I'd do the same thing.

Her hand feels dry and limp in my palm. I reach for the bottle of vanilla scented lotion on the nightstand, squirt some onto my fingers, and rub them into Gloria's skin. I have no idea if she feels it or if she detects scent, but I hope she can. I pray she can. I hold her hand to my cheek and for the first time, I'm aware that I'm crying. My tears seep into her skin—a part of me into a part of her.

"When the time comes ..." I breathe deeply, and all I smell is the vanilla. "I won't be here, so don't wait for me. I don't know what comes next, if anything comes next, but if there is something, it has to be better than this. You'll be free to be the person you truly are."

I let go of her hand, and it falls to her side. Leaning over her still body, I kiss her forehead. "I love you, Gloria. I always have. I always will. But I have to go now."

Holding my breath, I make my way through the darkness to the door, when a small, sleepy voice calls my name.

"Mr. Dooley."

I turn and face her bed. "Hazel. I'm sorry for disturbing you. I'm leaving now."

"So I hear." She sounds incredibly lucid for someone who was just asleep.

"What have you heard?" I ask, hoping she'll tell me about April.

"Apparently, there is some sort of bounty on your head." She closes her eyes and attempts to shift position. "At least, they make it sound that way. Not allowing you into the building. Of all the absurd things I have ever heard."

"And April?"

"She is frantic with worry." She opens her eyes and focuses on mine. "And guilt."

"She has nothing to feel guilty about." I pause. "Is she okay?"

"She will be when she sees you."

I shake my head. "I can't see her. The deal is I leave and nothing will happen to April."

"You know as well as I that will devastate her."

"Well, if it's any consolation, I think it will kill me."

"Then why are you doing it? You are a grown man. Why on earth are you allowing your daughter to call all the shots?"

"Hazel, you don't know my daughter's anger. Getting me banned from the building is only the tip of the iceberg. She could have April fired—or worse. I can't take that chance." I walk toward her and bend down so I can see into her face, lit by the small bedside lamp she often keeps on. "Besides, what future could we possibly have together? I'm an old man and she is—"

"Bullshit."

I feel my jaw drop; I've never heard a curse word cross Hazel's lips.

"Forgive me, Mr. Dooley, but you are old, she is young, so what?" Taking a deep breath, she continues, "Do you love her?"

"I do."

"And she loves you. You are correct in that it makes no sense, but, my dear man, love does not. Trust me on this. When you are old and gray ..." She pauses, eyeing my bald head, and continues with a wry smile. "Well, *older*, anyway. It is what you haven't done that you will regret. I know you already live with some of those regrets. Some big ones, too. How many more are you going to subject yourself to, Mr. Dooley?"

"Her life is here. Her mother is here. A sister. You."

"I will not be here much longer."

"Hazel, stop—"

"Now, now. Respect your elders, my dear. No talking back." She places her right hand behind her head and considers me and this situation. "She would resign first before allowing this to happen."

"I know," I murmur. "Which is why we need to let her believe that Adrienne got the best of me and that I walked away on my own."

"Where will you go?" she asks.

"I don't know."

"Are you open to suggestions?" I raise an eyebrow as she reaches into her bedside table, pulls out an envelope with my name printed in block letters on the front, and hands it to me. "Because I know of a house in need of some plumbing. And a caretaker."

I open the envelope and thumb through a wad of cash—fifties and hundreds—and directions to—

"Mr. Dooley!" Mickey is at the door. "You need to leave. Now."

"Take it, Mr. Dooley," Hazel urges. "Take it and follow the directions. I will send further instructions upon your arrival. That's all I ask."

"But—"

"Please. Promise me you will."

*This is insane.* "And then?"

"Wait."

"Wait for what?"

"For me."

"But Hazel, I don't understand—"

"Will you do it?"

"I don't know—"

"There is enough money, I believe."

I finger the crisp bills. "Money isn't the issue. I don't understand how—"

"Hugh, please." It's the first time she's ever called me by my first name. "Go. For me. The rest will become clear. Soon. Very soon. I promise."

Mickey huffs and puffs, while throwing me a nervous look.

"And April?" I say quickly as I retreat to the door. "What about April?"

"I will take care of April."

"Mr. Dooley!" Mickey hisses.

I nod my acceptance to Hazel because what else can I possibly do, where else do I have to go? I give one final glance in Gloria's direction

"Do not worry," Hazel soothes while following my gaze. "She will be at peace soon."

*What's that supposed to mean?* All I can picture is Hazel shuffling toward Gloria's bed in the middle of the night and turning off and unplugging machines.

"You finally gave her permission to go, Mr. Dooley," she says, as if she can sense my thoughts and my fears. "That is all she has been waiting for."

# Chapter 50: Nigel

Considering my specialty is estate planning and that many of my clients are in the Ruth Frankenfeld age bracket, you would think I'd be used to wakes and funerals. I am not. The whole business makes me queasy, even though I remind myself it's a part of life—for all of us.

Some wakes, of course, are worse than others. If it's for a young mother, father, or—God forbid—a child, you expect a long wait in line to view the body or casket, to offer your condolences, to pay your respects. For an old woman like Gertrude Collins, it's different. Still sad but bearable.

I'll admit, though, that I'm surprised by the size of the crowd for Gertrude Collins at the funeral home, until I realize that the people are not here for the deceased Gertrude, but rather for the living Trudie. It's a quarter to eight, and my goal is to pop in and out so I can get to an AA meeting. Problem is that's what you do at cocktail parties you don't want to attend, not wakes hosted by your former lover.

I sign the guest book, adjust my jacket and tie, and stand in the back, observing her. She wears her blonde hair in an elegant ponytail, and her black suit accentuates her thin frame. Her cheeks are flushed by what I imagine is a combination of tears, overwhelming emotions, and the heat emanating from the room. She convulses in a sob and dabs the corner of her eyes with a tissue. I take two steps forward, thinking I should go to her, because, well, I should. How can I not? Trudie Collins is bright, articulate, and beautiful. We talk easily together. We get along well in and out of bed. So why did I walk away? Or, in this case, why don't I walk to her now?

The answer comes in the form of a cleaned up Happy Byrd, who's dressed in an oversized gray suit he probably bought off eBay. Having materialized out of nowhere, he rubs his hand up and down Trudie's spine, and she leans into him, the way she does when she wants to feel close to someone—the way she did when she wanted to feel close to me. He doesn't pull back or stand up straight. Instead, he leans into her.

"The way it should be," I whisper, and I turn around and walk out.

#

By the time I knock on Maggie's door, it's past eleven o'clock. As the doorknob turns, I consider making a break for it and running down the hall, but I don't.

Her eyes open wide. "Nigel!"

"Hello, Maggie." She's still in full makeup from the show. In her left hand, she holds two pairs of jeans. On the couch behind her is a suitcase. "Going somewhere?"

"What?" she asks. I point to her hand and the suitcase. "No." She pauses. "Well, yes. I guess."

"Right." I stuff my hands into my coat pockets. "Glad we've cleared that up."

"I'm going to April's. For how long, I'm not sure."

"Is everything okay?" I, of course, already know the answer to this. Hazel explained what was going on, and even Ruth heard the rumors about Hugh Dooley being kept from seeing his dying wife.

"I'm not sure." She studies my face carefully. "You know, don't you?"

"Yes. But it will go no further, if that's what you're worried about."

She shrugs. "Everyone at Saint A's knows about April and Hugh."

"How do you feel about it?"

"Protective." She smiles, but it quickly fades. "And angry that he's disappeared without so much as a phone call to April. She's frantic."

"I'm sure it will all work out."

"Maybe." She waves me inside and throws her jeans on top of the suitcase. "Anyway. What's up with you?"

"With me?"

"Well, you are standing in my home at eleven o'clock at night. I'm assuming you've come to give me a piece of your mind or perhaps—"

"Or perhaps?" I interrupt.

"Or perhaps your agreement to co-produce the documentary?"

"Oh, we're co-producers now, are we?"

She grins. "Well, it is my baby." Smacking her hand against her mouth, she cringes. "Shit. Bad choice of words."

"Agreed," I nod. "But I can forgive."

Dropping her hand to her side, she searches my face. "Yes, but can you forget?"

We stare at each other for what feels like an eternity.

"No," I murmur. "I don't think I can forget."

"I see."

"However—"

"Yes?"

"I believe that I can move forward now. That I *am* finally moving forward. And have been. For four days, two hours, and—" I stop, pull up my sleeve, and look at my watch. "Seven minutes."

"What are you talking about?"

"You're not the only who carried around a secret all these years, Maggie. Difference is, you faced yours. You knew it was there. I didn't have the guts to do that. Until a few nights ago."

"Nigel, I'm still not following you."

I move closer to her. "Take a deep breath."

"What?"

"Just do it." She shakes her head disbelieving, but obeys anyway. "What do you smell?" I whisper.

She wrinkles her nose. "Yuck. Cigarette smoke. Again." She backs away. "Is that your secret? That you're a closet smoker?"

"No. The smoke is from the meetings I've been going to for the last three months."

"Meetings?"

"Yes. Drinking voluminous amounts of coffee and smoking endless packs of cigarettes might look like requirements for membership. To the outside world, anyway."

"But ..." Maggie says slowly, and I can see her wheels spinning. "Those aren't the requirements."

"No. The only requirement is alcohol. And admitting you have a problem with it."

"Nigel. What are you saying? That you're—"

"Yes," I interrupt. I close my eyes and take a deep breath. "I'm an alcoholic. I've been dry for the last eighty-nine days and sober for the last four days, two hours, and—"

"—seven minutes," she says, finishing my sentence.

I command my eyes to open. "So, you see you're not the only one with those ugly skeletons."

She reaches for my arm and places her hand on the sleeve of my jacket. I lean into her touch and keep my eyes on hers, determined not to look away.

"I think the hardest thing about skeletons," she finally says, "is hiding them. If we let them be, if we let the people we care about know about them, then they—and we—could finally find some—"

"—peace," I whisper.

She nods and smiles.

"So it looks as if we're both trying to move forward from our skeletons. Our pasts," I say.

"I'm glad. No one deserves to be stuck in the past."

"True, true." I stroke my chin and pretend to look thoughtful. "I don't think, however, that I want to move forward alone."

"Nor should you have to." She lets go of my arm and attempts a smile. "Trudie Collins is a lucky woman."

I smile now, too, because for once it's nice to have Maggie think she has all the answers when she really doesn't.

"You're right," I say. I'm amazed at how light I feel, how high. "She's luckier now that I'm out of her life. I dragged her down. Poor girl."

Maggie rubs her eyes, her face confused. "Nigel, what are you talking about?"

"Why, Trudie Collins, of course. Looks as if she's getting involved with her producer or some such person. Quite scandalous, if you ask me."

"So just now, you weren't referring to Trudie."

"No."

"You were referring to ..."

I lower my head, trying to catch her eye as she stares off into space. "You, Margaret Rose Prescott. I was, always have been, and—God help us both—always will be referring to you."

*April*

# Chapter 51: Maggie

Somehow, the one or two nights I'd promised to spend with April has morphed into a month. We never talked about it; it just happened. I sleep in April's childhood bedroom in a queen-sized bed with a pink canopy.

"After Jimmy and Vinny died and I moved back here, there was no way I was going to move into the room that I had grown up in," she'd explained when I came over. "Even though Mom had turned the room into a guest room of sorts, it still reminded me too much of my little girl bedroom. The colors, you know?"

I did know, but I didn't mind. On more than one occasion when I squeezed my eyes shut at night, I imagined that I was ten again and this was my room.

The rest of the house has become familiar to me—the squeaky floorboards on the third and fifth steps leading to the second floor, the refrigerator's hum, the way the sunlight pours through the kitchen in the morning, the cat fur you'll find on your clothes if you leave the closet door open.

I haven't had a roommate since college. It's different this time around, of course. The space is one hundred times larger than the dorm room I shared with my roommate at Emerson my freshman year. My roommate and I were on opposite schedules—she was a night owl, and I liked to go to bed early. She pulled all-nighters, and I had my projects and papers done days in advance of their due dates. We couldn't wait to be rid of one another at the end of the year. Now, opposite schedules are a blessing: April's been leaving for work earlier and earlier—a distraction, I'm sure, from thinking about Hugh. She's out of the house by seven most mornings, leaving me to get to know this old house one-on-one. At night, she's often in bed when I get home. I'll poke my head into her room, and if she's awake, we'll talk, but most of the time, we're satisfied knowing that there's another person around, even if we don't need each other yet. Today, though, as April and I attempt the sad task of emptying Hazel's dresser drawers I know that'll change: we'll need each other now, more than ever.

#

I stop and sit on Hazel's bed, which is ready and waiting for a new patient. The room is so different now, and not only because Hazel is physically gone—she's not here in spirit, either. I remember doing a segment once, years ago, on paranormal investigators. We followed them around on their ghost hunts. One of them—I think his name was Dakota—explained that most spirits go to the next world on their own, but some linger behind as "earthbound spirits." *Why would they choose to stay here?* I'd asked. He simply shrugged and said sometimes it's not because they want to stay but rather because someone here refuses to let them go.

#

As April bends over the bottom dresser drawer, her shirt rides up her back, and I can count her ribs. I've tried to stock up her fridge with food, but there's only so much I can do. I'm not the world's best cook, either. Nigel came over that first Saturday night I was at April's and made chicken parm for both of us, and even though she thanked him numerous times and attempted to eat, Nigel and I both noticed that she simply moved her food around the plate.

"I want you to know," April whispered to me as we cleared the dishes that night while Nigel was in the living room fiddling with the CD player, "that it's okay with me if Nigel, you know, wants to stay."

"Yeah?" I smiled. "Because I was thinking of kicking him out right about now."

She giggled, the first time I'd heard her do so all week. "You know what I mean."

"Are you sure you're okay with that?"

"Of course." She stopped scrubbing a plate and looked at me. "This is your house, too."

#

Everyone has a breaking point. I often catch myself staring at April, trying hard to discern her cracks. I used to think my life had more than its fair share of sadness. Now, I realize that anything I went through is nothing compared to the losses April has endured: a father, a husband, a son, lovers, a wonderfully close friend who was more of a mother to her in the last three years than her own.

We mourn in different ways, April and I. For me, the last five months have been a wonderful, surprising gift—having reconnected with Hazel this final time. Any sadness is countered by my firm belief that somehow, somewhere, Hazel and Mack are together, as they should be.

*What will be, will be.*

Despite spending years studying different world philosophies, Hazel's famous little phrase lurks like a piece of sand lodged in my inner ear, throwing me off balance. I'm not sure I believe in destiny or fate, but it's hard to make an argument against it considering that Nigel and I are together despite everything.

"Well, that's it, I guess." April closes the flaps on the cardboard box and sits next to me on the bed. She glances behind us at the other empty bed.

"What are you going to do with all of it?"

She shrugs. "Some of the residents could use nice dresses. The rest I'll give to Goodwill."

"What about Gloria's stuff?"

"Adrienne emptied out everything. The nurses said she came when we were at Hazel's funeral."

April mentioned once, months ago, that deaths at Saint A's always happen in threes, and so it is here: *Gertrude Collins, Gloria Dooley, Hazel Cooke*. Many people in television—like Serena—believe in this superstition as well. Back in New York, we had obituary segments for some older famous people ready to go, knowing their time was near. It was always a good project for interns to work on—putting together feel-good pieces by weaving clips and sound and commentary. No deadline in sight, just the knowledge that we'd need the segments sooner rather than later. So they would work on them, researching the person's history and early years, life's highlights, and—occasionally—some lowlights, for context, knowing that the final frames would be filled in fast, on the run, on deadline because deaths, even when they're expected, never really are.

"I still can't believe she's gone," April whispers.

Logically, I know she means Hazel, but I suspect there's a part of her that means Gloria as well. The two women died within forty-eight hours of each other—first Gloria, then Hazel. Gloria was alone, in the middle of the night. Well, she wasn't alone—Hazel was there. But Hugh wasn't. Or Adrienne. When Hazel died, April and I were together, each of us holding one of Hazel's hands, and even some of the regular nurses and aides stopped in and paid their final respects to a woman who had spent the last ten years of her long life at Saint Anthony of Padua Healthcare Center.

April wanted to go to Gloria's funeral, but she knew she shouldn't. I went in her place, standing in back, studying every person who came and went, hoping—as I knew April did, too—that Hugh would appear. But he never did.

#

Joelle walks in now carrying a black marble container, less than a foot long and about six inches high. She stops in front of us and holds out her arms to April.

"What's this?" April asks, as she runs her hand over the smooth top.

Joelle takes a deep breath. "It's Hazel."

"What?" April jumps back. "Joelle!"

"Well, you asked what it is. Hazel's attorney's office delivered it to me."

"Why you?"

"Hazel's wishes. I'm supposed to hand this off to you." She continues holding out her arms, but April stubbornly crosses her own.

"I don't think so."

Joelle shakes her head. "Oh, there's more to it than this."

I take the urn from Joelle and place it on my lap. Joelle pulls an envelope from inside her jacket. "Here. This came with it."

"What is it?" April asks suspiciously.

"A letter from Hazel. Telling you what she wants you to do with her ashes."

April sighs, reaches for the letter, tears it open, and pulls out a sheet of creamy white paper. As she reads the letter, she shakes her head. "I don't believe this."

"What?" I ask.

"Hazel wants me to spread her ashes. In Georgia." She looks up at me. "At Tallulah Gorge State Park."

"Makes sense," I say.

"Yeah, but she wants me to do it soon. Like, this month. She has an exact date. She says there's an airline ticket." April turns the envelope upside down and shakes it. "Nothing here."

"That must be what this is." Joelle produces another envelope from her jacket.

"Is that it?" April asks. "Or is there more in there?"

"That's it. Hazel was specific in her wishes about what order I was to give these to you."

April opens the second envelope and pulls out an airline ticket. "It's for early next week. How did she—"

I place my hand on April's. "She knew, April. She knew she was dying. You know that."

"But this is so weird. I can't leave now."

"Why not?" Joelle asks. "How much vacation time have you lost because you haven't used it?"

"I dunno."

"A lot, I bet. And I know you have a lot saved that you should use or else you'll lose that, too."

"But what about here?"

"We'll be able to hold down the fort without you."

April wrinkles her nose and hands me the letter so I can read it. "Maybe. But there's no way I can get time off on such short notice—"

"Too late," Joelle interrupts, and this time she pulls a folded piece of paper from her back pocket.

"I thought you said that was it," April sighs.

"That was it for you, April. But this here is a letter from Hazel to *me* requesting that I ask administration that you be given time off so you can scatter her ashes and fulfill her last wishes."

"Which you've—"

"Which I've already done."

"Great. Just great." April turns to me. "Will you come with me?"

I shake my head and point to the letter. "Hazel wants you to do this on your own." I hold out the urn. April rolls her eyes and takes it.

"When did this become my life?"

Joelle laughs, and I smile. "Hang in there, sister." I put my arm around her shoulders and squeeze. "It may surprise you yet."

# Chapter 52: April

I stand on one of Tallulah Gorge State Park's outlook points and peer over the railing's side into the canyons of rock and river below. This particular waterfall is called L'Eau d'Or Falls, French for "water of gold." I'd taken the North Trail to get to this point, as instructed in the letter awaiting me at my hotel room. It's my first trip to Georgia—my first trip outside of Massachusetts since my honeymoon a lifetime ago. Hazel and I used to talk about going to Tallulah Falls together. "I'll be your chaperone," I'd joke. "Your own personal flight attendant." I never thought it would happen, though, or that it would be like this if it did, with Hazel in a box and me still me.

I'm so tired of being broken, so tired of being forgotten.

I don't know how else to say it, don't know how else to feel. What hurts the most is that I thought I had gotten past all this brokenness when Hugh came along. Therein lies the problem, I suppose: you can't rely on anyone else to get you through things or past things. You can only rely on yourself. Which, in my case, doesn't help.

I miss Hugh. When Vinny and Jimmy died, it seemed unreal in one moment, surreal the next, and then nothing. In my core, though, I always knew they were gone and never coming back. It's different now. Right after they posted that silly notice saying Hugh was banned from the building, I kept turning the corner to Hazel's room, expecting to see him sitting by

Gloria's bed, defiant and strong. He loved her too much to leave. He loved me too much to leave. Didn't he?

I thought for sure once Gloria died that he'd make contact with me somehow—a call, a letter, a sign of sorts that he was okay and he'd be coming back. Didn't he say that night when we were sitting on my front porch steps that he wasn't going anywhere? Or had I imagined that, wishing he had spoken the words? I'm not sure. I'm not sure of anything anymore.

"Maybe it's for the best," I'd said a couple of weeks ago to Maggie.

"What?"

"Hugh leaving."

She put down the Sunday paper and watched me as I drank my coffee. "You actually believe that?"

"No."

"I didn't think so."

"But I should."

"Why?"

"Because." And I rolled my eyes and waved my hand in the air as if that were explanation enough.

"Am I supposed to understand what that means?"

"It's crazy."

She smiled. "Yeah, well. That's love. No sense to it at all."

"But at least you and Nigel—"

"Whoa. Be careful about making any assumptions about Nigel and me."

"But you're at least in the same age bracket."

"Is that your only concern? The age difference?"

"Well, it's a big one. I mean, you know ..."

"I don't know. Enlighten me."

"Kids," I said. "What if I—"

"Oh," Maggie nodded. "That's a legitimate concern. Did you ever talk about that with Hugh?"

"We never got the chance."

"Maybe you will."

"Yeah, right."

"You never know, April," she'd said. "You just never know."

#

I do know. Hazel's words haunt me: *What will be, will be.* Maybe Hugh was supposed to have left all along.

Closing my eyes, I breathe deeply and exhale. The month of April feels different in Georgia—warmer, the air thicker somehow. The hotel desk clerk said it'd get up to the mid-70s today. "Man, what's it like in July?" I asked.

"Blistering," he answered. He's wrong. It already feels that way to me now.

*Well, Hazel. This is it.* I bend down, reach for the urn, and close my eyes, but a noise disturbs me and my eyes flutter open. I jump and practically trip over the urn.

"Nigel!" I grip the railing for support. "You scared the bejeezus out of me." Nigel lets go of my arm, which he caught when I started to tumble. "What the hell are you doing here?"

He's dressed in the most casual wear I've ever seen him in: jeans, white polo shirt, and his trademark cowboy boots. "She asked me to come," he says.

"Who?"

He gestures to the black marble urn at my feet. "Hazel."

"What? But why?"

"I'm representing my client."

"Your client?"

"Hazel Beatrice Cooke."

"You were Hazel's attorney?"

"For the last four months, anyway." He stops and assesses my face. "Shocking, I know. But Hazel was a wise woman and knew a fine attorney when she saw one."

"Why are you here?"

"Hazel changed her will."

"She did?"

"Yes. You are taking care of Hazel's last wishes. For her ashes to be spread—

"—at Tallulah Gorge State Park," I finish for him.

"Right. April, didn't you wonder why it was so easy for you to take possession of the ashes?"

"I had the letter from Hazel."

"Yes," he nods. "All done through my office."

"But why are you here now?"

"Hazel did indeed ask me to come. Actually, ask is not the proper term. She hired me to be here when you were."

"And, of course, you knew the date. You knew exactly when I'd be here. Even the time," I murmur, thinking of the letter tucked in my back pocket. "But how did she know she was going to die? I mean, how did she know this was all going to work out?"

"I suspect," he says slowly, "that you of all people would have a better understanding of that than I."

I shake my head, overwhelmed. "So, why are you here?" I ask again. "Am I not doing this right?"

Nigel laughs. "I don't think there's any wrong way. Unless this place requires a permit for spreading ashes." He pauses as if it's the first time he's considered this scenario. "Ah, no worries. If that's the case, it'll be much easier to ask forgiveness than permission."

"Nigel, you still haven't answered my question. Why are you here?"

"I'm here simply because my client asked me to be. She asked me to be present so I could bequeath the rest of her estate."

"Bequeath what?" I think back to my final conversations with Hazel. "The money from her house in Wellesley is going to the Saint A's activities department. At least, that's what she told me."

"Indeed it is," Nigel confirms. "But then, there's the matter of her other house."

"What other house?"

"The house that Mack built for her."

"But it's Mack's *sister's* house. At least, it had been up until—"

"The beginning of the year. When the sister decided she and her husband would retire to California to be near their children and grandchildren." He nods. "I know the story."

"Right. I had always assumed Mack's sister was going to sell it."

"Why would she? It didn't belong to her."

"Nigel," I sigh. "I'm not following you."

"When Mack died, he left the house that he had been building to his wife: Hazel Beatrice Cooke."

"His *what*?"

"Before Mack had gotten divorced, the land and the house were in his sister's name so that it wouldn't become part of the divorce settlement. His sister was completely on board with this. After Mack's divorce was final, he came back to Boston, and he and Hazel were married by a justice of the peace." Nigel shrugs. "Who knows? Maybe he had a premonition. Anyhow, they kept their marriage a secret because Hazel's father was sick at the time, and they decided they wouldn't announce their marriage until her father regained his strength. So, Hazel stayed in Boston, and Mack returned here to finish their house."

"Except," I say, piecing things together, "he never made it back to Boston for Hazel."

"No. He died before he could. However, he did transfer the property in Tallulah Falls to Hazel, both in deed and in his will, before he died."

"And then?"

"And then." Nigel shrugs. "Hazel said she always planned on going down to her house, but for one reason or another—at first pain, and then the responsibilities of taking care of her ailing father, then mother, her aunts, nephew—life happened, and she never did. But the whole time, she allowed her sister-in-law to live there and raise her family."

"So every time Mack's sister called or visited Hazel and said, 'Come home,' she really meant home."

"Correct. No one in Hazel's life knew about the house, but Hazel knew that when she died she'd have to leave the house to someone. For a long time, Hazel had named Mack's sister, Lena, as the beneficiary. Lena is a wonderful woman. She was grateful to Hazel for the house, but she didn't want it forever. Too big, too far away from her children. She wanted Hazel to do something more meaningful. When Hazel met you, it became clear that you were the more meaningful thing Hazel had been looking for. But the problem was her nephew."

"Michael had already taken over Hazel's Wellesley house."

"Exactly. He had taken over the house in everything but deed, knowing that when Hazel died she would name him as the beneficiary simply because she had no other family. But what would happen when the nephew discovered that Hazel owned this other property in Georgia and that she had left it to the activities director of Saint Anthony of Padua Healthcare Center?

Hazel knew her nephew would have contested it in court. He probably would have won—or at the very least, caused years of legal wrangling, which you wouldn't have been able to afford." Nigel stops and gazes at the falls. "You worked at Saint A's," he continues. "A major conflict of interest."

"But now," I begin, while trying to process the information, "her nephew is gone. Nigel, what are you saying? That once Hazel's nephew died she changed her will and left this house to me? That's crazy! How did she know Michael Cooke was going to die? And still, someone, somewhere will have a problem with this."

"No, April," Nigel says, still staring at the falls. "Hazel had no idea her nephew was going to die. For a while, she kept Lena's name in the will, with an understanding that the house would transfer over to you at some point, when the dust had settled, so to speak." He pauses and glances at the urn by my feet. "But Hazel knew you well and figured you'd somehow wriggle out of taking ownership. And there would be no way you could be forced to take it since the agreement Hazel had with Lena was strictly verbal—she didn't want a paper trail that her nephew could contest."

"So the house still belongs to Mack's sister, just like I thought."

Nigel shakes his head. "Hazel recently found someone else she could leave the house to—someone else whom she could trust with nothing more than a verbal agreement to then transfer the house to you when she died. Someone she had had a history with, albeit long ago, but one that could be verified nonetheless if her nephew decided to squawk. Someone who would have more clout in making sure you accepted the house as Hazel's final gift."

"Who?"

He's quiet before finally facing me, a wide grin on his face. "Your sister."

I barely hear Nigel as he explains the legal process and what will happen next. All I hear is that I have a house in Tallulah Falls. My own house—not my mother's house, the one I grew up in, but a house that was built plank by plank—brick by brick?—with love.

"April," Nigel says, pointing at his watch and then the urn. "It's time."

#

I follow Nigel down back road after dusty back road until we come to a stop on a dirt driveway where an old mustang sits next to a large, rustic log cabin. Nigel waves me past his car and motions for me to park next to the mustang. He then expertly maneuvers a three-point turn until his vehicle is pointing the way we just came. He pokes his head out the window, and I jump out of my car and run to his door.

"Whose mustang?" I ask. "Don't tell me a car comes with the house."

"It's the caretaker's."

"Caretaker?"

"Someone needed to watch over the place once Mack's sister left."

"What am I supposed to do with a caretaker?"

Nigel turns to the passenger seat. "Here." He thrusts an oversized yellow envelope into my hands along with a white business envelope. "I believe these will tell you."

I take them, and Nigel puts the car into drive. Panic sweeps my body. "You're leaving?"

"I have a flight to catch. Hazel was very specific in her wishes. She wanted me to come, tell you, and then leave."

"But don't you want to come inside?"

He shakes his head. "I have to get to the airport."

"But what am I supposed to do? How am I supposed to get inside?"

"Keys are in the big envelope. The letter should explain everything else."

"What about the caretaker?"

Nigel tilts his head, revs the motor, and grins. "You are indeed Maggie Prescott's sister. Always asking questions." And with that, he drives away, leaving me staring at a house. *My house.*

I walk back to my rental, lean against the bumper, and open the large yellow envelope. Two keys fall out—one gold, one silver—which I turn over in my hand. Holding the other envelope to my nose, I hope to catch Hazel's scent. Nothing. I tear it open and pull out a letter.

*My Dearest April,*

*If you are reading this, then I am gone. Cry, my dear, but not too much. You have shed more than your fair share of tears in such a young life, and now it is time to concentrate on smiling. I imagine you spoke to Nigel and that you are stunned by the truth. I am sorry that I did not tell you everything in person. Unfortunately, it did not work out that way.*

*I am not sure you will ever know how much your friendship meant to me over the last decade. I love you as if you were my own daughter, and I pray for nothing more than your happiness. So, to start, I give you the house Mack built for me. It was built in love, and I give it in love. Take care of it, my dear, and everything you find in it.*

*With all my love,*
*Hazel*

I don't realize that I'm crying until two teardrops fall onto the stationery and spread across the fibers of the paper in small broken circles. Wiping my face with the back of my hand, I turn and face the house, which overlooks a large fenced-in yard. Woods surround the property. I do a 360 and can't see another structure in sight. I shake my head, incredulous. Mack built this house over fifty years ago, and his sister raised her family here, in this private oasis in Northern Georgia. I can almost hear the laughter of children from the happy times they spent in this home.

*Home.*

My stomach knots in an odd combination of giddiness and anxiety as I walk to the front door. The keys feel warm in my hand, and I wonder if I'll guess the right one on the first try.

"The door's unlocked."

Whipping around at the sound of his voice, I practically trip over my own feet.

"But it's the gold key," Hugh continues. "For future reference."

# *Chapter 53: Hugh*

Whenever Adrienne looked at me after that summer day when we found Winnie, I didn't see the hatred and anger that glazed the surface of her irises; I saw the sadness and disappointment lodged deep within the black abyss of her pupils. I could handle the anger. I could even shoulder the hatred, but witnessing such utter despair in my child was almost more than I could bear.

Now, April stands before me, arms crossed, and her eyes become Adrienne's—it's the same sadness, the same disappointment, the same heartache. I reach for her.

"No," she says, shrinking into the door. "Don't."

"April, I—"

"You what, Hugh? You want to tell me why you walked away? Walked away without so much as a note, a letter, a phone call?" She shakes her head, and the tears come. "For three decades you stuck it out with Gloria, even when the going got tough. But when things started getting sticky with us, you left."

"I had no choice."

"There's always a choice. You choose poorly, that's all."

"Adrienne was going to—"

"Hugh! How long are you going to let Adrienne control your world?"

"It wasn't my world she wanted to interfere with, April. It was your world. Gloria's world, too."

She rolls her eyes and says nothing.

"I can handle Adrienne hating me, but I wasn't about to let her destroy you or dredge up the past. She would have, April. She would have."

"You left," she whispers. "You. Left. Just like everyone else I've ever loved."

I step toward her, knowing she has nowhere to go. "You're right. I did. But I'm here now."

She pushes past me and sits on the front step. "How did you get involved in all this?" she says, gesturing to the lawn.

I sit down next to her, our knees touching. "Hazel asked me to watch over the place until things settled back home."

"Back home?"

"Yes."

"*Home*?" she presses.

"What else should I call it?"

"You tell me."

For most of my life, home has been with Gloria, for better, for worse. For eighteen of those years, home included my Pana. Now, that one link—the home base connecting Adrienne and me—is gone.

"I don't know, April. I don't know."

We're quiet for a while, watching a gray squirrel bound across the grass and disappear into the woods.

"She's gone, you know," April murmurs. "Gloria is gone."

I nod and stare ahead, even though I know her eyes are on me.

"How could you stay away? How could you not attend her funeral?"

"I did it for Adrienne." I face her now. "I love my daughter, April. That's never going to change. Yes, she would have—may still—try to hurt you. And me. But I'm hoping now that Gloria is gone Adrienne can find some peace." I rub my hands over my face. "In trying to protect our children, sometimes we parents screw up. Make bad decisions."

She nods, and I know she understands deep down. It's what her mother did. It's what Gloria and I did. It's what April would have done, I'm sure, if given the chance with Jimmy.

"This is crazy," she finally says. "This house. Everything. What does Hazel expect me to do?"

"What did she say?"

"She didn't. I didn't find out about any of this until after."

"Was there a letter?"

April glances at me. "Yep."

"What did it say?"

"It says," and she pulls it from the envelope she's carrying, "that she wants nothing more than my happiness. And to start, she's giving me the house Mack built her."

"That it?"

"No, there's more. She says I should take care of it and everything I find in it."

I smile. "I knew I should have waited for you inside."

April throws the letter to the ground. "What if I hadn't come, Hugh? What if this plan of Hazel's had backfired? Or what if she ended up living another year—or ten? What then, Hugh? Would you have stayed here waiting forever?"

"No."

"What would you have done?"

"I would have gone home."

"Yeah?" She closes her eyes, squeezing out two more tears. "And where's that?"

I take her hand and lace my fingers with hers. "With you." She's crying now. Hard. "April. What I said, that's supposed to be a good thing, you know."

"But," she sobs, and I lean into her so I can make out what she's saying, "How can this work? I still want ..."

"You still want what?"

"Kids!" she wails, and I laugh. She sniffles, looks at me, and laughs, too.

"Is that all?" I say. "Well, that's something we can talk about. And work on."

"But you're ..." She throws her hands up in the air, gesturing toward my naked head.

"I'm what?" Cupping her chin, I direct her face toward mine. "Old? Is that what you're trying to say?"

"Well. Older."

"April," I chuckle, "My greatest joy in life has been being a father."

"But—"

"But maybe now," I say, touching my lips to hers, "we'll both get a second chance to make it right."

# Chapter 54: Maggie

As I sit with Kate in the kitchen as she finishes her dinner, I note the time: five o'clock. It's hours after the time Hazel directed April to scatter her ashes. Nigel was at her side when she did this, also per Hazel's request. Nigel was also instructed to escort her to Hazel's house, where she would find Hugh. Of course, I only discovered all this yesterday, after April had left for the airport.

"Nigel. What is going on?" I demanded.

"Client confidentiality, Mugsy. I couldn't reveal to you what was happening until April was on that plane. Per Hazel's instructions."

"This is crazy," I said. I hadn't realized how hard I was pressing the phone to my right ear until I moved the receiver to my left one. "What sort of man is this Hugh Dooley anyway?"

"Apparently a man whom Hazel trusted with her house, which says something, and a man whom your sister loves, which should tell you something else."

"Humph."

"I'll tell you more when I get back. And there's something else we should talk about, too."

"Yes?"

"Staying on track for that documentary of yours."

"Task master."

"Yes, but admit it, Mugsy—you like my whip."

"Well." I smiled into the phone. "What time will you be home tomorrow night?" There was a long pause. "Nigel? You still there?"

"I'm still here," he whispered. "If my flight leaves on time, I'll be home between seven and eight."

It wasn't until after we hung up that I realized what had startled him: the word *home*. Nigel was coming home.

#

Kate's plate is empty, and I gather our dishes and bring them to the sink. I had mentioned to April that I wanted to take a few days off from work and spend some time with Kate in our house.

"That's fine," April had said. "But ..."

"I know." I took her hand in my own. "I know it's not easy. I don't know how you did it for as long as you did, but I'd like to give it a go. Even for a day."

She'd nodded, trying hard not to cry. "It'll be good for her. For both of you. Maybe for all of us."

#

When I glance toward the kitchen table, Kate's gone, and I panic, even though it's been only a few seconds since I turned my back.

"Kate?" I call, even though I know she won't answer me. I race through the hallway, through the living room, and into the hall in the back of the house.

"You frightened me," I say, when I find her standing there, staring at the ceiling. "What is it?"

I follow her gaze to the pull-down stairs that lead to the attic where April and I had pored over photo albums a month ago.

"Nothing up there, Kate," I sigh. "April and I already looked."

She turns to me—a normal movement for anyone else, but a jarring one from her: it's as if she understands what I said, and the look on her face indicates I'm wrong.

"Well," I murmur. "What's it going to hurt, right?" I gently move Kate out of the way and pull down the stairs. "You should go first," I say, directing her to them. "You know how to climb stairs, right?"

At first, she doesn't budge, but then she lifts one leg and then the other, climbing. I hold her butt in my hands, nudging her up. When we emerge in the attic, she doesn't stumble or fall, even as I trip on a nearby box. It's as if her body remembers the layout, even if her mind can't. She glides to the pile of photo albums and sits on a stool. I crouch next to her and lay the top album on her lap.

"We looked through these already," I say. "Did we miss something, Kate?" I hold my breath, hoping she'll flip through the pages and point to a picture, a letter, a clue—something that will reveal my background, my history, what happened a half century ago to this old woman sitting before me. Instead, she surveys the page, mumbling in her "Kate speak," as April calls it.

I flip the pages for her, slowly at first and then faster when it's clear she's not focusing on the photos anymore. I allow myself to settle on the floor, and, seeing that she's occupied in her own invisible world, I thumb through the albums again: first day of school dresses, homemade Halloween costumes, prom dresses lovingly sewn and altered. I'm so engrossed that I don't notice Kate's movements until I catch her crouching by the small porthole looking out onto the spring night.

"Whatchya doing, Kate?" I yawn. She's on her knees pulling at the pink fiberglass insulation below the window. "Hey. What are you doing?"

I crawl toward her and pull her hand away. Even though we're both on our knees, I tower over her shrunken frame. She gazes into my face. We connect—I feel it—but I tell myself that it's probably my imagination. As her eyes slowly turn downward to the insulation, I almost say aloud, "See, Maggie? It's all in your head," until my eyes follow hers and I spot something poking out from behind the wall.

It's another photo album, like the others.

I pull it free, all the while aware of my thumping heart, the sticky sweat on my brow, the gray shadows on Kate's face. Holding the album out to her, I will her to take it, but she doesn't. She simply sits back on her haunches, staring at it intently, trying to remember. Or maybe she does remember, the album's physical presence enough to jar the memory loose. Or maybe it's a red herring of sorts—another album with baby pictures, first steps, grade-school report cards, and nothing more.

Or maybe …

I start flipping. The first page is blank. So are the rest. Frustrated, I'm about to throw the damned thing across the floor, when Kate takes it from me and turns it over. That's when I see it: a slight bulge underneath the back cover.

# Chapter 55: Nigel

A couple weeks ago, I asked Max how he'd feel if I sold the loft.

"Okay."

"Just, 'okay'?"

He shrugged. "I guess so."

"Gee. That's convincing." I ran my hand back and forth across his newly shaved head. "I won't, you know. If you'd rather I didn't."

"Dad!" He pushed me away. "It's okay."

"Well, wouldn't you like to know why I want to sell it?"

"Mom says it's because of Maggie."

"Oh she did, did she?" So Anne Marie ratted me out. I had mentioned to her at Max's baseball practice that I was thinking of selling. "And what else did your mother say?"

"Nothing."

"Uh huh."

"I dunno. She said something like it was about time."

"About time?"

"Yup. She said it was about time you and Maggie got together."

Toward the end of our marriage, Anne Marie had brought up Maggie's name quite often. "I can't compete with her ghost anymore," she'd say. "You're not," I'd respond, even though we both knew, at that point, I was lying.

"What did you say when Mum made that comment?" I asked. I hated myself for badgering the boy.

Taking advantage of my high ceilings and the fact that I had a question on the table, Max threw his baseball in the air, caught it with his mitt, and grinned. "I said I thought she was right."

#

The plane lands at Logan on time and without incident. After gathering my overnight bag from the conveyor belt, I head to my Jeep in the garage. *Going home*, I say to myself in the rearview mirror, *I'm going home*.

Under any other circumstances, I would say I was moving too fast. Maggie and I have been together barely a month—and a tumultuous month at that, with her having moved in with April, my having effectively moved in with Maggie on the nights I don't have Max, and all of us having to deal with the aftermath of Hazel's death.

An old Randy Travis tune called "Forever and Ever, Amen" plays on my favorite country station and interrupts my thoughts. The song went to number one back in '87, the year Anne Marie and I married. We danced to the song at our wedding—a bone she threw to me, I know now, since she thought my love of country music exposed a personal flaw.

"It's shit-kicking music," I'd teased her one day when we were discussing the play list for the reception. "It'll spice up the wedding."

"Nigel, I don't know any woman in her right mind who wants to hear the word 'shit' and 'wedding' in the same sentence."

Hers was a simple, innocent statement that brought me back to 1973, on one of my first dates with Maggie. My college chums—Harvard, Ivy-League snobs that they were—chastised my interest in country music, which my mum had turned me onto during summer months and winter breaks when I lived with her.

"Tell me about it," Maggie urged one day after my college roommate met us for beers and poked fun at my musical tastes in an effort to impress Maggie.

"Why?" I sulked. "So you can ridicule me as well?"

"No," she said, while squeezing my hand. "So I can learn."

There wasn't much of a country and western music scene in Boston circa 1973, but there was a nightclub in Park Square across from the present site of The Four Seasons in Back Bay called Hillbilly Ranch. The name said it all. Maggie loved it. And I loved her. I knew it then. I know it now. Too fast it hasn't been. If anything, it's about bloody time. Just as Maxwell said.

#

April's house is in darkness as I pull into the driveway. The sun has set, and the night sky is a brilliant shade of purple and blue. Jogging up the porch steps, I push open the door and trip on Ming Toy.

"Maggie?"

I walk into the kitchen, and then back down the hall, through the living room, and into another hallway leading me to the back of the house. The attic stairs hang from the ceiling, and I detect noises above. Mounting the steps, I call her name again.

"Maggie?"

Breathless, I burst into the attic and spot Kate sitting on a chair beneath a single pale yellow light bulb. At her feet is Maggie, crying.

"Maggie? Mugsy, darling, what is it? Did you fall? Are you hurt?"

On her lap is an empty photo album, and in her hand, she clutches a piece of paper. "*Why*, Nigel." Our eyes meet. Her face is red and blotchy. I brush back hair stuck to her cheek.

"Mugsy," I whisper. "I don't understand."

"*Why*, Nigel." She opens her hand and reveals what appears to be an old yellowed letter. The date at the top reads "April 27, 1954," two days after Maggie was born, and the first lines, written in a delicate, faded script, say:

*Dear Baby Girl,*

*You were born two days ago, a moment I will never forget, in a month I will always remember. I held you once before giving you away, the hardest thing I have ever had to do, but the right thing, just the same...*

Maggie pulls the letter away from me before I can read anymore and holds it against her heart. She smiles through her tears. "I know why, Nigel. I finally know why."

*November 2022*

# Chapter 56: Adrienne

It's the first fall in over a decade that I've been able to appreciate autumn's scents: burning wood, apple crisp, damp leaves. I bring this up at one of the AA meetings, and some of the old-timers nod and tip their coffee cups in my direction. It still amazes me that someone who has always prided herself on her artistic sensibilities could be so out of touch with the perfumes of Mother Earth.

Rolling over in CJ's bed, I bury my face in his pillow and take a deep breath. I've washed the bedding since his last visit over two months ago, but I'm wondering if my newly-tuned nostrils will still be able to smell him. A mother can detect her child's scent, I'm sure, long after it's disappeared for everyone else.

My friend Lucy says I'm suffering from empty nest syndrome, and I have to remind her that this experience is nothing new since CJ chose to live with his father full time when he was fourteen, after the courts determined he was old enough to make that decision.

"Yeah, but it's more permanent now," Lucy said. "You had him on Wednesday nights and every other weekend. Now he's gone, living his own life, clear across the country. Unless something unusual happens, he won't be back."

"Are you trying to make me feel better," I asked, "or worse?"

"Just trying to get you to see the way it is."

#

Shitty is the way it is, and shitty is the way it's been. I blamed everyone else for the shit but myself: Daddy, Mom, Chris, CJ, the gallery owners, the critics, the courts. Lucy says I finally started to see things as they truly were when I ran out of people to blame. By then it was too late. Rock bottom isn't the cliché I always thought it was; it's a real place on the outskirts of Hell.

The thing I miss most about drinking is the curtain—the black velvet drape that obscured all the shit from my vision. Shrinks say that people drink to escape and that escape is not good. I disagree. Sometimes escape is the only way out. The problem is the mode of transportation. I agree that a bottle of vodka doesn't make the best ferry, but sitting sober in a pile of excrement is no picnic, either. I don't care how hard you try to psychobabble me into visualizing a tranquil blue lagoon. At the end of the day, it's still a pile of shit.

#

The digital clock on CJ's nightstand flips to two zero zero. I get up, not because I want to, but because I made a promise to Lucy.

"You're going to see him, right?" she'd pestered.

"Yeah."

"When?"

"Tuesday."

"What time?"

"In the afternoon, around two-thirty."

"I'm holding you to it."

"Okay."

"I mean it, Adrienne."

"I heard you the first time."

"You'll be fine." She patted my hand and sipped her coffee.

"Maybe," I'd finally said. "But, Lucy, what if he isn't?"

#

As I gather my purse and some tissues, I pause in front of CJ's old desk, the one I've adopted as my own, the one that holds the secrets to my parents' lives. Pulling out the bottom drawer, I spy the large yellow envelope from the Law Office of Craven & Hanks, LLC.

Carl Hanks was the attorney I dragged Mom to twenty years ago. "I don't trust Daddy," I told her when she resisted. "You need someone else to watch out for you. Let me be that person." She gave in, somewhat reluctantly, and I couldn't understand why she always stood by him despite everything. Four years later, she had her "accident." Was it a massive stroke and then a fall? Or did she fall—from drinking, perhaps?—and then have a massive stroke? And—more important—did she have any help in falling? I didn't believe that Daddy had simply found her, barely breathing, on the kitchen floor. And I sure as hell wasn't going to let him off so easy. Deep down, I knew Mom was gone, but I was not ready to let her go and watch Daddy walk away a "grieving" widower and into the arms of his current flavor-of-the-month. Putting her in that godforsaken nursing home and refusing to sign the DNR were the only forms of control I had. He wouldn't walk away if she were still alive because God forbid the world saw the real Hugh Dooley: a selfish, salacious beast. At least, that's what I thought at the time.

I discovered the envelope from Carl Hanks a year ago, when I came back from Newport where I dried out the last time. My circadian rhythms were off, and I was awake twenty hours a day it seemed, smoking cigarettes and doing my damndest not to break down and binge. Instead, I started a cleaning obsession: taking a toothbrush to the tile grout in the bathroom, scrubbing the pale pink ring around the tub, waxing the kitchen floor for the first time in years, and finally getting rid of some of the junk in CJ's old room.

In there, I came upon a box that I hadn't seen in years—it was Mom's stuff—the items we had for her in the nursing home: vanilla-scented hand lotion, extra blankets, a music box, the cards people sent. Her death certificate lay on top of the envelope from Carl Hanks' office, which I hadn't recalled receiving. But I also didn't remember much from that time in general—especially those last months when I discovered Daddy's relationship with April. It was two a.m. when I sat down on the old blue shag rug and opened the envelope.

*Dear Ms. Dooley-Whitmore:*

*Your mother, Gloria A. Dooley, requested that I forward to you this sealed letter upon her death. You will find it enclosed. I am sorry for your loss.*

*Sincerely,*

*Carl F. Hanks*

After all these years, the letter was still sealed. Either I hadn't seen it, or I didn't want to see it. *Escape,* I thought as I finally tore it open and found seven pages of creamy white stationery dated May 2002, right after Mom and I had squared away her new will. I sat and read and then re-read that damned letter for hours.

The next morning, Lucy barged in after ten. She found me smoking a cigarette while leaning against the wall.

"Don't you know how to answer the phone?" She squatted, stuck her nose in my face, and sniffed. Satisfied that I didn't reek of booze, she plopped herself next to me. "Where've you been? I've been calling since seven thirty."

"Been right here."

"Here?"

"All night."

"Why?"

"Because of this." I shoved my mother's letter against Lucy's sagging boobs.

As she read it, she kept murmuring, "Jesus, sweet Jesus." When she got to the end, she stared at me. "You okay?" she finally asked.

"What the fuck do you think?"

"Explains a lot, doesn't it?"

"Yep," I said. "Explains everything."

"What are you going to do?"

I took a drag off my butt. "Spend the rest of my life sitting right here."

#

I could spend the rest of my life sitting in my car, I think, right here in front of April's house, which is now my father's house, too. But then I spy him walking around the side, a rake in his left hand. He wears jeans, a sweatshirt, and a Red Sox cap over his bald head. I have no memory of my father ever having hair. Although the morning started out mild, an afternoon chill seems to have sneaked in, pushing the sun behind a thick veil of gray clouds.

Mental calculations aren't necessary—I've always remembered his birthday, known exactly how old he is. Still, it's hard to believe that I'm forty-six and that my father, whom I haven't spoken to in fifteen years, is seventy-three years old.

I've seen him, though, many times over the years, unbeknownst to him. "It's called stalking," Lucy always said. "Just keeping tabs," I replied, even though I didn't know what I meant by that.

When Mom died, I was certain Daddy would show up at the wake, or funeral, or both. I relished the idea of creating a big scene, exposing his sick and lecherous ways. But he didn't come. Chris had heard through the grapevine that April had taken a leave of absence from the nursing home and that she was taking care of an old woman's estate in Georgia.

"What if he's there? With her?" I'd bawled one night, while Chris held me tight. Chris said all he ever wanted to do was take care of me and make me happy.

"Look. What April and your father did was wrong. Two phone calls and everyone will know that."

"Who'd you call?" I sniffled.

"First, Saint A's corporate office. I know one of the owners."

"And second?"

"*The Globe. The Herald. The New York Times.*" He hugged me and whispered into my hair. "He shouldn't be allowed to get away with it."

But the "it" he was referring to wasn't the affair with April per se. It was the affair with—and death of—Winnie. Chris knew the stories. He had heard all about my father's philandering. Well, the two affairs I was sure of at the time: Kendra Jackson and Winnie Mansfield.

"Say the word, A-plus." Chris nicknamed me "A-plus" our senior year in college in honor of my 4.0 GPA. "And I'll do it. I'll make the calls."

I sat with his offer for several minutes before I'd answered. "No. Not yet."

#

What stopped me? I hated him enough, that was true. Yet for some reason, a fragment of a conversation I had with April kept swirling through my head: "*You know, your dad really cares about you. Loves you.*"

All my life—and especially after Kendra and Winnie—my mother used to tell me how much my father loved me. This I knew without a doubt up until I was thirteen. We weren't a perfect family. As a kid, I intuitively knew that. Mom was often sad or sleepy, Daddy was preoccupied with Mom, but we were together. For so long, the bad stuff didn't matter because I had my daddy, and I could count on him, morning, noon, and night. I knew, too, that my mother loved me, but, well, she was sick. Isn't that what Daddy would often say? Isn't that why he nicknamed me Princess Panacea?

When April spoke those words to me fifteen years ago, "*You know, your dad really cares about you. Loves you,*" it was the first time in years—decades, even—that someone else besides my mother told me that my father loved me. It was easy for everyone else to fuel my hate—Granddad, especially; Chris; my college friends—and have me believe that it was my father who was sick and that he wasn't capable of truly loving me while doing the things he did.

"It's warped, I know," I'd told my shrink-of-the-month, after I found the letter from my mother.

"Delusion often is," he replied.

"Gee, thanks."

"Question is, what are you going to do about it? How are you going to fly straight again?"

"Is that possible? To fly straight again?"

"Anything's possible."

"He should have told me the truth," I argued. "They both should have. A long time ago."

"Why are you telling me this? Why not tell him?"

"Because he'll have some story why he didn't."

"Seems to me," he said, "that maybe you need to hear his side."

#

A pile of leaves sits by the swing set in the side yard. Daddy pushes his cap back, scratches his pate, and surveys the area. When I was a little girl, I loved autumn, jumping in leaf piles, and throwing them high in the air. Daddy would be by my side, jumping and throwing, too. Chris and I used to do it with CJ when he was a little boy, and when I think back to those times, my heart aches because I was happy then, but I fucked it up anyway.

"Adrienne! You have to stop doing this to yourself to us," Chris implored. I'm not sure when he stopped calling me "A-plus" for good, but whenever he had to clean up my drunken ass off the floor, he called me Adrienne.

"I know. You're right. I will. I promise."

"You always promise," he said. "But you never do."

#

I slam the car door shut, but Daddy must not have heard it, since he's still staring at the pile of leaves as I approach him.

I stop, about six feet away. "Hello, Daddy."

At first, I don't think he hears me, but then—almost in slow motion—he turns and faces me.

"Adrienne," he whispers. "Pana."

My eyeballs swim in their sockets, blurring my vision. He waits for me to compose myself, or who knows? Maybe he's composing himself as well. When I'm able to focus on him again, I see that, up close, he hasn't changed all that much. He's still the same handsome man with a solid square jaw and liquid blue eyes. I detect laugh lines, and I'm both thankful and sad.

After Mom died, I drove by this house—April's house, not even five minutes away from the nursing home—three or four times a week for close to a year. It was the only connection I had to April, and I was convinced she was my only connection to Daddy. I never told anyone about the drive-bys, not Chris, not Lucy, no one. But I had CJ in the car a few times. Once as I slowed down, CJ piped up in the backseat, "Mama, whose house?"

"No one's," I said, as I sped up and drove away.

For many months, the only person I saw was a television news anchor named Maggie Prescott, April's half sister. She'd be walking up the porch steps, carrying groceries, shooing a calico cat out of her way, or holding hands with a man, whom I read about a couple years later in the celebrity pages of *People* after Maggie and he married. Nigel something-or-other was his name. A lawyer. A college sweetheart.

But then one day, about a year later, I saw them: Daddy and April. He had his arm around her shoulders as they walked up the steps to her house and disappeared through the door. They'd returned from wherever they had been for April's mother's funeral.

#

"You look good," I say.

"So do you. Haven't changed at all."

He's being kind or else he's blind. While Lucy reminds me that not many women in their mid-forties can claim the same weight they were as a senior in college, I know the booze and cigarettes have left their marks: leathery skin, permanent bags under my eyes, and long lifeless hair that I refuse to cut. It's the same length as it's always been—down to my ass, which, I've noticed in recent months, has started to sag.

He takes a handkerchief out of his back pocket and wipes his brow, and my eyes fall on his gold wedding band. I turn away.

"Yard looks good," I murmur.

He sighs. "I've been lazy this year. With the raking and all."

"You can hire people to do it, you know."

"I know. Keeps me busy, though. May likes to jump in the leaves."

He mentions her name as if he's said it to me a thousand times before, and I find it interesting that he assumes I know who he's talking about, which, of course, I do. At first, I don't move, convinced something is going to happen—an earthquake, pieces of sky falling, something. Nothing does, and, somehow, I'm still standing.

"CJ loved jumping in the leaves," I say.

"You did, too."

"Yeah. A lifetime ago." This time, the tears come, and I don't try to stop them. I simply brush them away and face him. "Why didn't you tell me the truth about Mom?"

We stare at each other for what feels like hours, even though I'm sure it's only minutes. My sense of timing has been off for years.

"You'll never know how many times I asked myself that question," he says.

"You should have."

"You're right. But by the time I wanted to—"

"What? Too late?"

"No," he says, shaking his head. "Too much damage. You were too angry. I don't think you would have believed me."

"You're probably right." A breeze stirs one of the swings, and I hear wind chimes coming from a neighbor's yard. "Don't you want to know," I say, "why I'm here now? How I found out?"

"I'm assuming it was your mother's letter."

"You knew about that?"

"Only after she died." He pauses and takes a deep breath. "I received a note from her attorney saying that she had instructed him to mail you a letter explaining everything."

"That was fifteen years ago."

"I know."

"Didn't you wonder what happened? Why I didn't come around then?"

He shrugs. "I figured you had your reasons. Maybe you hadn't read it. Or you hadn't believed it. But I always hoped that you would." He closes his eyes and takes a deep breath. "How's CJ?"

"Fine."

"He's what? Twenty-three?"

"Yep."

"Is he still around here?"

I shake my head. "No. California. Trying to break into film."

"Acting?"

"Directing."

"Got your creative genes, huh?"

I cough. "God, I hope not."

"And Chris?"

I look away, back at the leaves. "Chris and I are divorced. He's remarried."

His eyes are on me—I can feel them. "I'm sorry," he says.

"Don't be. I fucked that one up on my own. I'll admit, though," and this time I turn to him, "I tried blaming it on you. It was easier, you know? Than blaming myself."

"I imagine I had a hand in it and that I am deserving of some of the blame."

"Yeah, well. I'll let you duke that one out with my therapist."

He smiles, pulls up his sleeve, and peers at his watch. "April is at work, so I'm picking May up from school and—"

"Right," I interrupt. "No problem." I start to turn around, but he reaches for me.

"Hey," he says softly. "That doesn't mean you have to go." He holds my elbow. I don't pull away. "I don't want you to go, Pana."

"How can you want me here?" I shake myself loose. "After everything I've said and—"

Laying his hand on my mouth, he silences me. "Don't."

I push his arm away. "Besides, she … May. What will she think? I mean—"

"May knows all about you."

"She does?"

"Yes."

"But why? How—"

"You're sisters."

"But what does she think? I haven't been in her life." I shake my head and wipe my face with the back of my sleeve. "What did you tell her?"

"I told her that she has a beautiful, smart, talented sister. A sister who has some problems she needs to sort through before she can be a part of our lives, but that someday she will."

"Quite a gamble you were taking, telling her a story like that. What if I hadn't come around?"

"But," he says, as he lifts his hand toward my face and strokes my cheek with his thumb. "You have."

I follow him around the yard to the front porch, where he mounts the steps and turns to me before opening the door. "Come in," he says.

Nodding, I take a deep breath, climb the stairs, and follow him inside.

"I'm going to clean up. Make yourself at home. And then I'll introduce you to May Rose Dooley."

"May Rose," I say, tasting it. "Pretty."

"Her middle name is for April's sister, Margaret Rose."

"That's nice," I say, because it is. "And May is for what? Her birth month?"

"No." He looks at me, shaking his head, one tear trickling down his right cheek. "It's for yours."

For a half second, all I want to do is run to him, throw my arms around his neck, and never let go, but I don't, and the moment passes. We smile at each other through our tears, say nothing, and he turns and makes his way up the stairs.

I fish through my purse for a tissue, blow my nose, and wander into the living room. Before me is a fireplace, the mantel cluttered with countless photographs. Above that is a painting in a rich dark chocolate frame behind non-glare glass. It's one of my watercolors from thirty-five years or so ago. A little girl with long black hair twirls with a man in the center of a vibrant forest. The forest's been rejuvenated after a spring rain that forces the oils from the parched earth to ooze up and produce a glorious fragrance called—what?

Suddenly, I'm ten again, standing in the rain, Daddy's arm wrapped around me. *"Petrichor,"* he whispers. *"It's called petrichor."*

And standing here now, I swear I can detect its sweet scent.

###

# *Acknowledgements:*

There are so many people to thank, but here's the short list:

The Nobscot Niblets, my writing group, both past and present members who read either parts or full versions of this book: Dawn Swann, Colleen Cox, Steve Tannuzzo, Catherine Hathaway Mack, Patty Hebert, Donna Fisher, Jen Zuba, Paul Ashton, Rob Borkowski, Dave Retalic, Karen Low, Susan Weiner, Deb Kurilecz, Deb Mackey, and Laura Matthews. Laura was instrumental in editing the final version. Thank you, Laura, for your professional insight and for your friendship.

Early readers (my apologies if I've missed anyone): Kevin Bradley, Mitch Bradley, Skyla Bradley, Sue Bradley, Erin Bradley, Kristin Bradley, Beth Inman, Lisa Clay, Bette Gioffre, Don Kelley, Gay Vernon, Holly Vietzke, Rob Lynch, Larry Starkey, John Willis, Bronwyn Ford, and FPS.

Two of my biggest cheerleaders over the last nine years: Robin Chapman and Moneen Daley Harte. I love you both.

My MFA buddies who provided much support, specifically Tavi Black, Megan Doney, Tracy Isaacs, and Christine Junge.

Alan Chapman's guidance over the course of six months during a fundamental rewrite was invaluable: thank you, Alan, for your insight and prodding.

My cat, Dorian Gray, who loved me even when I was grumpy and unshowered.

My family, in general, which is as large in love as it is in size.

And my parents, specifically. This is for you, Mum and Dad.

## *About Robyn Bradley:*

Robyn Bradley has an MFA in Creative Writing from Lesley University. Her work has appeared in FictionWeekly.com, *Metal Scratches*, *Writer*'s *Digest*, and *The MetroWest Daily News*. When she's not writing or sleeping, Robyn enjoys watching *Law & Order* marathons, drinking margaritas, and determining how many degrees really separate her from George Clooney. Visit www.robynbradley.com for more info.


## *Like what you've read?*

Lend it out and/or tell others. Consider leaving a review at Amazon, B&N, or Goodreads. Become a fan of my Facebook page: http://www.facebook.com/RobynBradleyWriter.

Thank you for reading my work!

Made in the USA
Charleston, SC
21 June 2011